Everly

A Romantic Adventure

By

MORGAN VALENTINE

ISBN: 978-1-956441-20-8 Paperback version
978-1-956441-21-5 Digital version

Dedicated to:
Mary McLean,
who showed me I could tell a story.

Special thanks to Julie Thomas for her excellent editing assistance and advice.

Cover courtesy of
Tubs of Slaw Productions

Special photography courtesy of
Marcus Ranum

EVERLY

A Romantic Adventure

1

"My dear Mrs. Ramsey, you have been so good. I apologize for leaving you like this. I don't know what would have happened to Mama had you not been here for her, and I know I can never repay you. Maërlys has promised to stay until everything can be set to rights." Emmeline Blanc pulled on her gloves. "Oh dear, there is the coach now. Maërlys darling, you should be able to leave tomorrow if everything goes as we expect. You have enough money for the coach and your meals. Please write me if there is any problem."

Maërlys smiled at her cousin, "Go Emmy, everything will be fine. I'll be back to help you in the shop by Wednesday at the latest."

Emmeline hugged her young cousin and was gone.

Maërlys turned to Mrs. Ramsey. "I am sorry, also," she said. "I would have gone for her, but it is Emmeline the customers come to see. I like to believe I am some help, and Emmy assures me this is so, but I will never be the designer she is. She makes every woman who comes to her look so beautiful. I do not wonder they feel they cannot do without her."

"Never mind, dear," Mrs. Ramsey answered. "Your aunt was so easy to live with, never any trouble between us. I was afraid you and Emmeline might not arrive in time, especially as she was so ill on Thursday, but she waited to see you and then died almost immediately. It was as if she wished to be of no trouble to anyone, even at her death. I will miss her and would take up Emmeline's offer to move somewhere near your shop, except at my age I cannot face the noise and bustle of London. Come, help me finish these cards; there is only your visit to the lawyer tomorrow morning before you can leave."

Maërlys was at Mr. Carroll's office promptly at ten on Monday morning, as the lawyer had requested at the funeral the day before. Unfortunately, it was nearly twelve before he arrived himself. In any case, the meeting was a mere formality, at least as Mr. Carroll explained it.

It appeared that the house belonged entirely to Mrs. Ramsey. For the last two years Mrs. Blanc had paid rent out of her meager annuity, and when this was not enough, out of her principal itself. In fact, the actual legacy, after final payment to Mrs. Ramsey, amounted to only twenty-three pounds, four shillings and thruppence.

"Will I take that amount to Emmeline?" she asked, stunned.

"No, that would be most irregular. If you will provide me with the direction of Miss Blanc's bankers, I will see the full amount, less expenses, is forwarded to them. Would you be good enough to sign here?" He placed three documents before her, and she wordlessly signed her name where he indicated.

Maërlys left the lawyer's office in a daze. She hadn't realized how much she had counted on Emmy's legacy. She had been confident of at least several hundred pounds, and she had hoped that, receiving this, Emmy would have allowed her to investigate possibilities for Reynard and Ambre. Reynard would be of military age soon and she was sure it would take at least a hundred pounds, perhaps more, to bring the children to England. Now there would be no money.

True, Emmeline Élégance was doing well, better than they had expected three years ago when Emmy opened it. However, payments on the shop itself and costs of materials, such as the little dolls they depended upon for fashion guidance, ate up their funds almost as quickly as they were received. To say nothing of customers who paid slowly, if at all, and whom Emmy was so hesitant to dun. Maërlys knew there was less than a hundred pounds to Emmeline's credit at her bank, and that was needed for emergencies.

Thinking of these things, she paid little attention to her feet and was surprised when she looked up and found herself approaching the docks. A packet, possibly from the Americas, was swarming with activity. Wouldn't it be nice if she could bring Reynard and Ambre to England? Perhaps they could go to America and start a new life far away from Napoleon and his war. She stood watching as a gentleman and his dark-skinned servant came down the gangplank. The servant arranged the disposition of their trunks on the carriage which was waiting for them. She looked again at the gentleman as he opened the door to the coach and stepped up. Dear heavens, it was him!

Maërlys mind raced back a year. He had come into the shop and he was so handsome that she had watched as Emmy had waited upon him. Not only handsome, he was well-spoken and not the least top-lofty. He had treated Emmy as an equal rather than a shop-girl, smiling and bantering with her as she assembled a package for someone who had sent him. Maërlys had gone to bed that night with his face in her thoughts, dreaming dreams of him as a handsome prince who would come and sweep her away to his castle.

The dream had been so real to her, just turned eighteen, that she had taken the trouble to find out more about him. Emmy had told her his name was Everly, and Maërlys had found him in "DeBrett's Peerage." He was the younger brother of Baron Cherille, who had ascended to the title on the death of their father about a year earlier. They were an extremely wealthy house, very conservative, and seldom appeared in gossip columns. They were never connected with the scandals that plagued so many noble families.

All these things flashed through Maërlys' mind as the black man called out their destination to the driver on the box, then swung inside the coach to ride with his master. That was odd. Should he not have ridden postilion, hanging onto the rear like a proper servant? In any case, Maërlys saw him gazing directly at her from the window of the coach as it rattled away. She was startled by his look, almost as much as by the idea that next occurred to her. She'd heard him tell the coachman where they were going. It was a crazy idea but she was out of options and afraid of the future.

"Did you see him?" Jarrod Everly asked.

"The man in the doorway across the way?"

"Yes. The one dressed like an undertaker or an MP."

Henry frowned. "An MP?"

"Minister of Parliament."

"Oh. They never come to Jamaica. Is that how they dress?

"Invariably."

"May we go back to Jamaica?"

Jarrod laughed. "Point taken. Let us, for the moment, avoid undertakers, MPs, and French spies who dress like them, at least as much as possible."

"What about the young woman?" Henry asked.

"Young woman? I didn't see a young woman. Was she pretty?"

"Very. Makes it hard to believe you didn't notice her. After all, she was staring at you."

Jarrod stuck his head out the window and looked behind them. "Damme," he said. "Probably the only thing worth seeing in Portsmouth and I missed it. D'you think she was a spy as well?"

Henry shrugged. "Funny kind of spy, standing on the boards staring at you as if she'd seen a ghost. Pretty though. You'd be hard put to avoid her if she was a spy. If she is, we are beset. Have you those poison papers?"

Jarrod patted the breast of his jacket. "They die with me."

"Let us hope you can dispose of them without that extreme."

"Well, no sense worrying about it now. Where are we going?"

"You have a room at the Maiden's Tear, on the London road, for yourself and your man-servant, meaning myself. They have not been informed of my distressing color."

"Portsmouth is used to all colors, seaport that it is. Even London might not be too bad. It's the countryside where we'll have trouble about it. I do want to get to Cherille Hall as quickly as I can, but we must go to London and give Sir Charles our report. He hasn't recalled me from the islands for my health."

Henry looked around and shivered. "I should think not, if you call this June. More January, you ask me."

Jarrod laughed again. "True, the resemblance between English June and Kingston January is remarkable. But you will adapt, I trust, once you get the feel of it."

"I feel it now," Henry answered. "It feels cold. Is your family expecting you at the hall?"

"They will hardly know I'm in England, yet. I thought we could go up tomorrow and spend the night at Cherille House in Berkeley Square, see Sir Charles first thing, and perhaps get to Wiltshire Wednesday night."

"How will they take to your new man-servant?"

"Less of the man-servant business, Henry. I shall make it clear to them I owe you my life several times over and they shall treat you with the respect you deserve, or I'll know why. Don't worry, Christian will never allow a friend of mine to be mistreated in his house."

Maërlys shivered as she sat back against the cushions of the hired coach but not because of the cold; on the contrary, it was unseasonably warm, even for June. No, she admitted to herself, it was fear. The hire of this coach was consuming a part of her money, and a room at the inn would require even more. If all went as planned, she was about to wreck her hopes for the life she'd wanted. After tonight, she could be an outcast; the possibility of a home, a man she could love who would care for her and love her in return, all gone.

Unless her nerve failed her. No, she resolved, too much depended on her plan to accept failure. It was time to throw the dice and pray. Concentrate on Reynard and Ambre. She took a deep breath, opened the door and jumped down from the coach.

The driver turned to look at her, a slight frown creasing his face. "All set, Miss?"

"Yes, if you will just bring my trunk."

Inside, she wordlessly gave him a three-penny piece and watched as he scowled at it. Embarrassed she gave him another shilling. He went back out, whipped up his horses and was gone. Maërlys instantly regretted the shilling.

She tried to be inconspicuous as she scanned the room. There, in the corner, as far from the fire as possible. She turned as the landlord bustled up. "You have a room?"

"One, ma'am, only one left. Sorry it ain't as big as you might like, but we just had a gentleman come in and take the last regular guest room for himself. Still, it's clean and near the chimney, so it won't be cold no matter what. I'll take your trunk up. Supper'll be on the table in just a moment. Would you like to freshen up first?"

She felt her courage slipping. "I, ah, no, I'll just wait here. May I have a quiet table away from the fire?" She fought the muscles in her neck as they stiffened and her head started to move toward where Mr. Everly was sitting.

"Of course, of course, just over there, ma'am." He gestured in the direction she expected, and she felt a bead of sweat start to run down her back.

"Thank you," she said. "And may I have a glass of something cool? Not ale," she added hurriedly. "Perhaps you have some light wine or, or something?"

"I'll find you summat, ma'am. Just take a seat. Back in a moment."

Careful not to look at Everly or his servant, she went in the direction indicated and sat down at the small table. She could feel his presence only a few feet away. After all her dreams, she was so close. Now, if only she could be pretty enough.

The landlord interrupted these reflections, returning with a plate, cutlery and a glass of negus. "We have a joint just coming off the fire, ma'am, if you care for mutton, or there's a pork pie and even a portion of steak and kidney in the kitchen."

"Mutton would be fine," she answered, as a voice to her left spoke up.

"Mutton for me, too, landlord, but my man will take that bit of steak and kidney, if the lady has no wish for it."

The landlord raised his eyebrows at her and she said, "By all means, let the gentleman have it."

"You are very gracious, ma'am," the voice said, forcing her to turn in his direction.

The first thing she saw was his servant, frowning at her in a thoughtful, concentrated way, just as he had earlier. It drove everything out of her mind, and she found herself stammering, "Uh, n-no, not at all, I prefer mutton, thank you, I mean, ah—" All speech deserted her as his handsome, smiling face appeared, only a foot or two from her own. She felt herself flushing bright red and quickly turned back to her own place setting, lowering her eyes to the table.

"I apologize, ma'am. I am too free. We have not been introduced, and I have embarrassed you. Please forgive me. My name is Everly. Jarrod Everly, of the Wiltshire Everlys. We are not so well known as some houses but are considered respectable, I believe. Please forgive me; I don't know what the family will say when they hear I have been embarrassing ladies at country inns."

Without raising her eyes from her place she murmured, "Please, sir, it is nothing at all. Please."

"Sir—" she heard the servant say, but his voice was cut off, perhaps at a look from Mr. Everly.

She could feel his eyes on her and knew this was the moment, but her paralysis was complete. The moment stretched, she could feel him relaxing into his chair, and then it was too late. She felt the tear coming, and watched, horrified, as it dropped into her plate.

He was beside her in an instant, on his knee next to her chair. "Oh, my dear lady, please, I beg you will forgive me. I had no idea, I mean, I never meant to, I mean, you must allow me to make it up to you in some way. Please, Henry here will vouch for me. Speak up, Henry. Tell the lady I am not a highwayman or someone who accosts respectable women."

"I believe the lady can see you are a gentleman," Henry said drily, and his tone brought her head up, heedless of the tear still working its way down her cheek.

She met Henry's eyes and was taken aback to see the studious frown change to a look of wondering surprise. By a supreme effort of will, she managed to turn and face his master, whose face was again only inches from her own. "Yes, sir, I am assured of it. I regret that my emotions overcame me." She felt herself flushing, then going pale, then flushing again. "It is I who beg your forgiveness. I, I am Maërlys, Maërlys Blanc. I regret, regret...." It was all she could manage. She was staring at her plate again.

"I do apologize, ma'am. We will allow you to dine in peace. Again, my deepest apologies for embarrassing you. Please let me know if there is any way I can serve you. It is the least I can do. Come Henry, we are completely *de trop*. Landlord," he called, "we will eat in our room." He bowed to Maërlys. Now the lady can have some serenity."

She looked up as they moved away, trying to find a voice to stop them, her tongue frozen. She'd come this far and now it was all ruined. Fool! the voice screamed in her head. Reynard. Ambre. What of them? She struggled, but no words came. She was alone as the landlord brought her dinner.

2

"Good heavens, Henry, what a beautiful girl, though I'd swear I've seen her before. Somewhere. But how could I forget such a face? As I would imagine an angel must look. Did you notice? Where, Henry, could I see a woman like that and not remember. I am at a loss. Perhaps I am mistaken."

"You may be mistaken, but I am sure I am not."

Jarrod whirled on him. "Whatever do you mean?"

"Just that I have not had time to forget her. Not when I see her twice in one day."

"Twice? Today? Be clearer, man."

"Staring at you on the dock."

"You mean...?" Henry nodded. "But she's following us?" He was rewarded with another nod. "But she sat right next to us. Why would she do that if she's not trying to scrape acquaintance?"

"I believe she is. You heard the tiny French note in her speech."

"A spy? Surely not. You heard her stammering. She had me begging for her acquaintance, and said nothing."

"I didn't say she was a good spy."

"Oh, please, Henry. Surely the French are not sending out anyone so inept as that. She was blushing. Spies don't blush."

"Irregular, I admit, but the tears were good. Very good. We haven't heard the last of her."

Jarrod flashed a grin at his companion. "Now, see, you are an optimist after all. I may not remember whether or not I've seen her before, but I'll never forget her again. She may haunt my dreams tonight. In fact, I pray she does."

"I'll offer you eight to five we see her again before your dreams enter into it."

"You're covered and here's my fiver. I wish you may not have to give it back."

"Fine. You'll allow me to load a couple of pistols, in case she's not alone, and when she comes, please remember to take one with you, whatever pretext she uses to tempt you to her room."

"You interest me. I might even say you delight me. Will I take the poison papers, as well?"

"By all means. Please enjoy yourself to the fullest, but be careful. Don't eat or drink anything, and don't fall asleep. Just because she knows how to blush, stammer, and weep doesn't mean she can't handle a knife."

"I promise to follow instructions like a good boy. If you're finished with those pistols, can we eat? My stomach is on the verge of making those noises you dislike so much."

They had just finished eating when there was the gentlest, tentative, knock at the door. Henry winked at Jarrod, reached over, picked up the banknote lying on the dresser, and put it in his pocket. With a jerk of his head, he indicated that Jarrod should open it. "Be good," he mouthed silently.

When Maërlys reached her room, she found she had to squeeze by the door in order to close it. The trunk prevented it from opening fully, allowing just enough passage to scrape by between the bed and the trunk. Two nails hammered into the wall above the trunk evidently served as a closet. The bed was narrow, pressed against the window sill. The window was shut tight, and the end wall of the room, made of chimney bricks, was hot to the touch. Fortunately, the bed failed, by a few inches, to touch that wall. There was no room for a chair. She pushed at the window but it wouldn't open.

Her first thought was to sit on the bed and cry until the next day. She examined her purse, counted her money, and decided she had enough to reach London travelling post, though she'd likely have to spend some time on top. The thought of this embarrassment redoubled the urge to weep. The inner voice berated her. Fool! it said. Fool! Over and over. It was true. Her plan was a failure. Perhaps, if she was lucky, she might cook to death in this little airless room and be spared further humiliation.

The desperation of her plight gave her courage the necessary impetus. She knew which room belonged to Everly. She had seen them go up the stairs, and there was only one room they could have entered. How much worse can it get? she thought; perhaps there was still a chance for Reynard and Ambre.

Gathering the last of her moral strength, she reached over the trunk and opened her door, squeezed through and walked to their door. She stared at it a moment, considering. What would she say if the black man answered? She would look imperious and ask to speak to his master. She nodded, took a deep breath, and knocked, timidly at first, then with gathering strength. After a pause, the door swung open and that handsome face appeared, smiling at her. She wanted to cry, to fall into his arms and beg for his help, to sink into the floor and disappear. She did none of those things.

"I'm sorry to disturb you, but you were so kind before. I have a little problem which I don't like to bring to the landlord's attention. I would be very grateful," she tried to stress those two words seductively, but was afraid it didn't sound quite right, "if you could...."

He raised his eyebrows and blinked. "Let me get my coat," he answered. He reached back into the room and the coat was in his hand. His man, was it Henry?

must have handed it to him. He followed her pulling it on. Quite a feat, given how tightly it was tailored.

Looking back, she noticed there was something heavy in one pocket and some paper sticking out of the other. "You won't need your coat," she said. "That's the problem I'm having."

"With my coat?"

It was too much for her nerves. She giggled. "Not exactly, but you'll see." She opened the door and stood back for him to enter. He looked in, then squeezed past the door. She followed, realizing she hadn't thought this part through. She squeezed past the trunk, and he backed up to give her room, which placed him against the chimney. He stood it for a moment, then came off the wall rather hurriedly, bumping into her in the process.

"I beg your pardon," he muttered, backing into the chimney again. He managed to keep about an inch between himself and the bricks this time, with about twice as much space to spare himself pressing up against her.

The thought came into her head that it was lucky she wasn't one of those deep-chested women, then that it might be better if.... She bit that thought off. Reaching behind her she pushed the door closed, squeezed back between the bed and the trunk, and stood in the space left by the closed door.

Jarrod moved forward into the space she'd left him, smiled at her, said, "Warm, what?" and waited for a response.

Maërlys had almost nothing left. "I, I," she stammered. Then the words came in a rush. "I mean, ah, that's the problem. I can't open the window. I thought it might let in enough air to allow one to breathe but it won't budge. The chimney keeps it very hot in here, and I think the landlord likes it that way so he probably wouldn't care to open it, and I didn't know what to do, and then I thought maybe you, maybe you, maybe you...." She ran out of steam.

His eyes were fixed on her, and they were so blue, a blue such as she'd never seen and she wanted (well, she wasn't sure what she wanted), but she knew she had to do something. Anything. She moved back through the space left by the trunk and pressed against him. She looked up at him, closed her eyes, and waited. She could feel his heart beating, his chest was pressed so closely against hers, and he wasn't retreating, wasn't trying to get away from her, and she could feel him looking down at her. Her eyes were closed and she could feel him there. What was taking so long?

"Miss, ah, Blanc, isn't it? I must tell you that you are quite the loveliest woman I can recall meeting and, pressed together as we are, it takes every ounce of strength I have not to wrap you in my arms and kiss the breath out of you, but I fear that such an action would hardly relieve the singularly oppressive heat in this room. If you'll allow me...." He took her by the shoulders, then, reconsidering, placed his hands on her hips, encircled her waist and lifted her over the length of the trunk, setting her on her feet in the space behind the door.

Her eyes popped open and her hand flew to her mouth. She had never been handled so, and she liked it. She was looking into his smiling eyes and, without realizing it, her face beamed at him, a radiance he found so bewitching he almost forgot what he was doing. Then, shaking himself, he turned to the window.

After a moment's consideration he removed his coat, laid it gently over the trunk, papers uppermost, then climbed on the bed into a kneeling position. He pushed gently against the window, then more firmly. There was no movement. Edging closer and sweeping the curtains aside, he examined the window frame. There was a bolt at the top of each side. He slid these up, and tried again. There was still resistance. He found two more bolts at the bottom and opened them. There was another latch in the middle, and when this was lifted he was able to push the window open a few inches on each side. It refused to shift any farther; however, he had a space of about six or eight inches of open window, and the warm night air felt like an arctic breeze.

He turned and found Maërlys examining him, almost as if he were a side of beef in a butcher's window. She had never noticed before how tightly a man's breeches could fit him in the rear, or how pleasant, even attractive, the sight could be. She found herself longing to reach over and touch him and was actually considering whether or not she could do that when she realized he was looking at her, his eyes quizzical.

"You'd better come up here and get some of this air," he said, "because in a moment I intend, unless you stop me, to make it very difficult for you to breathe. I am not a man to take advantage of a woman's weakness, Miss Blanc, but I am a man, and only human. I believe I have already remarked on how lovely you are, and if you mean to try me any higher without recompense, I wish you will warn me at once. Even here in the window, I find my breath coming in gasps. Will you join me?"

Her eyes were shining as she climbed onto the bed next to him. As his arms encircled her, she watched his eyes until his lips met hers and she felt his tongue caressing them gently, finding its way into her mouth. Her own tongue seemed to have a will of its own and leapt up to caress his. She reached up to his hair and touched it, losing her fingers in it. She was pretty, she knew that, and had been kissed before, but it had never felt like this, this hunger. Her heart felt as if it would burst through her chest.

She suddenly realized that her other hand had gone where she had not dared to put it only a moment ago. Was it only a moment? It seemed an age that she had been in his arms; it felt as if she had come home. She pulled at him, trying to get him even closer, and felt his hands drifting gently along her body, His thumbs caressed her breasts lightly, teasing her nipples through the cloth, as his hands moved down to her waist again. Then his hand was on *her* bottom, and it felt so good, she found herself rubbing against it, caressing his at the same time. She lost all track of herself, just feeling. Some part of her knew this was what she wanted, this was the culmination of her plan, but she could not remember what the plan was or how she had gotten here or anything but the sensation of touching him and being touched.

His hands moved down her legs, gathering her skirt and her shift, moving the fabric up her legs. She could feel the air, his hand caressing her thighs. She somehow knew it was wrong, but not wrong, this was the plan. She gave into the feeling as his hand moved between her legs, stroking the soft silkiness of her skin. Then his fingers explored the fold between her legs, trailing through the hair, and he touched the very place she felt pulsing. Her breathing was fast, now, and she burned.

She moved her own hand up his thigh, felt the bulge and seized it, moving her fingers along it, exploring its size and shape. She was rewarded with a groan from him and a new frenzy. It was so much bigger than she expected. She'd seen them on men, their tight breeches sometimes outlining the shape, her brother when he was young. Never like this, so big, so firm. Would he push it up inside her? That was the plan, she remembered. Would it hurt? It didn't matter. She had to do it and, right now, she wanted it, to feel it inside her. And she felt his hand there, his finger moving up into her; it felt so good, and then, suddenly, a stabbing pain and she cried out.

3

He jerked his hand away as if he'd been bitten. He stared down at her, her dress bunched up above her waist, her hand still clutching him, softening as he looked down at her. "You're, you're...," it was his turn to stammer. "You're pure. Unspoiled. I mean, new, I mean, I didn't know, I'm so sorry."

She was confused. "Why?" She wrinkled her brow, trying to work it out. "You mean, because I'm a virgin? I thought men liked that. Do you not like it? You don't want me to be a virgin? You don't want to be first? I don't understand."

"But, I thought you were an experienced woman. You were following me. You were at the docks today." He was starting to get angry. "Do you know what almost happened to you here? Do you?"

She was still holding him. She squeezed, gently, and he gasped. "I thought you were going to put this in me," she said. "Don't you want to?"

"Of course I want to! Why didn't you tell me you'd never, I mean, why didn't you try to stop me? Did you want to make me into a rapist?"

Yes. That was exactly what she'd wanted; that was the plan. Now it was all spoiled, and she would never be able to convince him to give her money to go away. She was still a virgin; she couldn't convince anyone that he'd raped her. Even Emmy would laugh at her. She'd made a mess of the whole idea, and she didn't even know what she'd done wrong.

She looked up at him, he was so beautiful, and he'd been so kind to her. She remembered how it had felt, how she'd wanted him so much she didn't care if it hurt, even if he split her open. The plan hadn't even mattered. All she'd been able to remember was that she had to let him do that to her, and she'd wanted it. She had. And now, he hated her.

She glanced at his face again. He didn't look mad anymore; he looked sad and reached out to touch her face, softly, caressing her cheek. She realized her dress was still bunched around her waist, and he could see things she'd never let anybody see since she'd outgrown her nanny. But he wasn't looking at that. Just her face, his hand on her cheek. She turned and nuzzled the hand, kissed it.

He jerked it away, as if it burned. Then he looked at her, and her expression must have affected him, because suddenly his eyes were full of concern. He put his arm around her and pulled her to him, crooning in her ear, "Oh, my darling, my beautiful darling, I am so, so sorry. If you give me the chance, I will make you forget this business, and we will find a way to love each other. Please, please, give me that chance. Will you promise?" And he was looking into her eyes with his beautiful blue ones. And then, as if something he'd forgotten crossed his mind, they changed.

He drew back, "You followed me. You were on the docks, waiting, and you followed me to this inn. Why?" He shook her, not hard, but meaningfully. "Why?" he asked again. She put her face in her hands and began to cry. He pulled her to him, cradled her head against his shoulder, and stroked her hair. "You see, I have to know. You do see that, don't you?"

And then it all came out, between sobs, broken, incoherent, but understandable bits and pieces, names, lifetimes, tumbling out in chunks. They sat on the bed, and he held her close and stroked her hair. She told him of Reynard, her brother, and Ambre, her sister. Her parents, revolutionaries lost at the end of the revolution, murdered with the rise of Bonaparte. Reynard was thirteen and, soon, they would look for him and put him in the army; he would be forced to fight for the people who killed his parents. She didn't know what would become of Ambre. She needed to find them, but it would take money, lots of money.

She knew he had money. She had seen him at the docks, and he was so beautiful, and he had lots of money. She thought it would be all right if she let him...and then, when he was finished, he would give her money and she would use it to save her brother and sister. Finally, she ran down, her sobs lessened, and she fell silent. And she looked up at him again.

"I didn't know you wouldn't want me if I was a virgin. Nobody told me that. Everybody says men want virgins, but, I guess that is for marriage. I didn't know. I mean, I know you will not marry me but I didn't know you would not want me if I was not, I mean, if I didn't know how to, I mean, I guess I don't know what I mean." She smiled sadly, tears running down her cheeks. "I am such a failure."

"Oh, my beautiful, beautiful darling. Please forgive me for hurting you." He reached into her lap and pulled down her dress and shift, hiding her from his own eyes. "We have misunderstood each other rather badly, I'm afraid. We need to rest, think, and talk again in the morning. I promise, everything will be better in the clear light of day. Do you think you can sleep in this," he waved his hand, "closet?"

She gave him that winsome smile again. "Yes. Thank you. I will be all right. You have been very good to me and I will always honor you for that." She took his hand and kissed it. Then she gestured at the window. "And you have given me air. Already it is so much cooler in here. I thank you with all my heart."

He kissed her then, gently, just with his lips, and when her heart leapt up and her tongue reached out for him he pushed her carefully away and smiled. "Good night, my darling. I will see you in the morning." Then he reached out over the trunk, swung the door open and left the room, closing the door behind him.

"Wasn't expecting you back," Henry muttered when Jarrod opened the door. "Thought I heard a woman scream, but softly, the way they do sometimes. Would I be prying?"

"Yes. Would it stop you?"

"You left your coat."

Jarrod looked down. "So I did. Damme. Doesn't matter. I'll see her again in the morning and reclaim it. Expect it'll be there, even the pistol."

"She won't take the papers?"

"No."

"Then she is not what I feared or perhaps hoped?"

"No."

"You sound quite certain."

"I am not a complete idiot; I realize that I can be and sometimes am mistaken, but I will be very much taken aback if that should prove to be the case here. I freely admit to you the chit has turned me inside out and upside down. Henry, I have never felt so destroyed by a woman. She literally had me trembling with desire, and yet, faced with her innocence, I drew back rather than cause her any harm. I know the duty I owe my family, and my country, and I am not at liberty to indulge my own wishes without consulting those requirements. I must know more of her before making any rational decision, but, had I the right, I would beg her to marry me as soon as a special license could be obtained." He smiled at his friend. "You must watch out for me. I am not, at present, a sane man. But we shall know more in the morning. I have left the child to get what sleep she can, and tomorrow we will take her under our wing and investigate her situation to the fullest."

"But she is French?"

"Without a doubt. She freely admits it and tells me her parents were victims of Bonaparte's consolidation of power at the end of the revolution. She has a sister and a brother still in France whom she desires to rescue, and it was this that led her to seek me out. She knows I come from wealth and had some bizarre notion that she could offer herself to me in exchange for money to rescue her family. I swear it is the noblest thing I ever heard. Can such a one be duplicitous? And, though you will scarcely credit it, cynic that you are, I would swear she felt the same attraction for me that I did for her."

Henry smirked. "I'm told you are quite good-looking and, as you say, you are rich. I confess, were I a woman, I would feel a mighty attraction for you myself."

"You're a cold, heartless devil, Henry. That's why I rely on you to keep me safe. Now, let me sleep, if I can. We will have our work cut out for us tomorrow, and I look forward to my dreams tonight."

Jarrod Everly waited a long time for those dreams to come. Maërlys Blanc filled his thoughts, the feel of her, her smell, the softness of her breasts, her hair. He had touched every part of her and the memories kept him tossing and turning for hours, the sounds of which also kept Henry from sleeping. Jarrod thought he might be awake all night and expected to be up to greet the sun. Finally, his body defeated him; it was well after nine before he found Henry shaking him awake.

"What's the matter?"

"Your bird's flown."

Jarrod was alert in an instant. "The devil. I was wrong, then. I stand convicted of foolishness, taken in by an agent of the French. Though I'd swear, well, never mind. Anything can be counterfeited if someone is clever enough. Forgive me, Henry; I'll never mistrust your instincts again."

"Actually, you don't stand convicted of anything, since you're still lying down. And, as for the girl's guilt, that too is unresolved." He held up Jarrod's coat. The papers still projected from the pocket and the weight of the pistol was likewise evident.

"Are you sure she's gone? How about her trunk? I left that lying on it."

"I found it on the bed, apparently untouched. Perhaps I should have left it for you, so that you could see its exact attitude, but I was satisfied it hadn't been disturbed. The landlord assures me she left in the post-chaise at seven-thirty, the trunk with her."

"She left alone?"

"Again, relying on the landlord, yes. He says she was alone when she approached the driver about the fare. There were other people, including a pair of gentlemen, but he saw no reason to suspect she was anything but alone."

"Seven-thirty, and the coach goes all the way to London?"

"Yes."

"See what you can find in the stable. Give me some time to get dressed, and we give chase. Two hours' lead isn't so much. They'll have to stop to change at least twice. Find out where, if you can. I'll have our things sent to Cherille Hall."

4

"Fine horses, Henry."

"Well, I hope so sir, considering what you paid for 'em."

"Never stint, do I?"

"One of your many good qualities, sir."

"Please, Henry, can't you leave off the 'sir' when we're alone? Your deference never stops you bossing me around. To be honest, it seems a little hypocritical."

"Society is built on hypocrisy, sir. I hope I know what's right."

"You always win the arguments, too. Where are we going?"

"Landlord says they stop in Conford, most likely, but we have little chance to catch them there. With the change, they will probably leave there in about half an hour. If we make good time, we have a chance to catch them at Guildford for dinner. If we miss them, maybe Epsom or Croydon."

"Well, let us see if we can make good time, then."

They did not make good time. Not wanting to stop, they pushed the horses too hard and limped into Guildford a good forty-five minutes after the coach left.

By the time they found replacement mounts and had a
bite to eat, at Henry's insistence, they were still an
hour and a half behind the coach when they resumed
their saddles. They passed through Epsom at a canter
and reached Croydon only five minutes after the post
did. Henry dealt with the exhausted beasts while
Jarrod consulted the coachman.

"Lady, sir?"

"About nineteen or twenty, very good-looking,
well-dressed. You can hardly have failed to notice her."

"Oh, aye, the one with no blunt. I remember."

"That's probably her. Is she still with you?"

"No sir. Got off."

"Got off?"

"Aye, with the gentlemen."

"Gentlemen?"

"Aye. She come up this morning, looking to ride
with almost no blunt, like I said, and we was agreed
she'd go on top when the gentleman, well, they was
two on 'em, come and made up the fare. So, she rode
inside with 'em."

"Where did she leave you?"

"Guildford, in course. Didn't see her at dinner.
Gentleman came in and made me leave my meal. Took
his and t'other gent's luggage; took the lady's trunk as
well. Said they was in a hurry and couldn't wait
around for us all the day."

"Did you see which road they took?"

"Nay. Could have been same as us, mighta gone
north, like to Woking."

Rejoining Henry, Jarrod said, "That's torn it. We can't go to every town between here and Woking, looking for this particular needle. We will reach Cherille House tonight, see Sir Charles in the morning, and maybe even be in Wiltshire tomorrow night."

She had known she would probably have to ride on top part way but the coach driver was adamant. It was true she probably looked a little slovenly after her mostly sleepless night in the hot little room. Dickering for a place in the coach and arguing the cost for her trunk made her impecunious situation evident. She was just getting ready to climb up when the gentleman arrived.

"Here, here, can't stand to see a lady ride on top. Take that, my good man, and she'll ride inside with the rest of us."

"Oh, sir, you are too good. If you provide me with your direction, I will see you repaid after we get to London."

"Nonsense. A mere nothing. Let me help you in. Probably won't be comfortable, all squeezed in together and jostled as if we were cream in the churn, but at least you won't be wind-blown."

She did find herself crammed in, with the friendly gentleman on one side and another more taciturn man on the other. They looked similar, both wearing black breeches and coats, white stockings and shirts, black waistcoats. Not unlike ministers or undertakers. She pushed that thought away.

Across from them were a farmer and his wife, on their way to London to see an old relation, an aunt of the wife's. The farmwife had hopes of a legacy from her aunt and they believed they could push this along by visiting, now that the old lady seemed to be nearing her extremity. Neither had ever been to London and the woman was looking forward to it immensely.

The third traveler on that side, also dressed in dark clothes, was a recent arrival from the Americas on his way to London as a matter of business. The gentleman who had paid her fare, introduced as Mr. Caron, seemed very interested in this man, and they carried on a lengthy conversation about the news from Jamaica, business there and in London, crop prices, inroads made by the French into commerce. Lost in her own thoughts, Maërlys paid little heed and so failed to notice Mr. Caron's expression at mention of the baron who had traveled on the packet.

No one else paid her the slightest attention except the farmer's wife, a Mrs. Thomas, who used her as a sounding board for all her ideas about London, legacies, etc. Fortunately, she did not seem to notice if Maërlys paid attention or not, as long as she got an occasional nod. Maërlys managed to stay awake for most of the first leg of the trip, but after Conford, her lack of sleep combined with the drone of Mrs. Thomas' voice overcame her and she was startled awake by their arrival at Guildford.

Distressed to find she had been leaning on her benefactor's shoulder, she apologized.

"Never think of it, dear lady," Mr. Caron responded. "I see we are arrived in Guildford, and," he consulted his watch, "since it is the dinner hour, we must consider our stomachs." The man on her other side was first down from the coach, and by the time Mr. Caron descended, was already returning from the dining room, shaking his head emphatically.

Caron helped Maërlys down, saying, "My friend Mr. Broader seems to feel that this is not a suitable place for a lady to dine. But no matter, there is another inn only a few steps away down the High Street. I trust you will accompany us?"

"Oh, sir, I couldn't presume. I have already stretched your hospitality much further than is right."

"Nonsense," answered Caron, taking her arm and guiding her firmly toward the street. "I'd never forgive myself if I allowed a lady to eat in such a place as that. You'll come with us and I'll see that you're properly fed. Still a long journey ahead of us." He continued to prattle as they walked down the street and into a place called the Goat and Ox, which Maërlys had to admit was much more elegant than the post inn.

They had a delicious dinner, of which Maërlys ate freely, her straitened circumstances having pinched her at breakfast. She and Caron were still eating when Broader, who had said almost nothing during the meal, excused himself and left the inn. He returned as they were just finishing an apple tart Mr. Caron had ordered for dessert.

"Got one," said Mr. Broader, jerking his head toward the door.

"Excellent," answered Caron. "Now, Miss Blanc, we will continue our journey in style.

"Whatever do you mean, sir?"

"Mr. Broader has obtained a closed carriage, with comfortable springs and well-padded squabs. You also have a good pair, Mr. Broader?"

"I believe they will serve, sir."

"But you can't mean to leave the coach, with our fares already paid," Maërlys protested

"We most certainly do," answered Caron. "Come. You will find it infinitely more comfortable. Theo here is an excellent whip, and we will beat the post by an hour or more."

"Oh, but honestly, this is really impossible. I have imposed on you far too much already. You are most gracious, but I really cannot—"

"Come outside," he said, taking her arm, "and we will see what Theo has laid on. You needn't decide yet."

Outside, the carriage was standing in the inn yard. The door on their side was open, the horses ready, and no one else around except a post boy vanishing into the stable. With a firm grip on her elbow, Caron led her to the carriage and brought her up to the door.

"See, young lady," he said. "Climb up in there and see how it responds when you jump in. And be sure and feel the seats. If they do not meet your approval, we'll not go."

"Really, sir," she protested, allowing him to help her up into the carriage, "It is just too much. I'm sure it's very comfortable, but you can see, it just wouldn't be proper. I mean, after all, we hardly know one another, and a lady travelling alone—"

"Nonsense," he cut her off, climbing into the coach behind her, his presence crowding her into the seat. He closed the door behind himself, sat next to her, and as she opened her mouth to protest again, wrapped one arm around her body, pinning her arms to her sides, and clapped the other hand over her mouth. She heard the horses loosened and Mr. Broader climbing into the driver's place, then the carriage was in motion. She struggled, but Mr. Caron held her firmly in his grasp.

"Now, Miss Blanc," he whispered in her ear, "we have a long ride and a long conversation ahead of us. If you like, I have a knife I can use to convince you to converse with me, but it would be a shame to cut up such a pretty face and you can be of much more use to us with your beauty intact. Nod your head slightly if you recognize the hopelessness of your position and agree to a discussion of facts."

She was helpless. The carriage was in motion and Caron sat between her and the left-hand door. The other door was fastened tightly and she realized that

even if she were willing to jump from the moving
carriage, she would never get it open before Caron
dragged her back. Reluctantly, she nodded her head
and the hand over her mouth was removed.

"Excellent," Caron said. "Now then, my child, I
will tell you that we have been set to watch the
activities of a man, a Mr. Jarrod Everly, and we have
noted your association with him. I do not know if this
association is a political one but Everly is a very
dangerous man. If it were determined that you are in a
political alliance with him, your position would become
very delicate indeed. So now tell me who you are in
fact, how you support yourself and what is your full
relationship with this Everly. I warn you before you
start; we have a great deal of information and any
attempt to deceive us will be most unfortunate.
Proceed."

Maërlys was completely nonplussed. She had
little or no knowledge of English politics; she had
followed the career of Napoleon Bonaparte in France
for purely personal reasons. The idea that Mr. Everly
might be involved in political intrigue had never
occurred to her. She supposed it didn't matter, since
she knew nothing and would never see Everly again.
So, she told herself, she could do him no harm.

"My name is Maërlys Blanc, as you know, and I
became interested in Mr. Everly for my own reasons. I
knew him to be rich and had hoped to convince him to
provide me with money for a personal project. I failed. I
return to my cousin's dress shop to live out the rest of

my days in hard work and, possibly, penury. I know of nothing more I can tell."

"Oh my dear, you have only just begun. Tell me of this dress shop."

"My cousin's shop? It is Emmeline Élégance in London. It is certainly no concern of yours."

"I believe we know of this shop." He consulted a small book from his pocket. "Owned by Emmeline Blanc. Blanc. Why, that is your name. But of course, you said she is your cousin. But your name, then, is not really Blanc, is it? Already you lie to me. What is your true name?"

"I didn't mean to lie. Emmeline Blanc is my cousin's name and I have used it all these years I have been in England, but in France my family name was de Brissy. Is that what you mean?"

"Yes. You see, we get on. Now tell me how you expected to induce this Everly to give you money."

A wave of humiliation washed over her. Her face flushed, went ghostly, then flushed again. Her vision darkened, and she swallowed back the nausea. To expose her frailty, her foolishness, her very being to this horrible man would be too much. She looked around wildly, but she was just as helpless as she had been before. Tears began to run down her face, and then she was sobbing uncontrollably.

Caron handed her a handkerchief and waited patiently. "Don't worry, my dear. We have a very long journey ahead and you must see that when it is over there will be no secrets between us. Compose yourself.

Decide how to tell me of this attempt to draw Mr. Everly into your financial plan and then tell me all. We have plenty of time."

5

It was long after dark by the time they reached Berkeley Square. They led the horses to the stable in back and took their time finding grain and brushing the animals down.

As they worked, Jarrod apologized. "Sorry, Henry, we don't keep a regular groom here this time of year; hardly get any use out of the house these days, until after harvest in the fall."

"I can tend the beasts, sir, if you'd like to see to our welcome inside."

Jarrod frowned. "Don't be ridiculous. I accept you as servant when it suits our purposes, but not between ourselves. I can wipe down my own horse, just as well as you."

"Then why aren't you finished yet?"

"All right, all right, almost as well as you. Are you satisfied?"

Henry reached over with the currying brush. "Just this little area here," he said.

Jarrod seized Henry's arm with one hand, putting his other arm around his friend's shoulder. "Damn your impudence, Henry. Come along; let's see what's what."

Pushing open the door to the house they found a candle burning on a side table, and a voice behind it warned, "Stop right there, villains. Make a false move and this shotgun will make you regret it."

They froze. "That you, Thompson?" Jarrod asked.

The man beyond the candlelight moved forward, until his face came into view. He picked up the candle with one hand and thrust it into Jarrod's face, then suddenly backed up.

"Lor' sir, you give me a scare, you did! Heard you messin' around the stables. On the verge of callin' the watch when I heard you at the door. Didn't know you was in England. You been to Wiltshire?"

"Not yet. Urgent dispatches for the ministry. Why?"

"Ain't seen his lor'ship, sir?"

"Just got to Portsmouth yesterday. Speak up, man. What's amiss?"

"Had an accident, sir. His lor'ship, I mean. Pretty bad, from what I can gather. Course nobody tells me nothin'," he muttered.

"We'll go tomorrow. Is there anything to eat? If you could bring us something in the library, you can tell us about Christian then."

Jarrod moved forward and Henry followed, the candle illuminating his features for the first time.

Thompson fell back, startled, and the candlestick quivered in his grasp. "What's this?" he gasped.

Jarrod grabbed his wrist to steady the candle, then removed it from the caretaker's grasp and used it to light three candles in a candelabra on the sideboard. "For heaven's sake, man, steady on. Have you never seen a black man before?"

"Not in Cherille House, I ain't," Thompson answered. Then, remembering his place, "Least not but for the knives and boots boy we had back a while. About the year one, I believe. But he were just a lad and he didn't last," he added darkly.

"Thompson, meet Henry Winnow, my best friend," Jarrod responded, laying very heavy stress on the last words. "He and I will be in the library. Please bring us something to eat, and I expect to hear more about Christian's accident. That will be all for the moment."

He handed the candle back to the caretaker, picked up the candelabra, took Henry's arm with his other hand, and led him toward the library. Thompson shuffled off toward the kitchen, and they could hear him muttering. Jarrod looked apologetically at Henry, who grinned.

The remainder of the journey to London was a nightmare, and Maërlys remembered only bits and pieces. No matter what she told Caron, he had more questions, and it seemed to her that she was compelled to remove her soul and show it to him, naked and quivering.

"So, this Everly, he stopped his assault on you when?"

"When he, he realized I was, I was...."

"A whore?"

"A virgin!" she gasped, and began crying once more. She did not see Caron's startled expression, eyebrows almost touching his hair.

"And did he promise to give you money?"

"No, no, he only promised to talk to me again."

"So, he will seek you out?"

"He doesn't know where to find me."

He consulted his little book, in which he had been making notes. "But you said you saw him in your cousin's shop."

"He doesn't remember. I don't think he noticed me. I was only seventeen."

"Hmm," Caron muttered, clearly skeptical, making more notations. "If you need money so badly, why did you not wait and talk to him."

"Why? What have I left to talk to him about? My poverty? My foolishness? My, my virginity?"

"And what, pray, did you need money for?"

And so it went on to her last secret, the children. She told him almost everything; how her parents died; how the children had gone missing in France; the need for money to hire someone to help get them out. All she kept back was that she knew where they were.

That was a secret she had told no one, except Emmeline. Not even Everly.

At one point, after it had gotten dark, the carriage stopped on the verge of a lonely road. She had no idea where they were. Broader got down and looked in the window.

"What do you want?" Caron asked. "Why have we stopped?"

"Have you got what you need from her? I thought she might provide some pleasure for us. She's a pretty little thing." Maërlys shrank back against the corner of the carriage.

"Back away. I will come down and talk to you." Caron turned to Maërlys. "You will stay here. You will not move." He removed a pistol from under his coat, and showed it to her. "I will be watching the coach. If you come out from either door, you will be shot and left to die where you fall. Do you understand?" She stared at him. "Nod your head if you understand." Slowly, she nodded.

She heard them talking, but they spoke low and most of the words were unintelligible. When their voices rose she caught snatches: "virgin," "cause," and once "worth more alive." She huddled in the corner of the coach and discovered that she was whimpering. Once, she even considered jumping from the carriage, thinking that bleeding to death on the road would be preferable to this torture, preferable to any further horrors these men had in store for her.

When Caron came back, that's how she was. Curled up in the corner, feet on the squab, arms around her legs, face buried between her knees, whimpering. He ignored her, sat, and they started off again.

It took a thousand years, but the next time they stopped, he opened the door and stepped down. Then he reached back inside, took a firm hold on her hand and physically dragged her out, setting her feet down on paving stones. It was dark and they were on a city street. No one was in sight, and she knew it must be very late. She looked around, half expecting to see a guillotine, so much had the carriage begun to feel like a tumbril. Nothing looked familiar. From the rear of the coach, Broader brought her trunk, setting it down at her feet. She cowered as he looked at her, then he turned and resumed his place on the box.

Caron said, "We part for now, but we know where to find you. If we have to look for you, your cousin will suffer, as will your brother and sister. Do not speak of us to anyone and do not hide. You will only make it worse. *Adieu.*" Then the carriage was gone and she was alone.

She looked at the street again and forced her feet to carry her to the corner. The view to her right was familiar. She looked left along the empty street and saw Emmeline Élégance. Her mind in a whirl, she returned to her trunk and began to drag it toward the shop.

"Thank you for seeing me so early, Sir Charles."

"Not at all, my boy, not at all. We have been looking for you every moment."

"We came as quickly as possible. Portsmouth on Monday, London last night. Too late to catch you." Jarrod handed a sheaf of papers across the desk.

Sir Charles Blankenship lowered his ponderous bulk into the chair behind his desk and opened the packet. Laying the papers out before him he muttered, "Take a chair, Everly," and gestured vaguely toward the wall.

Jarrod picked up a chair, placed it near a corner of the desk, and waited quietly while Sir Charles immersed himself in the sheets before him. For some minutes, the only sound was an occasional "Hum," or, once "Good gad," as the information contained in the papers was absorbed by the minister. Then he raised his eyes, stared at Jarrod and tapped the papers. "But look here, d'ye mean the French have actually subverted Jacoby? And Randall? Good gad, man, Randall?"

"I was quite as perturbed as you, Sir, and would have taken steps, but it seemed judicious to leave them in place, at least for the time being. If you examine the accompanying second list, you will see that several of our best men are in danger of their lives, if these discoveries become known."

"Yes," Sir Charles murmured, glancing at the papers again.

"I am sorry. That is why I have come as quickly as I could."

Sir Charles frowned. "Were you followed?"

"We noticed no pursuit once we left Portsmouth, but there were definitely watchers at the dock. Henry helped me prepare this, in case we were taken." He handed a second sheaf of papers to the minister.

Jarrod watched him frown as he began to peruse the second set of sheets, then he smiled. At one point, he actually smirked. "Very good, very good," the minister chuckled, tapping the sheets. "Who is this Henry?"

"Henry Winnow, whom I met in Jamaica. He is a former slave who saved my life in a dicey situation two or three years ago. Since then, he has become my closest companion, as well as eyes and ears in communities where I am not welcome. His ability to suborn the servants of noble Jamaican houses, to say nothing of those in Fort-de-France, has been invaluable."

"A black man? You trust him?"

"I do. In fact, I have trusted him with my life, time and again, and helped him when he was in some tight places. We have chewed roots together when we were lost without food in a forest on a hostile island, pursued by the French. When I came back home at my father's death, it must be a year and a half ago, he kept my connections in the islands well in hand and added some threads during my absence. You have been paying him for years, although I haven't seen any need to mention it."

Sir Gerald looked startled and reached for a book in his lower desk drawer. He thumbed through it, frowning.

Jarrod smiled and went on. "We hold no secrets between us, and I honor his intelligence and discernment. As you can see from that poisoned report, he is both intelligent and subtle. It is too bad we were unable to get it into French hands."

"Yes, a pity," Sir Gerald answered, still thumbing his book. "Ah, here I see the pattern, now you explain it. I, ah, I mean, we, had thought some of these expenditures rather high, but I was able to point out to the committee that the results spoke for themselves." He looked up at Jarrod. "Perhaps I was wrong?"

"Only in detail, Sir, never in essence."

"Well, thank the fellow for me, but if you expect us to pay for him while he is in England...."

"Never in life, Sir. He is here at my behest and expense, though it's little enough he is willing to spend. I'll make another try to get him to enjoy himself, as soon as I can. For the present, however, I would appreciate any assistance you can give me in the matter of a young woman."

Sir Gerald looked surprised again. "That is not what we are here for. This fellow must find his own women. Have you been to the east end?"

"You mistake me, Sir. While we were in Portsmouth we met a young lady. Henry noticed her on the dock and then she turned up at our inn. We naturally mistook her for a French agent but I am convinced we were in error. She refused to take those papers, though they were thrust under her nose, figuratively speaking. I had an encounter with her, a sweet encounter, and I wish to extend the acquaintance. She is a French émigré and I believe you keep lists. She gave the name Maërlys Blanc. I intend to take other steps to locate her but would be glad of what assistance you can lend me."

"I suppose we owe you a great deal more than that, given your refusal to accept regular government recompense."

Jarrod drew himself up. "I believe I receive the usual pay of a soldier in the British Army."

"Yes," Sir Charles said drily. "Eight pence a day, rain or shine. We have it for you any time you choose to collect it." He consulted his book. "For the last five years, it comes to sixty pounds, sixteen shillings, and fourpence. Are you in immediate need of money?"

Jarrod blinked. "So little? Why do we pay such taxes, if that is all you offer these fellows who are dying every day to protect us from that monstrous Boney? A man takes the 'king's shilling' and has to work three days to get the whole thing? Well, never mind. I'll get it later. Right now, I have other business and wish to be on my way to Wiltshire as soon as possible. Christian has had some sort of accident, and

I must fly to his bedside. I will be back as soon as ever
I can."

"Bill, this is my friend Henry Winnow. Henry,
say hello to the best thief-taker in London, Bill
Nubbins."

Nubbins reached out his hand. "A pleasure, I'm
sure. Mr. Everly 'as done me many a favor and I 'ope
I've done 'im one or two in return. If you've been with
'im in those islands, I daresay you're aware of 'is little
ways." He grinned.

Henry grinned back. "I know exactly what you
mean. Wants watching every second, he does."

Bill laughed delightedly. "I see we understand
one another."

Jarrod said, "Well, I don't understand a damn
thing either one of you is saying and I don't want to.
What I want, Bill, is for you to find me a girl."

"Nothing easier. For a fine gentleman such as
yourself, good-lookin', well-dressed, with plenty of
brass, take your pick, I says. Dark? Fair? Tall? Short?
Plenty of curves," he illustrated with his hands, "or
more willowy-like? Will you want immediate service, or
delivery at some future time?" His smile was broad
enough to be mistaken for a wooden picket fence.

"I'm serious," Jarrod answered. "This is a
particular girl. She's about five feet high—"

"I think just five and an inch," Henry interrupted.

"Blue eyes that glow in the dark—"

"Pale gray-blue, fairly large, set wide," Henry added.

Jarrod said, "The face of an angel—"

"Oval. Straight, even nose turned up very slightly at the tip. Chin well-formed, with just the slightest suggestion of a cleft. High, strong cheekbones."

"The most alluring lips—"

"Small mouth, full lips, lower slightly pouty, if you understand me."

"I do, I do," said Bill, hurriedly making notes. "So good to get sensible instructions."

Jarrod ignored them. "A perfect figure."

Henry shrugged, "Hourglass, leaning ever so slightly toward pear. No fat, to speak of."

"Very good, very good. 'Er 'air?" Bill asked.

"Like silk," Jarrod said.

"Long, straight, dark brown with some golden highlights. Too dark for chestnut, but tending that way," was Henry's contribution.

"Anything else you can tell me?" Nubbins asked.

"Don't forget the French accent," Jarrod added. "Just the slightest undertone. Listen closely or you'll miss it. Otherwise, her English is excellent, gentry at least."

"Royalist *émigré?*"

"Almost certainly. Check royalist circles."

"May take some time, but if she can be found, I'll do it. Want 'er brought to you?"

"No, just locate her, if you can, without making her aware she's been noticed. We have word that she left Portsmouth in the company of two gentlemen. I would give a great deal to know who they were. Anything you can tell me about who she associates with, her friends and relations, would be useful, but use caution. I don't want her frightened, and any associates must not know of our interest. I have no idea whether she is in any danger or not."

"We'll be like mice. No one will notice us at all. Where can I reach you?"

"I must return to Wiltshire immediately. I hope to open the town house as soon as I can, but my brother is ill. I must remain by his side for now. You will let me know if there is anything you need, or if you find out anything I should know. This matter is quite urgent to me, but be very cautious. It is possible the French watch us at this moment, and they will certainly attend your movements. Be circumspect."

"I understand, sir. You realize, one of you may be needed for positive identification. I think, upon reflection, I would prefer you, Mr. Winnow."

Henry smiled and bowed. Jarrod scowled.

6

Facteau glowered at his lieutenant. "What do you mean, you let him go? Your orders were to keep him in sight at all times. Do my orders mean nothing to you?"

"We had a stroke of luck and I thought—"

"Do I pay you to think or follow orders?"

Caron drew himself up. "In view of the ultimate goal, I decided this contact was more important. It was not possible to follow both. I was compelled to make a decision, and I did. If I have done wrong, I accept the responsibility."

"What contact?"

"A girl. A French girl. She was watching for him just as we were. She—"

"How is that possible? Is she connected to the ministry?"

"No. Of that I am certain. She told me she saw him on the dock, recognized him as a rich man, and made contact. She is really a clever girl, except for some lapses in her understanding. I think these are merely due to youth and inexperience. Properly handled, she will be an excellent tool."

"What is her connection to Everly?"

"She knows of no connection to him before Portsmouth. Her knowledge of the de Brissy history is as limited as his knowledge of the family Everly before the conquest. Neither knows anything of the Leissègues. She merely hoped to pry money out of him, blackmailing him with her body. It is an attractive body, and it may be that her plan might have worked, given time, but she is too inexperienced to understand that. She lured him to her room, offered him her favors. He was pleased, thinking her experienced. She is, in fact, very lovely. Unfortunately, or indeed fortunately for us, he discovered her innocence before the damage was done. He is a very conservative gentleman and drew back, intending to discuss the matter with her the next morning."

"He refused her?"

"*Oui.* Is it not strange, the value these *Anglais* place on this little bit of flesh which, after all, is only in the way?"

"Bah, you should see the Americans; they are worse. Did he take it up with the girl the next morning?"

"*Non.* She felt humiliated, was convinced she had failed, and took to her heels. She knows nothing of men. She told me he had rejected her because she was unspoiled. Such a child."

"Did he not?"

"It is my belief that she has sown seeds with this Everly. He will be intrigued, perhaps even fall in love with her. Her beauty and obvious innocence will draw him, and he will find her. If he does not, we will throw her in his path, but it would be better if he finds her on his own. We will watch them both, and wait for our chance."

Facteau continued to glower. "Our time is not infinite. Leissègues could sail at any moment. We must be active, take our opportunity and be away before he returns to France."

"True, but we call the tune. If hurry is needed, we can hurry, but as long as he remains in Santo Domingo, we can take our time. A man who has lost an entire fleet can be in no hurry to return home."

"What steps did you take with the girl? You are very confident of her."

"Theo and I spirited her away from the coach. She had little money and would have been forced to ride outside except for our intervention, so it was easy to get her alone and bundle her off. I questioned her at length and, in fear for her life, I believe she was truthful with me. I have not told you the best part. She wished for the money from Everly to bring her brother and sister from France to England. Children of the de Brissy. Does that remind you of anything?"

Facteau's sour look changed to one of surprise. "From Cholet? Near Nantes?" He rose and turned to the map on the wall. "But the treasure...."

"*Oui*. As I say, a piece of luck. Divine intervention, perhaps."

Facteau glowered again. "Counter-revolutionary nonsense. How do you know you can control the girl?"

"That idiot, Theo, stopped the coach and asked if he could rape her. If all I had said before had little effect, and I believe she was already in our power, that was the final straw, as these *Anglais* say. I told her I would shoot her like a dog if she tried to escape, spoke privately with Theo, and when I returned she was abject. My heart would have gone out to her, were she not royalist *merde*. She whimpered the rest of the way and was confused when we left her on the street. She certainly expected to be killed."

"You warned her?"

"In the strongest terms. We can lay our hands on her whenever we wish. Her cousin and siblings are forfeit, and she knows it."

Facteau began to pace, then returned to the map. "What about these de Brissy children? Can we lay hands on them?"

"That I have not had time to explore, but will do so as quickly as possible. The boy is close to military age, and that may be the best chance."

"Then go. I will think upon this new tool, and how we may best use her. You have taken steps where Everly is concerned?"

"*Oui*. He must have gone to his family home and it may be difficult to get close there, but we will do what we can and also watch the London house. We will pick him up soon enough."

"Good. See if our contacts at the ministry can provide copies of his report."

Facteau returned to his desk and proceeded to examine papers, paying no further attention to Caron, who turned and left, closing the door carefully behind him. The look on his face was, of course, unseen by his master.

It was after sunset when Cherille Hall came into view. No lights shone on the ground floor, and only three windows on the first floor were lit. Henry held the reins while Jarrod bounded up the steps to the front door and pulled the bell. No one responded immediately, and after a short wait, he tried again. He was about to pull it a third time when he heard a bolt thrown back, and the door opened to reveal the butler, holding a candle and peering into the darkness.

"Early to bed, Marrin?" Jarrod asked.

The startled expression on the butler's face told Jarrod he should have warned them, but he'd gotten so wrapped up in the events at Portsmouth that he'd completely forgotten.

"My goodness, sir, I mean, you must forgive me. We had no idea you were yet in England." He opened the door wide. "No luggage?"

"It's being forwarded from Portsmouth; probably arrive tomorrow."

"Hmm. Very well. You'll be needing clothes, then. Be patient with us, sir, and I'll have someone prepare a room." He looked at Henry and raised his eyebrows. "Your valet, sir?"

"Call him rather my friend, and please prepare accommodations close to mine. May I present Henry Winnow, late of Jamaica, without whom I would not be here to brighten your evening. He too, could use a change of clothes, if you could arrange that. Lord Cherille is at home, I trust?"

"Yes sir, and his lordship will be that glad to see you, as are we all. We didn't know if you'd received word of the accident, but you've arrived in time, thank the good Lord."

"Thompson gave me a hint. Is it serious? What do you mean by in time?"

"You did not receive our letter?"

"No. What's amiss, man?"

"His lordship took a bad fall from his horse and there have been complications. I'm sorry to tell you, the doctors seem at a loss."

"Good heavens! Where is he?"

Marrin turned to the footman who had come up behind him. "Take care of Mr. Winnow, and find some clothes that fit him. Good clothes, mind. I'll take you to his lordship," he went on, turning back to Jarrod. "This way."

Instead of the larger master bedroom, Jarrod found his brother ensconced in the big guest bedroom at the front of the house. It was well-lit and there was even a fire, despite the warmth of the spring. As he came into the room, Christian, Lord Cherille, turned to look at him from the bed.

"Jarrod. Good to see you, and not before time. Pull up a chair and let me get a look at you." His hand reached out from under the covers, and Jarrod took it with both of his, staring at his brother's pale, sweaty countenance.

"Christian. What's all this? What have you been doing to yourself?"

"Just a stupid fall; think I'd never been on a horse before. Damn foot caught in the stirrup, twisted me around, and here I am."

"How long? What does the doctor say?"

"How long, Marrin? Nine days?"

"Yes sir."

"Thank you, Marrin. You may go. I expect you have things to take care of. Jarrod is sudden, as always."

"Yes sir. Thank you, sir." He closed the door behind him, leaving the two brothers alone. Christian turned his gaze on Jarrod.

"Afraid you're in for a bit of a turn-up. Glad you made it in time."

"In time for what? How long will you be stuck here?"

"The doctors are, I guess you would say, guardedly pessimistic. I am afraid I will be stuck, as you put it, for the rest of my life. Oh, don't worry," he added, as Jarrod made to question him further. "That won't be so very long. It's a good job you showed up when you did, or you might have missed me."

"You mean they can do nothing? A fall from a horse? Is this some sort of a joke?"

"Afraid not, brother mine. You'll probably be a baron before the month is out and possibly much sooner. It's turned septic, d'ye see, and it's gotten up where they can't just cut it out, as there won't be anything left. Hurts like the devil, I can tell you, and I won't be sorry to leave it behind." He tried to smile, but the effect was ghastly. He must have realized it, as he gave up the effort.

"But what about Susan?"

"Put it off too long. Should have married her a year ago, when there might have been a chance to spare you the responsibility. Too late now. She visits, and she's probably in her room down the hall, but we've both accepted what we have to accept. She's a beautiful woman, still young, and she'll be all right. I expect you to see to that. Promise me." His hand clenched Jarrod's.

"I don't know what to say. Of course, I'll do whatever is necessary, for, for, are you sure? Can we get another doctor? Have you sent to London?"

"Sorry. London doctors have been and gone away, shaking their heads. You're for the high jump this time, little brother, and no mistake. Promise me you'll do better than I did. Marry, start a succession. Don't wait. We know not the hour, as they say. You could marry Susan if you wanted. I'd feel better, knowing she was taken care of." He looked hopefully at his brother.

Jarrod shook his head, "She loves you, not me. It was always you and no one else, as you know full well."

"That's the only thing that worries me. I know I can trust you to take care of the estate, I just feel terrible about letting Susan down this way. She doesn't need money or the title, the Arvilles will be fine, but I hate to think of her alone. She's social, y'know; likes the bright life. I need to be sure you'll help her get over it and move on. Her whole life is ahead of her."

"I swear on my life, Christian, I'll do whatever she needs to make her happy. But maybe there's still hope...?"

This time the smile came unbidden, melancholy though it was, but vanished almost immediately. "Can't blame you for trying to weasel out of the responsibility. Afraid this time you won't escape, but it's not like you to pretend in the face of bad news. Always do what you have to, that's what I rely on you for. Guess that's what you've been doing in the colonies. Well, you'll have to chuck it. Got a home to look after now. Sorry, but that's how it is."

There was a soft knock at the door, then it came slowly open and Susan Arville, Christian's fiancée, pushed her head around. "They told me you were here," she said to Jarrod. "How is he?"

"As well as can be expected, Susie," Lord Cherille answered. "Just been giving young Jarrod his marching orders. Promises to look after you and Cherille when I'm gone."

"I'd like to avoid any such subject," she said, still looking at Jarrod, "but he won't let me. 'Got to face facts, old girl,' he says, and I suppose he's right. He usually is. These last two days he's been giving me instructions for you, in case you didn't make it in time. Thank God you got our letter."

"Actually, I never did."

"See," Christian put in. "He's just lucky, as always. Turns up wherever he's needed, our Jarrod." His face twisted as he was seized by pain. The hand in Jarrod's clenched and relaxed.

Susan rushed to his side, and felt his brow. She took a cloth from the bowl on his bedside table, and washed his face with it, then looked up at Jarrod. There were tears in her eyes.

"That's how it is," she said. "He tries to talk, tell us what we need to do, and he wears himself out. Then the pain takes him and he passes out. I hate it, I hate it, I hate it." She put her face in her hands and began sobbing.

"I'm sorry," Jarrod said, opening his arms to her. "I'm so sorry."

7

Jarrod stared at Susan. "But I cannot leave now. He sinks every day. What kind of brother would I be?"

"The kind you are. The best any man could ask. You have to understand, he feels so bad about leaving all of us. The responsibility wears straight through him. Part of that is his belief that you don't want the title...."

"Which I don't."

"Yes, but he feels it a failure that he cannot protect you from it, as he feels it a failure that he cannot now make me a baroness. As if that mattered. Well, never mind. As long as we hang about moping, it just makes it harder, and he clings to life, despite the pain. You know I cannot leave him, no matter how much he might wish it, but you can. Please. Talk to Marrin. He has a number of things he wants done in London, things he cannot trust to a servant. Take your friend Henry, show him the town. Spend a few nights at Cherille House. I promise it will ease Christian's mind to know you are not constantly fretting over him."

"You make it impossible for me to refuse. How long must I stay away?"

"Don't take it like that, Jarrod, please. Just spend a couple of days in London and then come home. You can find something to do."

"But surely, Maërlys, you can trust me. All these years we have been like sisters; at least, I have looked on you as a sister. But to vanish for days on end? To come back in the night, looking as if you have lost your last friend? Moping around the shop? And your dress! I found it, you know. Oh, my dear, whatever did you do to that dress? It was so lovely, and now, anyone would think you had slept in it for a week, and in the open, to judge from the stains. I find you here on Wednesday, and it is now Saturday, and still I am no wiser. Cannot you tell me anything?"

Emmeline Blanc was an elegant woman of twenty-four and would have been called handsome by any impartial observer. Without her cousin Maërlys' startling beauty and first bloom of youth, she had the same rosebud mouth and dark brown hair, but her nose was slightly more Roman. Her taller, slender figure was not as full, nor was she as obviously aware of her attractions as her cousin. The light of mature intelligence shone from Emmeline's grey eyes, and her moods were less mercurial.

"Oh, Emmy, you are so kind to me, and I do not deserve it, I do not. I am a ninny, a fool of the lowest order, and whatever fate befalls me cannot be as hard as I deserve. I wish I had gone to the guillotine with my parents. It would have been so much kinder. I live, but am of no use to anyone."

"Oh, please stop, Maërlys. You will have me in tears. You know I love you, and I need your help here. You have a place, a good one. Never speak of death. You have so much to live for."

At this, the younger woman burst into tears, her face still turned up to her cousin's. "Do I? Do I have anything to live for?"

Emmeline's eyes sharpened, and she frowned at the girl. "It's a man, isn't it? You've fallen in love and he's deserted you." Her lips twisted. "He tricked you into running away with him, promised you Gretna Green, and instead took you to some low place and had his way with you. Oh, my poor darling, do you think, I mean, do you think you, you'll have a, a baby?"

Maërlys stared at her, her tears drying on her cheeks.

Emmeline stood back, then began to pace. "He won't get away with it, he won't. He may try this with low-class women, but you and I are respectable. We'll find him out, and he'll marry you. You won't have a natural baby to be looked down upon by other children. He'll marry you, at the very least, and then, if he won't support you both, well, we'll do without him. We'll pretend he's dead and raise the child ourselves. Men, pah! They only cause trouble. I hope the child is a girl."

Maërlys put her hands over her mouth and began to giggle. Now it was her cousin's turn to stare. "I'm s-sorry," she stammered. It's just so, so, well, you've got it all wrong. I promise, there's no baby. At least, I think not. You can tell me more about how that happens, and we can see, but I don't think so, no." She was shaking her head now, quite distracted from the last four days of misery.

Then she looked up. "They have to put that, their thing in you, don't they? To make a baby, I mean. They can't do it with their fingers, or, or, anything, can they?"

Emmeline's eyes narrowed, and the look on her face told Maërlys that her secret was out. Her cousin's hands were on her hips now, "What exactly did you do with this man, Maërlys? Who is he?"

Maërlys looked at the floor, and her answer came in a croak. "It doesn't matter; it was all my fault. I followed him and tried to, to, get him to, you know, but he wouldn't. He was so kind, really. It wasn't at all as you think. When he touched me, he realized... I think he thought I was a, one of those women, for sale, but then he saw that I wasn't and he was so kind. It must have been terrible for him. He was so hard and swollen, and it must have been painful, but he didn't do it to me, not really."

"What do you mean, not really? Did he or did he not put himself inside you?"

"No, yes, I mean, not his...you know..., but his finger. And when he did, I cried out because it hurt,

and up to then, it had been so nice, and I wanted him
to do it, I really did, but then it hurt and he stopped
and made me tell him the whole story, and then he
kissed me, a sweet kiss, not like the ones before."

Emmeline's head was on one side, now, and one
eye was almost closed as she frowned at her cousin.
"The ones before?" she repeated.

Maërlys tossed her head. "Well, it's not as if I
was never kissed before, you know. I'm not a child."

This was too much for the older woman. She
knelt down and took Maërlys in her arms, kissing her
brow. "Are you not, my dear?" she murmured. "Are
you not? Tell me everything, darling, tell me all."

And Maërlys did tell her, except the part about
the two horrible men who brought her home, the ones
from the English government, because they'd told her
everyone would suffer. And she was the only one who
deserved to suffer.

When Maërlys finally paused, Emmeline said,
"Enough. This is a happy shop. We will make you
happy too. Come with me." She took the girl's hand
and pulled her out of the back room to the front
window. It was a quiet day, and only a few customers
had been in. At the moment, the shop was empty
except for the two of them. "*Voila.* Look outside. All
fashionable London is out this beautiful day, passing
by. Perhaps some rich peer will stop in, be swept away
by your beauty, and all your troubles will end."

Maërlys' eyes brimmed, and Emmeline hugged
her. "Ssh," she whispered. "I know this is a fairy tale,

but, after all, beautiful princess, you belong in a fairy tale. Try it. Imagination can give hope, and hope can lead, well, who knows where? Look, there is a handsome gentleman. See, he turns toward us."

Maërlys looked up, glanced out the window, gave a gasp, and shrank back in fear. It was him! Jarrod Everly. He must not see her. She looked around wildly and ran for the room at the rear. Her cousin watched, wide-eyed.

"Look at this shop, Henry. No doubt they offer the latest Paris fashions, in spite of the war. I hear that dolls wearing dresses in the latest mode are smuggled in every day for just that purpose, and this looks a very fashionable place. 'Emmeline Élégance,' indeed."

He thought for a moment. "If we ever catch that little beauty from Portsmouth, I'll dress her up with something nice from a shop like this. All about appearances, isn't it? If your skin were as pale as mine, I'd be the one carrying those parcels." He frowned at Henry. "After all, there is no question which of us is higher in the instep."

He looked curiously back at the shop. "I believe I was in there once, picking up something for Susan. No doubt owned by some well-to-do *emigré*. I wonder if Nubbins knows about it. We must ask him at the first opportunity. Now, I believe, this shop up here is the one we need. You have Marrin's list?"

"Right here, sir. We've got almost everything, except the special candlesticks, and there they are." He pointed toward the window. "At least, they match the description he gave you."

A brief exchange later, Jarrod emerged from the shop and Henry reached for the candlesticks. "I can carry them. You must let me share the burden, at least," Jarrod said.

"It isn't seemly, sir. People will notice. Give them to me."

Jarrod frowned at him for a moment, then gave up. "Very well, let us return to the house and gather our things. I've had enough of London, and the sooner we're back in Wiltshire, the better. We can make an early start tomorrow."

In the event, they had to deal with some trouble about the horses, and a problem with the off-side rear wheel, and it was afternoon before they left London. Traffic was terrible for a Sunday, the road was slow, and it was past five before they arrived at Newbury. By then, they were both hungry.

"Henry, does it appear to you that we've been followed?"

"I think so, but with all these carriages and horses it's hard to be sure. I have my eye on that fellow back there on the dappled gray."

Jarrod glanced casually around, taking in the dappled gray as he did so. "We will wait until we get to

Speen. The Raven will give us as good a supper as we can find anywhere, and the traffic will have thinned out."

"Means darkness across the downs."

"We're ready, aren't we? A little action might keep us sharp."

Henry glared, "If we aren't knocked on the head. Wouldn't like the title to go out of the family, would you, your lordship?"

"I keep pointing out, Henry, that we're friends. Less of that 'your lordship' bilge and more Jarrod, if you don't mind. As for the title, I'd be best pleased if it went out of the family before it got to me. But don't fret; I believe I've a distant cousin, Gerald, no, Harold, that's it. I think. Anyway, last I heard, he was still rolling along."

"How long ago was that?"

"Ten, maybe fifteen years. I was just a lad. Father told me of him. Don't believe we ever met. Of course, I'm not sure what generation he is. Might have been father's cousin, rather than mine. Ah well, bound to be some issue."

"You relieve my mind immeasurably."

At the Raven, the landlord refused to serve Henry inside, so, the weather being fine, they dined at a table in the garden.

"I suppose we must get used to this," Jarrod muttered.

"You could let me eat in the kitchen. Or invoke your heritage."

Jarrod frowned at him across the table. "You know better than that. I certainly have my faults—"

"Certainly."

"Your eagerness to agree should force me to consider adding another, but I suppose the list is long enough without the willingness to desert my friends. Besides, I've gotten used to keeping my name dark; it's sometimes better that way."

"Sometimes it doesn't matter." Henry didn't raise his head as he spoke. "There's that dappled gray."

"Check your priming before we leave. You might want to place that sword where we can reach it, too."

"The ceremonial we just bought?" Henry looked horrified.

"Got a blade, hasn't it? Mean more at a service if it were blooded."

"And the blade chipped? I don't know what to do with you, your lordship."

Jarrod grinned. "Just keep an eye on that man with the gray. French, you think?"

"Nothing to show it, but he's an ugly devil, and he never got that scar in King Street...what's this?"

"Should I look?"

"No. Just been joined by another. This one's never been seen in Mayfair, either. If they come at us together, you'll have all the action you're wanting."

"Big?"

"Very."

"Well, there's a long dark road between Hungerford and Marlborough, with hills in plenty. I know a good spot to wait for them."

It was well after ten as they left Marlborough behind. "See anyone?" Jarrod asked.

"Barely the hand in front of my face."

"Try mine." Jarrod held his hand up.

"Nice and pale. Catches the starlight. Best you keep it covered and, perhaps, put a pistol in it."

"You don't think we've lost them?"

"Where would we lose them? They must know our direction. I think they skipped ahead of us at Hungerford. They're on horseback and can certainly travel faster. I expect they're well ahead of us by now."

Jarrod frowned. "Yes, except for all this shopping, we'd be on horseback, perhaps even home by now. Well, we must make the most of it."

They were passing through a section of wood with trees gathering close to the road on either side. Henry's eyes suddenly darted to the left, then back. His head remained facing front as he drove. "Here they are now," he hissed through his teeth. "Take the one on the right."

Jarrod's hand came up with the pistol. Henry raised his whip and set the horses moving faster, turning them slightly to the left side of the road, just as a shadow moved out of the trees on that side. There was a shout of, "Stand and deliver!" followed immediately by two shots, almost simultaneous. On the right, a man clutched his breast and fell from his horse. On the left, the carriage horses rushed at the second man as his horse reared and plunged aside.

The man on the left had fired the second shot, and he hadn't missed, entirely. The reins fell from Henry's left hand as the feeling deserted it. He managed to hold on with the right, but the left-hand horse had its head and was frightened by the action. It lunged forward, bringing the other with it. To try to pull the other back would plunge them off the road into the trees. Henry flexed his hand, trying to get the feeling back.

Jarrod grabbed the other pistol and watched behind as the second attacker regained control of his horse and followed. Jarrod fired, and although he could discern no visible effect, the rider pulled his horse up short. As Jarrod reloaded, the horseman waited in the road and watched as they flew away behind the runaway horses. Then, slowly, he turned and went back to see to his companion.

Jarrod turned to Henry. "What now?"

"Scratch from a pistol ball. Dropped the reins. Here, hold this." He thrust the remaining ribbon into Jarrod's hand and stood up in the wildly pitching carriage.

"You've lost your mind. You'll never make it with a bad arm."

"You're too heavy. Hang on." Henry leapt forward and landed astride the left-hand horse. For a moment, his sudden weight renewed the animal's fear and it jumped ahead, but Henry leaned forward, wrapped his arms around its neck, and began to whisper in its ear. Slowly, the beast responded, and Henry, holding onto its neck for life, reached over with his other hand and began to stroke the neck of the second animal. Together, they slowed, Henry pulling at the left side of the right-hand horse and the right side of the one on the left, pulling them toward each other, slowing them until finally they stopped and stood panting.

Jarrod immediately looked around, reaching for the pistol beside him, but there was no sign of further pursuit. The road behind stretched empty and dark. The road ahead looked much the same.

8

"Well? Where are we?"

"We proceed, sir, we proceed," Caron answered. "We have Everly in our sights once more, after that nonsense on the downs."

"Fools. What can they have been thinking?"

Caron shrugged. "Perhaps they thought to enrich themselves, despite their orders. Perhaps they misunderstood their orders, although I don't see how. These English are so stupid; I wish we did not have to hire them. Either way, it no longer matters."

"They cannot be traced to us?"

"I doubt they can be traced at all. One was killed where he sat his horse. Everly is deadly with a pistol."

"The other?"

"I expect nothing will ever be found of him, at least nothing traceable."

"The Malay?"

Caron nodded. "I paid him. By now, that money is in the Malay's hands."

"Good," Facteau said. "So what about Everly now? Does he proceed with your little royalist?"

"Even before the incident on the downs, he was followed to her shop but he did not go inside. We believe his presence there was a coincidence and he has no idea of her direction. He returned to the estate in Wiltshire last night. His brother is expected to die at any moment and he will succeed to the title."

"The key?"

"It will come to him with the title."

"We must have it. It may solve all our problems."

"Of course. But we need to be careful. To attack a member of the house could be disastrous."

"Then have the woman steal it. What other use is she to us?"

"The children."

"Ah, yes, I had almost forgotten. You have found them?"

"Not yet. They do not appear to be at Cholet, as we had expected. Whether they were removed to Nantes or some other place after the execution of the parents, we are still searching. However, I have confidence we will soon have them in our power."

"Your confidence is all very well, but so far we have neither the children nor the key. Bring them together and we will be rich. Until then, we are all to seek. You say he was at the shop but did not go in?"

"Yes, he was with his slave. He went into the next shop and bought some candlesticks. No doubt for the bier. I expect he hungers for his brother's passing."

"Might it be best to throw the strumpet at him?"

"Perhaps when he returns to town. For the present, let us watch him and wait."

"Very well, but we cannot wait eternally."

Two days after the funeral, Jarrod rode to the Arville estate, where he asked for a private audience with Christian's fiancée. As soon as they were alone, he said, "Susan, I appreciate your giving me this time. I know this week has been very hard for you—"

"As for you, my lord," she interrupted. "You loved him as much as I did. As I still do." She looked down, then back up at Jarrod.

He winced and swallowed. "I would prefer you not address me that way, and certainly not yet. That is partly what I came to discuss with you. You know how much Christian loved you and you know, I trust, that his whole family shared his feeling."

She smiled sadly at that. "You are his whole family, my lord."

"Oh, yes, yes, but you know what I mean. Our parents always loved you. It was a source of joy and pride to them that you would one day be Lady Cherille, the perfect partner for Christian. The title is yours by right as much as mine. Christian was very particular in making his wishes known. I know that I can never replace him in your heart. Indeed, I would hardly wish to, but it was his desire that I see to your happiness and he was convinced that part of that happiness would be complete when you take your rightful place as Lady Cherille."

Her eyes widened, then narrowed as she frowned at him. "Are you making me an offer, my lord?"

"Please forgive me, Susan, I know it is too soon. If I were a free man, I would wait and woo you in the proper way, but there is the foreign office. You know I have a relationship with them and they expect certain services. If there were no war, I swear...." His voice drifted off.

Susan's eyes were mere slits, now. "You would swear what? That you love me?"

"Well, of course, I mean, as I said, we all have loved you since first Christian brought you home. I mean, how could I not love you, Christian's bride, my good sister-in-law? His only regret was that he never kept that promise to you and I am here to keep it for him if you will have me." He knelt next to her chair. "I want only your happiness; I swear it."

She studied him, staring into his eyes. Then, she smiled and slowly began to giggle. In a moment, she threw back her head and roared, as all the pent-up unhappiness of the last month caught up with her. Before she regained full control, she was pounding the chair arm with her fist.

Jarrod stared at her, emotionally off balance, trying to understand. She let out the last giggle, followed by a hiccup, reached out and put her hand behind his head. She leaned forward and kissed him full on the mouth, a kiss he was too startled to return. Then she sat back and regarded him, smiling.

"Thank you, Jarrod, that was so sweet."

"Then it is settled? We can marry whenever you like. I suppose there must be a suitable period of mourning, but I know Christian would have wanted it to happen as soon as possible. He did worry so about the succession, and, I must admit, the ministry does occasionally place me in danger."

"Not like this, I'll wager," she muttered. Then she said, "Of course there must be a suitable period of mourning. At the moment, I feel as though I could never marry anyone except Christian, though they tell me that feeling will fade with time. So, I will take time. I did want to be Lady Cherille, because Christian was Lord Cherille, and sometimes, I want to be dead, because Christian is, but they tell me that is cowardly and I must face life without him. The Arvilles are not cowards, whatever else we may be, nor do we need titles other than our own."

She paused at the look on Jarrod's face. "Oh, I am sorry. I'm not insulted, and I certainly do not mean to insult you, my lord, but you know it is too absurd. You certainly don't think I'm fool enough to believe you love me, and you must also know that I loved Christian, not his title." She reached out and took his hand. "We've always been friends, Jarrod, and I hope we always shall be so, but as for the succession, I mean, do you really think we could do what's necessary without dissolving into laughter?" She raised her eyebrows and looked at him. "Could you?"

He stood to his full height and looked down at her. "You question my manhood?"

She looked up at him for a moment, then began giggling again. "You try that on all those other ladies if you like, but not on me. I'll spank your little backside, your lordship."

"All right, all right, have your fun; I only meant it for your happiness." He sat down on the floor, next to her chair, and shook his head. "I suppose I did look ridiculous."

She smiled at him. "I believe we passed ridiculous a considerable way back. But I do appreciate it, Jarrod, I really do. You are a dear and quite brave to sacrifice yourself this way to Christian's wishes. He could be imperious at times, forgetting other people's needs in his own eagerness to make them happy." Her smile grew wistful and she added, "I often had to frustrate him when he got like that, and we must do it one last time. It may be that I will someday find a man who can make me forget Christian, and then I can be happy with him. Right now it seems incredible, but we do not know the future. However, it would certainly not be you, even if you didn't remind me so much of him. You're a good man, Jarrod. Find a wife who loves you, and take care of the estate. That's what Christian would really have wanted. Now, admit it, are you not at least a little bit relieved?"

"I only wish Christian could be here, to see how wisely he chose. But he knew that, so we will let him rest. And you must promise me that you will always, and I do mean always, treat us as family. I never expect you to call me 'lord' or 'lordship' again. I am

Jarrod and will be as long as we live, I hope. Call me anything else, and I shall know I've offended you."

She leaned over and kissed him again, this time on the tip of his nose. "You are the second-sweetest man I have ever met, Jarrod. We shall certainly be friends until we're old and gray."

"Your lordship, there's a message."

"Well, come in here." Jarrod led the way into the library and closed the door. "Now you can drop the lordship and tell me what I need to know."

"It's from Nubbins. He says he needs help right away." Henry thrust the letter at him.

"It is certainly a matter of identification. He's far too resourceful to need us for anything else."

"Shall we go?"

"I really am not at liberty. Not at once. Well, he did say he'd prefer you, anyhow. At all events, there's little I can do that you cannot. I'll give you a letter to Thompson, and he'll make you welcome at Cherille House or answer for it. This soon after the funeral, he'll be on pins and needles. He used to make things a bit rough for me when I was a lad, but he's a good-hearted fellow at bottom. His place is not really in danger, but you can imply that it is if he gives you any difficulty. Matter of fact, if he gives you *too* much trouble, he'll find himself wielding a scythe here at the hall. After that business last week, I've lost count of how many times you've saved my life."

"Thank you, but we had pretty equal shares in that little dust-up."

"Funny, I don't recall jumping through the air like an acrobat, with an injured arm, to stop a runaway pair. Perhaps I was asleep at the time, and missed it."

"You only missed it because I stopped you; I was thinking of the horse. How we should have gotten home after you'd broken its back, I'm sure I don't know."

"That'll do. You'll put me off my food. However, while you're in London, you might take the opportunity to enjoy yourself a bit." He went to the desk, opened a drawer, and took out a box. He removed a pile of notes and handed it to Henry. "We may be only barons, here at Cherille, but I wish I had a quid for every time we've loaned money to a duke or an earl. Whatever else, we won't starve. You could find a girl while you're in town. Nubbins will direct you. I've no doubt he knows someplace where you can stay with her, as well. Might be best not to have strange women at the house. However, it is your house while you're there, so don't let anything get in the way of your pleasure. Promise me."

Henry bowed. "I will try to enjoy myself in your big city."

"Excellent. I will follow you as soon as may be; two or three days, no more. Make no mistake, Henry. Were you not such an expert of survival, I would never ask you to go alone. London can be as dangerous as anywhere in the world."

Henry smiled. "You live in a free country, and freedom is always dangerous. Perhaps that's what freedom really is. I would never trade it for safety, which is usually an illusion anyway."

9

In spite of Jarrod's exhaustive descriptions and instructions, Henry knew that his birth in Jamaica and long experience in the islands of the Caribbean had not prepared him for London. He was relieved to find that he remembered almost every detail from his travels with Jarrod the previous week. He had no trouble finding his way to Mayfair, but decided to leave his mount at a public livery not far from Covent Garden, closer to Nubbins' headquarters in Blackfriars. It made him less conspicuous, which suited his natural bent. The slave trade may have been abolished, but not the institution.

Henry adopted the swagger he had noted in the comportment of London toughs and made his way on foot to Nubbins' neighborhood. With his cap pulled low, he leaned against a wall in a shady alley a half block down Feather Lane from Nubbins' address.

It became immediately clear that Nubbins was watched. A man, dressed as a porter, waited on the corner of Tudor Street doing nothing at all. Henry watched for over an hour, noticing that his eyes seldom left the direction of Nubbins' door. Midway through the second hour, another man approached the first, passed him by, and rounded the corner. As soon as the second man was out of sight, the first walked away. Henry watched as the second man came back, glanced around, and took up the same station on the corner. Henry went looking for the back door.

To avoid notice he took the long way around, and the shadows were growing before he found his way back to the alley parallel to Feather Lane. It only took him a moment to realize that this door was also under observation. Peering around the corner, Henry sized up the watcher and looked around at the nearby buildings. His quarry was in a doorway almost directly across the alley from Nubbins. Marking the place, Henry continued down to the next cross street and located the front of the building. It was a public house, just opening for the evening trade.

Unsure of the reception afforded dark skin in the area, Henry was careful approaching the landlord. Observing the tattoo on the man's forearm, he pulled off his cap. "All right to come in for a pint, captain?"

The proprietor looked at him, considering. "Be a sea-faring man, would ye?"

"Aye, and thirsty with it, begging your pardon, sir."

"A sailor's always thirsty, and it's me mission to remedy it. You'll never mind standing at the bar, will ye? There's an empty place down that end." He pointed to the far end of the completely vacant bar.

Henry walked meekly down the length and placed a gold coin on the bar. The landlord was there almost instantly, setting a pint on the bar and fingering the coin. "Been sailing in profitable seas, 'ave ye?"

"Oh, aye, and shipping a bit of water, as well. D'ye mind directing me to the heads?"

Still fingering the coin, the barman jerked his thumb toward a hallway, which ran past the end of the bar toward the back of the building. Henry knuckled his forehead again, bowed slightly, and set off down the hall.

As soon as he was out of sight, he raced for the back door. Quietly, he checked the latch. The door opened inward. From his pocket he drew a piece of wood, a little longer than his fist with a slight bulge at each end. He wrapped his fingers around it, raised his arm, and jerked the door open. Swinging his fist downward, the lower end of his weapon struck its target, just behind the watcher's left ear. The man dropped like a shot dove, collapsing in a loose pile of limbs and torso at Henry's feet.

He pulled the door quietly to, and rushed across the alley to Nubbins'. A light knock brought an eye to a lookout hole in the door, followed by the sound of the latch, then the man himself. With a finger to his lips Henry jerked his head at the door across the way, and was pleased by the quick intelligence in the other's eye. Together they rushed across, and in a moment the watcher was safely ensconced on a couch in Nubbins' parlor. With the door locked behind them, Henry and Nubbins smirked at each other.

"How long do you suppose?" asked Henry.

Nubbins consulted his pocket watch and said, "About an hour before 'e's relieved, if that's what you mean. I expect you've plans 'ow to best use the time?"

"Do we need information about them? Will we wake him up and ask him some questions?"

"Bless you sir, we know well 'oo 'e is and 'oo sent 'im. They're a nuisance but not an 'indrance, if you catch my meanin'."

"Is there another way for me to leave without being noticed?"

"I believe it can be arranged to your satisfaction," Nubbins smiled.

"Then it might be best to put him back, with perhaps an odor of something?"

"Will the landlord look for you?"

"He might, though I think he'll be well pleased not to find me."

"Then happen you should keep an eye on that door and, as soon as 'e's done looking, we'll put our friend back where 'e belongs. While we wait, I'll tend to that little niff you spoke of."

Henry put his eye to the door and was pleased to see the landlord open the one across the way after only a few minutes. He came out on the steps, peered around with a puzzled expression, then reached in his pocket and pulled out a coin. He examined it in the light from the doorway, bit it, looked at it again, glanced up and down the alley, shrugged and disappeared inside, closing the door behind him.

Henry turned back to Nubbins. "Oh, dear me," said that worthy, "I'm afraid the poor fellow's drunk more'n 'e can hold. Expect 'e'll sleep for a while yet. Care to take one end?" He arched his eyebrows at Henry, who seized the man's feet. They carried him back across the alley and propped him in the shadows at the tavern's rear door. Nubbins sprinkled the sleeping man liberally with gin, left a small bottle in his pocket, and shook his head regretfully. "Not the reliable sort of person you'd employ, is 'e, sir?"

Henry smiled, and they crossed the alley arm in arm, slipped inside and closed the door behind them. "You have some ladies you'd like me to look at?"

"One tonight, and a second tomorrow 'oo might be tricky. A moment and I am with you. Are you armed?" Nubbins asked. Henry nodded, and the thief-taker disappeared, returning in a few moments ready for the excursion. They slipped down the alley in the opposite direction from the watcher at the front, and soon were in a cab, rattling along the Thames.

Ensconced at a small table in a cheerful, noisy, and entirely disreputable ale house less than a block from the river, Henry sipped slowly at his pint until he felt Nubbins' elbow in his ribs. Looking up, he followed his companion's gaze toward a pair of young women, coming through the door on the arms of a well-dressed man. Henry noted the brown complexion and long dark hair of the one on the left, then turned his attention to the other. He was surprised at his own disappointment, unaware until that moment that his hopes had risen so high. It disconcerted him. Then he thought of Jarrod's feelings when they'd lost her on the road and his own ambiguity became clearer; Jarrod's happiness was important.

Nubbins said, "She's an 'ore, though expensive and discreet. We know she's a French agent, as is the man with 'er. D'ye recognize 'er?"

"No, but I'm glad you pointed them out. There's no telling what, or whom, we may need to know. I do see the resemblance, and you were right to check with me, but the one we want is less, ah, ripe and a bit shorter. I'm sure his lordship would say *more delicate*. What about the other girl?"

Nubbins winked, "Lovely, eh? Can't say I know much of 'er, though there are more rumors than you'd credit. She's not a regular sight in this part of London. Might be window-dressing, brought along for the evening. Maybe somethin' more." He looked at his watch. "We can await developments if you like. I fear we will not be able to see our other prospect before tomorrow."

"Then let us sit quietly, drink our ale and, as you say, await developments. I take it the other two are regulars in this establishment?"

"Like clockwork. Always been surprised the ministry don't take 'em up, but it's not our business. Sometimes nothin' 'appens we can discern, sometimes there is contact. Contact is usually fairly subtle, only occasionally clumsy, sometimes under cover of a diversion. We watch for anythin' out of the ordinary."

They didn't have to wait long. The gentleman brought his two companions to a table only a little way from where Henry and Nubbins sat, calling for wine as he did so. Henry glanced up as they came near and was surprised to find the dark woman's eyes upon him, frankly appraising. She didn't turn away as he looked up, but watched him openly. She smiled, winked and turned back to her companion as he helped her to her seat. She didn't say anything to the man and he took no notice of Henry and Nubbins.

The landlord, who seemed to know his patron well, brought the wine. He had barely left the table before a man, dressed as a seaman, came stumbling over and accosted the light-skinned girl.

In an instant the gentleman was on his feet, shouting at the intruder to leave them alone. He reached toward the sailor, and, as he did so, gave a hard knock to the other woman's chair, pushing it toward Nubbins' table. Henry saw his chance and moved quickly to catch the dark-skinned beauty as her chair fell over. He noted the exchange between the gentleman and the sailor as their hands touched, then turned to the woman he had rescued, trusting Nubbins to keep an eye on anything that passed.

Henry's breath caught for an instant as he found himself inches from the finest pair of intelligent dark brown eyes he'd ever seen. Lord, the woman was lovely. Don't let her be a French agent he thought to himself, even as he realized she almost certainly was.

She smiled up at him. "Thank you, sir, you are most kind," she said. He could discern no trace of a French accent, nor the tones of the London streets he had expected, but there was something else, a trace of accent he did not know. The far east, perhaps?

He smiled back, "Are you hurt, milady?"

She shifted slightly in his arms, still smiling. "Not in the least, so I suppose you must put me down. The matter isn't urgent, however." She pressed her head against his chest, and breathed a deep sigh, then smiled up at him again. She reached up and touched his cheek with uncommonly long, graceful fingers.

Henry realized he couldn't remember what he was doing. The feel and smell of her had nearly overwhelmed him. She was light but obviously strong; powerful, he thought. She smelled, not of perfume, but of fresh, clean woman in a way he found delightful. He moved his arms parallel, so she could stand gently on the floor. She was almost exactly his height, perhaps half an inch shorter. "Thank you again," she breathed, kissed his cheek, and turned back to her table.

Henry was frozen in place, until he felt Nubbins' hand on his shoulder. "We really should be goin'." He pulled Henry's arm, and they were outside in the dark. Henry blinked. Nubbins peered at him and smirked. "Should I slap you? Gently, of course. Did you see the transfer?"

Recalled to his duty, Henry shook his head, "Only the beginning. What happened?"

"The Frog put it in 'is vest pocket, though 'e may 'ave moved it by now."

"Right or left?"

"Left."

"Should we try to recover it?"

Nubbins shrugged, "We 'ave time, though it ain't in my usual line."

"You know where they go?"

"Invariably." He pointed up the street, away from the water. "Two blocks, then left. Usually find a cab there."

Henry looked, "How about that next corner. Nice and dark. You stand across from me in the side street, we'll keep an eye out." They walked up, took their positions, and waited.

The side street was as black as a tunnel. They kept close to the corner, watching the light at the door to the alehouse, until their quarry emerged. The Frenchman was walking just behind the two women as they passed the corner. Henry used his wooden tool and retrieved the paper, along with a small bundle of banknotes, from the man's pocket as he collapsed.

The white woman whirled, reaching in her reticule. Henry tapped her solidly on the jaw, and she collapsed into Nubbins' arms. Turning toward the dark beauty, Henry was surprised to find she had disappeared, until he felt a metallic nudge at his right ear and heard the click as the pistol was cocked.

"Please remain still," she whispered. "I would dislike very much to shoot you, but I need that piece of paper. You can keep the banknotes," she added. Henry heard amusement and steel in her voice. He held still as long, agile fingers plucked the note from his grasp, then returned to examine his little wooden weapon. He felt her breath in his ear and realized he was straining for the smell of her. "You are most interesting. Perhaps we will meet again under better circumstances," she said.

There was no sensation of nearby motion, and it was hard to tell in the darkness, but it seemed to him she was gone. He looked around and put out his hand. Nubbins was still supporting the other female agent. The man lay on the ground. Henry helped place the woman gently next to him. "Did you see her?" he asked Nubbins.

"'Oo?"

"The other woman, the dark one, damn her eyes."

Nubbins thought he had never heard a man damn a woman in quite that tone. "It's very dark. I suppose she run away. Did you get the paper?"

"Only for a moment," muttered Henry. "Only for a moment."

10

"But *Monsieur,* the streets are so black. One moment I am walking down the street, the next I awake to find my money gone. Pfut. As if into the air."

"Bah. And your companions, they saw nothing either?"

"I told you, there was no moon; it was as black as the evil pit. Loren, she reached for her knife, then she remembers nothing. Sarah, she ran. She says she screamed, but no one came. She went to where are the cabs and returned to find us insensible. She managed to wake us and, with the help of the driver, we returned to the hotel. It is most distressing. Sarah says she will have nothing further to do with what she calls 'this nonsense;' claims it is too dangerous."

"Money will bring her to her senses. What about Loren?"

"She is frightened also. She was hit very hard and has a large bruise on her jaw. She says she cannot be seen for a week and demands we pay her for such a loss as this will cause. These thieves, they were most imposing. They must have been very large men to dispose of us so quickly."

Facteau rounded on him and snarled, "How do you know they were thieves? Perhaps they were English agents."

"Surely English agents would have arrested us. These men lay in wait in a dark street. They took my money. They did not take the papers. They got away with almost a hundred pounds in notes. That is more than..." he frowned, counting on his fingers, "two thousand francs. A fortune."

"Bah," Facteau repeated. "Fools. I have only fools to help me. Get out of here." He waved his arm and the man bowed himself out the door.

Then Facteau turned to Caron. "Three of our agents rendered unconscious in the same day and not one of them sees a thing that we can pin down."

"Placide was drunk."

"He did not appear drunk when he was questioned."

"But he stank of gin and was completely dead to the world when our relief man arrived," Caron said.

"Would a Frenchman drink gin?"

"Placide is only French in name and connection; he has lived in this benighted country all his life. Such a man would drink harbor water."

Facteau shook his head, "Perhaps, but I mistrust coincidences. Had this other business not happened I might agree with you, but it is worrisome. And our watcher swears to the return of Nubbins to his establishment shortly after this bizarre robbery."

"Nubbins is a thief-taker, out at all hours. I told you he was too clever to be fooled by our watchers; they have been there too long. Still, this is not the work of a thief-taker; this is either common robbery, as it appears, or espionage."

"That fool was right to say it is a strange kind of espionage. The information was on the man. If arrested, he would have been hanged. Yet he is robbed of money only. A fairly large sum, if he is to be believed, but the information is worth far more. And what of the Malay? This is strange behavior for such a one, surely?"

Caron shrugged, "It would appear so, but if the men were as large as our man insists, appearances, as you say...." He let the sentence die, then added, "I will look into it more thoroughly."

"Good. Is there any reference to Lessègues?"

"It is considered possible he will sail before the summer is out."

Facteau began to pace. "The sands are running. You must ready your creature, this royalist girl. We need the key and we need it quickly. The transfer must be made before the end of summer. There must be nothing to find when Lessègues returns."

"Very well. Everly is the baron now and will almost certainly come to London, at least for a visit. If he follows tradition, he will wear the key. The Cherilles have always treated it as a badge of office, worn constantly by the patriarch of the family. If he does not go directly to the girl, I will push her into his arms.

Also, I mean to send Theo to take a look at their house in Berkeley Square. There may be something we can use, and while it is closed, there should be little to get in his way."

"Very well," Facteau said. "Make it so. But we must move."

Henry was discouraged. Nubbins had awakened him at six in the morning and they had lingered in a Mayfair street for five hours to catch a glimpse of a lady's maid, an émigré whom Nubbins believed might answer the description given. Unfortunately, when the woman finally appeared she was only vaguely similar to the girl he and Jarrod, now Lord Cherille, had encountered in Portsmouth.

"Do you have any more promising leads?" Henry asked, as they walked away.

"Not at the moment. This is a large city, and she may not even be 'ere. She could be anywhere in the country. Needles and 'aystacks ain't in it."

"What about shopkeepers? His lordship and I saw a French dress shop, called Emmeline something. Élégance, that was it. Not too far from here, I believe. Do you know of it? Could the proprietors be émigrés?"

Nubbins frowned, "Can't recall the name just at once. That means I likely know nothing against 'em. On the other 'and, although I 'ave 'elped Jarrod, I mean 'is lordship, begging your pardon, once or twice, this spyin' lark is new on my list. Ain't what I'm used to, so I could be caught out. I should look at my notes when I get back to my place, if it ain't been ransacked by now." He placed his finger alongside his nose and winked.

Henry smiled. "Probably the best plan. I'm expecting his lordship tomorrow or the next day and, tell the truth, that little excursion last night left me fair winded. I'll leave you to return home and check your notes. I'll take myself back to the library in Berkeley Square and see what I can learn of the history and geography of your delightful city. Perhaps one or both of us will call on you tomorrow to see what else you've found. I look forward to another sojourn in the nighttime streets. Never had so much fun in a strange city, though it could have turned out better."

Nubbins agreed, and they shook hands. Henry went back to Cherille House, where he was careful to use the servant's entrance, and spent the afternoon and evening in perusal of the excellent library. It was close to two in the morning when he suddenly snapped awake, aware that something had changed in the room. Because of the warmth of the day, there was no fire, and the candle next to him had guttered out sometime after he had fallen asleep in the armchair. Shouldn't make the damn things so comfortable, he thought.

Then he turned his mind to what had awakened him. He felt movement off to his right, and brought the layout of the room into his recall. Besides the usual furnishings, a small desk stood between the two

French windows. He listened as the desk was opened, the writing table lowered for access to the cubbyholes behind it. He heard a rustle of paper. He didn't know who was there, but he could tell that one of the windows was open, though he had left them both closed.

The situation now clear, Henry silently retrieved the little weapon from his coat on the table beside him and whirled around the chair; jumping to a spot immediately in front of the desk. As the intruder raised his head at the thump behind him, Henry brought the wooden knob down behind the man's ear. The upward movement of the man's head increased the force with which the blow landed, and he dropped, his chin connecting with the desk as he fell.

For a moment, Henry was afraid he had killed the burglar, but a check of breath and pulse reassured him. Turning his comfortable chair around, he heaved his victim into it. A length of strong twine from the desk enabled him to tie the man's thumbs together behind the back of the chair, and his ankles to the sturdy legs. A quick trip through the almost empty house to the kitchen secured him a basin of water and a cloth, which he used to bathe the sleeper's temples until the stranger's eyes fluttered open. There was a flurry of muscle tightening and strain against the bonds before the man subsided. Henry watched, saying nothing.

Finally, the man spoke. "Say, darkie, what's this all about?"

Henry allowed his eyebrows to rise, but gave no other sign that he had heard. The two men stared at each other for what seemed a very long time. The prisoner cracked first.

"Let me go. Got no right to keep me here like this. Me thumbs is asleep. Who d'ye think y'are?" Henry didn't respond. The larger man sank back into the chair with a sulky expression. "Can't keep me here forever."

Henry nodded and walked over to the fireplace. Thompson may have been a surly caretaker but he was thorough and knew his duty. The fire was laid, even if it might not be needed before October. Henry used the matches on the mantel and a spill from the fire bucket to light it. Ignoring the prisoner, he crouched before the fire until it was going well, then took up the poker and placed it so the tip sat in the center of the blaze. Rubbing his hands, he turned to see the man watching him, his head twisted around.

Henry winked at him. "Won't be long," he said, "and we can get down to work." Taking a large handkerchief from the pocket of his coat, he began twisting it into a ball around a length of twine.

"Say, what are you about?"

"Keep still," Henry replied, approaching the intruder with the twine stretched out and the handkerchief in the middle. As he opened his mouth to protest, Henry shoved the handkerchief in and began to tie the twine behind the man's head. At this, the intruder began to thrash wildly, and it took all Henry's strength to hold him still enough to fasten the gag in place. When he was done, he stepped back and examined his handiwork with evident satisfaction.

"Sorry," he said, "but this may hurt a bit and there's no need to wake the house. Thompson needs his beauty sleep. In fact, his beauty being what it is, he may need every bit of sleep he can muster. Can't have you waking him up, and screams in the night are so disturbing." He walked back to the fire and took a look at the poker. The end was glowing red. He took it out of the fire, and waved it in the prisoner's face, watching as the man shrank back into the chair.

"Another few minutes, you think? Quite right." He smirked, returning the poker to the fire. "Want to get it white-hot if we can. Burns right through the flesh before you even feel it." He waved his arm. "Was hoping you'd just tell me what was going on before we had to do this, but have it your way, says I. No skin off my nose. Bit off yours, though, hey?" He leaned forward and flicked the end of the man's nose with his finger, watching as the widened eyes crossed, trying to follow the motion. Sweat glistened on the prisoner's forehead.

Henry tilted his head and looked at the burglar quizzically. "Oh, I see, you're wondering how you can tell me what this is all about while you've got that gag in your mouth. Is that so?"

The man's head nodded enthusiastically. Henry said, "It's a point well taken. I haven't really worked out all the details. I expect it will come to me once we've burnt a few spots, just to show you that I'm serious. Do you think it's ready now?" He looked toward the fire. A choking sound came from behind the gag.

Henry looked back, his eyebrows high again. "You want to go ahead and explain without the hot poker?" The head bobbed up and down. Henry cocked his own head to one side and regarded the man, frowning. "Are you sure? If I take that gag out and don't get good answers, I might get angry. No telling how I'll behave if that happens. Better, I think, to burn you a little, show you what I mean." He went back to the fireplace and returned with the poker, now almost white at the tip, and waved it before the man's eyes. Those eyes followed the iron, rolling back and forth with each wave. The horror in them almost melted Henry's resolve. The sounds behind the gag became more frantic.

"Against my better judgment," he said, "I'll give it a try." He returned the poker to the fire, came back and reached for the man's gag. As he did so, the prisoner's relief overmastered him, and he sank back against the chair, his entire body going limp. Henry pulled his hand back. "Wait a minute. You called me a *darkie*, didn't you? I owe you something for that." He stood up and turned toward the fire. The renewed sounds from behind the gag reached a slightly hysterical pitch. Henry bent over him once more, frowning. "You'll apologize?"

The man's head bobbed rapidly. Henry pursed his lips. "Oh, very well," he said pettishly, pulling the prisoner's head forward and beginning to work on the knot. "You better not make me mad. It's late, I'm tired, and I'm hungry. I can be mean when I'm hungry. You understand?" He pulled back, holding the gag, and stared into his victim's eyes again.

11

"Sir, you cannot stay. I expect my cousin every minute." Maërlys was flustered. It had been over a week since they had dropped her off on the street in the hours before dawn. She had almost convinced herself it was nothing but a bad dream. Now, here he was in the shop, Emmy was gone, and there were no customers. She felt her heart sinking into her shoes.

"Nonsense. She left only moments ago and she is watched. You are alone and it is time we spoke. You have work to do."

"Oh, sir, please...."

The words hung in the air, but they did not affect Caron's frown. "There is no time for you to be silly. You have been warned of the stakes. Your brother and sister are in France. They will end on the guillotine if we expose them. Your cousin may be taken up here and hanged as a French spy. Your whole family is forfeit if you disappoint me. We expect your lover back in town every day. You must be ready to go to him when he comes. Are you ready?"

"M-my lover? But sir, I told you, he is not, I mean, I don't, I mean he cares nothing for me."

"I warn you, I have no time for this. Look at yourself, girl. You can easily entice a man. If he is, in truth, not your lover, then you must make him so. You will do this thing or you will regret it as long as you live, which may not be so very long. Do you understand me? Had I known you would act so silly, I might as well have given you to Theo when we were on the road. I can still take you to him if you continue to defy me."

This threat froze Maërlys' next objection in her throat. She felt feverish, cold, then hot again. She felt nauseous. She stumbled to the chair behind the counter, sat down, and put her head in her hands. "Oh God," she murmured, "oh God."

"Fine," Caron scowled, "Pray to whatever you like. Just be ready. The summons may come at any moment. Do you know he was outside this very shop only a few days after we brought you here? We watch and we know. He will return or, if he does not, you will be sent to meet him. Do not disappoint me. I warn you; be ready." He whirled and left the shop, leaving her there, tears flowing through her hands.

That was how her cousin found her. "Maërlys, you must explain this to me. You must. How can I help you if you won't tell me all? Was that man here?" The eyes she looked into were red and there were furrows down the girl's cheeks. A tear dropped from her chin and splashed on the counter.

"Please, Emmy, don't. You don't know, I mean, oh God, I wish I was dead." She put her head down and began to sob again.

"Oh, darling, forgive me. I don't mean to be harsh with you but you must see this cannot go on. You had been so much better I thought it was all over, and now this. What did he say to you? Who is he?" She came around the end of the counter and took Maërlys in her arms.

"Emmy, please, please, I can't tell you, he's from government, he can do anything he wants to us, I have to do what he says. We're from France, he can do anything, oh, Emmy, what have I done. I didn't know he was a traitor. What have I done?"

Emmeline held her close and stroked her head as she cried. "It's all right, Maërlys, it's all right, you just cry. When you're done we'll have a cup of tea and you're going to tell me everything. If this man knows all these things, there's no reason I shouldn't know as well. You just go ahead and cry, and then you'll tell me the whole story and we'll decide together what is best to do. I am your family and I am with you and you are not alone. Together, there is nothing we can't handle."

This little speech brought a renewed rush of tears, sobs, and hiccups. "I'm such a ninny, Emmy, such a fool," the girl cried, resting her head on Emmeline's breast. "There is nothing we can do. I've made a complete mess of everything. You'll never forgive me. Why should you?"

In the end, it took over an hour for Emmeline to calm Maërlys down enough to get the whole story. Born in France, Maërlys' earliest memories were of the terror and then the deaths of her beloved parents. She had no trouble believing in the ill will of government officials. Emmeline, born and raised in England, was not so easily persuaded.

"Who did he say he was, exactly?" she asked.

"His name is Caron. Felix Caron. He never said, exactly, but those dark suits." She shuddered. "Who would wear such things except government officials?"

"Does the name Felix Caron sound English to you?"

"I cannot tell. Your name is Blanc yet you are English. And there are the Welsh, Irish, and Scots. Some of them have quite outlandish names and they are all of the British nation. Is it not an English name?"

Emmeline snorted, "It sounds French to me. What about the other one, the one who threatened to rape you?"

"He was called Theo. I never heard his family name."

"Theo indeed. An Englishman *could* be called Theo, but I think a man in the service of the British government would hardly offer to rape and kill an innocent young girl in the performance of his duty. No, it will not do. We must find someone to whom we can apply, who will give us more information."

"But whom?"

Emmy wrinkled her nose, "There, I admit, I do not know. You still have not told me the name of the man who..., the one you tried to..., well, you know whom I mean."

Maërlys, who had been recovering, went pale again. "Must I? You will think me such a fool. And I swear, it was not his fault; it was all my own doing."

Her cousin smiled at her, "I am well aware, my dear, and I also know the noble cause that led you to it. You have no reason to feel shame and, in my eyes, you are a heroine of the highest standing. Boadicea come to life. I would not be the least surprised if the gentleman feels the same. It may be that he will help us, after all. But you must tell me who he is, and where you saw him first."

"Well, as to that, it was right here in this shop."

Emmy's eyes widened, "You astonish me. One of our customers?"

"Well, I think he must have come here for someone else. And I didn't actually speak to him, I just listened while you waited on him. I don't think he even saw me. At least, he didn't seem to recognize me when, when...." Her voice trailed off.

"When he put his, well, never mind. What is his name, dear?"

"Everly. Jarrod Everly."

Emmeline frowned, "Everly. That reminds me of something. Perhaps it will come to me. Why did you decide to apply to him?"

"Oh, Emmy, he's so handsome. I looked him up and found he was very rich. When I saw him again, I just thought, if I had to, you know, with a strange man, it would be nice if it was such a good-looking one, and he looked so kind. I have heard it is painful when it happens the first time, and I thought he might be gentle, and you know," she was studying the floor, her finger teasing at the corner of her mouth, "understanding. He looked understanding. And kind. Did I say kind?"

"Yes, dear, you did. Excuse me, I want to look at the paper." She returned from the other room quickly, after a rapid perusal of the recent papers, carrying the Times of two days earlier.

"Look, Maërlys. I knew I'd seen something with the name Everly. Christian Everly, Baron Cherille, was buried at his ancestral home in Wiltshire. Poor man, he was only thirty-five, and quite handsome and well-thought-of, by all accounts. Here it is: 'He is succeeded to the title by his younger brother, Jarrod Everly, who will be installed as Baron Cherille,' etc. It goes on to say that although barons are usually regarded as the lowest rank of the peerage, the house of Cherille is renowned for its wealth." She looked at her cousin. "Did you know?"

"Well, I told you he was very rich. That is why I thought he might be willing to help us. I know the wealthy are a pinch-penny lot as a rule, but he looked so—"

"Kind. Yes, I know. Well, he has only just succeeded to the title, perhaps he is not yet completely given over to farthing-squeezing. And he is a peer of the realm. And those men told you he was a traitor?"

"Cannot a peer be a traitor? After all, at the time, he was only a younger son, with no prospects, his brother being so young himself. I believe he was expected to marry and produce heirs, oh...." Her hands flew to her mouth. "Do you think he had something to do with his brother's death? Could that be considered treason, if he killed a peer?"

"According to this," Emmeline answered, "he was out of the country at the time of the accident, and did not even know of it until his arrival home. Apparently, he was as devastated as anyone by the news."

"I knew it. He could never do such a thing." Maërlys eyes had taken on a gleam. "He's much too—"

"Kind," her cousin finished in unison with her and they laughed. "Oh Maërlys, it's so good to hear you laugh again. It's the music this shop has missed these last two weeks. Come, I will find out his direction, and we will lay our case before him. At the very least, he will have contacts in government who can reassure us about the nature of these men who are troubling you. But, whatever is the matter?"

Maërlys was blushing to the roots of her hair. "Oh, must I see him? I mean, he had his fingers...I mean, oh, Emmy, I can never face him, after what I tried to do. He will think me a criminal. He may have me taken up."

"He will never have you 'taken up,' as you put it, my dear. I am confident that such a *kind* man will be glad of the opportunity to help us. And, in any case, he can do you no harm. You have committed no crime."

"But he's seen me...my dress, it was...."

"Please, my darling, I am trying to not think of it. Help me, will you, and don't speak of it any more. Try to forget."

It seemed impossible but Maërlys face became even redder. "Oh, I don't think I could ever do that; he was...I mean, it was so, so...."

Emmeline managed not to laugh. "You did like it, didn't you? However that may be, you must forget it. It was a bold plan, and I honor you for it, but you are a lady, not a, well, you know. The gentleman found that out, and you must never forget it again. Even if we do meet him, which, frankly, I find unlikely."

"This is it," Nubbins said.

Henry looked around. "They dropped her off here? There's nothing here."

"Let us try the corner. It's an important street." They walked to the corner, and looked both ways. "Ain't that the shop you asked me about?"

"Yes," Henry answered, "I believe it is." He started to move down that way, but Nubbins' hand on his arm restrained him, then guided him back into the side street. "What is it?"

"A man down there," he pointed toward the shop, "looks as if he don't really belong. Let's watch for a few moments."

"I see what you mean; pacing back and forth. Do you think he's watching that shop?"

"'Ard to tell from this angle. Let's us go round the block and come from that direction," he nodded his head. "If 'e's watchin' 'e'll still be there, which'll be tellin' in itself."

He led Henry on a pleasant walk, pointing out objects of interest as they went, explaining the history of various buildings and shops. Nubbins' knowledge of London was vast and covered both the lower ends, where he did most of his work, and these more fashionable sections as well. Henry found him interesting company and listened to his discourse with pleasure. Eventually, they found themselves at the corner of Oxford Street, looking south toward their original position.

The object of their curiosity was still in place, although he had abandoned his previous backing and filling and was now lounging at a corner as if waiting for someone. As they watched, another man came from the side street and, without a glance at their quarry, took up a similar position. The first man looked at his watch, glanced up and down the street and set off directly toward them. Henry and Nubbins both examined him covertly as he went by.

"See?" Nubbins asked.

"I do. From a distance it looks all right, but close up you can see he's no gentleman. Should we follow?"

"I think not. Lot of work and no reward. T'other one's taken up the place, and it's definitely Emmeline Élégance they're watchin'."

"Then so should we, I suppose." Henry looked around. "Is there somewhere we can be less conspicuous than that lout?"

"A black man and a fat thief-taker? Conspicuous? I'll 'ave to put someone else on it. Neither of us 'as any more business 'ere than those fellows. I propose we come back tonight. I'll get someone over 'ere right away."

12

Facteau was angry. "Who is this *negre*?"

"We are not sure, sir. There was a slave with Everly at the inn in Portsmouth. And we know Nubbins is associated with Everly. It may be a coincidence."

"Bah. There are no coincidences. In any case, if Nubbins was there..." He whirled and poked his finger into Caron's chest, "Are they sure it was Nubbins?"

"Absolutely. Our man walked right past them. He had been on the Nubbins station but was changed after the incident...." His voice trailed off.

"Yes, yes. Then they have located your Miss Blanc. That is as you wished, is it not?"

"Oh, yes sir. I believe we are progressing nicely."

"Do you think they spotted your watchers?"

"No. Tim says he almost brushed against them as he walked by, and they gave no sign."

"Then we have only to wait for Everly to make contact. Is he in town?"

"No sir, although he will probably come up soon enough. He has had time to settle affairs in Wiltshire."

"All right. What did Theo find at the house?"

"Ah, well, sir, ah, there we may have a problem."

Facteau glowered at him. "Explain."

"I have had no report from Theo. He has not been seen since I last spoke to him, and charged him with the examination of the house."

"Is anyone watching Cherille House?"

"No sir, no one is there, as far as we know, except the caretaker, and our men are stretched thin as it is, watching Emmeline Élégance and the Nubbins house."

"So, you don't know for sure if he went to the house?"

"No, but he is one of our most trusted men, and we had agreed that he would make a try that night. He seems to have vanished. He is not at home."

"Consult the Malay. We must know what has happened to Theo. He knows far too much to disappear."

"But after the incident at the river...?"

"Never mind. We know she has an extensive network. If he has gone out of our control, she can do what is needed."

"Very well. I shall see to it." Caron bowed, and left the room.

"You are sure the place is empty?"

"Well, the older one left just at five o'clock, and they put up the shutters. She often visits a friend nearby, usually stayin' all night. 'Er friend is an elderly invalid of long attachment. A light showed in the room over the shop just after six o'clock and went out about eight. There was a smaller light, a candle maybe, burnin' for another hour or so. We think the girl Maërlys retired then." Nubbins looked pleased with himself.

"What about the watcher?" Henry asked.

"Layabout. Took 'imself off as soon as the light went out. Probably in a public 'ouse somewhere, stuffin' 'imself with beef and ale at 'is master's expense."

"Any idea of his master?"

"Now that part is interestin'. Followed one of 'em to the Ambassador. It's an 'otel full of Frenchies, well-known as a royalist gatherin' place and consequently full of Boney's boys as well. My man wasn't able to positively identify to 'oom their watcher reported, but the Blanc's are known as non-political royalists. I mean they 'ate Boney but don't get involved, if you understand me."

"That would confirm what I learned from that fellow Theodore. Any trace of the man Caron at this Ambassador Hotel?"

"My man checked the book and there's a Felix Caron registered there. 'Owever, 'is room is a small one on the fourth floor, and my man swears the fellow he followed lost 'imself on the second. My guess is it's someone 'igher up than this Caron who can afford to dwell on a more expensive floor. Probably 'as a suite."

"Hmm. We can look into that tomorrow. Right now, I'd like to take a look inside. Think we can arrange that?"

Nubbins bowed. "Come with me. I've sent my man 'ome, so there should be no one about but the two of us. I'll keep watch, but it will be quieter in back." Henry followed him to a door in the dark alley behind Emmeline's shop. After a bit of jiggling, the door opened and Nubbins handed him a bulls-eye lantern. "Shall we both go?"

Henry said, "I'll feel safer if you keep watch outside. Shouldn't be anything in there I can't handle. Whistle if you see a problem."

Nubbins touched his cap, a motion barely discernible in the darkness. "You do the same. Good luck."

Inside, Henry quickly realized that the back room of a dress shop was even more foreign to him than the city of London. He bumped into a dress form, then a rack of dresses. They didn't cause much noise, but enough to make him a little more nervous than he had been. So, when he heard a clatter to his right, he covered the lantern and moved carefully in that direction.

He was rewarded with a seam of light along the floor in front of him, repeated more faintly above, indicating a door with light behind it. He was standing directly in front of it when it opened. The light almost blinded him for an instant and he had barely time to recognize Maërlys before the pistol exploded.

Maërlys came to herself sitting on the step, the empty pistol dangling from her right hand, the other still clutching the candlestick, the candle miraculously still burning. There was another noise at the outside door and she looked that way. The pistol was useless. She could never reload in time.

Then there was a thump, followed by something heavy falling against the door. More sounds. She sat there, staring. In front of her she could see the intruder's corpse, but it wasn't Caron or Theo. She peered into the gloom beyond the candle; it was a brown-skinned man. The only such man she could think of was the one she'd seen accompanying Mr. Everly. She pushed that thought away as the outer door opened and another man came in. She shrank back against the stairs.

"Who are you?" she squeaked.

"Me name's Tim, missus. Got a bit of a fix here, ain't we. Well, never moind. G'wan back to bed and old Tim'll handle it. Gimme that pistol, willya?" He reached toward her. She had no use for it, but her fingers wouldn't work properly and, in the end, he had to pry it from her hand. Then he seized the corpse under the arms and dragged it out the door.

He was gone for a few minutes, then he was back. "Still here? Whyn'tcha go ta bed?" He was staring at her.

"I have to tell Emmy. Do I need to tell Bow Street? Please, what must I do?"

He put his hands on his hips. "Ye need ta g'wan ta bed, and be leavin' the rest ta me. Ain't yez listenin'?"

"No, we can't just leave him there. I can't go back to bed now. Please, help me."

"Bloody hell, beggin' your pardon, missus." He stared at her, sitting on the stair in her nightgown. "D'ye have a long coat?"

"You're up late, M. Caron. Or early." The slight sneer in her voice was just enough to be insulting without any obvious cause for offense. Her golden skin glowed in the candlelight.

"*Madame.*"

"*Mademoiselle.*"

"Very well. We require your assistance. You know of my associate M. Broader?" She raised one eyebrow, and he went on. "He is missing. We wish to determine his location and remove him if he is in danger of revealing himself to our enemies."

"Cannot you handle this yourself?" Again, the hint of condescension.

"This is a case where your methods would serve us. If you no longer wish to serve us, merely say so. We pay generously, as you know.

"Very well, I will look into it. Where was he last seen?" Caron told her of his conversation with Theo and the assignment. "But you are not sure if he went or not?"

"I think it highly likely."

"Then I will start there. Is there any—"

The knock at the door was insistent.

"Come," Sarah Dane said.

Her butler, Simon McInnis, opened the door and stuck his head in. "There is someone to see *monsieur*," he said. "It is reckoned most urgent."

"At three in the morning?" Sarah looked at Caron, who shrugged. "Send him up," she said.

Evidently the man was right behind Simon for he thrust his way into the room. Simon looked at Sarah, who nodded slightly. He closed the door, leaving the other three alone, but remained immediately outside.

"What is it, Tim?" Caron asked.

"Please, sor, they's been a rare takin' at the shop."

"Emmeline Élégance?"

"The very one."

"Well, out with it. What's amiss?"

"The darkie, sor." He turned to Sarah. "Beggin' your pardon, missus. He bust in and she shot him, like."

"She what?"

"Had a pistol, sor. He sneaked in and she done him."

"Does anyone else know?"

"There was the thief-taker, sor, on the lookout. But I took care o' him, sor, so I did."

"You what?"

"Hit 'im, sor. Dusted him off proper."

"Where's the girl now?"

"Got 'er in a carriage, sor. Out front."

Sarah had been watching the scene with some amusement. At this intelligence she came to life. "Who is this girl and what is she to you?" She glowered at the two men.

"That is not your concern, *Mademoiselle*," Caron snapped.

"If she's shot someone tonight and is sitting in a carriage at my doorstep, she is most certainly my concern." Her brow furrowed. "Did you say she shot a black man?" She stepped to the door, opened it and whispered something to McInnis. Then she closed the door and turned back to her guests. "Now," she frowned. "Quickly. The full story."

"We have been grooming her for a little job we have in hand. Our opponents must have discovered her whereabouts and become curious. She is inexperienced and must have panicked. Steps will have to be taken."

"Indeed. And the darkie?" It was impossible to miss the emphasis.

"Of no importance. A servant. He was becoming a nuisance. He will not be missed."

Caron turned to Tim. "How was it left?"

Tim smiled. "Oh, as to that, sor, it was all settled, though I say it meself. Moved the corpse into the alley, put the pistol in the hand o' the fat thief-taker, laid 'im on the body, and left 'em. Let the watch make o' it what they will. Locked the shop back up and come away. Would o' left the girl, but she wouldn't 'ave it, and was making such a fuss, so she was, I brung 'er along. Didn't want to do nothing what wasn't authorized, sor, beggin' yer pardon."

"You should have strangled her and left her with the other two." Caron turned to Sarah, who was scowling at him. "Would you be so kind, since she is here? We will pay the full price, even though she has been delivered to you."

"You are too kind. Very well. I will take care of your problem for you. You still wish me to investigate the other matter?"

"Certainly."

"Fine. I will advise you when I have something of substance."

Caron turned to Tim again. "Bring the girl up. Be careful not to frighten her."

"That will not be necessary," Sarah Dane said. "The matter has already been attended to. Take your carriage and go, the sooner the better."

Caron stared at her for a moment but realized he had already been dismissed. "Come, Tim. Let us be off."

"Wait," Sarah said, "there is the matter of payment."

Caron bowed stiffly, then reached into a pocket, removing a small purse, which he handed to her. "Do you wish to count it?"

"That is not necessary. If there is any shortage, you can correct it when next we meet."

As their footsteps receded down the hall, she touched a bell rope. McInnis was there in a matter of seconds.

"Send her in to me at once but watch them. Make sure they leave. If they delay for any reason, I wish to know immediately."

McInnis left and very soon there was a gentle knock at the other door, the one in the alcove at the back of the room. For the first time, Sarah Dane raised her voice. "Come in."

The door opened, there was a slight flurry of movement and Maërlys seemed to pop into the room. She was wearing a long coat with what appeared to be a nightgown underneath. The door closed silently behind her. She looked around as if bewildered, then reached for the handle of the door through which she had just come; it was locked. She had grown very pale and the sight of the tall, dark, beautiful woman in front of her seemed to do nothing to reassure her.

"W-who are you?" she asked. "What is this place?"

"The house is mine," Sarah Dane answered, "and I am the one paid to kill you."

13

"Nubbins, my good man. Thank heaven you're here. I was beginning to think the town deserted. Tell me, have you seen anything of my friend, Henry Winnow. I sent him to London a while ago, and have now heard nothing for two days. My caretaker says he didn't come back to the house last night. He sent me a note that he believed he had located the girl, then, nothing. Was he in contact with you about the matter?"

"Yes, your lordship, 'e was. We did, in fact, locate the girl in question, but I'm afraid it went rather wrong after that."

Jarrod waved his hand. "Less of the lordship, if you don't mind. You can at least hold off until I'm formally seated. Do you know where Henry is now? What happened to the girl?"

"I regret that the girl, sir, 'as disappeared, but not before shootin' your friend."

"What? Shot Henry? That little slip of a girl? You'll never tell me Henry is dead! Trying to help me? Where is the body? He'll have the finest funeral London's ever seen. And I'll wring the girl's neck when I find her. Where do you think she's gone? Oh, God, Bill, this is all my fault. I should never have let him come to London alone." He sank into a nearby chair and put his head in his hands. Then, looking up at Nubbins, he said, "He wasn't used to really large cities, you know. Kingston, Port-au-Prince, those places don't compare to London. Still, I'd have bet my life Henry was the best survivor I ever met. Tell me how it happened. Was it quick?"

"No, sir, it wasn't quick at all. 'E still lingers, as a matter of fact. It 'appened in the wee hours last night, and there was some stir, but I 'ave every 'ope 'e'll recover. Would you like to go up and talk to 'im?"

Jarrod was on his feet in an instant. "You damned rogue. Of course I would. Take me to him at once. I'll not forget your playing with me this way. If you knew how many times he's saved my life, well, never mind, where is he?"

"Sorry, but your lordship was speaking very 'asty, if you don't mind me saying. Right this way." He led the way upstairs, explaining the circumstances as he went.

"I woke up and found 'im underneath me and the pistol in me 'and. When 'e came back to life, as it were, I got 'im into a cab and brought 'im 'ere. Doctor's been round, and thinks 'e'll do well enough with a day or so of rest. Clipped 'im good, it did, and plenty of blood, but not deep, and the ball never went in, so there's not much chance it'll turn bad. 'Ere 'e is."

He opened the door to a bedroom and they walked in. Henry was sitting up, with a very serious-looking bandage around his head. Jarrod gazed at him. "I thought we agreed you were to duck in these circumstances."

"Your concern is appreciated, your lordship," Henry answered. "As it happens I did, but apparently not enough."

"Bill tells me it was Maërlys who shot you. You must have done a great deal to anger her. She was gentle with me." His eyes grew dreamy. "Very gentle indeed."

"I fear I may have startled her. Certainly I meant her no harm, but I was never given the chance to explain. I opened my mouth to say, 'Begging your pardon, ma'am,' and she let fly. It's the last thing I remember until I woke up to find Nubbins on top of me. Not an experience I hope to repeat."

"Where did this shooting occur?"

"In the back of the shop where she works with her cousin, Emmeline Élégance. You may remember pointing it out to me?"

"And you woke up in the alley? Surely that child never carried you out, rendered Bill unconscious, and laid him on top of you with the pistol in his hand—"

Nubbins broke in. "We knew they was watching the shop; I must 'ave gotten careless. I saw the watcher leave and never noticed any relief, but that's what must 'ave 'appened. 'E 'eard the shot and caught me from be'ind as I started to go in. Must've taken the girl away as well."

Jarrod turned to him. "This was last night? What about the other woman, the cousin?"

"I have a watcher over there but haven't heard yet. Would you like to go look for her with me?"

"I would, as a matter of fact. I have a letter from that cousin which I picked up this morning; I believe we have much to discuss. Is there anything else I need to know?"

Henry took this for his cue and told him all about his meeting with Theo. Jarrod found himself blinking. "Henry, I have been too hard on you. I thought you had spent your vacation in London lying in bed or occasionally being shot at by beautiful young girls. This sheds a completely new complexion on the matter. This Theo was unable to tell you what they wanted Maërlys to do?"

"Only that it was connected to you. What they might want from you is still a mystery."

"Any other adventures?"

"Well, you did tell me to find myself a woman and I did so, but she too has eluded me. We saw an exchange of information between two French agents and attempted to place ourselves in a position to profit by the experience. Unfortunately, I was outwitted by another woman, this one with dark skin."

Nubbins interjected, "I've done a little research since then and believe 'er to be Sarah Dane. Little is known of 'er save that she is respected in the criminal world, although she seldom does anything truly criminal 'erself, or at least nothing what can be proven. She may 'ave something to do with gambling among the upper classes but I've not been able to get a full report as yet. If you 'ave connections at the ministry...."

"I see it all now, Henry. I had over-estimated your abilities because, so far, you had only been matched against men. I still believe that in that field, you have no equal. Unfortunately, when matched against the fairer sex, you have come a cropper. You must remain here in bed. Bill and I will venture out to speak to this woman, and we shall see what is to be done. I have an appointment at the ministry later in the day. If I do not arrive it will be because I too, and possibly Bill as well, have fallen victims to the women of London. Pray for us, will you Henry?"

"With all my heart, your lordship. With all my heart."

Sunshine was streaming through the curtains when Maërlys opened her eyes to see a stranger, a lovely woman only a year or two older than herself, sitting by her bed. Only it wasn't her bed. Where was she? Then, it all came flooding back like a bad dream, but it wasn't a dream. She felt herself getting cold, then hot, then cold again, nausea rising in her stomach. The stranger reached into a basin on a small table next to the bed and, wringing out a soft cloth, cool with water, laid it gently on her forehead. "Who are you?" Maërlys croaked, and realized she was desperately thirsty.

The stranger put an arm behind her head and lifted her up, rearranging the pillows to support her. She placed a glass of water into Maërlys' hand and said, "My name is Julia. You've been through a lot. Drink some water and then we can talk."

Maërlys sipped the water, faster and faster, until she had drained the glass. She felt the panic rising as she handed the glass back to Julia. "I-I'm in that house! She's going to kill me!" Her hand was at her throat. Had she taken poison? "Who are you? Where am I? What are you going to do to me?"

"Be easy. You must try to calm down. No one is going to hurt you. You are in the safest place in London, I promise, and no one, least of all Siti, is going to hurt you. She asked me to call her as soon as you woke up so she could apologize, but I won't call her until you calm down. You have nothing to be frightened of, I promise."

"Who are you? Please tell me."

"I am Julia Harley. I live here with Siti. It may be that you will come to live here also, at least for a while, until it is safe for you to leave. Please, let me call her. She will explain better than I ever could."

"Siti?"

"You may prefer to call her Sarah. Most of us do; that is the name she uses in London. She is very special; you must watch out. Everyone who knows her falls in love."

She smiled at Maërlys and looked so kind that Maërlys could not help but believe her. And, she thought, what have I to lose? If she wished to kill me, I would be dead already. "Very well," she said. "You may call her. I will try to behave."

Julia smiled again and reached for a bell rope hanging by the bed. When she did Maërlys noticed a scar on her neck, running from just below her ear down into the collar of her dress. She pulled three times, paused, and pulled once more. Then she sat back and refilled Maërlys' glass from a pitcher, watching as Maërlys slowly drank it. It was clean, cold, tasteless water.

It was less than five minutes before there was a gentle knock on the door. Julia opened it and admitted the beautiful dark woman Maërlys had met the night before. Unconsciously, she shrank back against the headboard.

The woman smiled at her and said, "Thank you, Julia," and held the door as the other woman left. Then she turned to Maërlys. "I am so sorry," she said. "I did not mean to frighten you. I wasn't thinking and am sometimes likely to be dramatic. You have been through so much. Can you ever forgive me?"

"Y-you mean, you, you aren't going to k-k-k...," Maërlys stammered.

"No, my dear. I am going to do everything I can to protect you from anyone who would hurt you." She reached out and brushed a stray bit of hair away from Maërlys' face. "You must help me by telling me the whole story and explaining why these men would want to hurt you. What happened last night? Do you feel up to it? Would you rather have some breakfast first?"

"Breakfast?"

"An excellent idea. You must be perfectly clemmed. I apologize again; I'm a terrible hostess." She reached out and rang the bell, this time two rings. "My name is Sarah Dane. May I know yours?"

"M-Maërlys. Maërlys Blanc."

"What a lovely name, Maërlys. Is it French?"

"Yes. I come from F-France, a place called, ah, called...."

Sarah smiled at her and placed her finger on Maërlys' lips. "There is no need to tell me anything you do not wish. In time you will come to know me and, I hope, to trust me, but I am not such a fool as to expect trust from strangers. I will not hold it against you, believe me. Ah, here is your breakfast."

The door opened and Julia brought in a tray, which she placed on the blankets across Maërlys thighs. Julia lifted the covers to reveal scrambled eggs, toast, ham, and kippers. There was also a glass of juice and a cup of tea.

"Is tea all right?" Julia asked. "Would you prefer coffee?"

"Oh, I, I, like tea...."

"Bring us a pot of coffee, would you Julia?" Sarah said. "And two cups, please." She looked at the tray. "Milk and sugar we already have. Excellent."

"Now my dear," she continued as Julia left the room, "my name, as I told you is Sarah Dane. Actually, it is Siti Zara Daeng, but this is difficult for most English to pronounce, so I am called Sarah Dane. You may call me Sarah or Siti, as you prefer. I am from what the English call the Malay States. My father was a king but his kingdom was small and caught between two larger kingdoms. He lost it with his life, along with most of my family. I escaped onto an English ship and so, here I am." She spread a pair of remarkably large hands with long powerful fingers and smiled, her smile so wide that Maërlys was dazzled.

"Now," she went on, "I live in London and do things for people, and they pay me well. Sometimes, I admit, the things I do are perhaps bad things, but I try to be very careful to whom I do these things. For example, last night some men brought you here and they told me they wished you to die. I told them I would solve their problem for them and I took their money."

She reached into her costume and withdrew a small leather pouch which she placed on Maërlys' tray. "Sometimes, I have to check very carefully to find out who the people are I am asked to hurt, and who are the people asking me to do this hurt. You, I do not have to check. You are young, lovely and I think, quite innocent. Are you quite innocent?"

At this, she reached out and ran her fingers along the blanket covering Maërlys' thigh. The feeling tickled slightly, but more than that, it was unlike anything Maërlys had ever felt except for a moment in

Mr. Everly's arms, and it made her shiver. Sarah laughed. It was a delightful sound.

"Yes," Sarah said, "I think you are very innocent indeed. Such a one must be protected. These men who brought you here are bad men. Sometimes, I take their gold and do things they ask me, but always to men like them. Bad men. This is the first time they have ever asked me to hurt a woman, so they do not know that I do not hurt women. Men hurt women. Some men, this is all they do, hurt people, especially women. Such men have much to fear from me but women, never."

Her eyes clouded over. "I will not lie to you; once I hurt a woman. She was my enemy and she would not be my friend. But even then, I would not hurt her until she tried to hurt another woman, a girl really. I tried to stop her and she would not let me stop her without, well, I stopped her. Sometimes we must make choices and sometimes we pay for those decisions. But this has nothing to do with you; one has only to look at you to see your innocence."

The door opened. "Ah, here is our coffee. Now you will finish eating and tell me the whole story."

14

"Yes, your honor," Nubbins' associate said, "it's been a rare dust-up. I got here about six-thirty, and the mistress come at seven. Come in the back, like usual. She goes in; locks it; she's in there about twenty minutes or so, then she's flyin' out the front door; lookin' all around. Sees a boy, gives 'im a coin and sends 'im for the runners."

"How did you know?" Jarrod asked.

"Well, I stopped 'im and asked, didn't I?"

"Of course. Silly of me. Did he know anything else?"

"Not a thing. Just go to Bow Street and bring 'em back was all she said. And 'e done it. Got 'ere about an hour later. They went inside; tore things up the way they do; looked all around, out in the alley and everywhere. Came out front and asked everybody they could get 'old of. They know me so I sent one of my people close so they'd ask and I could find out what the questions was. Wanted to know if anybody went in or out or seen the younger woman."

"Was that it?"

"Far as I could tell. They went away after a while. None the wiser, if you was to ask me."

Jarrod and Nubbins looked at the closed sign and the drawn shutters of Emmeline Élégance, and Jarrod shrugged. "Any sign of those watchers from the other side?"

"Funny, your honor, now you mention it. Nor 'ide nor 'air, come to think. Huh. You think they know somethin'?"

"Yes," said Jarrod, "I do indeed. Coming Bill?"

"Believe I will, if you don't mind, your lordship. Like to 'ear it from the mouth of the 'orse, as you might say."

They crossed the street and Jarrod knocked on the door. There was no answer so he knocked again, louder. The shutter was moved aside and a pair of eyes peeked out. "We're closed today," a lady's voice said. "Come back tomorrow."

Jarrod knocked again, and this time the door was unlocked and opened a crack. "I'm sorry," Emmeline said. She had obviously been crying. "There's been an accident and I can't open today. Were you supposed to pick up something?"

"No ma'am. My name is Jarrod Everly, Lord Cherille, and I have a letter from you." He held it up. "This is my associate, Bill Nubbins." Nubbins bowed.

"Oh! Oh, my goodness. Yes, your lordship, please come in. I hardly expected, I mean, I'd quite forgotten...." Her voice trailed off as she allowed the door to swing open, backing into the store. "I'm sorry, I haven't even cleaned up; the place is in a terrible mess. The runners, I mean Bow Street, were here...."

Nubbins closed the door, re-locked it, and arranged the shutters and the sign as Jarrod followed Emmeline inside. "Can you tell us what happened, Miss Blanc? You are Miss Emmeline Blanc, I collect?"

"Yes, yes, you met my cousin, as I said in the letter...." She stopped suddenly, and the blush began somewhere around her neck and moved slowly up her face. "I mean, well, I don't know what I mean, exactly."

Jarrod felt his own face flush. "Yes. I met your cousin. I look forward extremely to renewing the acquaintance."

Emmeline drew herself up and her face took on a stern cast. "Well, I hope you will forgive me if I say that Maërlys may have given you a false impression."

Jarrod held up his hand, his face still burning. "Not at all. Your cousin's innocence is unquestioned and I am under no illusion that the Misses Blanc are anything other than ladies of honor. Please do not let such thoughts disturb your mind. I am here to offer what service I can in answer to your letter, and to find out if I can help with what happened last night."

Her eyes narrowed and she frowned, "What do you know of last night?"

"I know you had the runners in this morning."

She looked down and began to twist her fingers together. "Oh, yes. If only you can help, but I fear the worst. I left Maërlys here alone last night, and when I came back this morning, there was no sign of her and there is all this blood. Oh dear, whatever will I do? I am so afraid for Maërlys...."

"May we see? My friend, Mr. Nubbins, is a very efficient thief-taker and has been of service to Bow Street more than once. Isn't that so, Bill?"

Again, Nubbins bowed. They followed Emmeline to the back of the shop, where she stopped at the edge of a large bloodstain on the floor. Nubbins looked at it, then to his left at the closed door. He walked to the door and opened it. It led to a stairway to the upper story.

He turned back to Emmeline. "Do you keep a pistol in the 'ouse?"

"A p-pistol? Why yes, how did you know?"

"Where is it kept?"

"Upstairs, in the closet."

He raised his eyebrows and she hurried upstairs. She was back down in a moment. "It's gone. The bag with the powder, caps, the shot, and the patches, they're all there, but the pistol is gone."

"You both know 'ow to use it?"

"Well, we know how to load it. I've fired a pistol once or twice, but not in years. I made sure Maërlys knew how to load it, in case…" Her eyes narrowed again and her chin came up sharply. "What is this all about?"

Nubbins reached into a pocket of his coat and withdrew the pistol he had found in his hand the previous evening. "Is this it?"

Emmeline stared then reached out for the pistol and pointed to some scratches on the butt. "My

father's initials," she said. Nubbins nodded and looked
at Jarrod.

"First of all," Jarrod said, "I think we can assure
you that the blood in the hall does not belong to your
cousin. In fact, it belongs to a friend of mine, Henry
Winnow, by name. For reasons of my own I have been
trying to find your cousin for almost two weeks now—"

She interrupted him, somewhat coldly, "I believe
I am aware of your reasons."

He bowed slightly, smiled and said, "Perhaps not
all of them. In any case, Henry was assisting me in my
search, and last night he became, shall we say, a trifle
over-zealous. In an attempt to ascertain if the Miss
Blanc who lived here was, in fact, the Miss Blanc we
were looking for, he entered this house without any
permission—" He held up his hand to forestall
Emmeline's objections. "Do not fear, dear lady, he has
been fully punished for his presumption; your cousin
shot him."

"Oh!" Emmeline's hands flew to her mouth.
From behind them she asked, "Is he...?"

"No, ma'am, but he is indisposed and will be so
for a day or two. I trust you will consider this
punishment enough. As you can see, he lost a great
deal of blood. Once he is fully recovered, I will show
him that it is his duty to come here and remove this,
ah, unsightly mess. He really is a good man and I am
sure he will wish to do what is right. Since it was I he
was trying to help, I am as responsible as anyone.

Perhaps I should start on it now. Have you a bucket?"
He smiled warmly at her.

Emmeline looked horrified, "Oh, good heavens
no, your lordship, that will certainly not be necessary.
I am sure it can wait until your man—"

"My friend, ma'am. The best friend I have in the
world. He is more like a brother than anything. I have
recently lost my real brother, and Henry is the closest
thing to family remaining in my life. Since you may not
be aware, I have every intention of marrying your
cousin, when and if I find her, if she will have me. It
behooves me to be on good terms with her family,
which I take to be you. Therefore, the removal of this
stain is not so far-fetched a task as you seem to think.
However, I believe no task is more urgent at the
moment than locating Miss Blanc. Would you agree?"

Emmeline was staring at him, her eyes wide, her
mouth slightly open. She realized this and closed it,
nodding in answer to his question.

"Then," Jarrod went on, "Do you have any idea
how we might proceed? Bill here has been helping us
also, and he believes your cousin has fallen into the
clutches of some Frenchmen, Bonapartists, in fact. Do
you know anything of this? Does the name Caron
mean anything to you?"

Emmeline was still staring at him. She shook
herself. "Did you say, marry? You want to marry
Maërlys? But I understood you only met her once,
didn't you?"

He smiled. "It was a lovely meeting."

"She said you.... Well, I can't say what she said, but...."

"Did she say if she disliked me, if she found me horrible, repellent?"

"Uh, no, quite the reverse, if I understood her correctly."

"I knew it! I knew she felt the same as I. Why did she run away? I must find her. Come, come, the name Caron. You have heard it before?"

"Caron? Felix Caron? He was here. That is why I wrote the letter. He is a Bonapartist?"

"So we believe."

"I told her no such man would come from the British government."

"Did you indeed?"

"Of course I did. Felix Caron, the name is obviously French. He led her to believe he was with the ministry and that you...."

Jarrod smiled and raised his eyebrows. "Yes, dear lady, do go on."

She looked at the floor. Her words came in a mumble. "He said you were a traitor to the crown."

"I? A traitor? The wicked dog."

He shifted his attention, "We will find him, Nubbins. I will stop his lying tongue. And if he's done anything to that girl, he'll regret it for the rest of his very short life. Did Henry say he lives at the Ambassador?"

"Oh, it is quite horrible; much worse than I expected! How could someone treat you so, innocent little kitten that you are? It makes me fume. Tell me about this man Caron threatened you with. The one who wished to rape you in the coach. Do you know his name?"

Maërlys looked up at the older woman. Now that she was no longer frightened, she could see the goodness shining from the other's dark eyes, the sense of humor clearly visible in the lines of her generous mouth.

Sarah Dane had skin the color of *café au lait*, a creamy golden shade. She was at least five feet eight inches tall, a full six inches more than Maërlys could claim, and obviously strong. Her long neck seemed to add to her height. Maërlys' attention lingered on her prominent cheeks, which, along with her wide mouth, saved her heart-shaped face from triangularity. Her breasts were not large. Not as large as Maërlys' own, of which she was, she knew, too proud. But there was something about them, an arrogance, that gave them a prominence they would not otherwise show. Maërlys thought they might be as hard as apples, not soft like hers.

But her attention kept wandering back to that mouth: the liveliness of it; the way it twitched at the corners, sometimes, as if its owner were amused but trying to keep it to herself, the deep cleft at the center of the upper lip, and the fullness of the bottom one. That fullness stirred Maërlys in a way she had not been stirred before, a feeling she quickly suppressed. At the moment that mouth was pinched into a firm line, as if the thought of Maërlys' abuse meant serious trouble for someone, and the thrust of her bold chin held a severe warning.

Maërlys shuddered and thought she would not like to be Theo in Sarah's presence. "Caron called him Theo but I did not hear any last name."

"A big man, was he?"

"Oh, yes, very big. I was afraid he might break me in two."

"Broader. They call him Theo Broader but his real name is *Brodeur*." Sarah pronounced the name in perfect French. Her mouth twitched in that knowing, amused way, and one eyebrow lifted slightly. "They think I don't know but I make it my business to find out as much as possible about those with whom I am dealing. It is surprising, sometimes, how much can be found out."

She looked down at Maërlys, and her mouth softened into a gentle smile, the corners almost disappearing beneath the cheekbones. "You see the bag on your tray?"

Maërlys looked down at the tray, now devoid of even the slightest crumb. She had forgotten the bag, partly obscured by one of the covers. She reached down and picked it up. It was surprisingly heavy. "What is it?" she asked.

"The price of your life, little one. It was given to me in exchange for your death. Since I intend to make it my business that you will live a long, happy and, I hope, prosperous life, it does not belong to me, and so must go to the one who holds that life: you. That money belongs to you and I give it to you on one condition."

Maërlys looked into Sarah's eyes and found only kindness and concern there. "What condition?"

"Promise me that you will use your life as you see fit, for your good and your pleasure, however that may come to you. And, if you are threatened, that you will not throw your life away but sell it, and sell it very dear. Will you promise me?" Maërlys nodded, her eyes wide, her lips parted.

"Good," said Sarah. "Now tell me about this man you shot. I was told his skin was dark. Did you know him?"

"No, the only black man I've seen lately was with Mr. Everly. It might have been him but I'm not sure."

"And then?"

"The man, Tim, came and took me away. There was another man lying in the alley, a fat man...."

Sarah looked at her sharply, "Bald?"

"Certainly his hair was very thin. Tim put the dark man's body under the other one, with the pistol between them. Then he brought me here."

"And here you remain, at least for now. Many questions must be answered, and if the Frenchmen were to find you alive, it would be unpleasant. Do you mind so much?" She walked around the bed, moved some more pillows into place, and reclined, her head propped up next to Maërlys, her lovely smile only inches from the younger girl.

Maërlys found her attention focused on that beautiful, full bottom lip, and her heart seemed to be beating faster.

"Tell me, little one, does the dark color of my skin repel you?" Unable to speak, Maërlys could only shake her head again. She drew a deep breath as she felt Sarah's strong hand at the back of her neck and saw those incredible lips coming nearer. She closed her eyes.

Suddenly, the hand was removed. "I think," Sarah Dane said, "that perhaps I am as bad as your Mr. Everly. Well, perhaps I am no worse." There was something wistful about Sarah's smile as Maërlys' eyes opened to see the older woman gazing at her.

Sarah rose and pointed to the bell rope. "Please stay here but ring if you need anything at all, books, company, anything. Whoever answers will help. I have work to do, but I will be back."

15

"So, your little whore has turned out to be a failure."

"Not entirely," Caron answered. "She has rid us of that troublesome slave, at no cost to ourselves."

"Except for the expense of the Malay," Facteau snarled.

Caron snapped his fingers, "A bargain."

"Also, you have forgotten about the children."

"I have not. The cousin will know anything we need to know. Let us keep our eyes on the key. For now, we still have our connections in France. They may make the cousin as unnecessary as the other."

Facteau's eyes narrowed, and he glared at his lieutenant. "You take too much upon yourself, Felix. If you had kept the girl alive, we could have used her to control the cousin. We would have the streets piled with corpses did we not keep paying the Malay's fees. Soon it will become too much and the Malay will have to be cut off. Are you prepared for that?" He watched Caron's eyes widen. "I thought not. Well, never mind for the moment. The key indeed. What of Cherille?"

"Ah, he is at last in town and we are watching. This morning he went to see the thief-taker. Tim must have only rendered him senseless. When the runners came in answer to the cousin's summons there were no bodies in the alley, nor any pistol. As far as we can determine they came only for the blood in the back of the shop and the absence of the girl. The man Nubbins must have awakened, realized his position and disposed of the other man's corpse. Perhaps he told Cherille some story to satisfy his curiosity. In any case, they went into the shop and spoke to the cousin."

"You told me the shop was shut."

"So it is, but she admitted them and they were inside for almost an hour. Afterwards, Nubbins returned home and Cherille went to the ministry. We are hopeful of some report from our man inside."

"Does Everly wear the key?"

"We cannot tell, unless we seize and undress him. We may yet do that some night, should the opportunity arise, but there is still the question of Theo to resolve. There may be something at Cherille House we do not understand. The Malay will report to us."

Facteau pounded his desk with his fist. "This business grows too complicated. I rely on you to simplify it, and quickly. We need the exact location, and the key is required. Except for Lessègues, those children may be the only ones who can direct us correctly, and the admiral will not take kindly to our interest. For all we know, he may already be afloat. Bring me that key."

"They are operating in London, as far as I can tell, with complete impunity. There is something very odd about the business I cannot lay my finger on, and I need a better view of all the actors. I hope you can help me, Sir Charles."

"Of course, anything I can do. What you tell me is most disturbing. This fellow Winnow, he will recover?"

Jarrod waved his hand, "Oh yes, right as rain in a day or so. Got him safely in bed and eating lots of beef; I almost envy him. But for some reason, he has become fixated on a woman and we hope you can help there. He and Nubbins ran afoul of her down near the docks, apparently in the pay of the French. She stuck a pistol in his ear and stole his heart as well as some papers. Name's Sarah Dane, according to Nubbins. Some sort of criminal gang leader, gambling mistress, I don't know what. Can you shed any light for me?"

Sir Charles looked surprised, then frowned. "Well," he said, "as to that...." He reached behind him and pulled a bell. There was a slight pause, then a knock. "Come," he said, and as his secretary entered, "Bring me the file on that Malay, will you Sadler?"

Jarrod noted the young man's expression darken at Sir Charles' characterization of Sarah Dane, and that it cleared before his boss could notice. He nodded and left the room without a word. He did not look at Jarrod. In a moment, he was back with a large folder. He laid this on the desk, bowed and left.

Sir Charles opened the folder and began to look into it. Jarrod paced the floor until Sir Charles grunted. He did not offer the folder to Jarrod but tapped it with his finger. "This is the file on Siti Zara Daeng, who goes by the name of Sarah Dane, a darkie from the east," he waved his hand vaguely, "and quite an interesting character. There is no doubt she's a French agent, although we've never been able to catch her with the slightest bit of evidence. On the other hand, though there is no mention of it here, we have tried to turn her to our own advantage and, once or twice, she's been willing to play our game. We don't think of her as our agent, more as an independent contractor. I daresay it is the same for the French, but there can be no doubt she does associate with them to some degree. We consider her totally untrustworthy but occasionally useful."

He gazed at Jarrod for a moment, then went on. "As I said, she comes from out east, and her father was killed in some native power struggle. She was very attached to him and fled here to escape reprisals. She runs a house for young women where there is gambling. It is not your usual pleasure house, and the women are apparently not for sale, as more than one intoxicated gambler has found to his cost. I believe the place is quite popular with the more adventurous young men of *ton*."

He continued, "She speaks French and English like a native, and I don't know what other heathen languages. She has an intimate knowledge of weapons, both edged and powder, as well as more exotic items, including poisons and, supposedly, unarmed combat as well. A very interesting and dangerous woman; your friend is lucky to be alive."

He frowned silently. "As for the papers you say she recovered from him, we may have them in our possession. That is to say, we have a copy of something she gave us. We are still researching its accuracy but it appears genuine. Since it is a copy, we are acting in the belief that they are unaware of our knowledge of its contents. Our faith in Miss Dane is limited but, if this proves to be genuine, it will be the most valuable thing we have acquired through her as yet. Oddly, she gave it to us without being asked; indeed, we hardly knew of its existence. It came by messenger just this morning, extremely queer."

He cocked his head, "It's put us in a bit of a quandary. In the past, we've had to practically force her to work for us, using every bit of blackmail and threats against her girls and house that we could muster. Then out of the blue she comes to us with this very lively bit of intelligence and hasn't asked for a fee, at least so far. We await the other shoe, of course, and we are checking it very carefully with our sources, I assure you."

"Thank you very much, sir. This is all very interesting. We seem to have dropped into a rather deep pit, and it may take all the digging we can do to extricate ourselves. May I ask if you have several agents who deal with this Sarah Dane, or is she the property of one person only?"

"It happens she corresponds only with my secretary, Mr. Sadler, and is, I believe, wholly unknown to the rest of the service, except as a possible French agent. I think he is a little bit in love with her and I would not be surprised to learn that he had, ah, been party to her, ah, favors, as it were. Indeed, when you refer to her as his property, I fear it may be the other way around."

Jarrod's brows moved. "Could he be the source of any leak?"

"I hardly think so. He is my wife's cousin and I trust his discretion completely. He would not be my secretary, else. Also, we have no reason to suppose Miss Dane has been very useful to the French in the way of intelligence. On the contrary, she is most often employed by them as a bodyguard and, possibly, assassin."

Jarrod's eyebrows rose even higher. "A woman assassin?"

"Do not under-estimate her for a moment. She is as stealthy as an adder and quite as deadly. Although, to be fair, we have no proof of her actual killings, since her supposed victims often disappear as completely as if they never existed. Certainly, no murder victim has ever been brought home to her roost, although, once or twice, we have wondered if evidence implicating someone else…. Well, certainly nothing has ever been proven. A thoroughly amazing woman. I ask you please to be extremely careful if you meet her yourself."

"I'll warn Henry. He was quite taken with her. I begin to see why."

Lincoln Sadler was drunk. He had begun drinking early in the evening, and it was now close to two in the morning. His companion noted that they had emptied three bottles and were deep into the fourth, though he had drunk very little himself. The servants had all gone and the doorkeeper was asleep in his chair in the hall.

"Come, old man, let's get you to bed."

"No," Sadler responded, shaking himself, "I need to see her."

"It's too late. You can see her tomorrow."

"No, now. She keeps late hours," he tried to enunciate. He flung his glass at the wall. "And her brandy is a thousand times better than this swill." He peered at his companion, placing his finger unsteadily on his lips, his head bobbing, "French, you know. Has connections everywhere. Believe she owns a boat somewhere to the south. Talked about a captain named Hornbeam or something."

"Personally, I should like nothing better than to take you there and roll you into her bed, but it is not her hours I am worried about. It is the number you have spent emptying the cellar of my best brandy, which you are pleased to characterize as 'this swill.' You can call on her tomorrow."

Sadler staggered as he tried to rise, then fell onto the couch. "She doesn't love me, anyway. God knows how many men she sees."

"She keeps a gambling house. Surely you cannot expect virtue from her."

Sadler raised his fist and tried to stand. The effort nearly overset him and his friend pushed him back onto the couch. "You don't know her," he snapped defiantly, though the effect was marred by the slur with which he spoke.

"Only what you've told me. She is a gambler and a spy; surely she does not draw the line at.... Well, you told me you thought she might, ah, surrender to you."

"But she never has. Even though she finally gave me something useful without even being asked."

"Oh?"

"Yes. It seems she stole some papers from the French. Very interesting papers, including some important names, both here and in the colonies."

"Gave them to you without your asking? Did they cost much?"

"No. Didn't even ask to be paid." He frowned. "At least not yet. There was no cover note. I need to speak to her. Perhaps she got them from some French lover. Damme, I wish I was dead."

"Keep drinking like this and you very soon will be. What was so important about these papers?"

Sadler managed to pull himself upright and placed his fingers to his lips. "Mustn't tell. Very hush-hush. Foreign office business."

"But I am in the War Office. We must know what is going on."

"So you will." Sadler's head nodded ponderously. "All in good time...." His head dropped onto his breast and he began to snore, still sitting upright.

Disgusted, his companion summoned his butler and together they put the drunken man to bed.

"Again, you trouble me at this time of night?" Sarah Dane's eyes were ice, her mouth a thin line.

"It occurred to me, if you had not yet disposed of the girl...."

"You think this is an hotel? You said you wanted her dead. I was paid. Begone." She snapped her fingers.

Caron was at a loss. He had come hoping to find the girl still alive, to use as Facteau had pointed out, but Sarah Dane was such a formidable woman. As tall as himself, she did not bend as other women did. He was almost afraid of her, he admitted to himself. He clung to the "almost," lest he be completely overcome.

"What of Theo? Is there any word?" He knew he was putting himself in the position of supplicant, but he must say something.

"I told you," the woman responded, her eyes flashing, "that I would advise you when I had something to advise. You have so far paid nothing for any information concerning M. Broader. Did you bring gold?"

Fumbling in his pocket, Caron brought out another leather bag. Sarah held out her hand, tapping her foot impatiently. Caron reluctantly placed the bag in her outstretched palm. She dropped it onto the table without examining it, as if it were beneath her notice.

"Fine. As I said before, you will be advised. Now please go away. You give my house a bad...name." She wrinkled her nose.

Caron pulled himself up to his full height, and was pleased to see that he was taller than the woman by almost a quarter of an inch. "You go too far, *Ma'amselle*; you are rude. How much of this sort of treatment do you think we will stand?"

He watched as the woman went to the wall and removed a blade from its place. It was a strangely shaped, outlandish, eastern blade with a fantastic jeweled hilt and an edge that looked as sharp as a razor. Such a knife, well wielded, could remove a head. She fingered the point and looked at him, much as he might look at a chicken he wished for dinner. Her eyes no longer blazed; they were frozen. He backed up a step. She said nothing but continued to look at him, as if deciding where to start. Sweat popped out on his forehead.

He backed to the door, feeling the handle behind him. "I will await your message," he said, as he pulled the door open, backed through, and closed it carefully.

16

She was ushered into his parlor and Lord Cherille turned toward her, then came over and took her hand, bending over it before meeting her eyes. His eyes are a rather remarkable shade of blue, Emmeline thought, before she recovered.

"I am sorry to bother you, your lordship, at this absurdly early hour, and I know it is none of my business, but I really must ask, before I go further, if you meant what you said about Maërlys."

"What did I say? That she is the most beautiful woman I have ever seen? Certainly I meant it. That she is both clever and bold, a woman to be reckoned with, despite her youth? All absolutely true."

"You are pleased to be humorous but I hope you understand that my cousin's life is not a matter of humor to me."

"A thousand pardons, dear lady. You correctly admonish me for my lightness of heart; but I have hopes that your lovely cousin will be well. I plan to take steps to further my belief today."

"And you believe it is no business of mine. I am only an elderly unmarried cousin of no account and you certainly do not have to answer to me, but I wish to know. She is my only relative in England and although she has a brother and sister in France, there has been no word for ever so long. We cannot be sure they still live. So we only have each other, and if I seem to act *in loco parentis,* it is only from the best of motives."

"Ma'am, I wronged you and now you wrong yourself. You are referring to my stated wish to marry your young cousin. If you are elderly, at the ripe age of, what, twenty-two, then I must appear as a complete grandfather. You object to the banns on that basis?"

Emmeline straightened her back. "I am four and twenty, your lordship, and I have learned a thing or two. You are, I believe, two and thirty, if I correctly recall what I read in the *Times,* and Maërlys is nineteen. Quite old enough to marry you if she wishes and you are sincere in your addresses. That is all I care to know. Are you sincere?" Her search of his eyes was unwavering.

Jarrod bowed briefly, then returned his eyes to hers. "You have every right to ask me that, ma'am, and the answer concerns no one more closely than you, unless it be myself or your lovely cousin. The answer is yes. I meant everything I said and it is my fondest wish to make Maërlys the Baroness Cherille, to ensure that my line does not perish from the earth, as Henry would say."

"Henry?"

"The man your cousin shot."

"Does he often talk like that?"

"Invariably, when he has the time. He has a great deal of time, at the moment, and if you visit him he will fill your ears with such nonsense. But he is a loveable rogue."

"Oh, I am remiss. I suppose I should visit him, since Maërlys is not here to apologize properly."

"No apology necessary ma'am. He was clearly house-breaking, and got what he deserved. Or, at least, some of it."

"But this is why I came." She reached into her reticule and withdrew a small, crumpled piece of paper. She smoothed it out as best she could, and handed it to the baron. He took it from her and read,

Have no fear for your cousin. She has come to no harm, nor will she, although there is some danger. Please show this note to no one, for her protection. SZD

Jarrod looked up, frowning. "This is most interesting. Where and when was it delivered?"

"It was in the shop this morning. I slept there last night in the hope Maërlys would find her way home and I was undisturbed, but it was on the counter when I came down. My first reaction was so violent I crumpled it rather badly, but it was clean and flat when I first saw it, weighed down with a small paperweight we keep on the counter. Whoever left it must move like a spirit. Do you know what *SZD* signifies?"

"Indeed ma'am, I might very well know. I believe I will take steps to confirm it. For the present it would probably be best to do as the message requests and show it to no one, or at least, no one else. I know how much Maërlys' welfare must mean to you, and am gratified you understand that it means quite as much to me. Your secret is safe with me, as will your cousin's future be, once I catch up with her, perhaps tonight. At any rate, I will do my best. Do you open your shop today?"

"I must. My resources will not allow any more loss of custom."

"Then I wish you well. I hope you will come to me at once with anything else that concerns this unfortunate business, especially if you hear from any of these Frenchmen with whom Maërlys was so troubled. I trust that you will not, but I have asked Mr. Nubbins to continue a guard on your shop. If there is any difficulty you need only shout from the doorway and help will come immediately. Do you understand me?" He bent over her hand again.

"Oh, yes, your lordship, you are too kind."

Retaining her hand, he said, "If we are to be cousins, call me Jarrod."

It took Jarrod most of the morning and several calls before he was able to find an acquaintance in town who was both free for the evening and knew of the house. Viscount Revis said he had gambled there a time or two but never noticed the dark-skinned woman Jarrod told him about. However, he was free for the evening and would be glad to serve as *entrée*.

When he approached the house at just after nine o'clock with the viscount, Jarrod was pleased to find a well-lit, fashionable place. Inside, their coats were taken by a large man with a twice-broken nose who eyed Jarrod carefully, though with no sign of hostility. Revis introduced this major-domo as "Charlie."

They were conducted to a well-appointed salon where a table was spread with a light supper and a very creditable bar occupied most of one long wall. Passing through this room, Revis led the way to another, where a group of men were gathered around a faro table. Both the dealer and casekeeper were attractive women, the dealer about thirty years old and the other somewhat younger, perhaps twenty-three.

The viscount abandoned him here, and it was clear to Jarrod that he found the casekeeper an irresistible attraction. Continuing to explore by himself, he found rooms dedicated to gambling of every kind. The games were all conducted by women, respectably dressed, with no indication that anything but gambling was on offer.

There was no sign of Sarah Dane. On two occasions, Jarrod encountered people he knew and asked them as casually as possible if they knew of a dark-skinned woman associated with the house. He had no luck until he entered the whist room, just as Lord Edward, Earl of Farlingham was rising from one of the tables. A long-standing friend of the house of Cherille and inveterate gambler, who had more than once been saved from financial ruin by Jarrod's father, he hailed Jarrod as soon as he noticed him.

"I was so sorry to hear about Christian," he said. "He was a good friend, just like your father and yourself. Are you playing tonight?" He swept his hand around at the tables.

"I like a game of cards," Jarrod answered, "but try to stay within my income."

"Far easier to stay within yours than mine," the old man responded. "I regret to say that I've lost the last bit I can afford this month and possibly a touch more. In fact, I'm down about five thousand pounds at the moment and devil take me if I can find so much before the summer is out. I believe I'll have to discuss my situation with the management."

Taking the old earl aside, Jarrod said, "Who is the management? Is it one of these women I see everywhere?"

Farlingham frowned at him, then leaned close. "To speak the truth, it is a woman, but you'll never believe me when I tell you she's a darkie. Fine-looking woman from the east, I believe. I don't suppose she really owns the place. All I know is if you get on your uppers and need to make concessions, as it were, she represents the management."

Jarrod grinned at him, "Are you under the hatches, your lordship?"

"Well, a bit. Still shy of the duns, I hope. Of course, a house like this can't really send the bailiff around, but a gentleman's a gentleman or he is not, hey? It is an attractive place, you'll admit. Well-run, and the service and the players as lovely as you could wish. Got an excellent cellar and the dinners are fine as well." He patted his stomach.

"Are you off to see the management now?" Jarrod asked. "I'd be glad to accompany you to get a look at this manager you speak of. Never heard the like. Besides," he smiled, "maybe I can help to reduce your embarrassment to something more acceptable." He patted his breast pocket.

The earl glowed. "You're a worthy successor to your father, Jarrod, and that's the truth. Come along and we'll have a talk with the witch." He winked. "Can't eat us, hey? Not done in England, whatever they may do at home."

They stopped a young woman passing with a tray of glasses filled with champagne. As they relieved her of the last two of these, Farlingham asked, "I wonder if we might speak to Miss Dane for a moment."

The girl nodded and conducted them upstairs to a closed door, with portraits mounted on either side. She gave two short raps on this door. At first there was no answer, so she knocked again, this time two quick raps followed by a third, heavier. Jarrod thought he heard a flurry of movement, then a woman's voice said "Come."

Inside the room, Maërlys had turned pale as she backed away from the peephole. Sarah looked for herself, then turned to the girl and frowned. "What's the matter? It's only old Farlingham and one of his friends. He's no threat to anyone, surely."

"It's him," Maërlys gasped. Her hand flew to her throat. "Mr. Everly, the baron. He'll have me hanged for killing his friend."

Miss Dane took another look through the peephole. "He seems very cheerful for such a grim mission." She looked back at Maërlys to find the girl was flushing. "Are you sure?" She moved aside and Maërlys put her eye to the glass again.

"He is very handsome, isn't he?" She turned back to Sarah, blushing furiously. "He kissed me. He t-touched...," her face was bright red, now, as she watched the other woman's mouth twitch into that enthralling half smile.

"I have not forgotten, my dear. And yes, he is very handsome indeed. I understand why you went to so much trouble." The twitch turned into a full smile. "But you are right; it would not do for him to see you here. We must know a great deal more of him. Go now, out that way." She pointed to the door in the alcove at the rear. "And don't worry. No one, no matter how handsome, will see you hanged while I live. Go back to your room and rest easy. I will come to you later, and tell you everything.

She watched as the girl hurried out the door, closing it after her. Sarah seated herself at the deal table, began to shuffle a deck of cards, counted to ten, and said, "Come."

17

Their guide opened the door and conducted them into a room, sparsely furnished, but distinguished by a selection of weapons hung on the walls. Mostly fine swords and knives, but here and there a pair of pistols, some muskets, and even an ancient hackbut that dominated one wall. A woman sat alone at a table, a deck of cards in her hand and a glass of something dark at her elbow. She raised her head as they came in, and Jarrod recognized her instantly from Henry's description. The serving girl left, closing the door. Sarah Dane stood up, looked questioningly at him for a moment, then turned and curtsied to the earl.

"It's good to see you again, my lord. I hope everything is to your satisfaction."

"Everything but my luck, ma'am. Allow me to name my particular friend, his lordship, Baron Cherille."

Miss Dane's eyes swung back to Jarrod. "Enchanted," she said, curtseying again.

"The pleasure is entirely mine," Jarrod answered, his eyes studying hers. They were a deep, chocolate color, filled with depth and flashes of light as well. They added to her beauty, which was quite singular; the reasons for Henry's interest became clearer by the moment.

"Well," she said, looking from one to the other, "may I ask what brings you gentlemen to me?"

"Since you ask, ma'am," answered Farlingham, "I would like to discuss some business with you."

Miss Dane raised her eyebrows slightly.

"The fact is," he went on, "my losses are somewhat embarrassing and I hope to make arrangements for some slight delay before payment in full might be forthcoming."

At this, the woman went to a bell-rope against the wall and pulled on it gently. Almost immediately, a side door opened and another woman came into the room, bearing a tray with a book on it. The woman with the tray retreated as Miss Dane opened the book to a marked page, scanned it rapidly, and looked back at the earl.

"According to this, you currently owe four thousand, eight hundred and fifty-two pounds, ten shillings. Had it gone the other way, I don't doubt you'd have broken our faro bank. How long do you think it will take to make this good?" She was smiling, but her manner was extremely business-like.

"Well, ma'am, I was hoping you might let some portion of the total ride for three weeks or so, until my income refreshes. In the meantime, my friend here has graciously agreed to make up the difference."

Sarah Dane looked again at Jarrod, this time sweeping him from top to toe with her glance, then cocking her head to one side and locking eyes with him. "How much difference are you considering?" she asked.

Jarrod said, "At the risk of being impolite, ma'am, I'd like first to know more about your establishment. For example, do you take a hand in the play yourself?"

She kept her eyes on his for a long moment before she spoke. "I used to but it didn't answer."

"May I ask why?"

Her eyes flashed with so much power that Jarrod felt almost as if he had been pushed. "I won too much. It is our experience that men do not mind losing to pretty young women, as long as they do not lose too much. On the other hand, when the woman has dark skin, they like it considerably less."

Jarrod smiled, "You are very frank, ma'am. I am grateful. And you won so often?"

"Almost always," was her reply.

"You intrigue me. I wonder," Jarrod said, "if you would consider playing with me. I have longed for a good game of piquet this age, and you may be the opponent I have looked for. Does your skill extend to that game?"

Again, that flash in the eyes, "It does."

"In that case, if you consent, I will take full responsibility for his lordship's debt, down to the last shilling, and we shall see if I cannot win it back. Does that suit you? And you, my lord?"

Farlingham blinked. "By gad, Jarrod, that is over the line. Decent of you, of course, but I never expected—"

Jarrod raised his hand. "Nothing, sir. You are an old friend of our family. Your credit has never been questioned in Cherille Hall. I am pleased to do it."

Miss Dane was still watching him. She frowned slightly but there was the hint of a smile at the corner of her mouth. "You can play for cash?"

Jarrod bowed.

"In that case, I accept." She reached for the bell-pull.

In a moment, one of the servants came in, chairs were brought, and the room was slightly rearranged, with Jarrod and Sarah facing each other over the table, now placed in the center of the room. Another table was set nearby and covered with various refreshments.

"A glass of Madeira?" Sarah asked, indicating her own glass. "Or would you prefer claret or champagne?"

The earl spoke first. A comfortable chair had been provided for him near the players, with another small table nearby, including a pipestand, humidor, and ashtray. "Madeira would be ideal," he said, leaning back and filling a pipe.

"Champagne for me," said Jarrod. "I believe I will need my wits about me this evening." He smiled at

Sarah, and was pleased when she smiled back. Whatever the foreign office may think, the woman in front of him was beautiful, charming, and bore no resemblance to any assassin of which Jarrod had ever heard. If the information was correct, it only added to his estimation of his opponent and spice to the game.

"Since you have a great deal to make up, I presume you will wish to play large. Will you name the stake, sir?"

"Since we are strangers, I propose we start relatively small. Shall we say half a crown a point?"

"Certainly, though it may take you some little while to recoup your deficit at that pace. Shall we agree to double it each rubber, up to say, a pound?"

He laughed at that. "First rate, Miss Dane, first rate. And an additional twenty-five pounds the rubber?"

"Certainly, my lord. Doubled, also?" Her eyes held his as she smiled at him.

"Limit?" he asked.

She shrugged, looked down slightly, and regarded him from under her lengthy eyelashes, "Why?"

He laughed again. "And damn the first one who cries, 'Stop! Enough!' What if I break your bank?"

"Why, then sir, it would be for you to name your prize." He suddenly realized that despite her still charming smile, under her lashes, her eyes were like dark brown ice.

Miss Dane won the first cut, but, contrary to all convention, designated Jarrod as first dealer. "Hospitality of the house," she offered in response to his single raised brow. Jarrod smiled, nodded, shuffled and dealt, setting the *talon* in the middle of the table. Miss Dane took her five, and Jarrod three. They exchanged, Sarah taking the usual five and Jarrod the remaining three.

"Point of seven," she said.

"Equal."

"Ace?"

"Equal," he said again.

"Queen?"

"Not good."

"Sixieme?"

"Good."

"Trio?"

"Equal."

"Aces?" she smiled.

He smiled back and executed a small bow.

Sarah marked her score of nineteen, and led the ace of diamonds.

Jarrod marked his own score of seven, and responded with the seven of clubs. Sarah then laid down ten more cards, including the remainder of her diamonds and the ace and king of hearts and spades, respectively. She smiled at him over her remaining card as he laid down ten of his cards to match.

"Am I capotted, ma'am?" he asked, and she laid the last card, a nine of spades.

She raised her eyebrows again, and watched as he laid his last card. "Rescued by the queen of spades," she smiled at him. "Well saved. We will have a game. For the moment, I am up forty-one to nine." She shuffled and dealt.

As expected, Jarrod did much better on the second hand, achieving something close to parity. The play continued back and forth, with the clear advantage always to the elder hand, and they finished the rubber at one hundred and twelve to one hundred and three, to Jarrod's advantage.

"Twenty-six pounds, two shillings and sixpence," he remarked. "We are evenly matched, ma'am. Shall we see how the second rubber goes?"

Again, Sarah took the cut, but this time kept the deal. With the rubber stake doubled to fifty pounds, and the point to a crown, she won by a total of eighteen points. She smiled at Jarrod, "That makes your total debt up to four thousand, eight hundred and eighty pounds, seventeen shillings and sixpence. You are going in the wrong direction, sir."

He cocked his head at her and returned her smile, "The night is young. Shall we continue?"

After the fourth rubber, with the point stabilized at one pound each and the rubber at two hundred pounds, set to double again for the fifth rubber, Jarrod found himself down almost two thousand pounds. It was too much for the earl.

"Damme, Jarrod, I can't watch this any longer. Call a halt, hey? Miss Dane will take your cheque, and I will repay you the whole amount as soon as may be."

"I have promised Miss Dane not to bother her with cheques." Jarrod reached into his coat and removed a bundle. He counted out fifty hundred pound notes which he laid on the table, restoring the rest of the bundle to his coat. "I'm sorry," he said to Lord Henry, "we have an agreement, and I must hold you to it. Your original debt of four thousand, eight hundred and fifty-two pounds—"

"And ten shillings," put in Sarah.

Jarrod bowed to her. "And ten shillings," he added, "are now between you and me, and you may repay me at your convenience. Put it in your will, if you like, and, as you know, I wish you a long and happy life. The bank," he waved at the pile of notes, "is now between myself and Miss Dane. I am enjoying myself immensely and flatter myself that Miss Dane also is receiving some small pleasure." He turned to her and bowed, which his opponent answered with a bright smile. He noted that, for the moment, the ice was gone from her eyes.

"Well, it's very kind of you, Jarrod, and I'm certainly grateful, but I can't continue to watch you ruin yourself. I'm an old man, and my bed has been calling me this hour gone. If you two young people will excuse me, I'll go and find it. You must call on me at your earliest convenience, my boy, and let me know the result. Either way, I'll show you something from my cellar that will make you feel better about it. You have my word, hey?" They both smiled at him, wished him good night and he withdrew.

Jarrod turned back to Sarah, "Not even midnight, yet. I trust you will allow me my revenge?"

"By all means," Sarah answered. She broke open a fresh pack, shuffled it, and laid it in the center of the table. "If you will cut, your lordship?"

The play continued, Jarrod's fortunes see-sawing with the deal, neither side gaining much more of an edge. At the end of the eighth rubber, Jarrod was slightly down, his debt, less the money on the table, which Sarah had allowed to lie, untouched, now totaled just over two thousand pounds, with the doubled rubbers now worth one thousand, six hundred pounds. The time was approaching two in the morning, and he suggested that they pause to take some refreshment.

"Perhaps we should call it a night. If we continue, you will likely only deepen your debt." She was smiling, but it was not an entirely friendly expression.

He gave her his most winning smile. "It's only money," he said, "and I hope I am not so mean. I like piquet because of the skill it requires and, may I say Miss Dane, that an opponent such as yourself makes the game a treat indeed."

"The feeling is mutual, sir. I admit that this is one of the games I have missed since I retired from dealing, although few gentlemen have offered me such sport. I venture to say that you are not some pink, but spend your time in more important endeavors. If I am not impertinent, may I ask how that is?"

"Certainly, ma'am," Jarrod said. Now they were alone, he was prepared to do battle in earnest. "With the recent death of my brother I have risen to the title and become a gentleman farmer, with large estates to the west."

"And before that? Were you the wastrel of the family, sowing a different sort of crop?"

"I hope not, ma'am. I have traveled a good deal, but mostly in the service of His Majesty." His eyes had hardened, and he noted that the flint had returned to hers, matching his steel.

"You are not here by accident," she said.

18

Jarrod held Sarah's eyes, admiring the flash. "No. Again I appreciate your frankness and hope I may deserve it. I am come in the hopes of finding a young woman in whom I have taken an interest."

"What makes you think I know anything of this woman?"

"I have made inquiries at the foreign office. They seem to regard you with a mixture of respect, caution and, as far as I can tell, even wonder. You are known to have associations with his majesty's enemies, and I daresay there would be repercussions, were government able to prove even one tenth of what they surmise."

"And this concerns your missing woman?"

"I am in touch with the young lady's only relative in England, her cousin. This morning the cousin received a note. Knowing of my concern, nay, my deep attachment to this young lady, she condescended to show me this message. The closing letters were most intriguing. Are your initials not *SZD*?"

Sarah Dane's eyes had gone from ice to stone. "You tread on dangerous ground."

"I believe, if you wished harm to this girl, you would not have sent the note. It was an act of kindness, the act of a friend, to allay the fears of the only person proven to have this young woman's interests close to her heart. I, too, hold the lady's interests here," he touched his bosom. "Her cousin knows of my attachment and was good enough to show me the note despite the warning included in it. Please understand I have no wish to cross swords with you, ma'am, although if I were to discover that harm had come to this young woman through your agency, that attitude would be revised. Indeed, I would seek your destruction with all the powers at my command."

Her eyes flashed. "Do you understand that your life is fully at my command, here in this room?"

"I suspect as much, certainly. I merely seek a frank exchange of views. My death here would almost certainly cause you embarrassment, as my presence is well known. Likewise, I would expect to sell myself dearly, and there might be other costs, as well." He shrugged. "For now, I merely wish to know if you acknowledge commerce with the young lady of whom I speak, one Maërlys Blanc, and if you can assure me that she still lives."

She watched him from under her eyelids for a long moment, her eyes once more as cold and hard as any he had ever seen. She appeared to be thinking and, although the wheels of thought were almost visible, he was unable to make the smallest conjecture as to their variety.

"Perhaps I should know more of your search for her. What is the nature of your association with her? If you are so attached, why is she not with you? You are a wealthy and powerful man, with sources within the government and without. Why do you come here seeking someone who apparently does not run to you for protection? Does your quarry fear you? Why? What of this cousin? Is she a gullible woman, fallen into your toils? I listen to you and hear no answers, only questions."

"I have promised to be frank and will keep that promise. I met the young lady for the first time only two weeks ago, in Portsmouth. I was misled into believing her to be other than she was, and took certain, ah, liberties. Discovering my error, I attempted to make what amends I could, but for some reason, the young lady fled from me. I have had no occasion since to discuss the matter with her, so cannot answer for her state of mind. I do, however, have reason to believe she fell into the hands, at least temporarily, of French agents. I sincerely assure you that my intentions are entirely honorable, as I have assured her cousin. I wish only the opportunity to see her, declare my intentions to her, and find out if she will have me or no. I am, as you point out, quite wealthy and would, I think, be considered a good match in even the finest homes, though I'm only a baron."

"You have not told me wherein the difficulty lies. Why did you not locate the young lady and present your case many days since? Why drag me into this business?"

"When the young lady fled the inn at Portsmouth, I gave chase but she eluded me. I was unsure of her direction and then personal matters intruded. The unexpected death of my brother put me into some obligations which must needs be resolved before I could follow her to London. My associate pursued her on my behalf but he became froward, and she was obliged to shoot him."

Her eyebrows rose. Jarrod could not tell if this was due to surprise. "Obliged to shoot him? Whatever did he do?"

"He entered her home by night, hoping to ascertain if she was, in fact, the young lady we sought."

"And she shot him? You astonish me. He must have frightened her dreadfully."

To Jarrod's eye, Miss Dane did not appear in the least astonished. "Yes, ma'am. I believe she took him for one of those French agents I mentioned, rather than an arrow from Cupid's bow."

"You take the death of your associate very lightly."

"In fact, ma'am, he is not dead. He will recover. He hopes you will be glad to hear that."

"I? What have I to do with your associate?"

"He claims to have met you four nights ago. He pines to renew the acquaintance."

Sarah's calm gaze changed to one of intense interest for a moment, then back to insouciance. "At some low dive on the docks, no doubt. Do I look as if I am in the habit of meeting strange men on the streets? You must be mistaken."

"Believe me, ma'am, I would not believe it myself, were not the description so exact. Henry is the veriest devil for faces and you made a strong impression on him. I suspect there is nothing strange in that, but he says you put a pistol in his ear and your hand in his pocket. He seemed to think you were interested in his dulodulo."

She stood up, placed her hands on the table, and leaned toward him. Her eyes were no longer icy; they blazed with fire. "You are frivolous. I think, sir, that despite your costume, your money, and your pretensions, you are no gentleman. Because of this house and what you have heard, you think you can insult me. I ask that you pay your debt and leave. I trust you will not make me call for assistance."

Jarrod stood, reached into his coat, withdrew another handful of notes, and flung it disdainfully on the table without counting it. He stared coldly at his opponent for a moment, then bowed, said, "Your servant, ma'am," from between clenched teeth, turned and left the room.

"Oh, Maërlys, my darling, I made a terrible mess of it. I snapped at him, and he stormed off. Men are so proud." She paused and reflected. "And, of course, so am I. It is my chief failing, I believe, although certainly not my only one. Can you ever forgive me?"

"Why, what happened? Does he seek to have me taken up by the runners?"

Sarah took the younger woman in her arms, "No, my darling. Of course not. He says you did not kill that man, but only wounded him, and he is recovering. But then he had the nerve to make insinuations about me. He used the coarsest word, one even I have never heard before. I lost my temper. Too many men have treated me as if I were for sale, because my skin is dark and my occupation seems to place my virtue in question."

She stopped and looked at Maërlys, her eyes soft and warm in the candlelight. "You do not question my virtue, do you, my sweeting? I admit I love my pleasure but I am no whore nor, I hope, seducer. You understand that, don't you?"

Maërlys face was reddening, and her breathing had quickened. She nodded her head and Sarah went on. "I simply refuse to be insulted and sometimes, perhaps, I take offense where none was intended. But to say such a thing to my face! It is beyond bearing. I cannot tell what he seeks, or guess what he means to do. I must think."

"Did he say anything else about me?"

"He wishes to speak with you and implied that he intends to make you an offer of marriage."

"What? Really? Marriage? Do you think he means it?"

"I cannot tell. His mind is closed to me. I believe we must sort out your situation first, so that you may approach him from a position of strength. If your enemies were to discover that you are still alive...," her face softened again, and she stroked the girl's arm, "so warm, and so alive." She shook herself, and turned away. "Tell me again about your brother and sister. And your cousin."

"What are you doing here?" Facteau's eyes were blurry and red. He was wearing a dressing gown. He looked up and down the deserted hallway, dragged the other man inside by his arm and carefully closed the door.

"I had to see you. I believe it is extremely urgent. I waited all day yesterday for an opportunity. I could wait no longer."

"If we are seen together we are both compromised, perhaps to the gallows. Are you mad?"

"No one will see me at this hour; London still sleeps. Listen to me! Your Malay has gone over to the British. Two days ago she brought them some intelligence of yours—"

"What intelligence? How do you know? Whom did she talk to? Speak."

"Calm yourself. I have not been able to see the papers, but she gave them to my friend, Sadler. He is

the only one there she trusts. The fool is in love with
her and thinks he can make her love him. Bah. She
loves no one but herself."

"Damn you, cease babbling about love and
speak of intelligence. If you have any."

"He wouldn't tell me what was in the
information. As far as I can determine, the foreign
office is trying to gauge its authenticity before
releasing anything to us. But he said it was excellent
material and that she had given it without asking for
money in advance. As you know, with the Malay this is
unheard of."

"Perhaps she plays some deep game of her own.
How can you know we are involved?"

"Of course she plays her own game," his visitor
hissed. "But if the information were not harmful to
your interests it would be of no use to them. I would
take my oath it is serious. Has the Malay done work
for you lately? Has anything passed through her
hands?"

"No. Ridiculous. You know we use her only for
guarding and assassination, things that compromise
her as deeply as they do us. We are not such fools as
to trust her. She never has access to any important...."
Facteau's voice trailed off and his gaze wandered, as if
he were thinking. Then, suddenly, he turned to his
companion. "Thank you. Now go. Before you are seen."

"Do you know—"

"Yes, yes," Facteau answered, opening the door and pushing his visitor through it. "Go. Quickly. Before you are seen."

"But I—" the other stammered as the door closed in his face.

Facteau whirled and began to pace. Then he moved to the desk and began to write something which he then crumpled in his hand and hurled into the basket at his feet. The clock on the table near the wall chimed very softly, five times. He began to pace once more, banging his right fist into his left palm over and over. He stood it for fifteen more minutes before he rang the bell, then he retrieved the paper from the basket and smoothed it out on his desk.

It was almost six before Caron came in, and Facteau was beside himself with rage. "Now your fat is in the fire!" he shouted. "Now we are compromised. "I misdoubt we may have to run for our lives. You fool. You, you traitor! We will all end on the guillotine, or the gallows, if you have your way. What have you done?"

"I, I cannot say. What do you suppose I have done?"

"Placed our lives in the hands of your Malay, that's what. She is a British agent. She will see us all hanged."

"Nonsense. We only use her for assassinations. She is as guilty as we. Were she to go to the government, she would be taken up in an instant. Their ridiculous old judges are with child to hang a woman. A beautiful woman like the Malay, they will have front-row seats with their hands under their robes. She never has any information we do not wish her to have."

"No? Can you think of any instance lately where she has behaved in what we might call an uncharacteristic manner?"

"What do you mean?"

Did she not tell us that she ran away on the night your toady was robbed of his money? Have you ever known her to run before?"

Caron frowned, "No, I was surprised. She is usually quite fearless."

"Suppose she did not run away. Suppose that while her companions slumbered, she removed the papers and made notes or committed them to memory."

"You have proof of this?"

"I am assured that she has handed valuable information to the British government. What else can it be?" He passed a paper to Caron. "Here are several points we can check quickly. Make inquiries to discover if these people are compromised. If they are, we will know and you will take steps. You understand me?"

"Yes, at once," Caron assured him.

"And find Theo!" Facteau shouted, as Caron hurried through the door.

19

"I'm sorry, Henry. I made a cock of it." Lord Cherille sat next to the bed, looking at the floor.

"Made her mad, did you?" His friend was smiling.

"Blazing mad. I found myself thinking about the description of her from the foreign office, hoping I wouldn't have to draw my pistol."

"You had a pistol with you?"

"No. All the more reason to hope it wouldn't be needed."

Henry laughed. "Did she go so far as to threaten your life?"

"Not at that moment. She was a perfect lady. Said she hoped I'd not make her 'call for assistance,' if you can believe it, after earlier pointing out that my life was in her hands as long as I was in her house. A most interesting woman and one I do not care to have for an enemy. And apparently I have made her one."

"Something you said about the girl? Do you think she's disposed of her?"

"I hardly know what to think. On that point she seemed not to take me seriously in the least, though I practically accused her of willful murder. It was most confusing."

"So, what set her off?"

"When I told her she'd met you, she laughed and described the meeting place as if it were ludicrous. In that house, looking at that handsome woman, it was ludicrous. Absolutely unbelievable. Then I assured her that I could not be mistaken, given your clear description, and that she had stolen the papers from you. She became enraged. I cannot tell what it was that set her off but she seemed to think I was trifling with her in some way." He shuddered. "As if I would. A most formidable woman."

Henry laughed again, this time loudly and at length. "I told you she was to be reckoned with and yet you had the temerity to suggest a romance to her? I wonder she didn't cut your throat. I expect you're lucky she *is* a lady, or you'd be floating down the Thames with your face in the water this minute." He laughed again. "I love you, sir, but there is much you don't understand. Maybe I should not let you out alone. Although, to be sure, you fared better with my intended than I did with yours. At least, she did not shoot you."

"I thank my stars. Do you know, she has a hackbut on the wall? A hackbut, for all love. I would not be surprised to find she can shoot the enormous thing. It must be two hundred years old." He frowned at Henry. "But you'll never have the temerity to call her 'your intended.' Not to her face."

"The woman I met was the woman of the century. Beautiful, bold, with a weapon in her hand and laughter in her eyes. With her at my side we could rule the world, if we were stupid enough to care for it. I will have to convince her, of course. I wish you may not have set her face against me. But what of her intentions, and what of your intended? Do you know where she is? This Sarah Dane seems to play a very dark game."

Jarrod stared at him, shaking his head. "This business is getting deeper with every step and we may be sinking in it. From what I've told you, do you think the girl is alive?" He stood up and began pacing, kicking a chair out of his way. "I swear, I'll kill that harpy myself if I find proof she's harmed that innocent little baggage."

Henry pulled himself off the pillows, "Innocent? She shot me out of hand! I like that, 'innocent.' And you'll have to go through me to harm Sarah Dane. But I'll not believe she'd hurt that child without evidence. The woman I met was too strong to do so weak a thing. There is also the other question."

"What other question?"

"The Frenchmen. What did they want with your 'innocent?' From what her cousin said, it was all a plot to make her your lover. To what end? What do they want from you?" He started to get out of bed.

The baron looked at him worriedly. "Do you think you should?"

"I've been idle too long. No telling what trouble you'll get into, left to yourself. Let us find Nubbins and see what watch we can put on my future bride's house. She's too much for any one of us alone. Then we'll see what can be done about these Boney-boys. They annoy me. Re-instituting slavery for black skins only. Bah. No wonder General Dumas is dead; I suspect he spins constantly in his grave."

"My dear, I think it is time for us to take steps to improve your situation, and perhaps mine as well."

Maërlys looked up at Sarah, who was pacing the room. "Whatever do you mean?"

"You told me that it was because of your brother and sister that these Frenchmen were able to entrap you; force you to serve them against your will and even your better judgment. This is correct?"

"Yes. This Bonaparte is evil; he wishes to rule the world. He should be stopped. But they told me they could find Reynard and little Ambre. By now they may have captured them and will harm them if I do not do as they say. Of course, now I am thought dead, so for the moment, they may be safe." She looked at Sarah with tears in her eyes. "I owe you all our lives."

Sarah smiled down at her. "My poor child. I promise you, I could do no less and face myself in the mirror. You owe me nothing, but the situation is untenable, you understand? You cannot remain in hiding forever. What life is this? You are too young and beautiful to be wasted in a closet. What of this handsome nobleman, this Lord Cherille?"

Maërlys' hand flew to her throat, the tears left her eyes and found their way down her cheeks. "You must have misunderstood him or perhaps he misrepresented himself. He would never marry such as I. He is a rich peer and he thinks me a wanton. Perhaps he regrets that he did not debauch me when he had the chance and wishes to rectify his error. It may be that he finds me pretty, even if I am only a whore. Do you think I'm pretty?"

"Excessively so, child, and you make me wonder if you would object so fiercely to being, as you put it, 'debauched'." Sarah's look was tender and the smile flickered at the corner of her mouth.

"If only I could be sure of Reynard and Ambre."

Sarah knelt beside her and wiped the tears away with her hands. "Hush, little one. You have done nothing wrong; protecting your family is the highest kind of goodness. I believe this baron would understand that, and do his utmost to protect you from any consequences." She grew thoughtful. "It was not my impression that he wishes you to suffer. Quite the contrary. His attitude was more that of, well, I think a man in love."

"You're teasing me. You said he was rude to you."

"He was certainly impertinent and I became enraged. Because of my skin many people in this country believe they can be rude to me with impunity. But now that I have had time to think about our exchange, I believe he did not mean to be offensive. It's my opinion that he simply meant to give me a message." She tapped her cheek with her finger, looked into the middle distance, and a singularly sweet smile came to her lips. "I think I like this message and am glad to receive it."

Maërlys cocked her head and looked quizzically at her, "What message is that?"

Sarah patted her hand, "Never mind. That will wait until we receive confirmation. For the moment it is your case we must deal with. Would you be willing to take a risk in the hope of freeing your family?"

At this Maërlys' face took on a stern look so antagonistic to her youthful prettiness that Sarah had to restrain the tiny half-smile that threatened to turn into a laugh. "I would do anything. I have been bad but Reynard and Ambre are innocent. Their lives should not be wasted, whatever happens to me. If they can be saved, I would gladly go to the guillotine." Then the girl broke down, and began to cry.

Sarah held her close and stroked her hair, but she smiled. "Hush. We will hope no such extreme is required."

"I regret to say it, but I believe you are correct. One of the people on your list has disappeared, and another was seen leaving his home with someone who was like a bailiff, but not like a bailiff."

"What does that mean?" Facteau demanded.

Caron shrugged. "That is what I was told. The man carried himself like a bailiff, as if he were taking James Gooding to prison, but he did not dress like a bailiff. More like a city man, if you can believe it. Do bankers arrest people? Of course not, but the foreign office.... At all events, it is too much of a coincidence, and I do not trust coincidences."

"No more do I."

"Having ascertained these things, I called on the Malay."

Facteau, who had been pacing, stopped in mid-stride and swung around to face him. "You did what? Did you speak to her? What did she say?"

"I merely wished to decide if she would give herself away. I asked her about Theo. She said she had no news of him. I reminded her that I had given her a bag of gold. She asked if I would have it returned or did I want her to continue the search. I told her to continue by all means. She shrugged her shoulders at me, as if it were a matter of no import. A hundred guineas of no importance! It made me angry."

"Did you beat her?"

Caron's face went slack and he stared at his employer aghast. "Are you mad? Do you think *I* am? I was already so close to death I could feel his breath upon my neck. To have raised my hand to her...aiee! You have not been there; the walls are full of blades and firearms. I have no doubt the blades are poisoned. These Orientals are not like us. They are not civilized. I wonder sometimes…these people who disappear at her hands, does she eat them?" He shivered. "I would not be surprised if she had a room somewhere, full of heads, perhaps mounted on the walls. Perhaps even shrunken. Aiee!"

"You should have stripped her and beaten her with the flat of one of her own blades. It is the best way to handle women. However, it is too late now. You must do away with her."

Caron stared at Facteau. "How, I mean, when, I mean, do you really believe it necessary?"

"You should have done it today," Facteau sneered, "when you had her in your hands. Never mind. Do it tomorrow. They are up late gambling. Call at dawn with some of your friends from the docks. Tell them they can plunder this rich gambling house and you will not even have to pay them. Kill anyone who gets in your way. And search the house for the little whore from the dress shop. It may be that she is hiding there and was not eaten for dinner after all. I do not trust this Malay. She is a liar. If you find the doxy, bring her to me. Everyone else you should destroy. Let the child watch; it will make her more tractable. Go and assemble your men. I look forward to your report, preferably before noon."

"Missus is coming down." Jenny said. "Julia told me."

"High time," muttered Ella. "Hardly seen her since the new girl came, the Frenchie."

"Her name is Maërlys, and you know it. She's been through the mill, same as us. You know that too. You just miss Sarah cuddling you. Jealous is what."

"Well, I don't see what's so special—"

"Yes, you do. You know she always takes care of the new ones because they need it. Once you've got to stand on your own legs, ain't no need to be cuddled and tickled and...."

"You just keep your 'ands to yourself, Jenny Ennis."

"And you watch out, Ella. You know Sarah don't believe in jealousy. Truth be, I think she prefers men, if she has a preference."

"I think she should prefer me."

Julia laughed at that as she came in. "We all think that Ella, and you know, I think she does."

"Does what," Sarah asked, looking at the three faces suddenly turned her way. Ella's grim frown, Jenny's surprise with her hand over her mouth, Julia's quiet smile with one eyebrow lifted.

Julia winked, just as Bill stuck his head in. "Better come look, Sarah," he said. "Urgent, Simon says."

20

As she came down the hall, she noticed the two heavy bars across the door to the foyer. Simon summoned her to the parlor on the left. "What is it?" she asked.

"Caron," Simon answered. "I told him you were out but he was very insistent, so I made him wait in the foyer. I barred the door behind me, but he did not even notice; the moment I left the room, he opened the front door and summoned more men inside. They are disposed about the foyer waiting for my return. I believe they mean to overpower me and storm the house."

Sarah raised her left eyebrow, "You were watching through the peep, I collect?"

"Yes ma'am."

She tapped his shoulder. "Remember how you made fun of me when I installed the closets?"

He smiled and hung his head. "That is why I work for you, ma'am, and not the other way around."

She smiled back, "How many are there?"

"Six, including Caron."

"The foyer must be bursting at the seams. Have you filled the closets?"

"Martha is doing so now. Here are Jenny and Ella. Andy will join Martha on the other side."

They watched as Jenny and Ella came in and opened the closet doors in the wall alongside the foyer. Ella lingered, looking at Sarah, and Sarah went over to her. "Be careful, now; you know what to do," she said, and gave the girl a quick kiss. Ella brightened, smiled, and closed the door behind her.

Sarah turned back to Simon who was looking at the floor, trying not to smirk. She smiled and ran a finger down his cheek. "None of that now," she said.

"Sorry, Sarah, but you always know exactly how we all feel. We're ready now, I think."

"Excellent. Then I will go and talk to them. Have you locked the front door?"

"William is seeing to it."

She frowned slightly, then smiled. "Go check, will you. I'll wait another—" she glanced at the clock— "two minutes before I wake them up."

"It'll never take that long." He hurried away and Sarah reached into a drawer of the cabinet standing against the wall.

She withdrew a pistol, sniffed it, then quickly emptied it, carefully removing the wadding, ball, and priming. She had just finished reloading it when Simon returned and nodded to her. She held up the pistol and he nodded again, patting his coat pocket. She reached into the drawer once more, this time removing a wicked-looking knife nearly two feet long in a sheath and harness. She put her arms through the harness so that the sheath and knife hung behind her. She reached back with her left hand, pulled the knife partly out of the sheath, then rammed it back down again.

She nodded to Simon and they went to opposite sides of the door to the foyer. Each took a place at one of the peeps, which were glass windows set in the wall, concealed on the foyer side by pictures in glass frames. A speaking tube on Sarah's side ran to a vent in the ceiling of the foyer.

Caron had disposed his men, one at each corner of the room with himself and "Battering Bill," a giant of a man, in the center. Bill was placed so that anyone entering the foyer from the inside door would immediately be faced with his incredible might. When the voice came through the vent, all six men began to look around, surprised.

"This is a strange visit, M. Caron," Sarah's voice called down to them. "Is that Battering Bill you've got with you? Open the ports, boys and girls, and cover the corners, if you please."

At this, four holes appeared in the walls, just below chest high, and musket barrels were thrust through.

"Please remain very still," Sarah's voice went on, "too much movement will inevitably result in the immediate death of four of you. The other two will be disposed of before you can do anything about it. So please, I implore you, think of your wives and children and be still. Bill, you know me, do you not? You know Sarah Dane?"

Bill had stopped looking at the muskets and was staring wildly about, trying to locate the voice. "Yes, ma'am, I know you. I swear I didn't know it was your 'ouse. Woulda never come 'ere, else."

"I believe you, Bill. What did Caron tell you?"

Caron leapt at Bill but was easily swatted aside by the bigger man. "I swear, ma'am, he told us we was to rob a 'ouse. Said nobody would be 'ome but a servant or two and we wouldn't 'ave to 'urt 'em. Least, not much."

"It would be a hanging offense either way, wouldn't it, Bill? Of course, now you know it's me, you know it will never come to law. I take care of my own problems, do I not? Are you a problem I must take care of, Bill?"

Still staring around, Bill said, "No, ma'am. I wouldn't never 'ave crossed you. This feller lied to me." He turned a furious face on Caron, who backed away. The four men in the corners were staring at the muskets, each of which was leveled at one of their bellies. Caron placed his back against the front door and tried the handle. It wouldn't move.

"Both doors are locked and barred. Not even you could get through, Bill," Sarah went on. "Now here is what you must do if any of you wish to leave this house alive. Are you listening?"

"Yes, ma'am," Bill answered, his eyes still searching for the source of the voice.

"I wish to hear from your companions in the corners."

There was a murmur of submission from those quarters.

"Then, gentlemen, you must begin by removing your clothing. I wish you to stack your coats, waistcoats, and trousers under that table along the wall. Any weapons, jewelry and other items you may have in the pockets should remain in the pockets. Do I make myself clear?"

Cries of "Not our clothes," and "Let us keep our pants, at least," and, "Our money, too?" from the men in the room combined with giggles from behind the walls.

"If you need persuasion, we can easily kill one or two of you. Perhaps you there, next to Caron."

Both men in the corners near the outside door began furiously tearing at their coats. "No, ma'am! Please, we're doing of it. Please don't shoot," one of them cried. Caron was looking to either side, his mouth working.

"One of the others, then? How about you, Bill?" The voice sounded sweet but hard. Suddenly, all five men were disrobing, stacking their clothes and belongings under the table, retaining only their shirts and drawers. Caron was watching from the door, his face frozen in horror. "You too, Caron," came Sarah's voice.

Inside the house, Sarah turned to Simon with a smile. "Go outside and watch with William. Unlock the door when I give the signal and make sure no one leaves with their clothes on. Caron stays here." Simon smiled back, nodded, and left.

As Caron placed his clothes on top of the others, the voice came again from the ceiling. "Now, gentlemen, I thank you for your cheerful accession to my requests. If you will take a few of those cravats, and, is that a bit of rope I see protruding from one of those pockets? Excellent. Use those things to bind M. Caron tightly and place him in that chair against the other wall, if you please. He and I have much to discuss."

"No, you cannot leave me with that devilish woman!" screamed Caron, as the others seized him and began to follow Sarah's instructions.

"Feel free to gag him, as well," said Sarah. "There is no reason why you should listen to his importunities. It is his fault you are in this position and it is certain that you will never be paid. You all have long walks ahead of you so I leave you your shoes. Remember, if you think of revenge, who lied to you about your mission and deceived you about the difficulties. I believe I have been more than lenient with you all."

She pulled a rope, signaling Simon, and the front door swung open. "Go now," the voice told them, "and if you cross me again you will not be so lucky. Bill, we have had business before and we can still have business, if you like, but you must be more careful of your commissions in future. Do we understand one another?"

Bill looked around then, coming to a decision, bowed in the direction of the inner door. "Yes, ma'am," he muttered and followed the other four through the door, leaving the gagged Caron struggling in his chair.

The front door closed. The muskets were withdrawn and plugs replaced the openings in the walls. The inner door opened and Sarah stepped into the foyer. She stood in front of Caron who stopped his struggling and stared up at her, his eyes filled with fear.

"Oh dear, oh dear," said Sarah, tapping her left palm lightly with the muzzle of the pistol she held in her right hand. "What am I to do with you, *Monsieur?*"

Simon appeared in the doorway and she handed the pistol to him, butt-end first, reached over her left shoulder and drew the knife. She chided herself inwardly for the enjoyment she received from the way Caron's eyes widened at the sight of it. "Andy," she said to the wall, "please bring this gentleman into the parlor. Perhaps Martha will make us some tea."

"Have you thought of what I asked you?" she said to Maërlys. "About taking a risk?"

"I know you are right about my position, that is, its instability. And my first concerns must be Reynard and Ambre. If you can help me to free them, I shall follow wherever you direct and assume any risk."

"Good girl. I expected no less. It appears that my position here has also taken on that quality of instability you reference. So, if travel is indicated, let us travel. Have you thought of returning to France?"

The look on Maërlys' face told Sarah that the younger woman had not thought of it, at least as an immediate possibility to be considered soberly. She watched as the frightened look passed and was slowly replaced by serious resolve, followed by a slight pallor and a smile, the smile of one who has resigned herself to the gallows. Slowly, Maërlys nodded, "Anywhere you say." She gazed up into the older woman's eyes. "There is something...." Her voice trailed away and she looked down.

Sarah knelt next to her and took her chin in hand. "My little darling," she said, "you must speak to me of what is in your heart. I know we have not known each other long, and you have small reason to trust strangers, but we may be going into much danger together. It is all right to keep your own secrets, but if there are things about me that you would know to make your mind easier, please, trust me enough to ask. I will not hurt you. On the contrary, I wish only to make you safe enough in the world to live your life as freely and completely as you could and should. Will you try to believe that?"

Maërlys slowly raised her eyes to Sarah's and nodded. "Then tell me. What do you wish to ask me about?" the older woman said.

Maërlys looked down, then up again. The words came in a rush, as if she needed to say them quickly to get them out at all. "You, you looked at me the first night I was here." Her face had turned bright red, "I thought you were going to, to k-kiss me. You had your hand on my neck, just like Mister, I mean Lord Cherille, when he, I mean, I never thought of anything like that but it seemed as if, I mean...." her voice trailed off, and she was once more studying the floor.

"You mean, never thought of it with a woman?"

Slowly, Maërlys nodded.

Sarah's smile took on a rueful quality. "Perhaps I went too far. I did not mean to frighten you, but I admit, I find you so delightful that I may have pressed you further than was quite right. I hope you do not think I have brought you here to take advantage of your beauty. I swear, I would not wish you to do anything that did not give you pleasure, or that was not in keeping with your own desires. If I promise not to do it again, will you forgive me?"

"Oh, no, really there is nothing to forgive. It just took me by surprise, and I didn't want to, to d-disappoint you in any way. You have been so kind. There is no need to promise, um, to promise anything...." Her voice evaporated in confusion, her cheeks on fire.

Sarah's smile changed to one of open delight. "Splendid. Then let us go shopping; we need a great many things and I do enjoy spending money. You will never mind wearing a veil, will you? You must not be seen yet in London. I regret that we cannot go to Emmeline Élégance, so many beautiful things, but it will certainly be watched. However, I will make sure your cousin is informed of your good health before we leave. In fact, why don't you write to her now and I will take steps to see it conveyed to her as soon as may be."

As the thought of France returned to Maërlys, Sarah was treated to that brave, if somewhat ghastly, smile and an obedient nod. As she left the room, Maërlys moved to the desk and took up a quill.

21

"So, what have you found that can help us?"
Lord Cherille looked inquiringly at Bill Nubbins.
Henry, his head still bandaged, though not so
thoroughly as before, was seated on a couch against
the wall. The other two stood at a table nearby.

"Lord sir, what a nest of wasps you've set us to
watch. I went over to see my people were disposed as I
would wish, and arrived just in time for the fun. The
Adelphi ain't in it. First, there was a bunch of very
stout fellers went in the 'ouse after a little thin man.
That was our man, Caron. Then someone, maybe one
of the servants like, comes round the side and locks
the front door from the outside. After a bit, another
man comes around the outside and 'olds a sort of
parley with the first one. Then they unlocks the door
and this mob of boys what oughta be in the army
comes pouring out in their shirts and drawers. Never
seen such a thing. Last one on 'em was Batterin' Bill, a
very dangerous man. Dunno what 'appened to 'em in
there, but they 'ad the look of changed men. Wouldn't
be surprised they 'urried round and took the shillin'."

Jarrod laughed. "And the Frenchman?"

"'E were inside a while, but 'e comes out the same as the others, missin' everythin' but 'is shirt and 'ose. Though, come to think, all them others 'ad their shoes, but not Caron. Quite a sight 'e was. Kep' lookin' be'ind 'im as 'e 'urried off."

"You followed him?"

"That were easy. 'E collected a bit of a crowd and 'e'd a long way to go. Almost felt sorry for 'im by the time 'e got to 'is 'otel. The Ambassador, as you know; French plots on every floor and prob'ly on the stair landin's as well."

"An ideal place for Bonapartists to hide," Henry pointed out.

"True enough, sir. Believe I'd go there meself, was I one of Boney's sneaks. Soon know everythin' I wanted about what them royalists is up to."

"We must look into it," Jarrod said. "Are you keeping an eye on Caron?"

"Yes sir. When 'e arrived at the hotel he went immediately, dressed as 'e was, to a room occupied by one Auguste Facteau. 'E were only inside a few moments before 'e come out and my man followed 'im to a much smaller room on a more inconvenient floor. He waited 'til the feller came out, dressed more appropriate like, and returned to this Facteau.

"I think it is past time for a talk with Caron, Henry," Jarrod remarked, then turned back to Nubbins.

"Have your men keep an eye on him, Bill, and we will select an hour for an interview. I think very late in the evening would be ideal. Any other interesting comings or goings at the Dane house?"

"Well, I didn't see it meself, but some while after the Frenchman left, a carriage come from be'ind the 'ouse. Not one of these open curricles, so they couldn't be sure, but it looked like two ladies was in it. My man followed in our own carriage. Went shopping, they did, two on 'em, Sarah Dane 'erself and another one in a veil. Couldn't tell for certain like, but nobody were willin' to swear it weren't your little fugitive, sir," he said, giving Jarrod a significant look.

"Huh. What were they buying?"

"Clothing, mostly," Nubbins muttered, consulting his notes again. "Um, yes, if I had to guess, I'd say they was gettin' ready to travel, sir."

"Any idea where they might be going?"

"None so far, sir, but we'll keep after 'em."

"Excellent, you do that. Tonight, unless something more urgent comes up, we will visit the Ambassador."

"Well," Facteau muttered, eyeing Caron with distaste, "at least you look more like a Frenchman and less like a rag-picker's bundle. Are you ready to report in a coherent fashion? And before you speak, I will remind you never again to present yourself as you did today. Our association is at least nominally clandestine, and to have you running in my door stark

naked is hardly conducive to.... Well, just don't do it.
Ever. Now, have you managed to relieve me of the
Malay nuisance?"

Caron's left arm twitched involuntarily. "I regret,
sir, that I have not. Oh, it was most horrible. I went
there with my associates well founded to take over the
entire house if necessary and discovered them fully
prepared. More prepared than I would have thought
possible! Indeed, they might withstand the whole of
Bow Street in a siege of indeterminate length. It was
only through the quickest thinking that I managed to
escape with my life!" He blinked his eyes.

"If not your clothing."

A shudder ran through Caron's body. "As I say
sir, it was the most horrible experience of my life. And
I was at the Bastille in eighty-nine!"

"I trust your actions then were more creditable."

Caron straightened up and glowered. His hands
were twitching, "You are unkind, sir, and unfair. We
were outnumbered! We were attacked from ambush!
The cowardly dogs stole our clothing, weapons, money,
and everything else of value we possessed. I was
compelled to walk through the streets as you saw me;
hounded by children throwing stones and any number
of other unpleasant layabouts!"

He paused, apparently overcome by his emotion.
He shuddered and blinked again. "I was lucky, as I
said, to arrive home more or less uninjured and, in my
dedication to our cause, hurried here to apprise you of

the situation. As a reward, I was ejected from your presence. I deserve better, sir."

Facteau held up his hand, "Oh, please, spare me your whining. All you have to report to me in such a hurry is abject failure, which could certainly have waited until you were properly clothed. You have accomplished nothing, except to apprise this woman of our intentions. Is that not correct?" He looked at Caron with his most penetrating gaze, and scowled as the man backed away.

"I regret that I have failed but I warned you the woman is formidable. It was a mistake to make the attempt."

Facteau snorted, "Humph. Certainly, it was a mistake to entrust the business to you. Well, never mind, I have already made arrangements to resolve the issue in a more efficient way. You, on the other hand, are becoming a bit of a problem, having exposed yourself on the streets of London. I believe it best you return to France."

Caron brightened, "*La France?*"

"You remember those children of the de Brissy?"

"Of course. But with the Blanc woman disposed of, they will be more difficult to find."

"*Au contraire, Monsieur.* I believe the information we need can be easily obtained, if you think you are capable of handling a lone woman. This one has not the resources of your nemesis, the Malay. You will call on this Emmeline Blanc; she will tell you where the children are, and you will go to France and place them in your custody. Quietly. You will keep them unharmed," he waved his hand, "more or less, although you may use such methods as are necessary to obtain the information we seek. "Can you manage a pair of children? We will probably only need one of them. The older one, the boy, is more likely to have what we need. No doubt you can use the other one to force him to talk. You know what to do."

"Certainly, sir, certainly. I am sure I will not need to work too hard to awaken the boy's protective instincts. A finger or two, perhaps, or a heated iron will do the trick."

"As you think best, but keep them alive until we can obtain the key and make sure of our goal. I will send someone to join you as soon as may be. Report on the woman's information before you leave but your ship sails tomorrow on the afternoon tide. Here are your papers."

"So soon? What if the information is not forthcoming?" His eyes blinked again.

"If you prefer, I can report to our masters that you seem to lack, ah, commitment to our work. They have wonderful ways of inspiring zeal in the hearts of laggards. I regret that I cannot hold your hand through this affair, but I have other business. Not the least of which is taking over, or perhaps I should say, rescuing, whatever shreds may be left of your network after this day's performance. What is your decision? Time is precious."

Faced with these options, Caron bowed. "Your servant, sir."

"Good. Those papers include your travel documents and you know where the ship is to be found. I expect you to locate the children's direction and secure them. Advise me when they are in your power. Until then, get out of my sight."

Quivering, at least partly, with rage, Caron bowed again and left the room. Facteau paced for a moment, then went to the desk and wrote a quick note, folded and sealed it. He did not place any address on the outside. He rang the bell and gave the note to his servant with the words, "You know where. Quickly."

"Come little one. It is time."

Maërlys sleepily looked at the clock in the light of Sarah's candle, "It is past eleven o'clock."

"Adventure does not wait. It is an ideal time to confuse our enemies and begin our travels. Come. You must dress quickly. Arrangements are being made."

After dressing, Maërlys emerged to find the house in a bustle, although almost silent and poorly lit. People hurried up and down the back stairs and took care that no light should show at the front. Four carriages were waiting in the back courtyard, all apparently heavily laden. Julia led Maërlys to the kitchen and they sat together as they made a hurried meal.

"What is happening?" Maërlys asked, whispering not because she had been told to keep her voice down but because of the general atmosphere of silent hurry throughout the house.

Julia smiled at her. "We are closing the house. We always do in the summer, although not usually so early as this, and, of course, not in such a sudden and clandestine manner. I find it all quite exciting. Don't you?"

"If you mean my heart is beating like the surf and the blood is rushing through my veins and I feel I may faint at any moment, yes. It is indeed exciting. Yes."

Julia laughed. "There are four carriages waiting. We will all go off in different directions, and no one watching will know which carriage contains you and Miss Dane. I have no doubt we shall be pursued; I find it perfectly thrilling." She leaned forward and whispered, "Sarah will not even tell us where you are going. How delightful."

"Oh, as to that—" the girl began, only to feel Julia's finger pressed to her lips.

"Tell no one, my dear; leave everything to Sarah. She is wonderful, is she not?"

It was just after midnight when the first carriage rattled into the street, followed closely by the others. Both watchers near the front of the house were settling down for a long night's useless vigil and were completely startled by the unexpected traffic. The French agent, unaware of the presence of Nubbins' man, ran to the corner and began to look wildly about for a cab, giving it up as he watched the carriages turn at the cross streets, separating into four different directions. Had he been able to follow he would have found that each one made so many twists and turns that pursuit would have been easily exposed and quite difficult, if not impossible.

Each of the four carriages took a different road out of London; the one carrying Sarah and Maërlys heading in the most northerly direction. The other three went east, south, and west, respectively. The eastern and western coaches made arcs that brought them back south, so that all three were eventually reunited, the following afternoon, at Sarah Dane's house on the High Weald.

Sarah and Maërlys went only as far as Golders Green, where they remained at an inn until the following day. Then, after checking for pursuit and finding none, they drove south, moving quickly but carefully avoiding roads to the High Weald.

22

"There's no sign of light."

"Nor life. But look, this lock has been broken; Nubbins was right. Watch behind me." Jarrod pushed open the back door to Emmeline Élégance and stepped inside.

"Careful. Remember what happened to me last time I broke in here," Henry hissed in his ear.

"Even more dangerous this time, I expect," Jarrod whispered back. "Is this the door? Up we go."

Opening the door to the staircase brought muffled sounds from above, the creaking of bedsprings, and a man's voice. Henry brought out his little wooden weapon and Jarrod loosened his sword as he set foot on the first step. They went as quietly as they could and the noises from above covered their approach.

Upstairs, the door to the bedroom was open and a burning candle cast a glow from the right. Emmeline lay on the bed in her nightgown, her hands tied behind her and her ankles bound together to the post at the foot. Caron stood with his back to the door. He held a second candle, which he was moving slowly toward his victim's breast. Her gown had been disarranged to make that part of her fully visible. Forgetting his sword, Jarrod was upon him in an instant. The candle went out as he knocked it to the floor and forced Caron onto the bed next to Miss Blanc.

"Bear a hand, Henry. He's slippery as the devil."

"I've got hold, but he's still wriggling. Shall I knock him on the head?"

At this, Caron stopped fighting, and lay motionless on the bed. Henry's fist was raised above him, the small wooden device at the ready. "That won't be necessary. I couldn't stand it. Not today," the little man rasped, almost breathless from his exertions. "I am your prisoner."

Next to him, Emmeline was gasping, her eyes wide with fear. "Watch him, Henry. Be brave, Miss Blanc. You are in no further danger and we will have you free quite soon." He threw a blanket across her to conceal her nakedness, then drew his pocket knife and quickly cut the ropes binding her ankles. He moved around the bed to release her wrists.

"Oh, thank heaven," she breathed. "I can never repay you. However did you know I was in danger?"

"I told you we would be watching, Unfortunately, this, ah, creature did not give you time to call for help. Nevertheless, though tardy, here we are. Do you need something to help you recover? A bit of brandy, perhaps?" He cast his eyes about the room.

Her hands busy under the covering, Emmeline had sufficiently restored her dignity to allow her to shift the blanket and wrap it tightly about her shoulders. "No, I'm all right now, thanks to you and your friend." She smiled at Henry, noticing his bandage. "I presume you are the gentleman who was so unfortunate the last time you ventured into this house of horrors. I'm glad you have forgiven us for that."

Henry bowed. "It is a pleasure, ma'am. I'm delighted to be of service to a gentlewoman of such a hardy disposition. May I say you seem to recover quickly from a situation which might have left many another in a fit of the vapors."

"Oh," she responded, turning to Jarrod. "You are right. He is wonderfully well-spoken."

"He is a talker, indeed. It is well he is not enslaved; I make no doubt any responsible slave-master would have his tongue removed."

Miss Blanc acknowledged this speech by raising one elegant eyebrow, then turned back to Henry. "Your friend is pleased to be jocose but I assure you, you have my undying gratitude, sir." Henry bowed again.

"Ma'am," Jarrod said, "It is unfair of us to inflict our society on you so late in the evening, and I regret it, but it may be that this, this animal has fellows. I would be gratified if you would accept the hospitality of Cherille House, at least for the remainder of the evening. We three will remove ourselves downstairs so that you can complete your toilette. Then you can gather what you need and we will go there at once, if you do not object. Tomorrow, we will have a locksmith do what he can for your door." They bound and gagged Caron, and descended the stairs.

Within an hour they were back at Cherille House and Thompson had safely installed Miss Blanc in a quiet bedroom with a decanter of Madeira and a few other refreshments. Caron, his hands still bound behind him, had been brought into the library. Placed in a chair, he was confronted by his captors.

"All right then, sir," said Jarrod, lighting the lamp on the desk. "You owe us an explanation."

Despite his position, the man had evidently decided to tough it out. "I don't know what you mean," he said.

"Hit him, Henry, would you? Not too hard, this time, just enough to make sure he understands his situation."

"*Non*—" was all Caron managed before the blow landed. Henry tried to pull the punch, but the image of Emmeline, bound, with the candle approaching her breast, swam before his eyes. He hit Caron just below his rib cage, doubling the man up and causing him to gag and retch.

"Henry, that's a very expensive carpet," Jarrod chided him.

"I am sorry, your lordship, but I just do not like him. I fear I was overcome by my emotions."

Jarrod waved his hand. "Quite understandable." He seized Caron's hair and pulled him back into a sitting position. "To tell the truth," he said, putting his face very close to Caron's, "I do not like him either. I suppose it would be all right to hit him again, but don't break his jaw or anything."

Caron's eyes were wide, but again, "*Non*—" was all he could manage before Henry's little wooden tool struck him just above his left kidney. He lay back against the chair, gasping.

"So there can be no misunderstanding, you will begin by telling us what you hoped to achieve by torturing Miss Blanc. And have a care; she has already told us what questions you asked before you became so wickedly brutal with her."

Caron looked from one to the other, and seeing nothing to his advantage in their eyes, hung his head and shook it. "There are children in France, related to the Misses Blanc, or De Brissy, as their real name is. I wished to know exactly where they can be found."

"To what end?"

"They are believed to have knowledge of a location near their home." He looked at Henry and went on hurriedly, "A location which may bring great wealth."

"So, this is a personal mission, not one authorized by your government?"

"I am not sure. That is a matter for my superiors. They do not tell me everything."

"Henry," Jarrod said.

As Henry raised his fist Caron began to plead. "*Non, non*, I will tell you all I know."

Jarrod bent over him. "You, sir, are a spy, a sneaking agent of Napoleon, here in England. Your life is completely forfeit. A word from me, and the gallows constitutes your whole future. The amount of pain you suffer before you reach it is also at my command. Do you understand me?"

Caron, his eyes wide, nodded.

"Do you further understand that neither I nor my friend cares for you in the least, and that we must restrain ourselves from beating you to death at this moment? When I think of how we found you, torturing that innocent woman...." He ground his teeth, and took hold of Caron's hair again. "Do not toy with me," he said coldly. "You will not like the result."

Caron's eyes bulged as his pale, sweating, face swung from Jarrod to Henry and back again.

They took their time over dinner at Ashford, and it was full dark by the time they reached Dymchurch. They stopped at the Scarecrow, and Sarah narrowed her eyes at the big man who approached them, "Where's Captain Hornbeck?"

"He's on board, ma'am. I'm Billy. He left me'n Tom Chancy to meet you. Tide's on the turn and we're ready to sail the minute you're stowed. Said that's how you wanted it. Let me help with your luggage."

When they reached the boat, Chancy was there to help them get seated. The boat was small but their trunks were squeezed in and the two men took up the oars. Maërlys was pleased that they were good at their work and rowed tolerably dry, careful of the ladies' dresses. Sarah was still frowning, though not as much as before.

The sloop lay in the offing, and a ladder was already rigged when they reached it. A third sailor helped them aboard, and the way he looked at them gave Maërlys a slight shiver, the first qualm she'd had since they left London. Sarah started toward the stern, but Billy ushered them toward a doorway and a ladder going down.

"Best get your things stowed. Be underway before you know where you're at, else. Captain'll be in to see you once we're into the first tack, bring you up to the deck."

Sarah shrugged and they followed him down into the dark. He pulled a lantern off a hook, lit it and led them along the lower decking to a bulkhead with a door. He opened the door, went in, and hung the lantern inside. The two other men were right behind with the trunks, and the little cabin was jammed with the three large men. Billy shooed the other two out, showed the hammocks to the two women, bowed and left.

Sarah started to follow him to ask something, the question forming on her lips as the door was slammed in her face. A loud thump sounded as a bar was placed across the door on the outside. Sarah pushed at it, but it was quite solid. Male laughter came from the other side, then the sound of retreating steps. She turned and looked at Maërlys, whose eyes were now wide with fear.

"Our adventure begins sooner than expected," she said, tenting her eyebrows and flashing a quick smile. "At least they left us a light; we must be ready when they return." She began to look around, picking up things that puzzled her companion, some pieces of rope, another lantern. There were several barrels that Sarah checked. She opened her trunk and rifled through it, bringing out two pistols, a bag with a powder horn, wads and balls, and two knives, one about six inches, the other more like a small sword. The knives gleamed in the light as she unwrapped them. Even from across the little room, they looked as sharp as any blades Maërlys had ever seen. They could feel the sloop move under them as Sarah closed the trunk, sat down on it, and began to load the pistols.

She handed the second lantern to Maërlys. "Light that," she said. "The brighter, the better. Now, little one, we must find out what you can do. You shot that beautiful man," she clucked her tongue and smiled, "but you did not kill him as you thought. We can allow no such mistakes this time. Had you used pistols before?"

Maërlys, staring in wide-eyed astonishment at Sarah's preparations, shook her head. "No. At least, I never fired one before. I was surprised at how it knocked me over."

"That was because you were unprepared. They do kick, but you must know that and be ready for it.

You will hold the pistol in two hands," she demonstrated, sighting along the barrel, "and you will keep it firm and steady. You will be very close to your adversary but you will not touch him with the weapon. It must be an inch or two away; otherwise, they can feel its presence and move away from the danger between the click and the bang of the powder." She shrugged. "I do not really believe these sailors are such quick thinkers, but they are good movers, and it is always a mistake to underestimate your enemy. Do you understand what I am telling you?"

"I, I think so. What will I have to do? I was so upset when I shot that man, but I was sure he would have me tortured or killed, and I did what I thought I had to do. I was glad when you told me he was not dead. He was not whom I had expected. He did not seem like such a bad man to me, and you have saved me from the fear of being hanged."

"I am sure you are right, *ma chére*, and I too am pleased that you failed to kill him; however, we must take no such chances with the men we face now. I have been betrayed in some way, and these men have stolen this boat from my loyal Captain Hornbeck. At least, until I find otherwise, I will continue to believe in Mr. Hornbeck's loyalty. But all that is no matter to us now. We must take this ship back from these evil men and we must do it by whatever means we can find. We are fortunate they did not suspect that we have weapons. Men make mistakes about women. We must take advantage of those mistakes."

She looked up at Maërlys and handed her one of the pistols, butt first. "You must hold it and get used to the weight. I wish we could fire it but we must not alert them before time. In fact, the longer we can keep from undeceiving them, the better it will be. When they come, you must stand behind the door, out of sight, so they will see only me as they enter. If one comes alone, you need do nothing, unless I make some mistake and am overcome. We will hope that does not happen."

The smile she flashed was beautiful, and Maërlys received the injection of confidence Sarah intended. "You remember how to cock and fire it? You must place it close to, but not touching, the ear of the person you wish to control, and then cock it so he hears it clearly. In most cases this will be enough to make him freeze in his position, and you will say 'be still' sharply as you do this. If he does not obey instantly you will shoot him dead. We have no leeway, as the sailors say, no room for error. I am sorry but, for now, we have only each other. You understand?"

23

"Are you sure you should 'ave released 'im, your lordship? 'E could cause trouble." Nubbins was frowning.

"We pumped him dry. Good Lord, the things he told us. Like a fairy story, much of it. Wouldn't have believed it, but we went over and over it with him, and although the words were different, the story never varied. Amazing, wasn't it, Henry?"

"Quite."

"See? Even Henry is rendered almost speechless. Still, we really couldn't do any more to the fellow and expect to claim any vestige of what we are pleased to call our humanity, could we, Henry? He was a sobbing wreck and had soiled his linen. Not sure we did him much of a kindness to push him out of doors before dawn in such a condition. Given what you told us of his experience at the Dane house the day before, I expect he will be hard pressed to retain his sanity, if he ever had any. That twitching was quite unnerving, eh, Henry?" Jarrod shuddered.

Nubbins bowed. "Very well, sir, I suppose you know best."

"Know enough to hope for it, at all events. Now, speaking of the Dane house, tell us what transpires. We would have liked to converse longer with you last night, but given what you told us, it was well we hurried. We were barely in time to save the maiden from the dragon, if I may speak lightly of what was a very grim scene indeed."

"I'm that glad you was in time. As for the Dane 'ouse, it's deserted. At least, in its essentials, like. The doorman, a man named," he referred to his notebook, "Clegg, Charlie Clegg, assured me the 'ouse were closed for the rest of the summer. Suggested I come back in September."

"They've flown? All of them?"

"As I started to tell you last night, there was four coaches what left at the same time, and each took a different direction. Four points of the compass. Our man realized at once it wasn't no use. Saw another watcher, too, prob'ly one of Boney's; 'e threw up 'is 'ands as well."

Jarrod frowned. "Could they distinguish the occupants?"

Nubbins shook his head. "Never a glimpse, although my man swears the coach 'e saw go west was driven by a woman."

"Doesn't prove anything in that household. Expect they've got women with all sorts of skills. Likely that would be the coach that belongs to the house, and equally likely it wouldn't contain the most important fugitives. Any idea where they might normally go to escape the London heat?"

Again, Nubbins referred to his notes. "Got a big country house on the south downs, up on the 'igh Weald."

Jarrod thought about it. "What do you think, Henry?"

"Well, sir, knowing all that, I'd guess the three coaches that went east, west and south probably went to the house, as they do every summer. I expect they don't do it quite so theatrically, most years. The one that went in the exact wrong direction is most likely to have your fugitive, or fugitives, in it. Can't tell, though, since we do not know what their plans may be." He paused and looked down, tapping his left-hand fingers into his right palm.

"If it were me, assuming your little friend is still with her, and I think she is, I'd try to clear up this business with the sister and brother. Maybe try to get them to England. Probably mean a trip to the continent."

"In the middle of a war?"

Henry shrugged. "They're women, less conspicuous than men. They both speak French like natives, in fact Miss Blanc is a native. There is plenty of smuggling traffic, war or no war, and Miss Dane almost certainly has connections. Did you mention the brandy at her establishment?"

"Indeed, it was very fine," Jarrod said.

Henry nodded. "Just so."

Jarrod looked at Nubbins. "What do you think, Bill? Any idea how they might go?"

"Sorry, your lordship. They's ways to find out, but not quick."

"Never mind. The port of departure doesn't matter. What matters is their destination. And here is the very person we need." He looked up as the door opened and Emmeline Blanc came into the room.

She curtsied. "I am so sorry to disturb you gentlemen but I really must be going, and I couldn't leave without thanking you for all your kindness and hospitality, your lordship."

"None of that, none of that, my girl," Jarrod answered. "Has Thompson given you breakfast?"

"Oh, yes, quite the best breakfast I've had for some time. Again, I can't thank you enough."

"Actually, it is we who are in your debt. After our conversation with our other guest, it appears I am to blame for much of the trouble."

"I knew they wanted Maërlys to get something from you, but what?"

"A family heirloom, but we can go into that later. For now, we must determine where to find Maërlys' brother and sister. Do you know?"

"Oh, you remind me," she said, fumbling in her reticule and handing him the letter from Maërlys. "I would have let you see this last evening, but I was under a strain...."

Grimly, Maërlys nodded, "I will do exactly as you say."

"Good. If there are two of them, I will handle the first one and you must take the second. If we are lucky no one will be hurt and we can subdue them. Even if we do not have that much luck, and it is foolishness to count on luck, it may be that I can dispose of the first one in such a way that the second will be awed and easily controlled. If there is a third, you will watch for him. I am hoping very much you do not have to fire your weapon, as it will alert the others, and we do not know how many they are. You understand? We will be silent if possible, but if there is the least danger, you must fire your pistol and kill your man. Are you with me on this?"

Again, Maërlys nodded. "I will not let them hurt you; I swear to you."

Sarah grinned and clapped her hands, "You are just the woman to join me in this adventure. Together, we will bend these evil men to our will. They will wish they had never undertaken this commission, and they will curse their masters for delivering them into our hands." She sobered. "I am sorry I did not plan this better. I see now it was wrong of me to come to Dymchurch. I should have arranged some other place where I am less known. I let myself be rushed and handed the advantage over to my enemies. Now we must take it back."

She stood up and began to undress. Maërlys' eyes showed her surprise. "What are you doing?"

"When they come, they will have some plan of their own. We do not know what it is, although it may not be so hard to guess, at that. We must distract them from their course so it will be our plan they shall follow."

She removed her dress and unlaced her light corset. She then pulled her chemise over her head, and stood before Maërlys. Maërlys felt her mouth drop open. She had seen women before, of course, but she had come so much to think of Sarah as a figure of authority that the sight of her nakedness was unnerving.

And she was lovely.

Maërlys right hand, holding the pistol, dropped to her side. Her left hand went to her breast, and she realized she was comparing its softness with the upright firmness presented by the sight of Sarah's. The long slender body drew her eyes, and she had to force her gaze from the bushy patch of raven hair at the base of Sarah's flat belly. She looked at Sarah's face and found amusement there.

"Do you like what you see, *ma chérie*?"

Maërlys found her voice, "Oh, you are so beautiful! So very beautiful!"

Sarah smiled. "Thank you my dear. High praise from a true beauty like you." She looked down. "But, one must keep something for oneself."

She turned back to the chest and Maërlys found herself admiring the firm curves of the older woman's bottom. She wondered if her own derrière could withstand such scrutiny. She remembered Jarrod's hand and the thought made her blush. She watched as Sarah found a pair of drawers in the chest and pulled them on, lacing the ribbons tightly to keep them up. Then, thinking better of it, loosening them, allowing the bloomers to slip slightly down her hips, the dark patch clearly visible through the thin material, presenting a particularly wanton picture.

A noise outside drew both of the women from their thoughts. Maërlys' face showed fear followed by grim determination as she looked at the door, then scurried to her place beside it. Sarah snatched up the two knives and retreated behind the light, her face taking on a hardness completely at odds with her enchanting deshabille.

"Here we are ladies, our pricks at attention," the sailor called Billy sang out as he opened the door. He walked in and froze, staring at Sarah, his mouth hanging open. Behind him was the sailor whose look had so disconcerted Maërlys at their arrival. No third man was in evidence.

The second man almost ran into Billy's back as he came in, staring around the bigger man, trying to get a good look at Sarah in the half-light behind the lanterns. He turned to stone when he heard Maërlys' whisper, "Be still," and the cocking of the pistol in his ear.

Billy was likewise immobile, Sarah's short sword just touching his throat, a very thin line of red trickling toward the top of his dirty shirt. "One sound, one movement, will be your last," she hissed, and the look in her implacable eyes was thoroughly convincing.

She drew back from him, slightly, "If you wish to live a moment longer, you will do exactly as I say. On the deck, face down, both of you. Move very slowly and keep your hands away from your bodies. Maërlys, shoot the first one who makes any threatening motion. I will cut the other's throat."

The sailors' confusion was complete. The second man was almost crying as he pleaded, "Don't kill me; I beg you."

"Shut your gob," hissed Sarah, "and get down." They did as they were told. Sarah stood over Billy, pulled his wrists behind him and tied them tightly with one of the bits of rope she had collected.

As she did this, her body came into full view of the second sailor and drew his attention, his mouth falling open. He was quite unprepared for the fierceness of Maërlys' whispered hiss in his ear, "Close your mouth as you were told or I'll put this pistol in it." He moved his head so that he was looking down at the deck and began to whimper softly.

It took only a few silent moments for Sarah to have the two men completely helpless, wrists and ankles bound separately, joined with additional bits of rope, then fastened to the bulkheads on opposite sides of the small room. She motioned to Maërlys to close the door and used the small knife to cut pieces from their filthy shirts to form gags. She patted them for weapons and relieved them of their knives. Billy's was in a leather sheath attached to his belt, and she took the whole belt. She had to cut the end off and make a new hole to fit her slender body. An idea occurred to her; she took a blanket in her hand and crouched next to the second sailor. She removed the slimy gag from his mouth and held Billy's knife in front of his face.

"What's your name, sailor?"

"Uh, Lem, Lemuel, ma'am," he croaked, his eyes wandering from the knife to her breasts.

"You wish to live, Lemuel?"

"Oh, yes, ma'am, please," he begged, his eyes now firmly focused on hers. He saw only cold steel there. She said nothing further and pushed the gag back into his mouth, re-fastening the cord behind his head. Then she whipped the blanket over his head, wrapping it several times about.

Next, she crossed to Billy, and knelt beside him. She pulled his head up by the hair and held her other hand in front of him. She whispered in his ear. "I'm going to hold my fingers in front of your eyes. When I hold up the number of the rest of the men on the sloop, you will nod your head. If I hold up the wrong number, you will shake your head. A lie will cause you deep regret for the remainder of your short life. You understand?"

Billy nodded. She held up all five fingers. There was a slight hesitation before Billy shook his head. She folded her thumb across her palm, and held up four. He nodded enthusiastically. She let go of his hair, and watched his head drop back down, then returned to Lem. Careful to keep herself between him and Billy, she removed the blanket. The sailor drew in a deep gulp of air through his nose.

She took his head by the hair, held up her hand and repeated her instructions in his ear. He nodded enthusiastically when she held up five fingers. "You may live a little longer," she whispered in his ear.

She went back and knelt beside Billy. "I gave you a fair chance, did I not?" His eyes were wide with fear. She took out her own small knife, and held it before him so he could see how sharp it was. "Maybe I will take something so you remember me." She put the knife close to his right eye. "You will remember if I take your eye?"

The man was sweating, his eyes rolled, then he shut them tight. She reached down and patted him between his legs. "Maybe I should take these to insure you never hurt another woman. What do you think?" She took hold of his hair again. "You consider it; I'll come back and we will discuss it. Maybe I let you choose. Maybe not."

She turned to Maërlys, "We need to do something about that dress; we must be able to move quickly." She raised one eyebrow, and the corner of her mouth curled slightly, "Are you wearing drawers, my darling?"

24

"A musical name, is it not, Henry? Maërlys? A man could get used to calling such a name. A beautiful name for a beautiful woman. Not so fond of *Blanc*, but that's easily remedied...."

"Provided you ever see her again. Especially if she's gone to France with Sarah Dane."

"Which reminds me, I had a chat with Sir Charles. D'you know, her real name is Siti Zara Daeng? Goes by Sara Dane so as not to tax our British ears. Kind of her, what?"

"Now that's music," Henry replied. "Siti Zara Daeng. Delightful."

Jarrod frowned. "You're making game of me, Henry."

"Perhaps. I remind you, this Maërlys of yours isn't really *Blanc*; *De Brissy* was what Caron said. You'll not complain of *de Brissy*.

"Quite right, Henry, I had forgot. Anyway, combining the notes of Caron, Nubbins, and Emmeline, it seems likely they have sailed for France to rescue these young siblings of Maërlys'. We must follow them to see they don't get into trouble, lest we remain bachelors all our days. A lonely thought, is it not, Henry? Sweet, perhaps, but melancholy. I love you like a brother, but I believe I would much prefer to share my declining years, not to mention my blanket, with Maërlys De Brissy."

"You'll not have forgotten that a French scaffold, whether it contains a rope or a blade, might easily reduce those declining years of yours, not to mention my own, to a mere fever dream."

The baron frowned again. "Adventure, Henry, adventure. You'll never stick at a little danger. Think of these poor feminine castaways adrift in a hostile land. It is our manly duty to rescue them from their folly."

"I believe one of these 'poor feminine castaways' is a noted expert in weapons, both explosive and edged. The less dangerous one recently shot me. And I thought you had an estate to manage."

"Pooh," answered Jarrod, "it will be fine for a month or two. What is an estate without a mistress? I undertake this mission as my duty to extend the Cherille line."

"I hope it has not the opposite effect, but I can scarcely let you go alone; you'd have no chance at all. When do we leave, and from where? And did you say 'pooh'?"

Sir Charles scowled at the newly minted peer. "Our military services are not for the amusement of lonely young barons, Everly. Nor are they panders to assist with assignations."

"All I want is passage on a mail boat. We will not take it out of its way. It can service the fleet, run in at night to drop us off, and we will be on our own after that."

"'Run in at night', forsooth. Under which battery?" He pointed at a map on the wall. "You're not in the Indies now. The whole coastline fairly bristles with guns, many of them thirty-two pounders. Do you know what just one thirty-two-pound ball can do to a sloop? And God forbid it should be heated. Have you been staring at the moon?"

"But these two women—"

"Confound your damn women. What are they doing in France? Can you be sure they are not French agents? Perhaps they are returning to their masters. Or, if they are not, how do you know they have not already been taken up? Although there are still gaps, rapidly closing gaps, I might add, Napoleon has the most efficient secret police on the continent. Possibly in the entire world, for that matter. Such an expedition is madness, lunacy." He pointed to Cholet. "Forty miles or more from the coast, depending on where you land. You have no support of any kind, no horses, nothing. You know not a single living soul, and you're looking for some children who were in the town six months ago, maybe."

He banged on his desk. "If I even attempt to help you, I shall have to explain to Government why one of our peers lost his head, quite literally, over some gel. No sir, it will not do, and there's an end to it. Now get out of my office."

Perhaps I was a bit rash, Jarrod thought as he left. Maybe Nubbins will come up with something. He was beginning to regret opening his mind to Sir Charles. Lost in these thoughts, he scarcely noticed Sir Charles' secretary, young Sadler, until the other took his hand, said "Good day," and walked on down the hall, leaving a slip of paper in the baron's palm. Jarrod found himself staring after the younger man for a moment, then he closed his hand over the message and hurried away.

Even with the poor light in the corner of the inn, Jarrod could see the flush of the secretary's cheeks as he stood leaning across the small table. Has he been drinking? Jarrod wondered. How much?

"I can help you," the young man insisted. "I have many contacts. I can find us a boat. We can leave tomorrow evening, if not before."

"I wish you will stop saying 'we'. Sir Charles was incensed at the idea of my going to, ah, you-know," Jarrod said, looking around. "If I take his secretary, I'm confident he'll have apoplexy, and he means a great deal to me. As I'm sure he does to you," he added.

"Nevertheless, it's all or nothing," Sadler replied. "You have the money but I have the contacts."

"You must tell me why you are so keen to go on what might be a very dangerous game of blind man seek."

His companion looked down. "That's my business."

Jarrod wanted to bang his fist on the table, but that was both an uncomfortable reminder of his interview with Sir Charles and likely to create a disturbance. It seemed impossible they could be inconspicuous in any case, given Sadler's intensity, but the baron saw no reason to make it worse.

"Sit down," he hissed, "and think. It's almost impossible as it is, but if you believe I'm going into an enemy country with someone whose motives are unknown, you must reconsider. I may be the fool Sir Charles thinks I am but I am not so crack-brained as that."

Lincoln Sadler subsided, slowly. He sat back down on the bench and the flush gradually drained from his face. He stared at Jarrod, who almost fancied he could see the gears turning in the fellow's head. At last, he seemed to deflate completely and nodded.

"I apologize," he said. "You're right, of course. If we go we must understand each other so there can be no surprises. Very well. It is quite simple, really. I believe my motives are the same as yours. You are in love with Miss Blanc, are you not?"

Jarrod was startled. "You seem to know a great deal. Perhaps even more than I do myself. I admit I was quite taken with the person you mention. Now, having learned more about her, I am convinced that she has been the victim of unscrupulous men and barbarously used indeed. I feel not only compassion but some responsibility, since I was the target of her attack."

The other man raised his eyebrows. "Attack? From what I heard, we might all wish for such an attack."

Jarrod's face froze and the look he gave Sadler caused the younger man to sit back on his bench, pressing his shoulders into the wall behind him. Jarrod glared for a long time, then said, in arctic tones, "We were speaking of your own motives. I tell you, sir, if you have designs on that girl, you will answer for them tomorrow morning, at a place of your own choosing."

Sadler raised his hands. "No, no, you mistake me entirely. I am upset, and spoke ill; please forgive me. I merely meant you to understand that my motives are like your own in that I am also in love. With Siti, with Sarah Dane.

Now it was Jarrod's eyebrows that attempted to scale his forehead. He stared at the younger man. "The French assassin? Are you mad?"

"Oh, I know." Sadler put his face in his hands. "Her skin is dark, her motives obscure, her past unknown." He shook his head. "I don't give a damn.

She's everything to me and without her, life is meaningless. I've never met a woman like her, nor expected to. Never even one who came close. I would sell my soul to the devil for her, sell two, if I had them. I must go and find her; she may need help."

Jarrod cocked his head, "I know the question is impertinent, but may I ask how old you are?"

"Six and twenty. Why? What does it matter?"

"Don't know that it does, old fellow, just that I met Miss Dane. You call her Siti?"

"Siti Zara Daeng. It's her real name. She's a queen. A goddess. She deserves no less that to be known by her own name. Siti Zara Daeng!"

Jarrod held up his hand. "Of course, of course, I have met the lady, and I bow to no one in my respect for her. A very remarkable woman, indeed. But I did get the impression that she may be a year or two older than you. And, of course, your family—"

"Damn my family," Sadler shouted, jumping up and banging his fists down in front of Jarrod. "I tell you, I don't care. She means the world to me. I won't hear her called 'darkie' or 'that Malay.' She's the finest woman I ever met. I'll go with you and, if need be, die for her. I'll show her what I'm made of, and she'll see that I'm worthy of her, that I'm the only man who truly loves her."

Jarrod looked around and raised his hands placatingly, "Easy, easy, my dear fellow. Let us not rouse the countryside. You must see how I am placed. I walk into the unknown. I do not know if Siti Zara

Daeng is an enemy or a friend. If I take you with me, blindly, it is hardly reassuring."

"On my life, I assure you, sir, that I love England, and would never imperil her. I promise you that whatever tasks Siti may have accomplished to amuse the enemy, she would never intentionally harm our nation. You have met her but I have worshipped at her feet for a long time. She is the very embodiment of virtue, whatever her profession or reputation may mislead you into believing. Again, I swear it on my life."

Jarrod considered. "Your argument is compelling, but I must take advice. I am not alone in this venture, and something is owed to any others who place their lives in your hands. Here is my offer: Go, now, and make what arrangements you can. It would take at least three or four hours to reach Dover, twice as long for Bournemouth. If we left tomorrow night from one of those places, we might make the bay by the following night, but only with luck. More likely, it will take two days, even with fair winds. Did you tell me you have contacts in Nantes?"

"Yes. Most people have welcomed Napoleon for bringing stability, but there are still some who see him as the embodiment of the government that sent Carrier to them. The intervening years have not softened those who lost relatives to that one's cruelty. They tell me skeletons are still found in the river."

"Then go. Meet me here tomorrow morning for breakfast, shall we say seven o'clock? Then we compare our progress and decide. Is that fair?"

"Oh, yes," Sadler replied. "I'll be back in the morning. You won't regret it." He wrung Jarrod's hand and hurried out.

Jarrod stood up, walked around the wall on which Sadler had been leaning, and looked at Henry. "You heard?"

"He is a fanatic, at least where Miss Dane is concerned. Fanatics are unpredictable and dangerous. On the other hand, he is probably our best chance for an early start and a quick passage." He smiled. "He, or should I say you, may get us both killed."

Jarrod shrugged and smiled back. "I only promised you excitement, never safety."

25

The sound came from forward; the gruff voice was new to them. Sarah motioned Maërlys to silence with a finger across her lips as they heard the order, "Tom, go see what's keeping them two. They need to let the rest of us have a chance before we drop the bitches in the Channel. Tell Billy to get up here and let Lem guard the wheel."

Pointing at a position to the right and slightly behind the ladder, Sarah watched as Maërlys took up position, the pistol held in both hands as she had been shown. They had cut the bottom off of one of Maërlys' shifts, and she now wore it as a tunic over a pair of bloomers. Her costume was cinched at the waist by Lem's belt, cut nearly in half, which also held his small knife. Sarah was still wearing her bloomers alone, hoping to take advantage of the costume's shock value, although she had tightened the strings around her waist so they did not interfere with her movement. She carried the short sword in her hand, with a pistol and her dirk stuck into Billy's belt. His longer knife swung in its sheath at her side.

Repeating the motion for silence, she shrank into the shadows on the left, positions and possibilities flashing through her mind. She decided they were too exposed, and a noise might bring the others down on them before they could be ready. It would have to be the hard way.

She tested the edge of her sword and watched silently as Tom came down the ladder. He reached the lower deck and started toward the closed door in the bulkhead. Without a sound, her bare feet brought her within two feet of him, her sword catching a beam of light from the hatch as she swung it up to the left.

There must have been some displacement of air as the downward swing began because Tom started to turn his head to the left. He was far too slow. The blade caught him from the left rear, driven by Sarah's surprising strength and the desperation of knowing how entirely their lives depended on the stroke. The blood spouted back toward her. Her blow cut through the spinal column, but caught in the muscle on the right side.

Her feet were braced, and she pulled the blade free as Tom collapsed, his head hanging at an impossible angle, blood gushing from the wound. He had no chance to cry out; there was only the slight thump of the body hitting the deck and a faint gasp from Maërlys. Sarah glanced up at the hatch, then at Maërlys.

Maërlys' eyes were wide with horror, the gun at her side forgotten as she covered her mouth with the other hand. Sarah was beside her in an instant, shaking her, whispering in her ear, "Courage, little

one. Maybe we can avoid more bloodshed but we must
see. Do not look at him. He cannot harm us any
longer. Now, be still and watch; if I misstep you must
be ready. Understand?" Her hand was over the
younger woman's mouth, placed atop Maërlys' own.
Slowly, Maërlys nodded and the expression in her eyes
became more nearly sane. Sarah smiled at her and
watched her face resume its resolution. "Good," she
whispered, and removing her hand turned to the
ladder.

Very slowly, she crept upward. There were four
more men and she must locate them. Knowing there
were men forward, she looked that direction first,
raising her head just enough to see. Two men stood
there, looking away from her to the sea. Knowing that
quick movements draw attention, Sarah slowly turned
to the rear. There were the other two, one at the wheel
and a very large man leaning against the rail looking
at his companion. There was something odd about the
way they held themselves, but Sarah was unable to
determine what it was. She was turning this over in
her mind when another voice spoke from forward. She
dropped her head back out of sight and listened.

"If we keep on this tack much longer, we'll never
weather those rocks you told me about. Are your men
ready to come about?" Sarah's heart was in her mouth
as she heard the footsteps moving toward her. She
knew that voice. Had Captain Hornbeck sold her to her
enemies? She ducked back into the shadows behind

the ladder. There were more footsteps, not hurrying, then the other voice just above, in the hatchway.

"Lem, Bill, get up here. We need to go about." His feet were on the ladder, his head came under the hatch and peered into the gloom. There was no more time.

Sarah swung in front of him, her sword lunging toward him. He must have seen something that warned him, for he threw himself back out of the hatchway, shouting. She felt her sword hit something hard and glance off, then he was gone, and she was after him, shouting for Maërlys. Maërlys crossed herself and followed, her pistol held in one hand. She hit her head as the hatch came down.

Sarah was on deck, the big man backing away from her. She registered Captain Hornbeck to her left, frozen. To her right, the man who had been against the after rail had slammed the hatch closed, trapping Maërlys. He was reaching for his knife, but seemed stunned by her appearance, as was the man in front of her, backing toward the rail. Her sword in her right hand, she lunged that way, and the seaman lost his balance as he backed. She saw him reaching for his knife, and jammed her sword into his shoulder, feeling it wrenched from her grasp as she pulled back.

Without looking, she fired her pistol at the big man, watching as the other regained his footing. Dropping the now empty pistol, she drew the two knives and prepared to deal with him as best she could. He had her sword and was moving quickly when the hatch flew up into his way. He howled as he slammed it back down, and the sound of Maërlys falling down the short ladder reached them.

Then the seaman was on Sarah and she twisted, feeling the sword graze her side. She folded back as he came, throwing him off balance. She'd hoped he'd pass over her, giving her a chance to turn and attack, but he landed on her, his weight pinning her to the deck. Then suddenly, the weight was gone.

The man at the wheel had jumped away, and the little sloop had suddenly flown up into the wind, her sails flapping, the deck lurching under their feet. The sailor with her sword had rolled off of her, and she jumped to her feet to pursue him. It was too late.

She had paid no attention to the big man while this was happening, and she felt herself seized from behind, her right hand nearly twisted off as he forced her to drop Billy's knife. She slashed behind her with the dirk in her left, but met only empty air. She tried to duck, to throw him off balance, to get a foot into his groin, all to no avail. She was whirling, slashing, twisting, a fury in his hands, her body slippery with Tom's blood, when his fist crashed against her head.

For a second she was insensible and went limp. He twisted the dirk from her hand and pulled her upright. She looked in front of her for the other man, but he was lying face-down on the deck, motionless. Captain Hornbeck stood behind him, a belaying pin in his hand.

The man holding her shouted, "Put that down, captain, or I'll wring her neck. You, Gabe, get back to the wheel. The two of you get this boat under control or there'll be real blood. Move."

The man at the wheel resumed his place, the captain dropped the belaying pin and retreated toward the rail. The man holding Sarah advanced across the hatch, yanking her hands behind her and securing them in one huge paw. She felt his right hand move up and grasp her breast, squeezing, hard.

"That'll be enough of your capers, missy," he said. "I'm going to rig a grating for you and take all that pretty hide off before I stretch you from the rail. Likely I'll have to do something unpleasant with your little friend. Unpleasant for her, at least. Maybe I'll make you watch before you die." He shook her.

She was trying to get enough purchase on her thoughts to wonder what was making Captain Hornbeck's eyes widen, when she heard the click, followed almost immediately by the explosion of the powder, somewhere very close. For the second time in minutes she felt blood raining onto her, this time from above, and the hands holding her relaxed and dropped away.

She found herself standing on the deck, staring at Captain Hornbeck. The big man's body lay behind her. She wasted no time in contemplation, but reached to the deck, grabbed the knife that was lying there, and flew aft, the knife at Hornbeck's throat before he could move.

"Well, Captain," she said, "are you ready to die?"

He was staring at her, his mouth opening and closing silently. The man at the wheel broke the silence.

"Please, miss," he said. "Weren't his fault. It was them others. Made us do it, they did. Forced us onto the *Syn*, then brought you two aboard and told us to get under way. We couldn't find no way to stop 'em, and when Lem and Billy went down to get you, we thought it was all up. Captain dropped that feller Jemmy as was coming at you with that hanger. Please, miss. Please."

She glanced at the speaker, realizing for the first time that he was no more than a boy, perhaps sixteen. She stared into Hornbeck's eyes, and saw nothing there but fear. She stepped back. "Well. Have you a story, Captain?" She felt Maërlys come up beside her, glanced at her quickly, then back to Hornbeck.

"It's like he says, miss. I'm sorry you'd think I'd ever turn against you, if I had my own way of it. I was trying to get behind Big Ben there, but he wouldn't take his eyes off me. Was never so glad to see anybody in my life as when you come bustin' up from below, in spite of you looking so heathen and all. That's my nephew, Gabe. He was visitin' me when they come and they made me bring him. Was afraid they'd kill him, else. If I done wrong, I'm sorry, but I hope you'll take it out on me, and spare the boy. Wasn't none of it his doing."

"There were five of them against you?"

He nodded, "That's right, miss. Wasn't nothing I could do."

She nodded, "I'm sorry, too, Captain. This is all my fault. I should never have tried to leave from Dymchurch. It must have been easy for them to find you and do this. I put your life in danger, and that of your nephew. It is I who must apologize."

She looked down at her hands, then back up at him and smiled. "Sorry for my 'heathen appearance,' as well. If there's anything I can do to make it up to you, please tell me."

'Well, miss, if you wouldn't mind," the captain answered, "you could maybe clean yourself up some and put on some proper clothes. I'm afraid young Gabe's eyes might pop right out of his head."

She glanced at Gabe to see him looking sheepishly at the deck, and laughed. She went over to the wheel, took the boy's head in her hands, and gave him a kiss, full on the mouth.

"No," shouted Hornbeck, as the sails started to shiver. He looked pleadingly at Sarah and she laughed again.

"I'm sorry, Captain. Lightness of heart. There was a moment when I, too, thought it was all up. Let us get this one over the side, and the one below, and we will accede to your every request. Shall we tie that one," she nodded toward Jemmy, still unconscious on the deck, "to the mast?"

The captain bent down and felt Jemmy's wrist. He frowned, then examined the wound in the man's

head. He looked up at Sarah. "Sorry, Miss Dane.
Afraid I took it all out on him. Must have hit him too
hard. He's gone."

"We get him over, then. We've other business."

Together, Sarah and Hornbeck lifted Jemmy
over the rail and, with a little help from Maërlys,
managed to get Big Ben off on the other side. They
covered Tom in a sheet before maneuvering him up the
ladder and over the side, as he was too awful to look
at.

"Hard on him, weren't you?" the captain
frowned.

Sarah shrugged. "It was quick."

Sarah's shrug drew his attention to her
nakedness and he looked away. She laughed. "Sorry,
Captain. Miss Blanc and I will go and make ourselves
more presentable. May we use some of your fresh
water? And I suppose you will need our help at the
braces?"

"Are the other two dead?"

"No. We could make them work if you like. Lem,
anyway. I'd hesitate to trust Billy even that far."

He nodded. "Fair enough. Bring him up when
you're ready."

Fortunately, Maërlys had been spared the blood,
except for a drop or two when she'd blown out Big
Ben's brains. She helped Sarah wash herself, and once
or twice, found herself lingering over the process.

Sarah raised her eyebrows and smiled at her. "I see we shall have to spend some time together, *chérie*. I hope you will like that."

Maërlys turned bright red to the roots of her hair and looked away, but her hands kept on washing Sarah's right breast, gently and very, very thoroughly. "That horrid man," she murmured.

Sarah touched her cheek, "He was horrid, wasn't he? We shall find you a much nicer one."

Maërlys, whose color had slowly been returning to normal, flushed again.

26

"Begging your pardon, Miss Dane, but we've got to come about. If we keep on this tack, we'll be onto them rocks. Another hand would be right helpful." Captain Hornbeck was standing in the doorway, his eyes firmly fixed on the horizon outside the cabin door. Since that horizon was the bulkhead about eight feet away, it was clear he was desperately seeking discretion.

Sarah laughed. "It is I who must beg your pardon again, Captain. Give us two minutes and we are with you. But remember, we are no sailors and will need thorough direction. For the moment let us leave the real sailors where they are, if you think we can manage."

In the early morning light, they did manage to bring the vessel about, although Maërlys' hands suffered, particularly when a sheet escaped her grasp unexpectedly, taking a good bit of skin with it. Once they were settled on the new tack, Sarah washed and dried Maërlys hands and salved them with a cream from her trunk, the same ointment she had used on her own cuts.

She turned to the prisoners, still bound to opposite bulkheads. She cut Lem free, then watched as he removed his blindfold and gag, and rubbed the circulation back into his wrists. "You wish to work?" she asked.

He looked up at her and nodded, "Yes."

She slapped her thigh with the flat of the knife. "Yes what?"

He recoiled as if she had slapped him, "Uh, yes Miss?"

"Better. Your other three friends are all dead. The captain says if you behave yourself, you can work your passage, at least to France." She jerked her head toward the door. "Go on up. Remember, the least sign of trouble and you forfeit your life."

He knuckled his forehead, "Yes, Miss," and hurried to the deck.

She removed Billy's gag. "Have you decided?" she asked.

"G'wan, kill me, you bitch," he spat.

"Later," she said, replacing his gag. Then she returned to the bridge.

"Now, Captain, I have neglected you long enough. Tell me where we are heading and why."

"Well, Miss," he said, pointing to the chart, "they had me looking for this little cove here. From their talk I collected they'd some friends there, or possibly inland, maybe Gravelines." He moved his hand along to point out the town.

Sarah said, "I believe it would be best, then, not to do that. Have we provisions for a slightly longer sail?" Her own finger moved south. "We seek the Vendée, and have friends at Le Tréport or, if possible, even down here at Fécamp. I wouldn't object, if you thought you could bring us in safely, even south of Le Havre, perhaps Deauville? We might be able to avoid Paris altogether."

He frowned. "We left in a hurry, Miss. They didn't provision us, and I had no time to act on your message. I shouldn't care to be out too much longer. If you like, we could come in at Le Tréport and maybe take on some things from the Durand brothers. They usually have some brandy on hand, at the very least, and it would pay the expenses...." His voice trailed off.

"Watching my purse, Captain?" Sarah smiled.

He smiled back, "And my own."

"What about our two passengers, Lem and Billy?"

"Can't take them regular. Far as I'm concerned they're nothing but mutineers and pirates. We might find a merchant ship going far foreign, out east like."

"Excellent idea. Best leave Billy where he is, then. Can the three of you get in? Could you get some men at Le Tréport?"

"Getting in will be tricky; we may have to lie off and send in a boat. And there's the watch to consider, meddlers without enough to do. For the rest, probably the Durands will help if they can and they usually can. Enough to get home, anyway. And we can get close as

long as you're willing to haul on a rope." He looked
down. "I hate to ask it of you, Miss, but you can do it,
and your friend, well...."

"I understand. Pleased to be of use. We'll try the
Durands and see where we go from there. Agreed?"

"Aye, Miss." He smiled. "I'm that glad you're
here. Sorry I let meself get caught that way, and sorry I
lost faith in you."

"Those things were my fault, Captain, not yours.
I apologize again, and I will make it up to you. You
have my word."

"He's coming about on the larboard tack, sir."

"Yes, damn him. Send for the passengers, will
you Ned?"

"I'm sorry, sir, but you see how it is." The
captain gestured at the frigate, now settling into its
new course.

"French flag?" Jarrod asked.

"Yes. May even be true. Hardly matters, in these
waters, if he finds you three aboard. Fish we can
explain. Might even get by with a bottle or two of
brandy, though they'd likely take it away. Anything
else, no. They find you, we'll all be finished. Hang us if
they're English, shoot us if they're French."

"Can't run for it? You're certainly faster than
they are."

"Not from under their lee with the wind dead
foul. We could come about, and the balls would start

flying as soon as we touched a brace. No, I'm sorry, but it won't do. The boat's already over the side. It's dark enough, you should have no trouble, as long as you keep us between you and them. I am sorry, but it's the best I can do."

Jarrod looked at the land, just a shadow to their right. "D'you know what the country's like?"

"Marsh, mostly, drying into forest as you move through. There's a fort on the headland there," he pointed, "but they can't see this far in the dark. Ten or fifteen miles, thirty-five or forty more to Nantes, depending where you come out. Turn right when you find the road."

"Can you lend us a good rower? We are all willing but maybe not as able as we might like. Except Henry, he's got some experience."

"I'll ask, but it'll have to be a volunteer. We may not be able to pick him up very soon. Depends on them." He nodded at the frigate, now less than half a mile away. "Ask the men, Ned."

"Célian has already gone down. He has a sister in Nantes, but he'll wait and see if they leave us here or if we can come back tomorrow night."

"Excellent. You'll like him. His English is pretty good. Now, you'd better hurry. There isn't a moment to lose."

In the boat, Célian acted as coxswain, speaking low to keep the sound from carrying. Under his instruction, they were able to row fairly dry. Jarrod caught a crab once, but the other three were

experienced rowers and they lost very little time. As
they approached the shore, they moved into the
shadow of the trees and followed the coast to an inlet
that allowed them to row directly into the swamp until
they were surrounded by woods. They could hear
voices across the water, but not the words.

Looking out, they were able to see the frigate,
now alongside the little sloop. Its gunports were open
and the light showed through, but there had been no
firing. The sloop itself was almost invisible in the
darkness, except for the lighter color of its mainsail
against the frigate's side. For a time, they held their
breath, staring at the ships, trying to make out what
was happening. If men were passing back and forth
between the two vessels, they were just shadows
against a larger one, impossible to make out.

Then, after what seemed forever, the frigate's
sails were braced up and the larger vessel came about
onto the starboard tack, gathering speed as its
gunports closed. The little sloop came about and
began to move off, more slowly, in the same direction,
but more northerly. The gap widened and continued to
widen as they watched.

"Can we rejoin?" Jarrod asked.

Célian shook his head, "They are watching and
will watch for a long while. You must go inland. They
are, ah, *ennuyé*, you know? Nothing to do. They will
watch because there is nothing else to see. Maybe, in
the morning. We see. But you must not wait. *Capitaine*

not take you on again. Not safe, now. You understand?"

Jarrod nodded, "Can you take us to something a little dryer?"

"*Oui.*" They began to row again, slowly now, threading their way through the trees, until they came to a slight rise. The boat could go no further. The three visitors, Jarrod, Henry, and Lincoln Sadler, shipped their oars, gathered their belongings, and said goodbye to Célian. Before they left, Sadler carried on a brief conversation with the sailor, in French.

They set out, hoping to cover ten or twelve miles before daylight. "Stay close," Jarrod warned. "If we get separated, we'll be lost by morning. And be as quiet as possible, though I expect we'll be mostly alone in here tonight." The trees were large and the undergrowth stunted, so it was comparatively easy going once they got out of the marshy areas. When they saw the dawn, Jarrod called a halt and they found a quiet, protected place with a flat, dry, and relatively soft floor. "I'll take the first watch," he said. "Wake you in four hours, Henry."

"You are sure?"

"No, I cannot be sure, but he has not been in the office for two days, and it is clear that Sir Charles knows nothing of it. His concern is quite palpable, though he says nothing. What do your people say of Cherille?"

Facteau ignored the question. "I thank you for this intelligence, now be gone. Quickly, and make sure you are not seen." He rubbed his brow and began to pace. He did that for some time, until he was sure his guest must be gone. Then he walked out into his sitting room, "Has he not arrived?" he asked.

The man on the couch looked up, then hurriedly rose. "He will be here momentarily, sir. He went to wash himself; ah, here he is." Tim Curley came through the other door.

Facteau turned to him. "Well?"

"Oi been watchin', sor, ever since them ladies all went away, but ain't seen any of 'em since the next day. They was all around, comin' and goin', and then they wasn't. Now, ain't nobody home but the caretaker, same as if they'd gone back to the country, sor."

"Describe them. Both of them."

Tim provided a detailed description of Lord Cherille and Henry Winnow.

The man on the couch asked, "This black man, he is a servant? A slave, perhaps? Cherille was in the colonies, was he not?"

Facteau frowned, "Slaves are illegal in England, just as in France."

"And I'm sure the law is adhered to most strictly, just as it is in France."

Facteau nodded, "I take your point. But our observation of them indicates the man Winnow is more than a slave."

Tim nodded his head. "Acts more friend than servant, he does. Seen him tell his lordship what he should do, just like he was the master instead of t'other way 'round. Seen him laugh at his lordship. Never known a peer what'd stand that in a servant."

"Thank you, Mr. Curley, that will be all. Maintain your watch on the house and let me know if anything occurs. Anything, you understand?"

"Oh, aye," Tim turned and went out.

Facteau watched the door close behind him, then turned, "My more immediate concern is the Malay. She should be dead by now, but I have heard nothing from my agents and fear they may have failed. If you hurry, you can be in Gravelines by tomorrow morning. Make haste and you may catch her. Her journey to France is certainly no coincidence. See what you can do. In any case, find Caron at Cholet and finish this. Leissègues will not wait forever."

27

"Damn that watch," Sarah muttered, as the coach wandered to the side of the road and bounced over a rut. Maërlys looked down and said nothing. She was still in awe of what had happened on board the *Doctor Syn* and even a little afraid of her companion. She was doing her best to not dwell on the moment when she had pulled the trigger and that sailor's head exploded in front of her, a picture that kept intruding into her thoughts, so she didn't immediately absorb the sense of Sarah's comment.

"What watch?" she asked, when the words penetrated.

Sarah smiled at her, "Those busybodies at Le Tréport. It is so much more comfortable to travel by ship. Had they left us alone, we could have provisioned and found some sailors. The *Doctor Syn* would have carried us to Deauville quickly and comfortably. As it was, they barely got the brandy off, and Fulbert had to go along to help."

Maërlys shivered. "I did not find the boat at all comfortable," she answered quietly.

Sarah laughed aloud at this and stroked her hand. "My poor little one, you have seen much these last days for which you were unprepared. I tried to warn you but I forget, not that you have been gently raised, but what that means. I have fought to stay alive since I was eight, no, seven. I am a crude, awful woman, and you should have nothing to do with me. But here we are. It will take us a week, at least, to reach Cholet and you have no one of your class to keep you company. Can you endure me for so long, *ma chére?*"

Maërlys felt quite another sort of feeling, one which had come to her several times over the last days, sometimes at the strangest moments. She seized the older woman's large hand and looked into those delightful brown eyes.

"Oh, please don't talk like that; I am sensible of how much I owe you. I know I would probably not be alive at this moment were it not for you, and my poor brother and sister would fall victims to that vicious Bonaparte. I owe you nothing but gratitude and, if I am a little frightened by what happened on the ship, it is true I have never seen such things before."

She stopped and looked down, her face reddening, then gazed once more into the other's eyes. "You were wonderful. I did not know a woman could do those things. Alone, I would have been, I mean…."

"Yes, my dear, I know what you mean. But you did splendidly." She touched her breast, "I still remember how tenderly you washed the blood from my body."

Maërlys face glowed with heat now, every bit of her neck and face as red as it was possible for it to become. Still, she did not take her eyes from Sarah's, whose own brightened. "I thought those Durand brothers were very nice, especially Constant."

Sarah looked under her eyelashes at Maërlys. "You think you might prefer him to your baron?"

"You are teasing me. You know I mean nothing to Lord Cherille. I make no doubt he has forgotten my existence."

A frown crossed Sarah's face, "No, my dear, I think not. You will enjoy his kisses again, I believe." Her face changed again, and she looked at Maërlys seriously. "Are you afraid of me, now that you have seen how I treated those sailors?"

"Oh, you mustn't think that."

"Even if it is true?"

"It may be a little true but I am no more afraid of you than I was of Lord Cherille, when I...."

"Do you compare me with your beautiful baron, then?" Sarah's eyes were full of mischief and she closely watched the younger girl's reactions.

Maërlys looked up at her, her face still glowing red. "I guess, I mean, I do wonder, sometimes. Do you remember how you spoke to me when I had just arrived at your house?"

Sarah nodded gravely without taking her eyes from Maërlys', "I do."

Maërlys could no longer face the clear eyes of her companion. "Did you, I mean, I thought you might, um, try to, um, do that."

Sarah took Maërlys chin in her hand and forced the girl to meet her eyes, "We must be clear with one another, *chérie*. Did you think I might kiss you?"

This time Maërlys did not look away and she nodded, ever so slightly. She said nothing, but her lower lip was caught between her teeth.

"It is true. You have earned the right to know this thing about me. I am attracted to men," she paused and grew thoughtful. "I especially am attracted to this friend of your baron's. I believe his name is Henry. He is a most interesting man and I believe we might have much in common. I look forward to the chance that, someday, I will have a long talk with him. And if he wishes to do things other than talk, it is possible I will wish to do these things also. Do you understand?"

Her chin still held in the long fingers of the other woman's hand, Maërlys nodded again.

"But," Sarah went on, "I could never be blind to your beauty. I have seen your lovely body on the ship and, frankly, I long to kiss your enchanting lips and might even do so if you will stop biting them. Do you think you would mind so much?"

This time, Maërlys shook her head, almost imperceptibly, "You have saved my life. I am yours to do with as you will."

"You are sweet, *chérie*, but that is not enough. Remember, you have saved my life as well. For me you have blown out a man's brains with your pistol and caused his blood to rain down upon me. Then, with your soft little hands," she picked up Maërlys hand in her own, "you have washed this blood from my breast, so gently and so lovingly. I confess I wished you would touch me in other places and I longed to touch you. But these things are mutual, or they are nothing."

She dropped Maërlys hand and sat back on the squab. "Please, my little one, if you care for me, you must think about this and decide what you wish to do for your own pleasure. I see the fire in your face. Does it travel beyond to other parts of your body?"

Sarah leaned forward, her face inches from Maërlys', her eyes grave, locked on those of her young companion, "Between us there could be no commitment except to give one another pleasure, and I would never ask you for more. I have told you what would please me. Now, you must decide what would please you, and if you believe they are the same, then you have only to tell me so. Until then, I believe we have said enough. Do you agree?"

Maërlys looked down and slowly nodded. "I have not conveyed it as I would have liked," she said, "but will do as you ask and think about it. In truth, I can hardly stop thinking about it. I am curious, but I understand that is not what you are asking. When I am sure, I will tell you."

"Fair enough, my kitten. We have a long journey ahead and will spend the nights together in rooms at inns. We cannot travel comfortably if we do not understand one another and this is why I have this conversation with you. Please understand that whatever you decide, I care for you deeply and wish you only the life you choose and deserve to have for yourself. Your decision about these physical matters will not alter that. You understand?"

Again, Maërlys nodded silently and sat back, but she retained her hold on the other's right hand and placed it gently in her lap. Sarah smiled, and put her left arm around the girl's shoulders, pulling her close. The jouncing of the coach seemed softer that way, and eventually they both fell asleep.

They spent most of the day in the forest, moving when they felt safe enough to indulge the inclination, but mainly sleeping. By evening, they had reached the edge of the trees and, at full dark, set out in earnest. Several times they met peasants on the road and pretended drunkenness to keep them from coming too close. They were pleased to note, as far as they could see, that their clothes were not particularly different from those worn by the natives.

Jarrod usually acted as if he were almost overcome and leaned on Henry for support. When spoken to he did not respond, worried that his inadequate French would give him away. They left most of the talking to Sadler, whose French was impeccable. Henry, too, had a full command of the language, but his color was a concern, so he kept silent whenever possible.

They excited no suspicion and, on one occasion, when a lone peasant attempted to join them, Jarrod reeled over to him and nearly fell on him, then lay retching in the grass. Henry and Sadler acted both bothered and tipsy, and Sadler explained that they had consumed all the wine and were unable to offer him a drink, but implied that he would have some down the front of his shirt if he stayed too close to Jarrod. It was enough, and the man moved on as they helped Jarrod regain his feet.

The next day was spent in the hedges, with one man on watch at all times. Although they were not traveling on the main road, they occasionally saw passersby. Fortunately, no one paid any particular attention to them, and that night they set off again, fairly well rested.

Henry and Jarrod were used to this sort of life in the islands and, the weather holding fair, even the heat of the day presented no difficulty. Sadler showed unfamiliarity with the constant walking and was inclined to sleep as much as possible during the day. However, aside from a tendency toward irritability, he bore it well enough.

They were a few miles past Bouée, hoping to get to the outskirts of Nantes before dawn, when they rounded a curve in the road and found themselves faced by three soldiers, evidently headed for the town. All three carried muskets and the leader had a sword at his side. Jarrod immediately staggered next to Henry and leaned on him. The leader, the smallest of the three, wearing the ensign of a *caporal*, demanded their names. Sadler appeared confused so Henry began to answer, but was interrupted constantly by murmurings and pawings from Jarrod. Finally, Henry pushed Jarrod so that he fell toward the *caporal*, who jumped back to avoid him.

Nonetheless, Jarrod managed to get his arms around the man, much to the amusement of the other two soldiers. They were attempting to pull him off of their leader when Sadler drove his knife into the back of the soldier nearest him. Immediately, Henry presented his pistol at the head of the other soldier. The *caporal* attempted to draw his sword, but Jarrod prevented this and Sadler killed him.

They dragged the two bodies to the side of the road while Henry kept the third soldier at bay with his pistol. They agreed to take cover in a large copse on the other side of the field. Relieved of his weapons, the remaining soldier was obliged to carry his fellow, and Jarrod bore the body of their leader over his shoulders. Once among the trees, the soldier was bound to a tree and gagged. The three Englishmen walked a little way from him so they could not be heard and discussed options in low voices.

"What now?" Jarrod asked.

Henry shrugged, "Leave them. We can be a long way from here before dawn. Make sure the knots are tight, he may still be there tomorrow."

Sadler was appalled, "Leave a castle in your rear? Are you mad? He'll have the whole countryside down on us! Kill him and take everything of value; make it look like robbery, and let us be away. We must be quick."

Jarrod answered, "The man probably has family near here. They were only headed to Bouée for leave. Check to make sure he is tied tightly and we will search the pockets of the others." This they began to do; Henry checked the *caporal* and Jarrod searched the second corpse. They took all the money they could find, a total of seventeen francs and twelve centimes. They had just risen from this task when Sadler returned, wiping his knife. He offered them an additional five francs and three centimes. Henry looked at him, then at Jarrod, and raced toward where the third soldier was bound. He returned in a moment, shaking his head at Jarrod.

"We agreed that I am in charge," Jarrod told Sadler.

Sadler shot back, "I will not stand by while you allow sentiment to lead us to the scaffold. We are in a very dangerous situation, whether you realize it or not. I am here to fulfill a purpose, not to reach the guillotine before we reach Nantes. We should be moving now."

This last was so obviously true that Henry took Jarrod's arm and shook it. Jarrod looked at him, frowned, then walked off in the direction of Nantes. Henry and Sadler followed.

They stopped a few miles short of Nantes and took to the hedges the next day. Conversation between the three men was desultory, when it existed at all. Once Sadler attempted to discuss the matter, but Henry pointed out that as they neared Nantes, traffic was more common and they would do well not to be heard speaking English.

They entered the city the following evening and Sadler led them to the house of a woman he swore could be trusted. Mme Bisset was a woman of about sixty with two girls, sixteen-year-old twins. She was wary but welcomed them. Sadler explained that, because of circumstances from the past, she had no love for the government. Like many Vendéens, she associated the new emperor with the revolutionary government. Young people, like Jacqueline and Julienne, the twins, had no personal memory of the war of the Vendée or its tragic aftermath, but many of the older ones still nursed their hatred.

28

Caron faced the official and twitched. He had been twitching a great deal, lately, including a tic in his eye. The official shouted, "Stop winking at me!" and Caron, silently, twitched some more. Finally, the official handed the papers back to him. "These seem to be in order," he admitted, his distaste for the twitching, blinking man in front of him evident on his face. "You may apply for a horse or, if you prefer, a carriage and pair. When you get to the Vendée, apply at Nantes, or someone at Angers might be able to assist you. Cholet will give you only trouble."

Caron snatched the papers and left the office without a word. He carried, in addition to his own papers, full authority from Facteau including arrest warrants for two enemies of the Empire, unnamed for *raisons d'état*. That these enemies were ages eight and thirteen was not mentioned. I will pay them all back, he thought. But not yet.

The old woman stood in the kitchen doorway, looking covertly at her guests and wringing her hands. Henry was the first to notice. "*Qu'est ce?*"

Jarrod followed the direction of his eyes, but Sadler was on his feet. "*Mme Bisset, c'est quoi?*" He took the old woman's hands as her eyes began to spill over.

Her answer was too rapid for Jarrod to follow but Henry translated while Sadler tried to calm the old woman. "She says we must go. She cannot protect her daughters and we must go immediately." He shrugged.

Jarrod asked, "She thinks we will attack her beautiful children? Cannot you reassure her, Mr. Sadler?"

"It is more complicated than that. Let me try to get the whole story. In the meantime, you two must prepare for flight, just in case."

He led the old woman to a room at the back where they were joined by Jacqueline and Julienne. Henry and Jarrod re-packed their small kits and checked the exterior of the house, finding no one in sight.

They had just finished these tasks when Sadler returned. "It is a story. Is anyone watching the house?"

"No," Jarrod answered. "We checked all sides."

"Good. It seems there is a man in town who lusts after the girls. He uses money to lure women to him, abuses them, then casts them out. In some cases, it seems they disappear altogether. According to Mme Bisset, it goes back to the drownings. If you don't know, the prisoners were often stripped completely before the boats were sunk. Sometimes, these disrobings were forced on the docks and, when the victims were women, men in the crowd were allowed to abuse them before they were murdered. The girls' parents were such victims."

Henry stared at him, "You mean they stripped women naked, raped them, then forced them onto boats which were sunk in the river? Who did this?"

"The revolutionary government, in the person of a man named Carrier. He eventually went to his own fate on the guillotine, but too late for a lot of people in Nantes, including many women and children," Jarrod answered.

"Exactly," Sadler agreed. "According to the old woman, the girls were brought to her by her daughter when she feared she might be arrested. Mme Bisset kept the children hidden and did not witness the murders of her daughter and son-in-law. She was told of the horrors by friends. They said this Victor Boucher, a young man at the time, brutally raped her daughter Aurélie on the dock, in front of anyone who cared to watch, including her husband, Louis Pelletier. They said the poor man went insane at the sight and was bound to the boat, screaming, while his ravished wife, naked and bleeding from her wounds, her hands tied behind her, tried to comfort him. The watchers told her it was the most fearful thing they had ever seen and they could only hope death came quickly as the raft vanished beneath the waters of the Loire."

"Dear Lord," Jarrod breathed. "And was this Boucher not punished in any way?"

"On the contrary, he flourished. He has become quite wealthy since then, trading in properties taken from the church. Our hostess believes he was driven a little mad himself by his actions that day, and this is why he has not married. Women are attracted to his money and are taken advantage of, but his tastes are too violent and disreputable for marriage. He has learned of the escape of *les nourrissons*. He knows they are the twin daughters of the beautiful woman he treated so dreadfully, since they are the living images of their mother. She believes he longs to repeat his crime. She has often seen him in this part of town, though it is not on any route he might normally travel."

"But she took us in. Where do we come into this?" Jarrod asked.

"He stopped her on the way home this evening. He said he knows we are fugitives and she is sheltering us. He gave her until midnight tonight. She must bring the two girls, their hands bound behind them, to his house by then or he will send the soldiers and everyone in the house will end on the guillotine, including the children. He said he would go to them in prison before they died, and have his way with them anyway. He smirked at her as he told her this."

"What do you think will happen if they are brought to him?"

Henry looked grim. "He might easily sequester the girls to prolong their agony, but the watch would arrive here all the same. It would be the best way to rid

himself of witnesses. I think, though, he will not send
them until the children are in his hands. He would
prefer to satisfy his lust in private."

"Do you agree, Lincoln?"

"I think Henry is completely in the right of it."

Jarrod said, "Then we must be quick. You and
Henry are the shortest, you will have to be the girls."
He looked at them, "You will need the thickest veils
you can manage, even in the dark. You look nothing
like those lovely children. Fortunately, your hands are
going to be hidden behind you. We must hide our
things elsewhere; if the watch should come, there
must be no trace of anyone except these innocent
women. What can Mme Bisset tell us of this Boucher
and his household?"

Sarah Dane looked around the room in distaste.
She spoke in French, as they had agreed would be best
for all conversation as long as they were in France.
"Well, perhaps we will do better tomorrow." She sat on
the bed, then jumped up, "Like a rock." She patted the
coverlet, "We must be grateful the dust does not rise
from it like a fog. Come, Maërlys, perhaps the food will
be more inviting."

Guillaume, the coachman assigned to them by
Constant Durand, was waiting in the dining room. The
two other guests, a young couple, kept to themselves.
The food explained the lack of custom; it was not in
the least inviting. They ate listlessly and drank

perhaps more wine than was right. As the food was finished, they were more relieved than satisfied.

Guillaume apologized. "*Je suis désolé*, but Constant insisted you stay here tonight; I promise we will do better tomorrow. At least the wine is better than the food and rooms. We can have an additional room at almost no extra cost, so if you ladies would like separate...."

Sarah spoke immediately "That would—"

"*Non*," Maërlys interrupted, then turned bright red and looked down at her plate.

Sarah smiled and shrugged, "Thank you, but it will not be necessary. We have far to go and money is not infinite. Why, do you think, Constant wanted us to stay here?"

"The innkeeper is an old friend, and, as I say, the wine is excellent. Constant comes here often. Fulbert almost never does. Likes his food too much, Fulbert. Also, I believe Constant felt that the lack of strange travelers would be an asset. You wish to travel quietly, I collect?"

"*Oui*. You will keep alert for us, will you not?"

He frowned, "You expect trouble?"

"We do not expect trouble but we do dislike it. And, when trouble comes, as it is wont to do, it is well to be prepared, *n'est-ce pas*?"

"*C'est vrai*. Will you wish an early start?"

"It is not so far to Cottévrard. Let us take our time, although it is unlikely we will sleep late in such a bed as that. Do not rise early for us, and we will go whenever you are pleased. We hope not to be two troublesome women and are sensible of your kindness in driving us the length of France."

"I hope I am not too forward if I say that it is a reward above my station to escort two such lovely ladies where ever they wish to go. I trust they will not be needed, but I have a musket, a brace of pistols, and a strong sword arm, all at your service. I am also advised that your ladyship knows how to take care of herself, and Constant insisted that I obey your orders at all times."

"Thank you, *Monsieur*. But no deference to me, if you please. I am this lady's maid," she smiled at Maërlys, "at least for this trip, and it would be best to have no indication of any other relationship."

He smiled, "Then it may be necessary for me to flirt with you from time to time, to maintain the fiction. No coachman could travel with such a maid otherwise. Not unless he were over eighty. Perhaps ninety."

Sarah raised her brows and tossed her head, "You do speak pretty, sir, but you must keep your hands to yourself."

He laughed, "*Formidable*. I shall try my best." He leered, then laughed again, genially. "I'll bid you good night. Shall we say, between eight and nine tomorrow?"

Back in their room Maërlys lingered by the door, watching Sarah remove her clothes and put on a nightgown. The evening was stuffy despite the open window, and the nightdress Sarah chose was a very light silk that clung to her body. She walked slowly over to Maërlys, smiled into the younger woman's eyes, touched her cheek, then climbed into the bed.

Maërlys, blushing furiously, removed her dress. Because of the heat, she was not wearing a chemise, but she had on the long drawers she made sure to wear ever since the incidents on the ship. She turned her back and began to remove the drawers, then, thinking better of it, slowly, and with what felt like an incredible effort, turned to face Sarah as she took them off.

Sarah sat up in the bed and smiled at her. "*Magnifique,*" she said, clapping her hands. "Will you come to me like that, now?"

Feeling as if her entire body was bright red, Maërlys forced her legs to move until they brought her to the side of the bed. Sarah, still smiling, her eyes bright, reached out and took Maërlys' hand, pulling her up into the bed with one strong arm while the other hand swept the coverlet and sheet aside in welcome. Maërlys found herself kneeling in the bed, looking down at her lovely companion, as Sarah's eyes devoured her naked body.

"*Bien.* You are ready?"

Unable to make a sound, Maërlys nodded.

"Do not be afraid, my kitten. If you change your mind, if you become frightened, or if you find it does not answer, you have only to speak and we will sleep quietly, cuddled here. I will love you even more for your honesty than I ever could for your body. Do you understand?"

Again Maërlys nodded, but this time she managed, "*Oui.*" It was a soft mew, an almost inaudible whisper.

Sarah put her hand on Maërlys' hip and slowly moved it up the side of her body, gently caressing the soft roundness of her breast, continuing upward to Maërlys' arm and shoulder. A sigh escaped Maërlys as Sarah touched her neck, then pulled her head down so their lips met. It was the softest touch at first, then Sarah's full lips surrounded Maërlys' upper lip, let go, and seized the lower. Sarah's tongue slowly wandered over the lower lip, the upper, then, gently exploring, pushed its way into Maërlys' mouth. At this touch, Maërlys' tongue found a life of its own, sought Sarah's mouth, and her body melted into the older woman's, the soft feel of silk and the firm breast beneath as it touched her own breast, her nipples rising to meet it, the warmth of the other's skin under her hand. She realized her hand had strayed under Sarah's nightgown and was caressing her bottom, but she lost track of everything as Sarah moved her hand between her legs and the sensation claimed her. She remembered moments of intense feeling, Sarah's lips squeezing her nipples; Sarah's hand on her bottom, moving down the cleft; Sarah's fingers caressing the soft lips between her legs. Then those fingers delicately teasing the pulsing nub before slipping inside, just a little; her own breathing coming faster, her heart pounding in time with Sarah's, and the ascent. Sarah's hair, Sarah's neck against her mouth, Sarah's nipple on her tongue, and the exquisite climb, throbbing, melting, yielding... and, then... the explosion.

29

The house was large, and only a short way from the river. *Mme Bisset* said, "*Prés ses plus grands crime.*"

Only one light shone from the window at the front. Jarrod placed himself in easy reach of the door, out of sight in the shadows. He almost laughed to see Henry and Sadler trying to make themselves small. *Madame* stood straight and proud.

A big man, dressed in the livery of a servant, opened the door and told her to leave the girls and go. She demanded to see his master. "*Ou est M. Boucher? Je dois les voir.*"

Reluctantly, the servant stepped aside and a smaller man, in a dressing gown, came into the light of the doorway. Mme Bisset nodded. Henry, on the left, struck the servant twice with his fist, holding his little wooden weapon. The man collapsed. Sadler clapped his pistol to Boucher's head. Jarrod whispered, "You go home, now," into the old woman's ear as he brushed past her and closed the door.

"May I hit him now?" Sadler asked. Jarrod ignored him and went to the first door on the right. A glance assured him that it was a parlor, and he held the door, gesturing the three of them inside. The fear was evident in Boucher's face and he made no move to resist as he was bound into a chair.

Henry knelt in front of the man and began asking him questions in rapid French. After a moment he turned to Jarrod and said, "He claims there are no more servants in the house tonight. Perhaps one of us should stay here while the other two make sure?"

"I'll stay," said Sadler.

Jarrod and Henry looked at each other. "I'll stay," Jarrod said. "You two start looking." He reached down and removed the rope from Boucher's dressing gown, handing it to Sadler. "The servant. Make sure."

Sadler looked from Jarrod to Henry, then back. His face was sullen but he nodded. Alone with Boucher, Jarrod took a chair nearby and waited, a pistol in his lap. He said nothing, nor did he react to Boucher's questions though he understood enough to answer, had he wished.

It was a large house and it was almost half an hour before Henry and Sadler returned. They had found no other servants or guests. "There is something you should see," Henry said to Jarrod.

Jarrod nodded, and turned to Sadler. "Stay with him but don't hurt him. It's important." Again, Sadler looked unhappy but nodded, and Jarrod followed Henry out of the room and back to the kitchen.

From there, Henry showed the way through a door and down some stone steps. They led in the direction of the Loire and, at the bottom, opened into a

large room hollowed out of rock. Torches were set in
the walls and Henry lit two. As the light came up,
Jarrod could see that an alcove to the right was
separated from the rest of the room by bars, and
behind these were two cells.

"Got his own dungeon, has he?" Jarrod
muttered.

"Go look."

As he came closer, Jarrod could see that one of
the cells was occupied. There was a sort of cot
attached to the wall and someone lying on it. He
brought his torch closer and the prisoner stirred, then
looked up at him. It was a girl. She had a piece of
blanket to cover herself, and appeared otherwise
naked. Her left wrist was secured by a stout and fairly
long chain to a bolt set in the wall next to the cot. A
stench came from a chamber pot on the other side of
the small cell. She stared at him in fear.

Jarrod breathed a curse and turned to Henry,
"Can we get the door open and bring her out?"

"She's a complication."

"Can you talk to her?"

"I tried before but she just stared at me.
Frightened out of her wits, I'd say."

"We've got to get her out."

Henry shrugged, "I can open that door but the
chain may take some time. Sadler will be hard to
control if he sees this."

"Do you think you can deal with her? She could
have your dress." He tented his eyebrows and smiled.

"Good thing I'm used to you, your lordship. Have Sadler find me some clothes. I'll see what can be done." He went over to a desk set against the far wall and began rummaging its contents.

Jarrod looked around and noticed another door, set in the far wall. "Does that lead to the river?"

"I didn't follow it all the way, but I believe it does. Getting ideas?"

"Hmm, perhaps a small boat on La Sèvre Nantaise. I'll go get the others, and we'll decide what's best to do. See if you can get her to talk to you."

Upstairs, he sent Sadler to find clothes for himself and Henry, taking the opportunity to speak to Boucher. In his halting French, he asked him for the name of the girl, and her history. Obviously frightened, Boucher's replies were often incoherent, and Jarrod was repeatedly forced to make him go over things again, more slowly. Finally, he determined a few facts.

The girl was named Claire, or perhaps Clara. Her family name was obscure. She had been obtained for him by someone, possibly the large servant lying bound and unconscious in the hall. He did not know, nor care, precisely where she came from but she was a country girl, from somewhere west of Nantes. He considered her beneath his notice and referred to her as "*la vache.*" He had kept her for almost a month. He intended to *se débarraser*, once he had the twins in his grasp. How he meant to dispose of her was unclear, but the closeness of the river was ominous. He used the word *noyer*, and his eyes lit up. It was difficult for Jarrod to keep his temper, and he thought it best to say nothing to Sadler of it. In the end, it made little difference.

Sadler returned with the clothes and the three of them went through the kitchen and down into the dungeon. Henry had opened the cell and was working on the girl's wrist chain. Sadler took one look and slammed Boucher against the wall. His head hit the rock; he bounced back and lay still.

The moment the shackle was released, the girl grabbed up the chamber pot, ran to where Boucher lay on the floor of the cavern and pushed it down hard over his face, screaming "*merde, merde, merde.*" Boucher did not move. Henry gently pulled her away, and held her close as she began to cry. The marks of the whip showed clearly on her naked back.

Over her shoulder, Henry looked at Jarrod, then at his dress, lying on the floor. Jarrod picked it up and they managed to get the sobbing girl into it. She went limp from time to time, which made the process more difficult, but they did it.

Jarrod and Sadler went upstairs and managed to bring the butler down to the dungeon. Sadler, who carried the man's head, dropped him against the hard stone steps more than once but Jarrod was past caring. They laid him alongside Boucher, still wearing the chamber pot, and went back upstairs to wash and gather some food. Jarrod had decided not to go back to Mme Bisset's until Henry showed him the next surprise.

He found it in the other cell, under another cot, concealed by a blanket. It was an iron box, about a foot square and six inches deep. When Henry opened it, it was full of *louis d'or.* "Not such a good revolutionary, after all," commented Jarrod.

"I don't know. Here's a napoleon," said Henry, holding it up. "I estimate about twenty-five or thirty thousand francs."

"It must be taken to *madame...* wait. Take out ten thousand for this poor child; it is little enough for her suffering. Henry, can you manage that and bring us our packs? While you are gone, we will find a boat and take care of these two." He gestured at the two unconscious men.

"Are they dead?" Henry asked.

"I don't know and I no longer care. An ordinary soldier is one thing," he glared at Sadler, "but these two have given up any claim to humanity. We will deal with it. Please hurry. We need to be on the river before dawn." Henry nodded, dressed himself in servant's livery, divided the money and left.

Maërlys was shy all morning, from the moment she awoke. Silent through breakfast, she found herself wondering what she should say, how she should broach the subject of what had happened. Sarah, on the other hand, was unperturbed. She bustled the younger girl along, helped her dress, repacked their

things, and prepared for departure. It was not until
they saluted Guillaume on the box and climbed inside
that Maërlys found her tongue.

"I fell asleep."

"So you did, *ma chère*. Is that why you have
been silent all morning? Did you not enjoy the
experience, and now you wish to know how to avoid it
in future without hurting my feelings?" Amusement
played at the corners of Sarah's mouth.

"Oh, heavens no! It was so wonderful. I never
knew... I never knew. Avoid it? Oh, dear me, why
would people not do it all the time, as much as they
could? I never knew." She grew thoughtful, "Though,
to be sure, I imagine people do it much more than I
realize. And of course...," she stopped and turned a
deep red.

"Of course what, my kitten?"

Maërlys looked down. In a very small voice, she
murmured, "I, I did nothing for you. You did
everything for me and I did nothing for you."

It was too much for Sarah's control. She began
to giggle and her attempts to contain it made it worse.
Soon she was laughing uproariously while Maërlys
stared.

"Is that funny? I don't understand. Is this
something else I don't know about? You must tell me.
Oh... I am so ignorant, I must be a sad trial to you."

Sarah managed to get her laughter under
control enough to gasp out, "I am sorry if my sadness

depresses you," before going off into another round of hilarity.

Maërlys could stand it no longer, and slapped the older woman on the arm, although not very hard. "You are making game of me. I don't think that's very nice, after you were so sweet to me last night. Is that all I am, a source of amusement?"

Sarah managed to stifle her mirth and pulled the girl into her arms. "You misunderstand, and I am no help to you. Please let me try to make you see. You cannot know how much joy it gave me to hold you in my arms, to feel you lose all control and allow me to give you so much pleasure. Your body is wonderful, capable of as much incredible satisfaction as any I have ever seen, and to be the instrument of such release, oh, Maërlys, my dove, it was delicious. Someday, you will learn."

"B-but, I know you were aroused as well; I could feel your heart beating, hear your breathing. Surely you wished me to serve you as you served me. Were you not disappointed that I failed you?"

Sarah looked into her eyes, and smiled, even as tears came into her own. "No, my love, I was not disappointed, and you have not failed me. It is simply that there are things you do not know as yet. You are innocent and that is no crime in the house of love. We will be together for some time, with more inns ahead of us. Tonight, perhaps, if you like, I will show you some other things, and we shall see. Would you like that, do you think?"

"Oh, yes, I'm sure I would. In fact, I don't see how I can wait until tonight, and if you want to show me something now...," she had placed her hand on Sarah's knee and was pulling at her dress, trying to get it high enough to get her hand under it.

Sarah gently slapped the hand, rearranged her skirts, and laughed. "Oh my, you little minx. I wish I may not regret unleashing a very tigress upon the world...at least upon mine. If I teach you too much, how will you explain it to your baron when you come to him. He too must treasure your innocence."

"Oh." Maërlys sat back against the squab. Do you really believe we will see him again? And do you think he will be interested in me?"

"I am quite certain of both those things, my dear. I believe he will have no choice in either matter."

"But surely if he wanted me innocent, he had me at his command, and he allowed, nay, insisted that I leave him as virginal as before. That surely does not speak of great desire on his part."

"On the contrary, it speaks of very great desire of the deepest and purest kind. The man loves you and when you meet again, I am certain he will do whatever he can to make you his own. Does that prospect not please you?"

"I, I don't know. I mean, I do find him very attractive, but now that I know how it is, I mean, with you, would I ever be able to leave you?"

"Well, my love, you must remember that his body holds surprises for you that I cannot supply. It is true that some women prefer to avoid those things, but I am not one of them, nor do I think you are. When you were in his arms, you were ready to let him do whatever he liked, even though you found that there might be pain involved, *n'est-ce pas?*"

"Oh, *oui*, but with you there was no pain. I might like that better, I think."

Sarah laughed again. "*Oui,* but the pain is only the once, and after that is a pleasure I can never provide. At least, that is my experience, and I believe it will be yours. He is a gentleman, your Lord Cherille. He angered me, but not intentionally, I am convinced. I think I will come to like him and you will learn to love him."

"He is very handsome," Maërlys said thoughtfully, "and kind."

"And you are still very young," Sarah smiled.

30

Caron loved the night. To walk the streets of a city, preferably a French one, at two or three in the morning was his delight. All the most interesting *citoyens* were on view in the darkest hours. It was his opinion that a small man had the advantage in the night. Secure in the darkness, his twitching stopped. He should have come at that damned woman this way, alone on the street at night. He could have run her through before she knew he was there and then showed himself to her as the light faded from her beautiful eyes. The thought aroused him; he might still get his chance. The night made him brave.

As he approached a corner, the shadows beyond the cross street drew his attention. The difficulty of making out detail tickled his senses. He moved directly into the shadows, not slackening his pace or adjusting his attitude in any way that might invite suspicion until he was secure in the blanket of the dark. Then he watched as the object of his interest moved out of the deepest shadows a little down the cross street to the left. His intuition intrigued him and he glided in pursuit.

He did not expect to meet anyone he knew but

all his senses were alert. When he realized the man he was following had dark skin, he mentally adjusted his interest from casual to careful. He found it angered him to see this African, this barbarian, walking the streets of his beloved France as if he owned them. He would learn his mistake. Then he blundered, trying to get closer.

As he saw the man move into the shadow of a tree and stop to check his boot, he realized the error. He had gotten too close and now this man suspected he was followed. He watched as the quarry, unable to confirm his presence, moved on. The man's walk, his build, pushed Caron's suspicions higher and higher, but could it be? He was almost sure when the man suddenly turned a corner and vanished.

Carefully, Caron approached the corner. Moving so slowly he was hardly moving at all, he followed the cross street a couple of feet before taking himself into the nearby hedge. From there, invisible in the dark, he studied the darkness, looking for variety. There, a little extra blackness within the blackness moved forward slightly though there was no wind. It withdrew.

Sure only of his quarry's location, he decided to act as if he knew. Careful to catch no light, he drew his blade, and advanced noiselessly to the solid darkness in the shadow of a large, low-limbed tree. Keeping his eye on the darkest shadow, he waited.

It was very dark and the city strange to him, but Henry's sense of direction was unerring; it took him only half an hour to reach the Bisset home. He detected a light glowing softly under the door, but the house was otherwise as dark as the rest of the street. He knocked softly and the light immediately disappeared. He heard rustling as the girls hurried back to their room, then the shuffling of the old woman as she came to the door, the light reappearing in the crack as she opened it.

"*Qui vient à cette heure?*"

He answered in French, "Your pardon, *Madame*, for the late hour. It is I, Henry. I bring good news."

The door came open, he was pulled inside, and it closed quickly behind him. "*Henri. Tout est bien?*"

"*Oui, Madame.* All is well. You will no longer be bothered by this devil, and he has apologized for his evil with a legacy for your girls." He handed her the box with the remainder of the coins inside.

She carried it to the table, set the lamp beside it, and opened it. Her hands flew to her mouth and she stared at Henry, "*Pour nous?*

He nodded. "That your girls may not want, but it would be good to keep it concealed for a time. Save it until it is needed, then invent a relative who has died and left it to them. Can you do this?"

"*Mais oui, bien sûr, oui.*" She flung her arms around him and kissed him on both cheeks.

He laughed, "You have been kind to us, and now we have other business. We must be away as soon as we can. My friends and I thank you for your benevolence to strangers. Be well and kiss your girls for me."

"*Ils doivent t'embrasser.*"

He laughed again and pushed her gently away, "No, your angels are too beautiful, and I am only a man. If I began kissing them, where would it all end?"

She looked up into his eyes and laughed too. "*Être bien, Henri,*" she said, shaking his hand with both of hers, "*et vos compagnons. Au revoir.*"

"*Adieu, Madame,*" he said, closing the door behind him and returning to the night.

The streets were nearly deserted and, as he had done on the first half of his journey, he moved into the shadows whenever he noticed anyone coming his way. Their packs were concealed in some shrubbery not too far from the Bisset house. He recovered them and was about halfway back to Boucher's when he felt himself followed.

He stopped and slipped into the darkness, expecting to hear footsteps behind him. There were none. After a moment he shrugged his shoulders and continued; instantly, the feeling returned. At the next corner he turned right, passed a house and slipped into the space beyond it.

The silence seemed to deepen as he dropped the packs and waited, crouched low, wood in his hand. Nothing. You are alone in a foreign, hostile city, he thought, you have not had enough sleep. You must return to the house as quickly as possible and see if you can rest before you have to leave.

Nevertheless, his eyes roamed the shadows before he stepped back into the street to check. His surprise was complete when he felt the rapier touch his throat.

The voice that spoke was French, but the language was English, "Hold, slave, we have much to discuss." Silently, Henry held still, his arms at his sides. The little piece of wood became invisible in his hand; he knew that voice too well. "Where is your master?"

Henry searched the darkness, but Caron was almost behind him, just a shadow in his peripheral vision. The rapier at his throat never wavered. No need to lie, except habit. "If you mean Lord Cherille, he did not come."

The blade slammed against his head. He winced, hoping his hair prevented it from slashing too deep. "Liar. He would not send you to France alone. You pretend I am a fool and it will be to your cost. Next time I take your ear, perhaps; talk sense."

"I am only a servant; he has loaned me to another for this trip."

"Still, you play with me," Caron's voice was rising and Henry felt the point of the rapier prick him. A trickle of blood ran down his neck. "These English dogs pretend they are your equals, even with a black savage. It is how they keep their heel on your neck."

"It is not an English heel I feel there."

"*Touché*. Perhaps I let a little more blood and you begin to speak more sensibly."

The street was empty except for the two of them. With a silent prayer that he had judged the length of the rapier correctly, Henry whirled and ducked toward the Frenchman. Unable to pick his point, he jammed the wood into the man's throat as the flexible steel whistled over his head. With his left hand, Henry seized Caron's right forearm and pulled, bringing it down across his knee. He felt the blade caress his cheek, but ignored it. Caron was choking from the blow to his throat and Henry's hand followed the arm to his wrist, twisting the sword from his grasp.

The Frenchman started to rise, but Henry's right knee connected with his chin, pushing his head back sharply. Then Henry heard running feet and a rattling sound. He moved quickly back into the shadows, leaving Caron and his sword lying in the street. As soon as he was sure he could not be seen, he recovered the packs and, taking left and right turns at random, hoped he was still heading toward the river.

Although the sound of the watch vanished behind him fairly quickly, it was some time later before Henry felt safe enough to stop, catch his breath, and get his bearings. He had been leading the Frenchman toward the Erdre, parallel, he believed, to the Loire. To find his way back, he must retrace his steps to find that part of the city near the Loire and across from the Island. He did not know which island, except that it was the easternmost, and they would have to cross the island and both *bras* of the river to reach the Sèvre Nantaise.

He set off, searching for the Loire. When he could smell the river, he turned east, watching for some landmark that might determine his course. Unfortunately, as he moved in that direction, he became aware of a brightening ahead of him. The sun was coming up. He was too late.

Sadler began to talk to the girl who, having finished crying, was looking about herself with interest. Discovering that Sadler spoke good French, she began telling him everything that came into her mind.

Leaving them to it, Jarrod went down the passage. It went on for some time but there were torches along the way. After almost two hundred yards, it opened out in a cliff face near the river. It was well hidden with over-hanging trees, and a clever iron door was made to look like rock on the other side. It was tightly bolted on the inside when he first reached it. A brief look around showed him he was only about one hundred yards down-river from a small landing with several boats tied to it. At least two looked suitable for his purpose, so he returned to the cavern.

When he got back, Sadler and the girl were still conversing, but at his entrance, she leapt up and kissed him, then stepped back and curtsied. She said something he was unable to follow, but the sentiment was clear, even had Sadler not translated.

"She thanks you and offers you anything she has, including her body, in gratitude for her rescue from these inhuman monsters. She has made me the same offer, and I have no doubt she intends to offer herself, even more fervently, to Henry, whom she sees as her chief deliverer. When he first appeared, and later with you, she thought you had been sent by Boucher to murder her. He had threatened to kill her many times and had made clear that he was expecting her replacement, which would render her unnecessary. She had resigned herself to death and hoped she would go to heaven, since she saw her time here," he waved his arm, "as Hell or Purgatory, after which suffering, God must certainly accept her among the blessed."

"Little do I know of the ways of God," Jarrod admitted, "but if He's got a spark of feeling in Him, I'd have to agree. However, since she will now be compelled to go on living, has she told you anything to the purpose? Her full name, perhaps, or the location of her home?""

Sadler frowned, "Of course. I'm not a fool. She calls herself Clara de Tiffauges, and her mother lives near that estate, about fifteen miles from Cholet."

"I apologize, Mr. Sadler; I was brusque and hope you will forgive me. Perhaps I am testy from lack of sleep. Have you checked the prisoners?"

"No," Sadler replied, wrinkling his nose. "Make yourself free of them, if you like."

Close inspection revealed that both men were dead. The butler must have succumbed to the repeated blows on the head he had suffered on the trip down the stairs. Boucher's windpipe had been crushed by the edge of the chamber pot. *Merde*, thought Jarrod, and decided justice had been served, at least in that case.

It was agreed that the bodies should be prepared for disposal in the river, so they carried the butler down the passage to the doorway. Returning, Sadler went upstairs looking for weights, and eventually came back with some stout sacks and twine, which he maintained could be filled with rocks. Jarrod accepted this compromise, and they carried Boucher down the passage. Jarrod was obliged to take the head, as Sadler steadfastly refused to go near that end of the corpse. The process was further complicated by Clara's insistence on walking along with them, spitting on Boucher and cursing as they went.

Jarrod gathered rocks which Sadler and Clara put into the two sacks until they had at least thirty pounds in each sack. They tied a stout rope around each corpse's waist and tied the sacks closed in preparation, but decided to leave the final operation until just before they traveled.

Leaving the bodies near the opening, they returned to the dungeon. Jarrod lay down on the cot in the second cell, telling Sadler to wake him in an hour.

Sadler fell asleep, with the girl in his arms, and it was almost dawn when Jarrod shook him. "It will be light in a few minutes," he said, "and Henry has not returned."

31

The sound of someone coming in woke him. His memory came back instantly, but more light came from the window he'd squeezed through just before dawn. He held very still. Whoever it was must be looking for something. He heard the clatter as things were pushed aside and replaced, footsteps coming nearer. He tensed.

Her eyes grew large and her mouth formed an O just before Henry's left hand covered it. His right arm closed around her back, pinning her arms and pulling her close to him. He spoke to her in French.

"If you scream, I'll have to hurt you," he said, as quietly and gently as he could. "I don't want to. Will you promise?" He could feel her heart pounding against his chest. She stared at him, and he tried to look reassuring. He felt her tension relax, slightly, and she slowly nodded, the movement restricted by his hand. He removed it, but continued to hold her close.

It was a large house, and he realized she must be a kitchen maid or servant of some kind. A very pretty one, too.

"*Qui êtes-vous?*" she whispered. He saw the merest trace of fear in her large green eyes, but mostly, he saw curiosity. He relaxed his arm so that he was still holding her but not so tightly. Her breathing, which had stopped when he seized her, began again. He realized that the swell of her breasts against his chest was distracting him and he relaxed his arm even more.

"My name is Henry," he answered. "A man attacked me on the street, and I hid from him in here. I mean you no harm. Please, will you let me hide here for a little while?"

She glanced around, as if reassuring herself that they were alone. Then, she raised her hand and gently touched the cut along his cheek. "*Africain?*" she whispered, withdrawing her hand as he winced.

"From the islands of America. I ran away from the English."

"*Esclave?*" She seemed fascinated. "You speak French."

"So do you," he whispered, and a small giggle escaped her. She put her hand over her mouth and looked around. Then her eyes returned to his. She placed a finger over his lips and began to wriggle her body. Henry took the chance, and released her. She did not back away. Her hand came up along his arm and caressed his bicep. She ran her finger along his undamaged cheek. Her lips were parted and her eyes held his.

Why not? he thought, and kissed her. Very gently, a question, not a demand. The eagerness of her response surprised him, as her tongue flicked out and stroked his own. He felt the rest of his body responding to her, and reluctantly broke the kiss and pushed her gently away.

She smiled and looked around again, then reached for a platter on the table next to them. It had two candlesticks and a small box on it. She removed these items, and took the platter under her arm. She turned back to him and placed her other hand against him, flexing the fingers slightly, feeling the hardness of his chest. She was smiling up at him and rose on her toes to kiss him again, gently, quickly, softly. Her finger moved across his lips again.

"*Tu es mon secret*," she whispered, "I will be back. You are hungry?" He nodded and watched as she walked back to the stairs. Her hips swung deliberately as she went.

The moment she closed the door behind her, Henry moved to a position from which he could make a dash if she came back with assistance. He was hidden behind the edge of an armoire, in deep shadow, near the base of the stairs. Through the door, he could hear her voice raised in that tone of indignation he thought of as particularly French.

"I had to look for it. It was covered by a mountain of useless things. It is dirty down there and there are spiders. Perhaps I will not go again."

He smiled. In fact, she did come again, about two hours later, with a plate of food, a mug of ale, a basin of water, and some cloth. She set them down on the table and put her finger to her lips. Then she ran the finger along his jawline, smiled, winked, and scurried back up the stairs. After he ate, he went back to sleep under the table.

It was dark when he woke. A quick look through the window was enough to tell him there was still traffic on the street, and he decided it would be best to remain where he was for another hour or two. He was still considering that decision when she returned once more, this time carrying a tray containing another plate, another mug of ale, and a candle. She placed them so the light would not show through the window and sat beside him, watching as he ate. She inspected the wound in his cheek, but seemed satisfied that he had cleaned it properly.

"How can I thank you?" he asked. "I believe you have saved my life."

She reached up and touched his ear, "Such a beautiful life, *Monsieur*. You must go on living, for me." She put her hand behind his head and drew his mouth down to hers. She placed her other hand flat against his chest. His arms encircled her, and they explored.

It had been a long time since Henry had a chance to give and receive pleasure this way. If, once or twice over the next hour, he might have wished that the circumstances were different or that the woman in his arms was someone else, they were fleeting instances that did not spoil the experience for him or, as far as he could tell, for her.

When they lay still in one another's arms, he kissed her pretty mouth again before he began to dress in preparation for departure. She was slower, knowing they had only this moment. But she too had other duties and stirred, wistfully caressing his chest, his arms, his shoulders as he dressed.

"Do you know of a wealthy man named Boucher?" he asked

She jumped back, her eyes were wide. "Victor Boucher?"

"*Oui.*"

Her eyes narrowed, "They say he is the devil. Sometimes, when I make a mistake, my mistress says she will sell me to him. They say he beats and sometimes kills his women. What are you to do with him?"

"I too, have heard these things, but I must see him. It may be that he will answer for his crimes. I cannot say, *ma chérie*, but we may hope. Perhaps I can convince him to change his ways, *n'est-ce pas*?

She reached out, squeezed his bicep, and smiled. "Be careful, *mon ami, mon amour*, he is a dangerous enemy." She gave him the directions he sought.

Before he left, she gave him a bundle of food. Not knowing in what circumstances the others might find themselves, or if he would even be able to catch them, he thanked her warmly. She returned his warmth with passion, smiling with tears in her eyes. He brushed them away with his fingers, kissed her again and left through the window.

Sadler was instantly wide awake, "We must be off. Hurry. We can leave the bodies in the river and steal a boat. We must go now." He was on the verge of panic.

"No. We wait for Henry. We need to prepare. I'll be back."

Jarrod raced up the stairs to the kitchen. Quickly, he located a sack, found the pantry, and, in the half-light, began looking for things to put in it. He had two loaves of bread, a pot of jam, two bottles of wine, some kind of potted meat, and half a roasted chicken when he heard voices. He had filled a small bucket with water, and he grabbed it as he went through the door to the basement. He set the things down, made sure the door was locked behind him, and descended as quietly as possible, his ears cocked for pursuit.

At the bottom of the stairs, Sadler and Clara were waiting, staring. He signaled silence and handed them the bucket and bundle. "We must make it last the day," he whispered. "If Henry is caught out, he may not be able to get back until tonight."

"How do we know he is not dead or in the hands of the watch?"

"We cannot know, but it does not matter; we will wait. We cannot leave now in any case; people are abroad. We must wait for darkness."

"Very well, since we are trapped, but tonight we must go. If he does not return, so be it." He glared at Jarrod and Jarrod glared back. Clara stared from one to the other, not understanding a word.

They made a meager breakfast of one loaf of bread and half the jam between them. Sadler took the first watch, hoping he might learn more than Jarrod could. He sat on the top step, his ear close to the door, and listened to the snatches of conversation that came through.

The servants were puzzled by the absence of the master and, more especially, his servant, but did not seem overly disturbed. Apparently, the man had strange habits and it was possible he was "below." Several times he heard "*en bas*" with a tone of warning. Occasionally footsteps would approach the cellar door, as if someone were listening, but no one tried to open the door. That the servants were afraid of Boucher was evident.

Over time, it became clear that the servants arrived every morning, made breakfast, and waited to serve it. If no one came, they ate what they wanted, cleared away, and made ready for the next meal. The process was repeated three times with the supper left on the table to be cleared away the next morning, if no one came.

"That's something," Jarrod said, when this was reported to him. "If we starve all day, we can expect a good meal tonight. All the servants leave at dark?"

Sadler said, "Earlier, if they can. The house has a bad reputation and the servants believe every word of it. Likely, it is all true, as poor Clara here can attest. They are in the habit of working through the day, but none of them are willing to stay in the house at night. They think it haunted by that animal's victims." He spat in the direction of the tunnel. "You can keep watch if you like, but they'll never come through that door." He jerked his head at the stairs.

It was a long day and Jarrod insisted on taking turns listening. Once, the girl became agitated, and Sadler took her down the tunnel to show her the bodies again. She kicked Boucher and spat on him. She was sobbing quietly when he brought her back to the cavern.

Finally, all the kitchen sounds ceased and, after about an hour of complete silence, Jarrod ventured out. He found a cold supper laid in the dining room and no other sign of life. He summoned the others and they made a much more pleasant meal than they had so far that day, although Henry's absence cast a pall.

Sadler said, "We must go tonight. It is foolishness to wait any longer. Someone will come looking for Boucher. He is wealthy and no hermit, despite his reputation. He is known to venture abroad regularly and even monsters have friends, or at least sycophants, if they're rich."

"We wait until two in the morning, when the city is asleep. Then, we steal out and drop the bodies in the river. If Henry has not come, you may steal a boat and take the girl home, by whatever means you can discover."

"You must come with us."

Jarrod gazed at him. "Henry is my friend. He would not leave me in danger; I can do no less for him."

"But your French is atrocious. Left to yourself, you will be clapped up in an instant and treated as an English spy. You sign your own death warrant if you stay."

Jarrod shrugged, "We must hope it does not turn out that way."

They were sitting at the table in the dining room, with only two candles. They had taken care that no light penetrated to the windows or the front of the house. In the quiet, the sound of the front door opening took them completely by surprise. Jarrod reacted instantly, blowing out the candles and moving next to the doorway closest to the hall. In the gloom, he saw Sadler approach and, touching his shoulder, directed him to the other side of the open door. Their blades were in their hands. They waited in the dark but heard nothing further.

"I'll go," Jarrod whispered.

Sadler's hand on his shoulder restrained him, "We should not be separated," he said in Jarrod's ear. Clara had risen and was quivering directly behind him.

Jarrod nodded and hissed, "But keep the girl back."

They checked the front door, which was closed. As quietly as possible they returned to the kitchen and went down to the basement. Sadler and Clara waited while Jarrod checked the tunnel. Satisfied it was empty of anyone living, he rejoined them, and they went back up. Silence reigned. Slowly, they went around the ground floor of the house. Nothing.

Undecided about the second floor, they were nearing the dining room when Jarrod pointed out the door they had left open. It was closed, and a thin wisp of light was visible beneath it. They listened but could hear nothing. Silently Jarrod motioned Sadler and Clara to the right of the door, then, his rapier in hand, he suddenly kicked the door open and leapt through. He landed next to the table, at the ready. Three candles were burning.

"You'd better have something to eat," Henry said, waving a loaf of bread at him. "You have a long night ahead."

32

The nights had been so pleasant, and the days so wearisome, that both Sarah and Maërlys had found themselves sleeping more in the coach than at the inns. At Rouen, it was clear that Guillame would have liked to linger, but after talking it over, they decided that evening comfort depended on movement, at least thirty-five miles each day.

The trip from Brionne to Gacé was particularly tiring. They had left almost at dawn and did not arrive until after dark. The next day's trip to Alençon was shorter, but Guillaume insisted that, because of the forest, an early start would be best. He was starting to wonder about his passengers.

"Surely the inn was not uncomfortable?" he asked, as the ladies dragged themselves into the coach a little before seven.

"Whatever do you mean?" Maërlys mumbled.

"You look as if you haven't slept a wink. Your maid looks only slightly more alert." His tone was respectful, with only a slight hint of the facetious.

"There were disturbances in the night. You know. Disturbances."

Guillaume's eyebrows looked ready to take flight.
"Yes, I see. Disturbances."

"Exactly. Disturbances." She climbed wearily
into the coach. Guillaume shook his head, jumped up
onto the box and cracked his whip. Inside the coach,
Sarah was already asleep and even the starting lurch
hardly bothered her.

They found dinner that day in a small town
called Marmouillé. Surprisingly it was quite good, and
the ladies were feeling much refreshed as they set off
on the way to Alençon. There was the usual—actually
Guillaume thought them quite unusual—afternoon
stop for pistol practice. Sarah and Maërlys would
vanish into trees at the side of the road, ostensibly for
reasons of hygiene. Guillaume would "rest the horses."
The sound of shots would issue from the trees at
intervals, and then the two women would return,
either laughing gaily or Maërlys intent as Sarah
explained some point or other.

That afternoon, after practice, they had been
riding for a long while in silence when Sarah broached
the subject. "In four more days, my dear one, we
should, God willing, be approaching Cholet. We must
be alert then, for it is possible that our enemies have
already made plans for us as well as your sister and
brother. Of course, if we are lucky, they do not care
about the children, and the attempt on our persons
aboard the *Doctor Syn* may have been an attempt to
avenge themselves for my previous behavior, but only
a fool relies on luck. In any case, it seems unlikely; it

was too well-planned, involved too many persons, and was too savage. It also seemed to me they thought to keep you alive, for what purpose I do not know. Do you? Have you secrets, *ma chérie*, which I should know?"

"I cannot tell. It is odd, the way that Mr. Caron treated me, as if I had something he wanted, and he was mad at me all the time for not sharing it. Always he was so angry, so mean. But he never asked me any specific questions, except about the children, and then mostly about where they lived. That first night, when he asked me so many questions and threatened to let that awful man rape me, he was particularly demanding that I be specific about their home. Who did they live with, where, how long, other relatives, everything. It was so odd for an Englishman to ask such questions."

Suddenly she sat up, her eyes wide, "He was not English; he was French! The children! He could be here now. Oh, what can we do? We must go faster. I have wasted so much time. *Mes pauvre petits.*"

"Peace, darling. We are going as fast as we can. Do you imagine I did not think of this? But if we travel by coach, by stages like the mail, we will be off our path and around and back. It will take just as long and we will arrive exhausted. I wish we could go faster, but we have already encountered delays not of our making. We hope there may be no more, but it is a long journey and much may occur. We do our best and when we arrive, if fighting is needed, we must be prepared to fight like tigers. Where I come from, there are tigers. We must be as like them as we can."

Maërlys looked down, "Do you think we are having too good a time, at night, I mean? Will it keep us from fighting as we may need to do?"

Sarah reached out and lifted the younger woman's chin with two fingers, looking directly into her eyes. "It is true, my love, that we are having a wonderful time, but it will stop whenever you say. It is also true that we are so tired in the morning that I believe Guillaume suspects we do more than sleep at night. But it is difficult for men to imagine the things we do together, so he will probably not reach any dangerous conclusions."

She brought Maërlys face closer and kissed her gently on the lips. When Maërlys attempted to deepen the kiss, she drew back.

"These four days, and the three already gone, may be all the time we have," she went on, "and I treasure it. Once we have collected the children, it will be hard, if not impossible, for us to find time alone. I say this not to threaten or cajole, but merely to insure you have all the facts in your head. I love you, I enjoy you, and will always remember our time, but it approaches its end. And it will, in all probability, be the end. Life holds many wonderful adventures for us. We must not miss them by holding too tightly to the ones we have already had. *Me comprends-tu, mon coeur?*

Maërlys looked confused, *"C'est oui ou non?*

"Both, my love. Each night we must decide again, but let us not decide lightly or thoughtlessly. We will discuss it further—"

The coach drew up suddenly and both women were thrown forward. Instantly, Sarah was at the window, "*Guillaume, que se passe-t-il?*" But even as she asked, looking out the window, she saw the tree blocking the road. Looking around, she saw they had entered the forest and dense trees were at every hand.

"A tree across the road," came from the box.

She was already reaching down for the pistols she kept loaded, checking the priming, and handing one to Maërlys. "Get down low," she hissed, drawing her sword with her left hand. "Do you see anything?" she called to Guillaume.

There was the sound of a shot, not close, probably from the trees, and a cry from Guillaume. They heard him tumble from the box, the clatter of his musket as it hit the ground. Two men came out of the trees on Sarah's side. Maërlys watched as a third came into view on the other.

"You're sure it was him?" Jarrod asked.

"Could I make such a mistake?" Henry paused. "I don't think he knew about *madame*. It was sometime later he picked me up. I'm certain I wasn't followed from her house."

"You should have killed him," Jarrod said.

"Well for you to talk; you know how you are. I remember that soldier in Port-au-Prince...."

"But we knew him," Jarrod said. "He had a family."

"Two families, if I remember correctly. Might have been three."

"My point exactly. All those mouths to feed. How could I kill him in cold blood?"

"It would have saved us a lot of trouble later, and he died anyway."

"In the heat of action. A different thing entirely."

Henry sighed, "I know. We are neither of us that sort. If we become the same as our enemies, then we become the enemy. Though it may be that in his case it would have been a kindness. Still, there was no time for consideration, and I cannot regret that I am not yet so lost."

They were speaking quietly though they were alone. They had left Sadler to "mind the baby," as Jarrod put it, and were moving along the river. It was approaching three in the morning. The conversation took their minds from the disposal task they had set for themselves. They had left the door to the tunnel open, the bodies ready. A boat was nearby and a small bag of gold had been tied to the end of the rope which previously moored it, a little way upriver. When the owner came in the morning, it would be as if his boat had melted into gold. A miracle.

"He spoke English to you?" Jarrod said.

"He insisted; said I was unworthy of the French tongue, and called my accent barbarous. Heavy bastard," Henry complained, as they heaved the body of the servant into the boat.

"Not so heavy as to call for such language," Jarrod said primly. "I blame the extra rocks. No doubt your command of French is barbarous, Henry, uncouth native that you are. I'd know better if I could get my tongue around the words at all."

"We are both mere foreigners, are we not? There," Henry said, as Boucher's body joined the other, "let's get them under."

They stepped into the boat and Jarrod rowed as Henry pushed against the pole. As soon as the pole failed to touch bottom, they rolled the two corpses overboard, one after another, gently so as not to splash too loudly. The rocks took them straight down. Henry waited, then felt with the pole. Encountering no resistance, he pulled it in and helped Jarrod at the oars.

"We will surely see him again at Cholet. We must be prepared and get there before him, if we can."

"Do you think he will search for us or try to beat us there?" Henry asked.

"He will certainly not waste time searching Nantes. He may already be on his way; however, he must search for the destination while we have a definite direction. We may have a chance. Do you agree?"

"I do."

"If we see him again, I fear we can show no mercy. Else we may never return to London."

"We may never return, regardless."

"You've a gloomy soul, Henry. Legacy of slavery, I make no doubt. Come on, let's get the passengers loaded. And not a word of any of this to Sadler."

"He worries you?"

"Not so much as he does you, I'll wager, but caution is usually a virtue. Tell him you ran into a footpad, to explain your cheek and the delay. By the by, how did you spend the day?"

"In bed."

"You have nothing more to say than that?" Jarrod was trying to frown while his eyebrows were rising.

"Nothing."

"You brought food with you. Was the food in the bed, also?"

"Yes."

"This bed, it was warm, was it?"

"Warm enough."

Jarrod shook his head. "I think you are not as gloomy as you pretend, old friend. I must attend you more closely. I believe I miss a great deal."

The others were waiting in the tunnel with the packs, now freshly re-provisioned. It was only a little after four when they found themselves in the Bras de Pirmil, and by dawn, they were rounding the bend into the Sèvre Nantaise.

Taking turns at the oars, they set out for
Tiffauges. In their guise of peasants and laborers they
could go no faster on foot and would draw less
attention on the water. The first day they found that,
other than occasional hails from boats headed
downriver, they were usually ignored. Jarrod and
Henry kept their heads down and let Sadler do the
talking when necessary.

Several times, Clara proved herself invaluable,
posing as Sadler's wife. The story that they were on
their way back to her parents' home, with two laborers
they had found in Nantes, made them as innocuous as
possible. She implied they were newlyweds—she was
apparently able to blush at will—and they were
hurried on their way with bawdy suggestions and good
wishes.

There was a bad moment the first night when a
stranger wandered into camp. He made no attempt at
concealment, so they were speaking only French as he
drew near. Jarrod was silent. Henry had slipped into
the shadows.

"I saw your fire," he said in French.

Sadler responded in the same language. "You
are a traveler?"

"*Oui.* I live near Clisson. I had hoped to get home
tonight, but I am tired. May I rest by your fire for an
hour or two?"

Sadler's eyes found Jarrod's, who nodded. "Why
should you not? Are you hungry?" Sadler asked.

The man shrugged and Clara handed him a bit of bread and the remains of the potted meat. He thanked her, and responded by producing a bottle of wine from his pack. He pulled the cork with his knife, took a sip, and passed the bottle to Sadler. Jarrod watched closely, but could see no deception. He took a small sip when the bottle came to him, then passed it to Clara. It tasted all right, though not particularly good. He excused himself, and walked into the bushes. He found Henry under a tree a little way from the camp.

"Anything?" he whispered.

Henry shrugged. "Never seen him. Alone, as far as I can tell," he whispered back.

"I'll relieve you, but be patient, and watch him until then. All right?"

Henry nodded, and leaned against the tree.

When Jarrod awoke, the stranger was gone. "Well?" he asked.

"He got up about an hour ago, packed his things and set off."

"Toward Clisson? Alone?"

"Yes and yes."

"Let us be gone in case he returns. Can you sleep in the boat?"

"At this moment, I could sleep anywhere."

"Wake the others. I'll pack."

33

"Wait Maërlys, until he puts his head in the window, then fire. Just as you did on the boat," Sarah whispered.

"Do not worry, Sarah, I will protect you," Maërlys answered, and Sarah turned back to her own window, both to check on the enemy and hide her smile.

She was considering their position. If they could lure both men to the windows, they may be able to dispose of two at once. Then quickly out the other side and try to catch the third man when he came to investigate. If she could get Guillaume's musket and if it was still loaded, they might have a chance to settle the whole thing. If the musket was not available, she might be able to hide her sword behind her until she could get close. If there are no more of them, she thought, if, if, if.

Then there was a shout and once again a musket roared. It was the forward man on her side, and he fired at something behind the coach. An answering shot came from that direction, and the man with the musket threw up his hands and fell on his back. His companion, an unusually large man, brandished his sword, ran to his fellow's side, and began to drag him back into the trees. Sarah turned to Maërlys.

On that side of the coach, there was a shot from the man who had been approaching. Another shot rang out from behind the coach, and he turned and began to run toward the trees. The carriage lurched slightly, as the horses reacted to the shots. A man raced by their window in pursuit, waving a sword. He was shouting in French, "Hold there, stand and fight, you dogs. *Lâches.*" He vanished into the trees after the brigands.

Sarah carefully opened the door on her side. There was no sign of anyone. Motioning to Maërlys to remain where she was, she climbed down, keeping her pistol ready, her sword now in the scabbard behind her back. Slowly she walked around the back of the carriage, then to Maërlys' side until she reached Guillaume, lying in the grass at the edge of the road, his musket nearby. She picked up the musket and checked the load. It was intact, but no longer tight. She pulled the ramrod, drove it into the barrel, then replaced it. Only then did she turn to Guillaume.

He was watching her, "I was worrying, *Ma'amselle.* I see I needn't."

Holding the musket by the barrel, with the stock on the ground, she knelt beside him and placed her other hand on his brow. She smiled down at him but her face was full of concern.

"You understand?"

"*Oui*. It would do no good to worry about me while they overwhelm us. Are they gone?"

She looked around, "I doubt it. How are you?"

"Took me near the shoulder and I've lost some blood, but if you can bind it up I may do."

She turned to the carriage door and called, "Maërlys."

The younger woman was beside her in an instant, "*Que se passe-t-il?*"

"We must bind his arm, stop the blood."

Without hesitating, Maërlys reached down, pulled up her dress and tore a strip from her chemise. Guillaume's eyes went wide and he looked away. Sarah had laid the musket gently aside and was examining the wound. The ball had torn a large piece of flesh from the muscle of the upper arm, and appeared to be still lodged in the bicep.

"I can't take it out now. We wrap it here," she pointed to a spot just above the wound, "and will try to stop the bleeding." She looked at Maërlys and held up two fingers, "Get me a strong but small stick, can you?"

She took the strip of cloth and began to wrap it while Maërlys searched the ground around a tree, returning quickly with two small pieces of wood. Selecting one, Sarah made the tourniquet and twisted it tight, ignoring Guillaume's grimace. Maërlys tore another strip of cloth, which Sarah bound over the wound.

"We must get him into the coach," she said, glancing at the horses, which were standing quietly, waiting. "Do you think you can walk?" she asked Guillaume.

"Sorry, *Ma'amselle*, I'm afraid I did an injury to my leg, caught it wrong when I fell."

She caressed his forehead with her hand, "It is not your fault. You have done well and are very brave. We will get you into the coach, but there may be some pain. I am sorry."

They were attempting to lift his shoulders as gently as possible when a man appeared from the woods. Sarah left Guillaume to Maërlys and picked up the musket, raising it to her shoulder and aiming it at the intruder. The man immediately threw up his hands, one of which held a sword. A pistol was visible in his belt.

"*Pardon, Mademoiselle*, I was unable to catch them. I thought I killed one, but they took his body as well."

"*Qui es-tu?*" Sarah spat. The man started to lower his arms, and she gestured with the musket. He raised them again. He was a slender man of about medium height with dark hair, a strong attractive face, and a small mustache.

"Jules Andre. I was walking this way when I heard the shot. I went after the villains, but they were too fast for me. *Je suis désolé.*"

"Where are you going?"

"Alençon."

"Where did you stay last night?"

"Sees."

"Lay your weapons on the ground and come help move Guillaume into the coach."

Andre did as he was asked, first returning his sword to its sheath then removing the sheath from his belt and placing it, alongside his pistol, on the ground. As he did, Sarah turned to Maërlys, though she held the musket steady on the stranger.

"Hide the pistols," she whispered, and Maërlys slipped up into the coach.

Andre strode past Sarah, who stepped aside, but kept the musket pointed toward him, and bent over the coachman.

"He will need a doctor, and it will be difficult to move him without pain."

"Do the best you can. My mistress will help, will you not, *Mademoiselle*?"

Caught by surprise, Maërlys was slow to answer but finally said, "*Bien sûr.*"

Together, Maërlys and Jules managed to get Guillaume into the coach, resting with his injured leg out on the squab, his back against the side of the coach. The bleeding had stopped but the process of moving proved too much, and he was unconscious by the time they had him settled. Leaving him with Maërlys, Jules descended again to the ground beside Sarah.

"What will we do with you now, *Monsieur*?" she asked.

He smiled at her, "I do not expect gratitude, since I was unable to catch even one to punish as they deserved, but I would be pleased if you did not shoot me."

"You can drive?"

"*Oui*."

"Would you care to drive us to Alençon?"

He shrugged, "It sounds better than walking, to me."

"Very well. See to the horses. Do not mount the box until I tell you to. I must consult with my mistress." She walked over to where he had left his weapons and picked them up.

"*Mademoiselle*," he said as she returned, "I am sorry to ask favors, but I threw my pack aside when I ran after those brigands. May I go back to retrieve it before we journey on?"

"Where?"

"Just around that bend in the road."

"Go ahead. I will be watching as you return."

"I hope so," he smiled, and set off in the direction from which he had come.

Sarah turned to the coach window and handed the newcomer's weapons in to Maërlys, "I believe we should drive off without him."

"Oh," answered Maërlys, "but he has been so kind. He did chase away those highwaymen. Surely we can allow him to drive us to Alençon. In any case, he will find us there when he arrives and it will be most embarrassing to have left him standing in the road after all his effort to catch them."

"Yes, I suppose we must endure it."

"Perhaps it will not be such a trial. He is very handsome, is he not?"

Sarah laughed, "Ah, my love, what will I do with you? Yes, I suppose he is, but you must not fall too hard. His appearance at just that moment bothers me. I do not like coincidences."

"You are a hard, suspicious old woman, and do not wish me to have any fun."

Sarah laughed again, "Perhaps, my love, perhaps. We shall see. But remember, you are my mistress. You must order me about, and, when thwarted, say *La, je dois avoir une meilleure femme de chambre.*"

"Must I indeed say *La*?"

"Perhaps not. You can say *Zut alors*, but you must not say *merde*. Only peasants say *merde*, and peasants do not have abigails."

When Andre returned, Sarah pointed her weapon at him again, "Empty the pack for me, if you do not mind."

"You are very suspicious."

"My mistress says so, also, but we are two women alone now, and we must be cautious. If you are a gentleman, you will understand."

"I try to be a gentleman and I do understand." He upended the sack and let its contents fall out upon the ground. Warning him back with the musket, Sarah approached and gently sorted the things with her foot. They included a small knife and a razor, which she confiscated. A copy of Rousseau, soap, brush, a small metal bowl and cup, and some clothing, she left alone.

He cocked his head and smiled at her, "Satisfied?"

"*Oui. Pardon, Monsieur,* but I am responsible for my mistress, now that Guillaume is hurt; I hope you will forgive me. We will return your things when we reach Alençon. Let us go now." She curtsied, and climbed back into the carriage.

Andre gathered his belongings, tossed the bag onto the box, and walked over to the tree blocking the road. Setting his coat aside, he went to work.

"You see, *Monsieur,* there was their fire. They were here."

Caron put his hand over the coals, "They have been gone for some time."

"It takes time. I must walk back to Clisson. I must find you, you must be awakened, and you must dress. We return as quickly as possible."

"How long?"

The man shrugged. "It is almost seven hours since I left."

Caron scattered the coals with his foot, "They must have left shortly after you did. You gave yourself away."

"*Non, Monsieur*, there was no trace of suspicion."

"How many?"

Pardon?"

"How many were there, you fool?"

"*Trois. Deux hommes, et la femme.*"

"*Trois? Femme?* Idiot. Describe them."

"They were all dressed as peasants, but did not carry themselves so...," he hesitated and cocked his head, thinking. "Except the woman. She, I think, was most definitely peasant and very attached to one of the men." He hesitated again, "Or perhaps both."

Caron's eyebrows went up for a moment, then he frowned. "*L'homme noir?*"

His companion was puzzled, "I saw no black man."

Caron cursed, "They must be the wrong ones. Did you hear any names?"

"The girl called her companion *Lin-cone.*"

"Lin-cone? Bah, the wrong...." He thought about it. "It is not French," he mused. "Did they speak French?"

"*Oui.* The girl and Lin-cone. The other one never said anything, except once, he muttered *pardon* when he went to make water."

Caron, who had begun pacing, whipped his head around, "He said nothing else?"

"Not that I heard."

"When he left the fire, was he gone long?"

Another shrug.

Caron began muttering to himself, "*Il n'est pas possible*. Lin-cone? Lin-cone?" He stopped pacing and cast his mind back over the people in London. "Lincoln? Could it be Sadler? But it was *le noir*, I had him in my hands. But they are not fools. Naturally he would be the one to hide, but *la femme*? Who could she be? A peasant?" He dismissed it with a wave, "We have wasted enough time. I must go. They had a boat?"

"*Oui.*"

"Here is your pay. I would give more were you not such an *imbécile*."

"*Monsieur* will take me back to Clisson?"

"You have legs. It is not on my way." He hurried to his carriage then turned around, "On second thought, I may have need of you. Come with me and I will pay you a gold napoleon."

The man held up his hand, "*Deux.*"

Caron stared at him for a moment, but the man stared back, "Oh, very well, two gold napoleons. Get in the carriage."

34

It was early in the afternoon when Henry pointed it out to Jarrod. "There, you see?" The coach was some distance away, almost a quarter of a mile across the marsh, but clearly recognizable as such. The road followed the river's course, rarely closer than this, often farther away.

"A coach, stopped on the road," Jarrod shrugged.

"Watch."

They were moving well, Sadler and Henry at the oars, Clara in the bow watching the river. They were slightly behind the coach's position but rapidly pulling even with it. Henry noted the flash again.

"Did you see?" he asked.

"What do you make of it?"

"Could be a musket or sword, even a fancy drinking cup of some sort, but I think a glass."

"Caron?"

"I would ask for odds, but I'd take the bet all the same."

"Do you see it, Lincoln?"

"I did that time, but couldn't say what it was. It could even be some appointment on the coach that catches the light when the horses shift."

"Any of those things would be a coincidence," Henry said. "A stopped coach, a flash of light, that we happen to be fugitives, that someone is looking for us—"

Jarrod broke in, "Well, we can do nothing but pull for the moment. Is it my turn, Lincoln?"

They kept watch after that but did not see any coach stopped on the road again. Several went by along the road, however, so when they reached Tiffauges, Henry insisted that they continue to row for at least another two miles. Since the sun was almost down by then, he was only able to convince them to go one more mile. Sadler complained even that was unnecessary.

As soon as it got to be full dark they turned the boat around and moved to shallower water to catch the current. Using the pole to keep off the banks and the oars to keep themselves in the current, they were soon back at their intended landing. Clara knew the country well and pointed out a high spot in the marsh and a path to her home. She assured them they would be welcome and her parents would help them re-provision for the remainder of their journey.

It took them about an hour to reach the house, which sat alone at the edge of a field of ripening wheat. She did not knock; she opened the door and went inside, while they sat on the ground a short distance away. She left the door open and they heard her say, *"Maman? Papa?"* A lamp was lit and light poured from the door, along with the sounds of surprised greetings, questions and sobbing. Then the door was closed behind her.

It was several minutes before the door opened again, and a man came out, carrying a lantern. Clara's father addressed them in rapid French, which Sadler translated, "He thanks us for returning his daughter. Although he has not yet grasped all the circumstances, he has collected that the situation as a housemaid she was promised, and for which they took money from the agent, turned out to be something quite different. I believe the full horror of it has not penetrated, or perhaps Clara has left out details to spare their feelings, but he welcomes us and invites us to come inside. His wife is preparing a supper for us, although they ate earlier."

As they ate, both parents expressed concern that their daughter, whom they'd thought well situated in Nantes, had run away. They had to be reassured that she had not stolen anything that did not belong to her and that the gold she had brought was hers in compensation for her sufferings."

"But so much money," the woman said, "were her sufferings indeed so immense? She has provided no details. Will no one come to seek her?"

Sadler explained, "Indeed, *Madame*, she has been only partially compensated for what she has undergone. Perhaps in time, she may tell you more of it, but it might be best to let it lie, to fade in her mind."

He continued, "She is a good girl and has clearly been raised by honest, God-fearing parents. You should save the money against need and not show it around, lest you attract thieves, *n'est-ce pas*? No one should follow her."

At this, Henry whispered in Sadler's ear, and he resumed, "It is possible that someone may ask about us. It would be well if you explain that we are strangers, that we found your daughter along the road, gave her protection to her home, and that she knows nothing more of us. We are a gentleman and two laborers, traveling to Cholet. My name is Loïc Salle. You need give no more answer than that and, indeed, it is only the truth." He turned to the girl. "Is that not so, Clara?"

The girl looked at him blankly for a moment, before saying "*Oui*," and nodding her head emphatically.

Her parents pressed them to take their bedroom, which consisted of an alcove separated by a curtain from the rest of the cottage. Due to the impossibility of the three of them squeezing into the couple's narrow bed, they courteously refused, and once again slept outdoors.

They were off at first light and approached Cholet a little after noon. None of them being familiar with the country, it was a bit of a surprise to come to a crossroads with a signpost pointing north to LeMay-sur-Èvre and indicating directions to Cholet, Tiffauges, whence they had just come, and the main road to Nantes.

"Could we get there today?" Henry asked.

Jarrod answered, "I expect it would reduce the distance by perhaps five miles, but we would be lucky to arrive much before evening. We would not be able to approach our goal except in broad daylight."

"I am against it," said Sadler, "we should go into Cholet, restore our packs, and seek transportation for leaving, if we expect to take these children."

Jarrod said, "In fact, we cannot leave until we find Maërlys. However, we do not know if she and her companion—".

"Siti, Zara, Daeng," Sadler hissed.

"Yes, yes, no offense meant, old fellow. I expect we are ahead of them, in spite of lost time at Nantes, but it would never do to be late. Then we would have to try and chase them, or worse, find them mistreated by our enemies. Of course, neither do we know what Caron may be planning; we must keep our eyes open for him."

"A coach is coming; let us step to the side of the road," Henry said. They moved to the grassy verge, and were keeping their heads low, as befitted peasants when a coach approached. As it drew abreast, Jarrod was startled by the face in the window staring directly at him. It was Caron. The face twitched, and both eyes blinked, then it was gone, the coach rattling past, following the road to LeMay-sur-Èvre.

"Good God, he looked straight at me," Jarrod said.

"And he certainly knows me well," Henry added.

"Who was it?" Sadler asked.

"Felix Caron, from whom you've pledged to defend your mistress."

"Was there anyone in the coach with him?"

"I couldn't see," Jarrod said. "You, Henry?"

"I couldn't see either, but given the sturdy look of that coachman, and the likelihood of a brace of loaded pistols to hand, I think he'll attack us if he can. We should make ourselves invisible and see what happens."

"Excellent idea," Jarrod said, "follow me." He led them hurriedly down the road to Cholet for a short distance, then turned right across a small meadow into some trees, which extended back toward the crossroad. They had barely hidden themselves when Henry pointed out the coach, returning. They watched as it turned down the road to Tiffauges, stopped, and disgorged its occupant.

Caron looked around. At that moment, no traffic was visible in any direction. He scanned the scenery all around, then ran back, got in the carriage and started down the road toward Cholet.

"I expect we should go to LeMay-sur-Èvre, after all," said Sadler.

"I believe we should wait here a bit, rather than draw hasty conclusions," Henry said. "At the moment, he does not know our location, although we do know his, at least roughly."

"I always agree with Henry," Jarrod said.

"Always is a very long time indeed," said Henry.

"Well, usually. And when I don't, I usually regret it."

They continued to wait. The carriage was back in less than half an hour. This time it took the road they had just walked, toward Tiffauges.

As it rattled away, Henry stepped out of their cover. "They can probably get to Tiffauges before the horses die of exhaustion," he said. I wish they were going anywhere else." He looked at the sun. "We cannot expect to get to LeMay-sur-Èvre today. Let us go into Cholet, find an inn, have a good dinner and a decent bed for the night, and set off in the morning. Perhaps inquiries may be made at the inn and we can proceed to LeMay-sur-Èvre in better style."

Sarah was lying in bed, thinking about Jules Andre. She could not make up her mind. He had been with them for two days now and she could find no fault with his behavior or manners. His story that he was on his way to Poitiers to settle the estate of his father was plausible, and she had no means at hand to disprove it. When he had told them, Maërlys had eagerly chimed in that their own destination was Cholet, which was not too far off his road. It was impossible to disagree that the speed of their coach would easily make up for any distance he might lose by the route through Angers.

Of course, in private Maërlys was quick to point out that the man was both handsome and charming, but the fact that he was not a nobleman seemed to be the main point in his favor. Comparing him to Lord Cherille had become something of a hobby with her. That was a great deal of the reason Sarah was lying in bed, enjoying the solitude.

For each of the last three nights, Maërlys had come to bed full of things that must be said about the delightful *monsieur* Andre. Each night, it had taken longer and longer for her to settle down and finally fall into Sarah's arms to make love and drift into sleep.

This morning the girl had bounced out of bed before Sarah even awoke, a thing new in their experience. Sarah had heard her shut the door, though Maërlys had tried to keep quiet. Instead of saying anything, she had determined to make the most of it; let Maërlys eat her breakfast with Jules. Sarah would enjoy the solitude and grab a quick bite of something as she went out the door. It was still another hour before they would leave.

She had heard steps on the stair and had expected the man to knock on the door, as he had done each of the previous days, to advise that the coach would be ready in an hour. The steps had retreated, however, and she supposed there must be some delay. She would relish this moment of peace. If only she could keep her thoughts from the man; he was just a little too perfect, a little too easy. Had she become a suspicious old woman? Oh well, never mind. If she could not enjoy the time, she may as well dress and join them.

Sarah came downstairs to find the dining room deserted. The landlord was half asleep at the bar. Puzzled, she looked into the yard. The coach was gone.

The landlord said, "Your lady went out to look at the horses with your driver, then I heard the coach leave the yard."

"How long ago?"

The man shrugged. "Ten minutes?"

"Did you see which road?"

He pointed west, "*Oui.*"

Sarah was on the stairs before he could turn around. "I need a horse, a fast horse. Have it here when I come back down. You will be well paid." She stopped and looked down at his astonished face. "Do not fail me," she hissed, "or you will be rewarded in a less pleasant way. Quickly!"

In ten minutes she was back, dressed as a man. Her hair was bound up under an old tricorn. Her smallclothes also had a military look, and there were bulges in the coat indicating the presence of weapons.

"Where is my horse?" she demanded.

"The groom is bringing it, *M-Ma'amselle,*" croaked the paralyzed landlord.

She laid a small bag of gold on the bar, "Now, let me see." She rushed to the door, to find the groom bringing two horses.

"I could not decide, sir," he said cheerily. "Which one do you like? He said it was for a lady so I put the sidesaddle on this one, but if you prefer—"

He stopped, astonished, as he realized that the person in front of him was no gentleman. Sarah grabbed the bridle of the unsaddled horse from him, placed her large hands on the animal's back, and vaulted up, a standing jump he was sure no man he'd ever seen could accomplish.

"But sir, I mean, *Ma'am*...," he stopped speaking and stood there with his mouth open as he realized he was talking to the wind.

35

"It was your suggestion we return to Tiffauges. I saw them go past this place. How could they be here?"

Caron answered, "Something has alerted them, *Monsieur*. They could have easily gone past, then let the current bring them back down after dark. When we saw them near Cholet, they came from the west. If they had passed Tiffauges they would have come from the south. The girl is no longer with them. Tiffauges?"

They were walking along the riverbank, Caron occasionally slashing at the reeds with his rapier. "I rely on you to spot the girl if she is here. If you wish to earn that napoleon—"

"*Deux*," his companion interrupted.

"None, unless we find the girl," Caron snarled.

"Eh, look *Monsieur*, a boat." They hurried to the vessel, pulled up into the reeds. "You see?" the man said proudly.

"Oui. Is it theirs?"

"Certainly it looks like theirs and has not been here more than a day or so. Look at the mud, the reeds." He looked around, then pointed. "See. Several people have walked up from here, not so long ago. They have left a path."

Together, the two men followed the track until it ran into a field of wheat. The path continued into the wheat, heading toward a cottage on the far side. Caron stopped and considered their position. To the left was a line of trees, dividing the field they were in from the next field. Their carriage was along the road to the west, out of sight on the other side of those trees.

"Go into the trees, just there, and wait. If you see me coming back with the girl, pretend you are hurt and lie down. I will bring her, and you will tell me if she is the one. *Tres bien?*

His companion nodded, "*Oui,*" and hurried off toward the trees. Caron continued to the house and knocked loudly on the door.

"*Au secours!*" he shouted. "I need help."

The door was opened by a young woman, no more than a girl, and Caron was instantly sure. This was the one he had seen through his glass, the one who had been in the boat with Cherille and his slave.

He spoke quickly, "*S'il vous plaît, Ma'amselle,* my friend has hurt himself. I cannot help him. Will you come? Please hurry, I fear he will die." He had seized her wrist and was pulling her through the door.

She looked around, but her parents were not there. She tried to pull back, but Caron's grip was strong, and he was moving quickly. Off-balance, she had to run along with him to keep from dislocating her wrist. "*S'il te plaît, Monsieur, s'il te plaît,*" she cried, as she tried desperately to keep from falling.

As they passed into the trees they became invisible to the house and there was the other man, lying on the ground. Caron thrust the girl toward him, and she stumbled to the ground at his side. Then she saw his face.

"*Alors*, it is the man who was at our camp," she said, and started to rise.

The man reached up and pulled her back down. "It is her," he said, clapping his hand over her mouth. Caron reached down and pulled Clara's hands behind her back, binding them tightly with a cord from his pocket. Clara bit the man's hand, and he jerked it back. She opened her mouth to scream but found Caron's handkerchief thrust into it. Another cord passed around her head secured the gag.

The man cursed, still lying on the ground, holding his hand. "*Putain*. She bit me." Then he laughed, "I am wounded after all. You will have to pay me three napoleons, now."

"That is no wound," said Caron. "What about the other?" He was holding Clara down, using only his left hand on her shoulder, forcing her toward the ground.

"What other?"

"Someone has run you through," Caron answered, thrusting his rapier directly into the man's breast.

With Henry driving the coach, it took only about an hour to reach LeMay-sur-Èvre. By mid-morning, they had drawn up in front of the house they were seeking. Henry waited on the box as Jarrod and Sadler went in.

The door was opened by an elderly lady and, behind her, a youth on the edge of manhood. He looked about twelve but had an air that made him seem older, and his resemblance to Maërlys was striking. So much so that Jarrod had to drag his sight away from the blue-grey eyes, the dark brown hair.

"*Pardon, Madame,*" Sadler said. "We have journeyed a long way in search of two children, whom we believe may be in some danger. You are Mme Rivet? May we come in and talk to you?"

The woman frowned but held the door open for them and they passed inside. Neither a wealthy home nor the humble cottage of a peasant, this house was free-standing and had several rooms, all on one floor. They were led to a sort of parlor where, seated on the floor, a young girl was looking through the pages of a book.

"Who has sent you here?" the woman asked, directing them to a table with four chairs around it.

Jarrod spoke up, "Maërlys de Brissy." At the name, the boy moved forward until he was standing next to Mme Rivet, the girl jumped up and took a place at the woman's other side. *Madame*'s arms moved immediately to surround them. All three locked their eyes on Jarrod.

"You have proof of this?"

"*Je suis desole, Madame.* I have perhaps spoken too freely." He turned to Sadler, and said in English, "Explain it, will you Lincoln? I haven't the language."

"My friend means that we have no token from *Mademoiselle de Brissy*, nor even any real authorization to be here. We know that *mademoiselle* is on her way here, with a friend, and we know that they are both in danger, as are these children. Learning these things, we have come to be of service should this danger develop before *mademoiselle* can reclaim her sister and brother," he nodded at the children, "and bring them to safety in England. Have you then no word of Maërlys?"

The woman shook her head. "*Non, Monsieur.* We did not know she was in France. Do you think these children are in danger from the regime? The terror has long passed, and it has been many years since their parents were taken. They are but children, yet. What can cause danger for them?"

"They are young, yes, but Reynard will soon be old enough to enter the army, and you must know how hungrily Napoleon seeks fodder for his cannons."

At this, the boy spoke up, "I am not afraid; I will fight for France. This is an English trick of some kind, Aunt Firoze."

At this, Jarrod smiled, and said in his halting French, "Well spoken, lad. As an Englishman, I respect brave Frenchman like yourself. It would be an awful thing to have to meet you on the battlefield, not only because it would take all my strength to meet your fierce and proper loyalty to your country, but also because it would be a shame for one of us to have to kill the other. I would not like to kill you and, I hope, you may come to wish you do not have to kill me either."

He switched back to English. "Tell him, Lincoln, that we would not keep him in England against his will and, when he is grown, he may return to fight for France, as any man should fight for his country. We only wish that he may not be forced into the army before his time and that he may go into battle with his eyes open, sure of his country and his cause."

Lincoln translated this, and the boy seemed to relax. The girl tugged at Jarrod's sleeve. "Do you know my sister?" she asked.

The girl resembled Maërlys in the color of her eyes and the extraordinary beauty of her face. Her hair, though, was fair, and her features altogether different from those of her sister, beautiful in a less delicate, more powerful way. Were it not for her fair hair and skin, Jarrod would have said she almost resembled a tiny Sarah Dane.

"I do," he responded.

"Is she beautiful?"

"*Oui. Presque aussi belle que toi.*"

The child smiled, and Jarrod felt his breath catch in his throat.

Sadler went on, "There is a question of greed, *Madame*. Some French officials have an idea that there is a treasure near here, to which the children have the key. Or at least, if not literally the key, certainly the direction. Are you aware of their relationship to the family of Admiral Leissègues?"

"*Mais non.*"

"It is as well. The less you know of these things, the safer you may be. We have come a great distance and we believe Maërlys and her companion are on their way here. It is our intention, with your permission, to await them here, and to keep you and the children safe, as far as it may be in our power, until they come. When they arrive, we hope to help them remove the children to safety in England, until they are of age and can be free to determine their own futures."

"How may I know you are in earnest? Why should I trust you?"

"We are only waiting for Maërlys and her companion. When they arrive, you may discuss everything with Maërlys and we will do as she dictates. Is that satisfactory?"

The woman looked at them, first one, then the other. When she spoke, she addressed herself to Jarrod.

"What is your relationship to Maërlys de Brissy?"

Jarrod looked her in the eyes, "If she will agree, I hope she will marry me once we are safely back in England."

"If she will not?"

"Then I must find another wife, though I," he paused, searching for the French words, "doubt I will ever find one I can love better."

"You too are well-spoken, *Monsieur. Tres bien.* We wait."

Maërlys was struggling with her bonds, as she had been doing for the last hour, when the coach suddenly stopped. Her capture had been so sudden and unexpected. Jules had seized her, bound her hands behind her, and thrown her onto the floor of the coach. She had started to shout, but he had thrust a cloth into her mouth and tied a piece of rope around her head to hold it. Another bit of rope had been wrapped around her ankles and connected to the one holding her wrists. It had taken fifteen or twenty minutes for her to work the gag loose, but there was nothing she could say. She had called out to Jules but there had been no answer.

The coach had been moving very rapidly, but it stopped suddenly and she hit her shoulder against the bench. Jules gave an order, and the door to the coach was yanked open. A huge man leered in at her and began dragging her out. Beyond, she could see Jules, his back to her, stalking across a field toward a wood. Another man followed him, leading three horses on a long tether. Then she was lifted by the big man in front of her. She yelled as he raised her, and a third man, standing at the head of the coach, turned around to watch, but Jules didn't even look back. No one said a word and the breath was squeezed out of her as she landed across the big man's shoulder, like a bundle of chaff from the field. She gasped and tried to keep her head from banging against his back as the giant carried her toward the wood.

Just beyond the first band of trees they came to a clearing. She was set on her feet against a tree. "What is the meaning of this?" she demanded, but she might as well not have spoken for all the attention anyone paid her.

"That one will do," said Andre, pointing to a thick branch just above Maërlys' head. A rope was slung over it, and she watched as the giant fashioned a loop in the end just above her head. Oh, dear God, were they going to hang her?

"Why are you doing this? What have I done?" she asked, but again, no one paid any heed.

The man with the horses had secured them nearby. He began to fasten the other end of the looped rope to the tree. Finished with the loop, the giant pulled her away from the tree, turned her around and untied her hands. Before she could react, they were yanked over her head and secured in the noose hanging above her. The other man adjusted the rope around the base of the tree, so that her hands were stretched to their utmost limit, and she was obliged to balance on the toes of her traveling boots. The giant backed away and examined his handiwork. The look in his eyes frightened her as much as anything that had happened yet.

Suddenly Jules was in front of her. "Now, my little miss, you will tell me what I want to know, everything I want to know, truthfully. You will very much regret any other course. What, exactly, is your destination?"

Confused, Maërlys said, "We told you, Cholet."

She was completely unprepared for the slap across her cheek, which stung like fire, and caused her to lose her balance, so the full weight of her body hung against the rope holding her wrists. The pain in her wrists and shoulders was shocking. She gasped, and the slap to the other cheek made her rock the other way, again tugging at her arms.

"Do not play with me, *ma fille*. You are helpless here. You will tell me where to find the children, or you will suffer as you have never imagined."

"Oh, please, I don't know what you mean," she begged, but at last she understood. He wanted to know where the children were. He was one of those evil men. Oh, why had she trusted him? Sarah had been suspicious. Where was Sarah? Had he already killed her? She remembered the moment when he had gone upstairs and then returned, before he invited her out to see the horses in the air. Beautiful horses, he had said, leading her to the off side of the coach. Now it was clear, and Maërlys' heart was a stone in the pit of her stomach. She thought for a moment she would vomit. Jules must be one of those Frenchmen who had wanted her killed. He had murdered Sarah. Now he was after the children. She realized how wrong she had been and the terrible commitment she now faced. He would kill her, of course, but she must not betray Reynard and Ambre.

"Come, come, little one. Do not make this worse than it has to be. For three nights I have sought, cajoled, tried to get the information from you the easy way. Now we are arrived at this. Tell me what I wish to know and I will not have to beat you. Tell me, and I will not have to strip you before my friends here, or let them have their way with you." He pulled the giant over into her range of vision. "But perhaps you wish to know how it will be with Armand?" The giant leered at her and her eyes widened. Suddenly, Andre slapped her again. "Where are they?" he demanded.

"I don't know what you mean," she gasped.

"Armand, release those ropes." Andre said.

Oh, thank God, she thought. He believes me. Finally, this will be over. Armand knelt and untied the ropes around her ankles, which had also held her dress tight against her legs. She spread her feet a little, and at last had her balance again. The pain in her wrists lessened slightly.

Then Andre moved around behind her, and, placing his hands on her hips, ran them slowly, almost sensually down her legs until he caught the cloth at her ankles. Then he stood, pulling the cloth up with him, gathering the chemise as he rose.

To her horror, she watched the giant in front of her lick his lips as her legs, then her belly, were completely exposed. Hurriedly, she tried to bring her legs together, to diminish the feeling of exposure, but as she did she felt Andre's hand on her bottom, caressing, squeezing, then disappearing for a moment, before he smacked her there, as hard as she could have imagined. She screamed again. The giant in front of her rubbed his hand over the swelling at his crotch.

"Must I use the whip, *Ma'amselle?*" Andre purred into her ear, holding the buggy whip up in front of her eyes. It was too much, and she felt the world going black around her.

When she came to she was soaking wet and the big man, Armand, was staring at her, holding an empty bucket. She felt the dampness of her dress, and her hair. Her dress hung down in front of her, but not as far as it normally would. Her calves were bare, and she realized the dress and chemise had been tied up behind, leaving her fully exposed from that direction.

Armand nodded at someone behind her; when the whip lashed her naked bottom, it was the most fearful pain she had ever experienced, coupled with appalling humiliation. It was unendurable, and she fainted again.

When she came around this time, Andre was standing in front of her, brandishing the whip, "Please, Maërlys de Brissy, do not make me do this to you. You have only to tell me the name of the town where the children live, and the name of the person they live

with, and your suffering will be at an end. If you do
not, you will be stripped naked, whipped all along your
body, and given to these men, one after another. If you
faint, as you almost certainly will, you will be
awakened before the next thing is done to you. You
will feel every bit of the pain, every bit of the
humiliation. Do you think you are Joan of Arc? Her
suffering was as nothing to what yours will be. I
promise you."

Summoning all her remaining strength and her
new hatred for this man, Maërlys glared at him
through her tears and said nothing.

Speaking in English, Andre said, "You spoiled
little minx. You think because you are pretty you are
safe. I admit that you are lovely. It would be a shame
to give such perfection to these animals I employ," he
gestured at the other two men. "It is easily mended. I
will show you how fragile beauty is."

Suddenly, he was holding a knife, waving it
slowly back and forth before her eyes. The blade
looked as sharp as a razor. Involuntarily, her eyes
followed it as it moved. Then it was gone, and she felt
a pressure against her right cheek. The blade was as
sharp as it looked, and for a moment she felt only a
gentle pressure. Then the air caught the cut, the blood
welled up on her cheek, and she felt the pain. Her
scream seemed to go on and on.

36

Henry had been inspecting their coach, and was not happy with what he found. After discussing the problems with Jarrod, he returned to the inn at Cholet, leaving Sadler and Jarrod to the hospitality of Mme Rivet. His plan was to return the next evening, and each ensuing evening, until the carriage was ready or the women arrived.

It was just after dark the next night when they heard a carriage pull up outside the house.

"That was quick work," Jarrod said, slowly rising and heading for the front door. He was coming into the hall when the door burst open and Clara de Tiffauges, bound and gagged, was thrust through ahead of Caron, who held a pistol pointed at the girl's head.

"Everyone stand before me or the girl begins to suffer. Attempt any trickery and she dies. Quickly now."

Jarrod had backed up into the parlor where the others were gathered. Caron forced him back farther by pushing the girl forward, practically shaking her in his face. Jarrod fell over a chair. Sadler had jumped up and reached for his sword, which was hanging on a hook on the wall.

"Leave it," Caron snapped, and Sadler froze. The children were backing into a corner, under the protective arms of Mme Rivet. "You," Caron said to the boy, "you are Reynard de Brissy?"

Reynard pulled himself to his full height. "*Oui,*" he said proudly. As he did, a large man came in behind Caron holding a knife and a coil of strong cord.

"Bind them all," Caron told him, "starting with that one." He pointed at Sadler, who appeared ready to fight.

"Easy," Jarrod said in English, "can't risk Clara."

Sadler seemed to deflate, "*Oui.*"

"Very wise, your lordship," Caron sneered, also in English. Then, reverting to French, "Where is *le noir?*"

"In Cholet."

"*Pourquoi?*"

"We left him to find transport for us."

"Perhaps you may not need it now. Are the men bound, Lutz?"

"*Oui.*"

"Bind the woman, then gag all three. He watched as this command was carried out. "Now bind the boy's hands, *et la petite.*"

At this command, Mme Rivet became agitated, stepping forward, trying to speak through the gag. Caron pushed Clara to the floor and slammed his pistol against the side of *madame*'s head, causing her to stumble. With her hands bound behind her she could not catch herself, and hit her head against a chair as she fell. She lay immobile on the floor. Clara also showed no sign of life except for shallow breathing.

Reynard's hands were bound behind him, and Ambre began to cry as she was seized by the huge Lutz, her tiny hands tied behind her and a loop of rope secured around her body, pinning her arms to her sides. A similar loop confined Reynard's arms. Caron reached out and pulled the boy to him.

"Open your mouth," he said. Reynard stared at him. "Do as I say or I shoot your little sister," Caron said, pointing the pistol at Ambre and cocking it. Still staring defiantly, Reynard slowly opened his mouth. "Wider." The boy complied and Caron shoved the pistol barrel into his mouth.

Immediately Sadler and Jarrod reacted, shaking their heads and trying to speak. Sadler lunged forward but was jerked backward by Lutz.

Caron held up his hand, "Calm yourselves. So long as you all behave no harm will come to him, but make no more sudden movements or an accident may occur. You understand me? Nod your heads." Both men complied.

"Very well. Go outside and get into the carriage. Lutz will go with you and secure you to your places. One on each side, Lutz. If there is the least sign of trouble, one of the children will die. You understand me?" He watched as the captives nodded silently, then jerked his head. Meekly, the two men moved toward the door, waited for Lutz to open it, then went outside.

Lutz followed them. Caron withdrew the pistol barrel from Reynard's mouth and gently released the cock on the weapon.

By the time Lutz returned there was an ugly bruise on Reynard's cheek and Ambre was sobbing uncontrollably. Neither of the bound women had moved. Lutz started to lift Clara but Caron shook his head.

"We do not need them any longer. Cut their throats."

At this Lutz's face paled and he shook his head, "I cannot. It is wrong. They know nothing. Leave them as they are."

Caron considered him angrily for a moment, then shrugged, "All right. Take them in the other room and bind them to the beds. Someone may discover them tomorrow. They are no longer our problem."

Lutz nodded and said, "*Bon.*" He picked up Clara and put her over one massive shoulder, then did the same with *madame*. He carried them that way, though he had to squeeze through the door.

After a few minutes, he returned. "Shall I take the children?" he asked.

"*Oui.* Rope them together."

Lutz strung a rope connecting the hands of the boy to the loop around Ambre's body. Then they were marched to the carriage and lifted in, Lutz grabbing the boy's collar in one huge hand and lifting him, his feet scrabbling to find purchase as his sister was thrown in after. They were pushed onto the seat

between Jarrod and Sadler, whose bound hands were
behind them, attached to leather straps at the corners
of the coach. Caron climbed in and sat on the other
side, facing his captives.

He turned to Jarrod, then reached out and
jerked open the baron's shirt. There, on a small gold
chain around Jarrod's neck, was a large, bronze key.
Caron took it in his hand, gently, caressingly, then
suddenly pulled sharply, snapping the chain. He
smiled, his teeth almost glowing in the blackness.

She saw the coach first, as she came around the
bend in the road. It was about two hundred yards
ahead and she drew on the reins, pulling the horse to
a stop it was glad to get. The coachman was looking
toward a line of trees. Sarah was too far to recognize
him, but she could see that it was not Jules Andre.
The coach, however, was unmistakable.

Her own position was almost invisible, next to a
tree, just at the bend. She watched the coachman
open the carriage door and climb inside. Then she
kicked the horse gently and moved quietly forward.
The soft grass in the field covered the sound of the
hooves. She went as close as she dared, then slid off
the animal's back. The beast immediately began to
crop the grass. Sarah moved to the back of the
carriage, drawing her sword from its sheath at her
back. No fencing foil, this was almost a cavalry saber,

though slightly shorter. She tested its edge, then ducked down beside the coach, reaching for the handle of the door with her left hand. She yanked it open and jumped inside.

The coachman was relaxing on the squab, already almost asleep. As Sarah entered his eyes opened and he reached for the pistol in his belt. He was far too slow. Sarah ran her sword directly into his chest, the blade feeling its way between the man's ribs. He attempted to cry out but all that escaped was a low gurgle and he sank back against the cushions, his eyes wide with surprise.

Sarah wiped her blade on his clothing and jumped down. She remounted and moved swiftly toward the wood. When she reached it, she slowed and, listening to the murmur of voices ahead, moved gently in among the trees. She worked her way toward the sounds until she came in sight of the clearing.

Maërlys was bound by her arms to the limb of a tree above her. Andre was facing her, his back to Sarah. Behind him were two other men, one very large and another man, smaller, holding the leads to three horses. They were all watching Maërlys intently. She saw the flash of the knife, followed almost immediately by Maërlys' scream.

Sarah was already in motion and the scream briefly covered the sound of her approach. That was all it took for her to make up the distance between herself and the giant, and she sank her blade into his neck. Driven with all the force of her anger, a lesser man

might have been decapitated. As it was, she had to
wrench her blade out of his thick muscular neck,
giving the other two men time to back away.

Sarah's next blow clove the rope binding Maërlys
to the tree. Sarah saw Maërlys drop to her knees as
the scream was cut off. Then she swung her mount.
Andre was moving toward the horses and fell
backward as Sarah reached unsuccessfully for his
chest with her sword.

The other man had his own sword out and
lunged toward Sarah. As she pulled her mount
around, the man's sword plunged into her horse's
breast, missing her thigh. The creature screamed and
twisted. Without a saddle Sarah was thrown from the
animal's back, losing her weapon as she hit the
ground. She found her feet as the other man jumped
over the dying beast, his sword reaching for her. She
pulled her pistol from her belt, cocked and fired as he
came, but she stumbled against the body of the giant
behind her and began to fall.

Anger, Sarah thought, as she saw the blade
seeking her breast. Now I will die. I have failed this girl
because I lost my head. The blade seemed to be
moving in slow motion when there was an explosion
just behind her head. Her enemy flung his arms
outward, a red stain blossomed in the center of his
chest and he fell forward, across Sarah's legs.

Glancing behind her she saw Maërlys lying
across the giant's legs, his pistol clasped in her bound
hands. Smoke was rising from the muzzle and Maërlys

tongue was protruding slightly from between her teeth, her eyes wide at the result of her shot. At the sound of hooves, Sarah realized that Andre was gone. She looked again at Maërlys to find the girl staring at her, then starting to shake, tears flowing down her cheeks, diluting the blood on the right one.

The house was dark when Henry arrived on horseback. He was later than he had planned but was surprised to see no light. Coming closer, he was surprised again to see the door standing open. Dismounting, he removed a pistol from his saddlebag and checked the priming. He stuck two knives into his belt. Lastly, he felt in his pocket for his little piece of wood before he faced the door.

He detected no sign of life while he tended these matters. Still, he was careful going in, keeping low and watching the shadows. It was darker inside and he allowed his eyes to adjust before making the turn into the parlor.

The disorder in that room filled his heart with dread. Slowly he moved to the back of the house. He found someone lying, no, bound, on a bed. His hands told him it was a woman, probably Mme Rivet. There was no response to his touch, but her breathing said she was alive. He decided to check the other rooms before dealing with *madame* or showing a light.

In the next room, the scene was repeated, but this time the victim was younger, smaller, more familiar in some way. He must have a light. He reached for the table, found a candle, and opened his tinderbox. That's when he heard the carriage.

Abandoning the candle, he moved quickly to the parlor, peering around the door jamb to see the front door. He had closed it when he entered, now it was opening. Framed against the comparative lightness of the outside was a man about his own height. Henry reached for his little wooden weapon and moved in quickly.

He was astonished to find his swing parried, and had to move as fast as he could to block the other's arm as it swung toward his temple. He spun right, only to find the other matching his move. He ducked low and rolled into the next room, coming up with his weapon at the ready. He moved toward his opponent, but his raised arm was blocked again. He swung his other arm in a brushing motion across his body, felt it contact something hard and go numb. He whirled again, trying to catch his antagonist off-balance. He was in the hall, the door still open. He felt a pistol barrel pressed momentarily against the back of his head.

"Hold very still, *Monsieur*," a woman's voice said in French. A familiar voice?

A light was struck. The man he had been battling stood there, one hand on his hip. His? Her hair had come loose in the struggle and fell around her shoulders almost to her waist. She held out her hand, the little wooden weapon in view.

"We meet again at last. I show you mine, *Monsieur*. Will you show me yours?" Sarah Dane said, smiling. "You like my little dorge?"

He smiled back and opened his hand to reveal the weapon in his palm. He placed it in her hand, next to the other. Looking into her eyes, he said, "I like everything I see. That little ridge, for instance," he said, pointing with his finger. "My left hand is slowly regaining feeling. You call it a dog?"

"Seldom used, but effective in defense," she answered. "I call it a *dorge*. What do you call yours?"

"Dulodulo."

She laughed, "Your baron called it such. I thought he referred to something else and took offense. I must apologize to him when next we meet." She cocked her head, "I enjoyed our struggle. You are very quick, for such a big, hard man." She placed her left hand flat on his chest.

"I wasn't hard a moment ago," he answered. "Will you ask Maërlys—it is Maërlys, isn't it—not to shoot me again? The first time still hurts when I shake my head."

"Be careful when you release the cock," Sarah said to Maërlys, winking at him. "We wouldn't want any accidents, would we kitten?" He felt the pistol removed and heard the slight click as the weapon was neutralized. "Now explain your presence and tell us what is going on."

"First we have two unconscious women tied to beds in the other rooms. If you help me unbind and minister to them, perhaps they can tell us more than I know."

They soon had Clara and Mme Rivet untied, and both responded to water and a little brandy Maërlys found in a cupboard. Neither knew the name of the villain who had brought Clara here and invaded the house, but their description was clear.

Clara told them of the murder of the man's associate. "I thought he meant to return me to Nantes," she sobbed.

Sarah looked at Maërlys, "He has beaten us. We do not know where he has gone."

"Do we not?" Henry asked. He told them of the questioning of Caron in London. He turned to Maërlys, "You are related to Admiral Leissègues. Caron is here to recover the treasure, which he believes the admiral had placed in the family crypt. Your family crypt."

He turned to Mme Rivet, "Can you lead us there?"

The woman stared for a moment then said, "*Oui*. But it is kept locked. I have no key."

"Lord Cherille is also a relative of the De Brissy. He carries a key, which, until we questioned Caron, he believed to be a useless family heirloom. It has always passed to the holder of the title. No doubt it is in Caron's possession by now."

Maërlys drew in her breath sharply, "Has he killed Lord Cherille?"

"I hope not. If he wanted to do that, he could have done it here. I think he has other plans for his lordship, though death may be at the end of the path."

Sarah asked, "Do you know anything of a Jules Andre?" She described the man to Henry.

"No. *Pourquoi?*"

"He scraped our acquaintance on the road, then kidnapped and tortured poor Maërlys. He was seeking the children."

She turned to Mme Rivet, "He sought your name, *Madame*. We believe he is coming here. We came as fast as we could, but we must expect him every moment. You should come with us."

"To the churchyard? At night? Do you think you can rescue the children?"

Sarah answered simply, "We must. Both of these men have proven themselves cold-blooded killers. I cannot think they mean to leave witnesses to their evil deeds. Come, we must be away. Mr. Winnow, you have a horse?"

Henry smiled. "I do, and I hope you will call me Henry, Mlle Daeng."

She smiled back, "Sarah. Or Siti, if you prefer. You three ladies are in the coach," she said to Maërlys and the others. "I am on the box. Let us be off."

Following Henry, Andre kept well back. As they approached the house, it was dark. As soon as Henry entered, Andre slipped off his horse and led the animal quietly to the rear, staying well away from the horse standing at the front. Securing his horse at the back, he crept to a window but could see nothing through the darkness. Then he heard the carriage and moved aside, placing his back against the wall. Inside he heard some sort of brief struggle, then lights began to come on all over the house. Returning to the window, he almost panicked when he saw Maërlys looking directly at him, until he realized she could not see him past the light.

Slowly, watching the scene inside, he put it together. The Malay. He had been warned but, traveling with them, seeing the pretense of servitude, he had been lulled. He fingered the hilt of his rapier. It would give him great pleasure to watch them each die as he pinned them with his sword.

Who were these others? Of course, there was the slave from the colonies, Cherille's servant. The older woman must be the nanny. The other? Never mind. She could die as easily as the rest, but where were the chief actors? Where was Cherille? Should there not be a man from the War Office? And the children?

The answer came to him: Caron was here first. Suddenly the people inside rose, almost as one, and went out. He heard them boarding the carriage. Now he would see.

37

It was very dark in the churchyard. The church had been empty for years, most of the clergy having suffered extensively, first under the Republicans, and later, Napoleon. Facteau had said no one could point out the mausoleum, nor was he sure if it was in Cholet, LeMay-sur-Èvre, or somewhere else.

The little girl, looking around at the gravestones, began to whimper, "*Il y a des fantômes.*"

Caron slapped her, "It's not ghosts you need to fear. Keep moving. You, Reynard, which one?"

Reynard glowered at his captor, "That one, *Monsieur*, ahead of us. The big one."

"Are you sure?"

"*Oui,* Maërlys showed me before she went away. She said our *père et mère* were in there and their spirits would look out for us. She told me to bring flowers when I could."

"Did you boy? Did you bring flowers?"

"*Oui,*" Reynard pointed with his foot. A small tin cup with wilted wildflowers stood at the door of the crypt.

Caron lifted his bulls-eye. There was no name over the door. He took the key from his pocket and tried it in the lock. It went in easily and when it turned at his pressure he felt it give, but when he pulled, the door did not budge. He went back to the key and forced it to turn until the loop at the end was parallel to the ground. This time, when he pulled at the heavy door, it gave a little, but he was unable to open it. He took a small bit of rope from his pocket, tied it to the rope connecting the two children, and tied the other end to the massive handle of the mausoleum door.

Crouching down to look the boy in the eye, he said, "If there is any foolishness I will cut your sister's heart out and make you eat it. Do you understand?" The boy nodded and Caron slapped him hard, "Answer."

"*Oui*," Reynard stared at him, his eyes as hard as Caron's.

"*Bon*," He turned and walked back toward the coach.

"Quickly," the boy whispered, and grabbing her hands with his own, guided them to the rope on the handle. He found the connection on the rope binding them together. They were careless knots, and in a moment, the children were no longer attached to the door. Seizing Ambre's hand again, Reynard led the way through the darkness, around the back of the crypt. Continuing to hold her hand, he pulled her into the bushes behind the church. He kept moving, the little girl's legs pumping to keep up, until they were almost on the other side of the church. "Ssh," he whispered, kneeling on the ground and pulling her close to him.

Feeling with his hands, he went to work on the knots binding her. After a moment, she began to tug at his.

When Caron returned to the crypt with Lutz, he cursed. Looking around, along the sides of the crypt, he swore again. With his bullseye, he could make out tracks along the side leading toward the rear of the mausoleum, but at the back there was a marble square, with stone surrounding it and stone paths leading off in several directions. A quick scan with the lantern gave him no clue. He swore again and returned to the front.

Lutz had the door standing open and Caron pointed toward the carriage. "Watch them," he hissed, and took his lantern inside the crypt.

There were carvings within, names graven into the walls. Nothing else. No sarcophagi, no coffins, just a marble railing at the back, and stairs. Stairs leading down, farther than the bulls-eye would reach. Caron started down into the blackness.

As he descended, the lantern picked out more carvings, some quite horrible and grotesque, along the walls. Not generally given to fanciful imaginings, Caron found that his experiences leading up to this moment had rattled his nerves. His hands were starting to twitch again, a thing that seldom happened at night, in the dark. He felt the tic in his eye. He kept on.

After what seemed an age, he reached another level. He swept the lantern around in a wide arc, revealing stone shelves let into the walls of a cavern, carved out of the living rock. Stone benches rose from the floor. Stone sarcophagi rested on the shelves and benches, except for a few that were empty, waiting perhaps, for the mortal remains of future generations.

The idea that he had brought three mortals with him who could rest here among their ancestors amused him, and he giggled. It was a strange sound in the silence, a sound even he recognized as madness, and he stifled it. But where was the treasure? It must be here. Facteau had been certain, and the names engraved on the sarcophagi and on the walls upstairs were those of Leissègues and de Brissy; this was certainly the right place. He began examining the sarcophagi.

In the last place he looked, right next to where he had come in, a shelf of what appeared to be recent vintage had been cut into the wall immediately to the left of the stairs as he came down. Examining it, he saw that the sarcophagus on it was also recent, with almost no dust, and the name was Leissègues only, with no Christian name. He looked around; all the others had Christian names in addition to the ubiquitous Leissègues on one side of the cavern and de Brissy on the other. This must be it. His twitching increased.

He pushed on the top. There was no movement. He laid aside his coat and, making a determined effort, pushed again. Again, it failed to move. This was too much and he paused to consider. As he did, he looked around at the walls, the crypt, the fantastic carvings lunging out of the gloom along the stairs. He took the

lantern and, counting, walked up the stairs and out of
the mausoleum. By the time he reached the coach, he
had counted one hundred and twenty-three.

"Lutz," he said, "bring them. Both of them."

It took a few moments to detach Jarrod and
Sadler from where they were tied to the coach, but
soon Lutz was walking behind the two captives as
Caron led the way, back into the mausoleum and
down the stairs to the crypt. Again he counted, this
time reaching one hundred and twenty-two before he
stopped in front of the sarcophagus with no Christian
name.

"Untie the big one, Lutz, the baron. Including his
gag. Then the two of you move this stone." He pointed
to the top of the sarcophagus. "You, Sadler, sit there."
He pointed across the chamber to the base of one of
the raised tables. "On the ground."

Between them, Lutz and Jarrod managed to
push the stone enough sideways that it swung across
the sarcophagus, revealing the interior. Caron shone
the lantern into it. It contained boxes, wooden boxes
with metal corners and locks. A quick count came to
two dozen. He reached in and shifted one. The weight
pleased him immensely.

He stepped back and took a pistol from his
pocket, "Now, gentlemen, this is what we will do. Lutz,
take up one of the boxes and you, Cherille, take
another. Lutz, when you get back to the carriage, see
to the stowing of the boxes. Cherille, you will return
and take another which you will give into Lutz's

keeping. You will continue this until all the boxes have been removed, you understand?

Jarrod stared at him a long moment before he said, "*Oui.*"

"Even a simple word like that sounds obscene in your English mouth. You will speak only English from now on. When you go, I will count. I will give you until I count two hundred and fifty; no, I am a generous man, make it two hundred and seventy. If you are not back here by the time I complete that count, I will remove something from Mr. Sadler." He shrugged, "Perhaps an ear, an eye, a finger. It will depend on how late you are and, of course, my mood. You will have twenty-two chances to be late, since that many boxes remain. Should you be late too many times, I fear your friend from the War Office," Jarrod started, and he went on, "oh yes, I know who he is, will be a sad wreck of a man. His fate is in your hands. Now go, I begin my count."

Jarrod glanced at Sadler, then hurried up the steps after Lutz. The box was heavy, but so was the responsibility, and Jarrod made good time. When he reached the crypt again, Caron was sitting on another sarcophagus, within easy reach of Sadler, his sword beside him and his pistol in his lap. Caron smiled at him.

"*Bon.* Take another box and we begin again."

According to instructions, Mme Rivet rapped on the ceiling of the coach when they were about fifty yards from the church. Sarah brought it quietly to a halt and leapt down. Henry drew up next to her and stepped out of the saddle.

"I'll go," he said. "You stay here and protect them, in case this Andre shows up." He nodded toward the coach.

"How will he know where to go?"

"He probably knows it is in the churchyard. In this town, that will not be hard to find." He pointed to the steeple, rising above them.

"Do you have a plan?" Sarah asked.

"The women said there are only two of them, but they have the children. I would like to see first if we can find out what they are doing."

"The coach will be on the road, the crypt somewhere in the yard. You go find the coach. Mme Rivet will show me the mausoleum. Maërlys will stay here and protect Clara."

"I am unused to taking directions from women," he said.

Sarah seized his ear and pulled his face to hers. Then, as her hand crept to the back of his head, she kissed him on the mouth, lingering perhaps longer than she originally intended. "Hmm," she said, "I think you'd best begin to learn."

He smiled in the dark, nodded and moved off along the front of the church, following the street.

Turning to the coach, she said, "Mme Rivet, you can show me the crypt?"

"*Oui, Ma'amselle.* I have been there many times with Reynard."

"You have your pistol ready, Maërlys?" The girl held it up. "*Bon.* Check the priming." Taking Mme Rivet by the hand, she moved into the shadows, heading for the church. When they reached the corner of the building, *madame* stopped her, and pulled her along the side.

"Can we approach the crypt from behind?" Sarah murmured into *madame's* ear.

"*Oui.*"

"*Bon, conduis moi.*"

They were approaching the back corner of the massive church, when Sarah noticed a rustling in the bushes. There was no wind. Quickly she pulled *madame* off the path, and into the shadow of a tree. They waited. The rustling came again, just beyond the corner of the church, in the low bushes that formed a border for the building.

Sarah watched and wondered. "Have you a signal for the children?"

After a moment's silence, *madame* whistled softly between her teeth. The rustling stopped. She whistled again, even more softly. A shadow detached itself from the wall of the church and stepped onto the path. *Madame* ran from the shadow of the tree and gathered Reynard into her arms. Sarah waited. After a moment, the bushes rustled again and Ambre joined them, all three sobbing with relief.

"Ssh," Sarah whispered, coming up to them. "The danger is far from over. Reynard, will you show me the crypt?"

He looked up at her, then at *madame*.

"She is a friend of Maërlys," *madame* whispered.

The boy looked her up and down, trying to tell if he had a man or woman to deal with. Finally, he nodded his head in a little bow, "Your servant, *Mademoiselle*."

Her smile was invisible in the darkness. She took his hand. "*Madame*, take Ambre to Maërlys, but keep a watch for *monsieur* Andre," she said. "Reynard and I will go and inspect this villainy."

In the coach, Maërlys and Clara waited. Maërlys was on edge and as the coach door across from her was opened, she swung the pistol in that direction. Clara cowered against the squab.

"*C'est moi et Ambre*. Please do not shoot us Maërlys." *Madame* helped the little girl up into the carriage. The child stared into the darkness at Maërlys.

"Are you my sister?" she asked.

"Oh, *oui, ma chérie, mon amour*," Maërlys gathered the little girl into her arms, hugging her so tightly the child gasped. Ambre didn't seem to care; she cuddled tight into Maërlys, pressing her head into her breasts, feeling the kisses the woman rained down on her head. "You were just a baby," Maërlys whispered, "just a baby."

Madame put her arm around Clara and they enjoyed the reunion. In the dark of the coach, they watched the two sisters trying to get even closer to each other. Tears ran down four pairs of cheeks. Then the door to the coach was yanked open and Maërlys, still holding Ambre, was dragged out.

Two women and the little girl screamed, almost as one. Maërlys brought the gun up, cocking it with one hand as Sarah had shown her, and fired back over her head. The ball whistled past Jules Andre's ear, and the powder burned the side of his face.

"*Putain,*" he hissed, as he flung her into the street. He kicked Maërlys as he grabbed the child and threw her over his shoulder. Ambre kicked at him and beat his back with her fists, but she wasn't strong enough to bother him. He ran toward the other coach.

Behind him, Maërlys dragged herself up and reached into the coach for the other pistol. She turned and pointed it at Jules but he was too far away, and was holding Ambre. She staggered to her feet and stumbled after them.

38

Henry moved into the shadow of a tree at the corner of the churchyard. He could see the coach and a big man standing at the open door on the side away from the road. Suddenly, a second man appeared, moving quickly from the direction of the yard, carrying what appeared to be a heavy chest. He was staggering under the weight and Henry wondered why he did not slow down. The big man reached out, took the chest, and the other hurried back into the trees. As he turned, Henry would have sworn it was Jarrod.

He kept watching as the big man stowed the chest inside the carriage. In a little under four minutes, the second man returned with another chest, passed it to the bigger man, and hurried away. This time, Henry was sure. Taking his dulodulo in hand, he moved toward the big man.

The screams, followed by the report of the pistol, brought the man's head around just as Henry reached him. He swung his massive arm across Henry's chest. Henry managed to block the worst of the blow but his balance was wrong, and the strength in the man's arm threw him backward against the carriage. He hit his head and slumped to the ground.

As they watched Jarrod coming back without the chest, Sarah pushed Reynard behind her and stepped into his path. Jarrod froze, looking at the pistol she held out to him. He shook his head.

"He's counting. He will be watching me closely. He'd shoot me, then kill Lincoln. I have to go." He pushed past her and went into the mausoleum.

She turned to the boy, held her finger to her lips, gestured toward the rear of the mausoleum and followed Jarrod inside. Within, the darkness was almost complete. She caught the movement as Jarrod started down the stairs, and flattened herself against the wall so that he would not see her as he re-emerged. It was only a moment later that she heard him.

She was on the stairs before he got through the door to the outside, moving down as quickly as she could without making noise. It wasn't silently enough. As she stuck her head around the edge of the stairs, a hand grabbed her and jerked her into the cavern. Something hit her wrist and the pistol flew from her grip. She was lying on the ground at Caron's feet, his sword at her throat.

"You," he breathed, "how could I have wished for more? Now, you harpy, you die." He drew back his arm, the sword-point aimed directly at Sarah's breast.

The screaming and the gunshot had Lutz's full attention. He left Henry where he lay and ran toward the source of the sounds. As soon as he came out of the churchyard shadows, he saw the coach and a man running toward him, carrying something that moved.

Lutz's mind moved slowly and none of this was expected. The man was running directly toward him, and now Lutz could see a sword in his hand. At last something he understood. He growled and drew his own sword.

The man came on but dropped his bundle, which lay still in the road. Lutz raised his arm and swung, a blow that would decapitate any man, but he hit nothing, the man had vanished. He felt it as the blade was withdrawn; he looked down and saw the blood. The pain built wickedly, paralyzing him. The man was past him now and had reclaimed his bundle, whatever it was. Lutz felt his strength seep away. His blade fell to the ground as he sank to his knees.

Jarrod, approaching the coach with his box, saw Lutz leaving the trees to his right. He'd heard the gunshot as he was wondering about Sarah Dane. She'd suddenly appeared in front of him holding out a pistol, like some sort of bizarre genie granting a wish.

He was glad he hadn't taken it, because at the bottom of the stairs Caron had been waiting for him, his own pistol leveled. A gun in his hand would have been his death warrant, but Caron had just smiled that vicious smile and watched as Jarrod picked up another chest and started toward the stairs.

Could Sarah have shot Lutz? No, the shot had been a moment ago, and Lutz was moving. If Sarah was here, where was Maërlys? He saw Lutz raise his sword and make some sort of noise in his throat. Where, in God's name, was Maërlys? He dropped the chest and ran after Lutz, all thought of Sadler forgotten. A man came from nowhere and bowled into him, knocking him down. He reached with his hand but missed, and the man was gone.

Rising, he looked around. There was Maërlys, coming toward him, staggering as if she were injured, a pistol in her hand. She raised it, aiming at him. He saw her cock it. She pulled the trigger.

The noise Sadler made was unintelligible through his gag, but it was loud enough to draw Caron's attention for an instant. Sarah rolled to her right as Sadler, his hands still bound behind him, charged toward Caron. With one eye on Sadler, Caron finished his thrust at Sarah's body, but she was gone, already springing to her feet to his left. The thrust was so hard, containing all his pent-up hatred of the woman, that the rapier snapped when the point hit the rocky floor of the cavern.

Then Sadler was upon him, forcing him to the floor. Caron shoved the remaining part of his weapon into Sadler's body with the last of his strength, just as Sarah's fist came down on Caron's head, driving her dorge against his temple.

Sarah knew the weapon intimately, and the chances of Caron's surviving the blow were incredibly small. At the very least, he would be immobile for a long time. She had no chance to worry about Sadler; there was Maërlys to consider and she was on the stairs and running. When she came into the relative light outside, she glanced left and saw the white face of Reynard, peering around the edge of the mausoleum.

"Stay," she shouted at him. "*Reste.*"

She kept running. Ahead, a chest lay in the path. A man at the carriage slammed the door closed and, bolting onto the box, whipped the horses. She redoubled her efforts, leaping for the back of the coach as it pulled away. She reached the boot, her hand grasped the rail along the top, and she hung on with all her strength as the coach gathered speed and raced off down the street.

Henry regained consciousness to find the coach starting to move. He managed to roll clear, then he was up, staring around, shaking his head. He looked at the coach just in time to see Sarah clinging to the rear of it as it clattered away. He ran for his horse, slowing for a moment as he saw Maërlys and Jarrod standing in the street, staring at each other. Maërlys was holding a pistol.

No time, he thought, and raced past them to his horse. He vaulted into the saddle, chasing after the coach. Jarrod and Maërlys still stood in the street.

"Kiss her, damn you," he hurled at Jarrod as he went by.

Sarah had both hands on the rail and began to pull herself up. At first, the jouncing of the coach was no help, but she managed to brace her foot on the wooden ledge at the top of the boot, wait, and then use the momentum as the carriage lurched to hurtle over the rail and onto the top.

She crawled toward the box. She had no idea who was driving, but was confident it was no friend of hers. She also had no real reason to stop him, except for the confidence that he was an enemy, and her enemies had already caused enough trouble on this trip.

Something must have warned him, because he turned and saw her, just before she reached him. Jules. Of course, he must have decided to cheat his masters or at least Caron. The whip flicked toward her and she barely managed to dodge, retaining her grip on one side of the coach rail with her right hand, warding off the blow with her left.

The coach lurched again and Jules returned his attention to the horses. Once again, Sarah found her anger overwhelming her cooler tactical sense. She pushed her feet against the rear rail, flew forward and wrapped her arm around the man's throat, using all her strength as she pulled back and turned her arm.

The coach leaned dangerously and he went limp in her arms. She saw the reins drop from his hands and the horses, given their heads, frightened by the noises and the situation, began to run in earnest. Jules' body fell from the box as Sarah dove toward the horses.

Maërlys recognized Jarrod just as she pulled the trigger and felt the hammer click down. It took them both a moment to realize that the pistol had misfired, and neither one noticed when Henry raced by, heading for his horse. They were staring at each other, barely able to take in all that was happening: the coach racing away, Henry riding by at top speed and yelling something unintelligible.

Maërlys looked around. Where was Ambre? The coach? Jules? She screamed, and began to sob, just as Jarrod pulled her into his arms. She beat her hands against his chest, still clutching the useless pistol, crying, "Ambre, Ambre, Ambre."

Jarrod looked around, holding her tightly. There was Lutz, still kneeling in the middle of the street, clutching his belly. Jarrod released Maërlys and went over to him, retrieving the big man's sword from where it lay beside him in the street.

"Did you see them?" he asked. "The man with the child?"

Lutz looked up at him. "He stabbed me," he said.

"Yes, and I will do the same again unless you tell me if he had the child with him."

"He had a bundle," Lutz moaned, "he took it with him. He stabbed me," he repeated.

Jarrod ignored him and looked into the darkness down the road. Everything would be up to Henry now.

He turned back to Maërlys, "We must wait and see, my darling."

He felt a tug at his coat, and looked down to see Reynard.

"Sir, if you please. The lady told me to wait, but I went down into the crypt. There are two men there. I think they are dead." As he spoke, his eyes shifted to Maërlys.

"Damme, I'd forgotten Sadler. Both dead?"

He turned back to Maërlys, who was staring at Reynard, "Please, my dear, we can do nothing for Ambre right now. Henry will take care of her; you will see. He is a splendid man, Henry. His eyes followed Maërlys' to Reynard. The two siblings were staring at one another.

Jarrod said, "I apologize, I am remiss. Reynard, this is your sister, Maërlys."

Reynard bowed, never taking his eyes from his sister's face. "You are very beautiful," he said.

At this, Maërlys crumpled, tears flowing down her face. She dropped to her knees and caught Reynard in her arms, squeezing him and sobbing. Reynard looked over her shoulder at Jarrod. His cheeks were glistening and his lips quivered. His hand went to his sister's hair, and stroked it gently.

The baron smiled at him and opened his mouth to speak. He was interrupted by the arrival of Mme Rivet, who dropped next to Maërlys gathering both the de Brissys into her arms. Clara was lagging timidly behind.

"*Madame*," Jarrod said, "please take care of all these people for me. You should keep an eye on that man," he indicated Lutz, who was now lying in the street, moaning. "Perhaps you could get Maërlys to look at the flints on that pistol, but I do not think he will cause any trouble. I must go back into the crypt and see what is there."

He turned to Clara, "Would you come with me? I may need help."

Her eyes widened, "Into a crypt? Oh, *Monsieur*...."

Maërlys had taken control of herself. She stood and looked at the flints of the pistol, then replaced the cap with another from the cloth bag at her waist. She thrust the gun into Clara's hand. "Watch the big man," she said. "Shoot him if he moves toward you. I will go with Lord Cherille."

   In the dark, Henry could just see the body lying in the road. He pulled on his reins as he drew up alongside, realized it was a man and a stranger, and jabbed both his spurs into the horse. He could hear the clatter of the coach and the pounding of the horses ahead.

   When he finally caught up, he could see no one on the box. He forced his horse off the edge of the road and raced the coach until he was alongside the team, the coach on his left. Reaching over, he managed to get his left hand on the rein near the mouth of the nearest horse, and began pulling it sharply back and to the right.

   As he did, he realized that the far horse was being pulled in the opposite direction, and he dragged on his own horse's reins until the carriage clattered to a halt.

   "You certainly took your time," Sarah's voice came from his left, and he realized she was astride the far horse. She had been so far forward, and to the left, that she was half off the beast. He had not seen her in the darkness. "I'd have stopped them eventually, but it wanted more weight," she added.

He bowed slightly, without releasing his hold on the near horse. "I am glad I could be of service, ma'am."

The voice from the carriage startled them both. "*On peut rentrer? J'ai faim.*"

39

When the coach arrived back at the church, Jarrod was waiting. "All well?" he asked Henry, who looked down at him from the box.

Henry shrugged, "We lost the pigeon but the rest of the game is here."

"Got away from you?"

Again, Henry shrugged, "Sarah removed him from the coach at high speed; she thought he was dead. I thought the same thing when I passed him in the road, but he was gone when we came back. We beat the bushes on either side but found nothing. It was too dark to see any trail and the child was hungry, so here we are. There might have been a farm nearby. If he stole a horse, he's gone. On the other hand, he was much mishandled; he cannot be a well man. How are things here?"

"We removed the last of the treasure, and Mr. Sadler is very badly hurt. The ladies and I got him into the coach and Mme Rivet undertook to drive them all back to her house. I waited for you."

"Climb aboard, then, and we'll join the others. All these horses are pretty spent, so we will not hurry. The child was hungry but she may be asleep now, so go quietly. What of Caron and his big companion?"

"I don't know what killed Caron but perhaps Miss Dane can enlighten us. Lutz was stabbed, apparently by your quarry. Perhaps we should have been more merciful to him, but Mr. Sadler occupied all our thoughts. By the time we came to check on Lutz, he had crossed over. We left the two of them in the sarcophagus marked Leissègues, as a surprise for the Admiral when he comes for his money." He smiled a little, "Perhaps he will not return this year. That reminds me, before we go, if you will help me close the mausoleum, we can let the horses rest a moment more."

At the house, Mme Rivet bustled about providing a meal for Jarrod, Henry, and Sarah. The others had already eaten, and they found it impossible to awaken Ambre. Maërlys sat to one side on a soft couch with Clara.

Reynard, who could barely keep his eyes open, insisted on sitting between them, pressed close to Maërlys, listening to every word. Since they spoke mostly in English for Jarrod's sake, it is unlikely Reynard understood much; though Maërlys occasionally whispered translations into his ear. For his part, Reynard reached out his hand constantly to touch Maërlys, as if to reassure himself of her reality.

"It would be good if we could arrive in England before this Andre," Jarrod said. "Do you have a way out, *Mademoiselle*?" They both looked at Sarah. She looked at them each in turn, then went on eating for a moment. Henry smiled as he watched her.

Finally, she put down her spoon and shrugged, "Should such fine gentlemen care to travel with the likes of me?" she asked the air. "Might not they find the company too low?"

"Speaking for myself," Henry responded, "I can think of no company I should prefer."

"That is very well," she smiled, "but you are a dark-skinned man and no doubt accustomed to occasional rough usage. Your companion, however, is a peer of the British crown. He will find no silk dressing gowns on what may be little better than a pirate vessel."

"I beg your pardon, Miss Dane," Jarrod answered, "but I have slept in the forest before now. I trust I am not so fastidious as to take exception to so much lovely company." His gesture took in the whole house.

Sarah became serious, "You must understand that I have many friends, and some of them may sometimes practice outside the, shall I say, letter of British law. If I take you with me, I expose them as well as myself, and must rely on your absolute discretion. Can I so rely?"

"I think, Miss Dane, that this night's work has taken us all into places that might best not be spoken of again. Deliver us safely to merry old England, and I promise you shall have no cause to regret it."

She gazed at him for a moment, then turned to Henry, "You will vouch for him, I believe?"

"Upon my life," Henry said.

She reached out and picked up his hand, turning it palm upward, then traced a line in his palm with her finger. "Let us hope nothing so severe is required," she smiled. "However, we have much to consider. We have some twenty or more boxes of what can only be called contraband, and to be discovered with it would almost certainly cost us all our lives. Also, quite a number of people join us on this journey. Mme Rivet believes herself safe and feels she is too old to make the journey, nor does she have any desire to leave her beloved France." She repeated this in French to *madame*, who nodded.

"On the other hand," Sarah continued, "Clara has had many bad experiences over the last months and believes she would feel more secure in another country. French lady's maids are much in demand in England, whether they know anything of fashion or not. Their very accent makes them fashionable. Is this not so, Maërlys?"

"*Oui*," said Maërlys, without looking up.

"Also, I have assured Clara that a place of some kind can be found for her, whatever the case. She is comely and would fit in well with my household, an idea that seems to appeal to her."

"So," Jarrod said, "we are seven, including the children. It is a large responsibility."

"Eight. We cannot leave Mr. Sadler, no matter how ill he is. His presence could never be explained and would endanger Mme Rivet."

"True. I had forgotten him again."

"He is my responsibility," she said. "He has saved my life, and it is my understanding that he undertook the journey expressly for that purpose."

"That also, I believe, is true," Jarrod said. "He is madly in love with you."

Sarah looked down, "He has told me so before. In England I could laugh at him, and it has certainly never been within my power to return his feeling, but I would be a very low person indeed could I not respect such a show of love as he has made. If he dies, I will owe him all my life. I will do my best to ensure he survives to reach his home and reclaim his life there."

"The responsibility grows larger and larger," Jarrod said.

"A responsibility which is mine alone, your lordship," Sarah said. "It will take a number of people and some very close work to make it happen. You understand why I am so demanding of your assurances?"

Jarrod stood, took her hand, and bowed over it. "It is not my place to speak for Henry in this circumstance," he said, "but for myself, I am entirely at your disposal. I will fetch, I will carry, I will rob or steal as necessary, and my sword is at your command. If this thing cannot be done, I am confident it will be no fault of yours, and if it can be done, then you are certainly the one to do it."

Henry stood and also bowed over her hand, although he took the liberty of pressing it to his lips. She smiled at him and raised her eyebrows to a sharp point. "I too, am at your service, lady, body and soul," Henry said.

"You are sweet," she said. "Shall we speak now of the treasure?"

"With your permission, ma'am," Jarrod said, "why do we not leave that for some future day? It is a long journey, there may be dangers, and even if we arrive safely with all our goods and chattels intact, there may still be trouble at the end of our way. M. Caron was not alone in this search, and we know of at least one other, possibly even now on his way to England. Once we are at sea, there will be time enough to speak of temporary storage, and final division can certainly wait until safety envelops us."

"You speak well, your lordship. So be it."

"And it please you, Miss Dane, call me Jarrod."

They left the next day, early in the morning. They felt the presence of two coaches would draw unwanted attention to Mme Rivet. Jarrod had recovered Caron's papers, and with these they were able to smooth the very few difficulties that arose on the way to the coast. It took six days to reach Lessay.

After several days delay in contacting Captain Hornbeck, they returned to St. Malo, believing the larger town would offer better facilities and greater anonymity. Plans originally made for two women and two children had to be revised to accommodate twice that number of passengers, and many boxes of very heavy luggage. Finally, they embarked from Cancale rather late one evening. A small boat took them all to Jersey, where they met the *Doctor Syn* to find their luggage already aboard.

As it happened, one of the boxes failed to make it to land, and was abandoned on board the *Doctor Syn*. No one mentioned it. Another had disappeared before they embarked, and somehow managed to find its way to two brothers named Durand. No one spoke of that, either.

It was close quarters on board, with special accommodation made for Sadler and all three women crowded into the cabin. The children enjoyed hammocks slung on deck. The weather was fair and they made a quick passage. Out of caution, they avoided Dymchurch and landed at Hastings, which was closer and offered quicker passage to the High Weald.

Throughout this time, Jarrod had been increasingly and repeatedly thwarted in his attempts to discuss his feelings with Maërlys. She was playing the part of leader of the expedition, with Sadler as her infirm husband, come to the sea for recuperation. She had little opportunity to be alone with servants, roles played by Jarrod and Henry, except for her maids, Sarah and Clara. She spent most of her time with her putative children. She usually wore a veil in public, to keep her youth from drawing difficult questions.

On board ship, they were able to drop these roles, and one night Jarrod caught her returning to the cabin she shared with the two other women. He took her elbow and guided her to the rail.

"I must speak with you."

She looked up at him. Her hair, worn long, obscured her right cheek, a style she had adopted since the beginning of their return journey. "I cannot imagine what you would say to me, my lord."

"You are unaware that I undertook this journey specifically to seek you out?"

She looked down, suddenly unable to meet his eyes. "What business could you have with me?" she murmured, her voice barely a whisper.

"You have forgotten an evening we spent together in Portsmouth? Only a month or so ago? Though I admit it seems an age."

She felt herself flushing and hoped it was hidden by the night, "You are unkind, sir. I made a mistake. I was desperate to accomplish the salvation of these little ones." She gestured toward the children's hammocks. "I did something I know is unforgiveable; I allowed you liberties a woman should not allow, without she holds at least certain promises. I admit this to you because I have no choice, but you must understand that I would be required to deny it to any other living soul. I suppose you could count on Mr. Winnow's testimony, were it needed."

"I doubt Henry would say the slightest word that was not sanctioned by your friend Miss Dane, and I would hope you know that they both have only your best interests at heart. As do I."

"If that were so, sir, why would you be so cruel as to remind me of indiscretions I am trying so hard to leave behind? If I have made myself a pariah by my actions, cannot I at least hope that the world will, in time, forgive and forget? Must I be hounded by mistakes made in a good cause, though without proper forethought? Would you ruin my life for such an error, if you indeed wish me well?"

"I wish to m—" he said, when they were interrupted by Reynard.

"Please, sister, come look at the sea with me," he said, taking her hand and pulling her toward the other side of the vessel. "Sorry I was so late..." Jarrod heard him say under his breath as he led Maërlys away.

Jarrod reluctantly released the tension in his body. It was not the first time he had made the attempt and not the first such interruption. He could count at least two others involving Reynard and three with Ambre, though the change in subject was usually initiated by Maërlys. Were they doing it on purpose? He thought a moment. Why would the boy apologize for being late? He frowned angrily. Tomorrow night they would be in Hastings. He and Henry must push off for London as soon as they could, but he would track the woman to her lair and demand she look at him while he got down on his knees. This frustration could not go on.

The moment they landed, Jarrod and Henry took their departure for London, leaving all else in the capable hands of Sarah Dane, with the understanding that they would contact the party at her country house as soon as it might be both convenient and discreet.

40

"Good of you to receive me on such short notice, Sir Charles."

Sir Charles glowered at him, "None of that, you nuisance, where have you been? Looked for you this month and more. Even had that fellow Nubbins in, raked him over the coals. Swore he knew nothing of your whereabouts. Mumbled something about a vacation."

"Exactly, Sir Charles. A vacation. Bit of the summer sun, what?"

"Vacation spots in France, was it? I don't doubt it was hot."

"Never mind the details, sir, I'm sure they'd bore you. Just got back to England this moment. Or at least, last night."

"I imagine the vessels you travel in prefer the darkness."

"Just so. Relieves the chance of sunburn."

"Less of it, you puppy. Did you think I wouldn't notice you took my secretary on this, ah, harrumph, vacation, damn your eyes? What have you done with Mr. Sadler, eh?"

"Ah, now there I'm afraid I have bad news."

"Did you get him killed, you damn fool? Or worse, leave him in the hands of Boney's bullies?"

"No, but he did suffer some, ah, misfortunes, and is still a little unwell. Sometimes these vacations can disagree with one."

Sir Charles banged his fist on the desk, "Damn you, where is he?"

"He is currently at the country house of a friend of mine, recuperating. I am confident you can have him back as good, well, almost as good as new, in less than a month."

"A month? He's been gone almost that long already."

"True, but these afflictions can take time to heal. It's no good hurrying."

Sir Charles put his head in his hands and looked at the desk. When he looked up, he appeared slightly more composed. Through gritted teeth he said, "And did you accomplish your goals, on this, ah, vacation?"

"Indeed, sir, indeed, thanks for asking. In fact, you bring me to the crux of my visit. Or should I say nub. No, I believe crux is most apropos."

Sir Charles wrinkled his nose and peered at Jarrod, "If I ask nicely, will you get on with it?"

"Of course, sir, it's quite simple. You'll never believe it, but we discovered that M. Bonaparte has spies right here in England."

Sir Charles grimaced, "Indeed."

"Oh yes, and in fact, though I hate to say it, one

right here in the ministry."

At this, Sir Charles lost his look of carefully feigned composure, "In the Foreign Office?"

"That I could not say, for sure, though I really suspect War."

"Of course there's a war, you imbecile."

"No sir, I mean the War Office. With tentacles, as it were, into the Foreign Office."

"You have my full attention. Can you prove it?"

"Not yet, but with your assistance, I believe it can be done." Leaning across the desk, he outlined his plan in low tones for Sir Charles, who sat back in his chair, blinked, and said, "Well, damme."

"Henry is working on the details with Nubbins, whom you said you have met. As you can see, I did not wish to directly involve ministry people. I believe my appearance here today will be enough to set things in motion, and I expect we may have results as early as tonight. Or at least before Monday, although it depends on what Nubbins can tell us. There is a wild card."

"Oh?"

"A gentleman we ran into on vacation. If he is here before us it may complicate matters. Can you check to see if anyone in the ministry has gone missing recently? Carefully, of course. Don't want to startle any hares not already on the jump."

"Yes, I see that. Very well, then, I'll look into it quietly. Send a boy with a message sealed with this," he handed over a small seal, "and I'll get it safely."

Jarrod took the seal, thanked Sir Charles, and left.

"Please, darling, humor me. I'm sure it will only be a few more days."

"Sarah, you have been so kind to me," Maërlys answered, "and so understanding about the children, but it is time we stopped draining your resources and returned to London. My cousin—"

"Your cousin's resources are nothing like mine. Besides, surely you understand that you are due some of the, ah, proceeds of the expedition."

"Surely that is Lord Cherille's. He undertook the expedition for that reason, did he not? My treasure is Reynard and Ambre."

"His lordship does not make decisions in my house."

"You should not underestimate him. The peerage in this country is often a law unto themselves, and he is very rich."

"And he claims to love you."

For a moment, it looked as if Maërlys' face would crumple, but she regained control, "You told me he said so, but that was before we went to France. I am a different woman now. I am a murderer, twice over. I am, I am, well, you know; I am no longer pretty."

The corner of Sarah's lips twitched, and her eyes shone, "Are you not, my love?"

"You warned me that you would grow tired of me, and I understand how you must feel. I am no longer the innocent woman you enjoyed. I have been, ruined, defiled, devastated."

"You are a delightful child, and every bit as spoiled as Ella or Jenny, or any of the rest of my household. Honestly, had I not sworn never to raise my hand to a woman except in direst emergency, I would spank the lot of you. Well, you may sulk if you like, but I think you are behaving very foolishly. Your baron is quite good-looking, and likeable, now I know him better. And understand the word, dulodulo," she added under her breath.

She walked over to the younger woman and pulled her close, stroking her hair, "I am not tired of you. Were it practical, I would keep you here always, like a princess in a tower. I warned you of the lack of solitude. You have no idea, really. Elise is so jealous I believe she will drive me mad someday. Were I to take you to bed now, I expect we would find her underneath it. No, darling, you have another life to live, and I hope I will always be some small part of it. For now, you will remain here a few more days yet. We still have enemies, and it would be best if they have no access to you. I must go to London. Your baron needs my assistance, and I trust he is putting your safety in train. We can discuss this further when I return. Would you give me a message for your cousin? I have no doubt she is worried about you."

"But the children—"

"Are delightful. You must have noticed how everyone has fallen in love with them. Both Simon and Julia speak excellent French, and I believe Julia has already begun their English lessons. Ambre said something to me just this morning. I didn't understand a word, so I'm sure it was meant to be English. Even Ella sneaks treats to them, since she can communicate in no other way. Take care of them, and I will arrange for the three of you to travel to London as soon as it is safe. And no more talk of my resources, if you please."

"You're late!" Jarrod shouted, as Henry drove the coach into the yard. "It is too late. We cannot take them to the bank today; now it will be Monday. We will have to store them here."

"I am sorry, your lordship. It was unavoidable; a wheel will not mend itself."

"Well, it's too bad, but we'll have to bring them inside. I'll get Thompson, to help. We can stack them next to the door here and move them back out on Monday."

"If you keep yelling like that they'll hear you at the ministry," Henry muttered, carrying the first of the boxes inside and setting it next to the wall.

"Best be sure," Jarrod hissed back as he went to find Thompson.

Together, the three of them managed to bring in the twenty-two wooden boxes, and range them along the wall in two stacks of five and two of six.

As soon as they were done, Henry went to the window, "Do you know your watcher?"

Jarrod pointed to a house opposite, which had a third floor with a view of the yard. A man was visible, with what appeared to be a glass in his hand. Then he raised it to his eye and Henry was sure.

"It will be dark soon," Jarrod said.

"I'll take her a cup and a cake, if you have them available."

"You could have brought Maërlys, as well."

"I have enjoyed our association these years, your lordship, but I draw the line at pandering."

"She was well?"

"According to Sarah. I did not see her."

"The children?"

"They were quite well. It was all we could do to keep them out of the coach. They appear eager to see London."

"And yet Maërlys did not appear. Is that not odd?"

Henry shrugged, "I will ask Sarah at the first opportunity."

"Let me know if you need help."

"You saw the chests?"

"Absolutely. They carried them inside with hardly a thought. It was like watching a parade. They are very stupid, the English."

"If they are so stupid why have they these chests instead of we? You are sure they are the correct chests?"

"Of course. They are the same ones. I had them for a time but they out-numbered me and—"

"You let the Malay take them away from you," Facteau finished for him. "You are sure no one recognized you?"

"The girl Maërlys and the Malay are the only ones who could do so. They were not there. They must have remained at the High Weald."

"So, we have until Monday. It was most obliging to bring them up on a Saturday past banking hours."

"It is the first chance they have had. Obviously, Lord Cherille had to come first, to be here when the chests arrived."

"*Le noir* did not come with him at once?"

"No. He was not seen until he drove in with the chests."

"Do you think they will expect us?" Facteau asked.

"They might. That is why we wait as long as we can, to allay their suspicions. By Sunday night, they will be relaxed. When we come, we will take them easily. Who knows? As we watch we may find some other edge to assist us."

"You intend to kill them?"

"Of course. It does not matter and will be safest. It may be days before they are discovered. By Monday night we will be gone."

Sarah turned from the window, "You expect them tonight?"

Henry shrugged, "We expect them every night. If it were me, I would wait until Sunday night."

The not-quite-smile played around the left edge of her mouth. "Do they always do what you expect them to do?"

"No. Sometimes they are not so clever as I, but we watch and are watched."

"So I see."

He laughed, "Yes, he's there almost all the time now. Is it him?"

"Yes. May I not go and cut his head from his shoulders?"

"Certainly not. This is a civilized country, and he will be hanged or shot. Beheading is rare now, and always reserved for the *crème de la crème*. Certainly, that man will never qualify."

"Europeans are so, ah...."

"Provincial?"

"Exactly the word. Tell me, Henry Winnow, how did you get such a delightful education?" She ran a finger along his jawline.

"I believe my father wished it. Although, of course, I never could prove he was my father. He never admitted it, nor did my mother."

"They are both dead?"

"I am a poor orphan boy."

"Perhaps not so poor, now."

He smiled, "Perhaps not. We shall see. It may be necessary for the ministry to know of the existence of some part of the money. A little here, a little there, it all adds up. Or rather, diminishes. Do you know, some boxes are missing already?"

"Really?"

He grinned at her, "I think you may be the most splendid woman I have ever met. When this is over, I hope we will become better acquainted."

"I too am hopeful. Speaking of hope, can you tell me anything of your friend's attitude toward Maërlys? I fear she is morose, and believes that her experiences in France have put her quite beyond the pale." She glanced toward the window, "I blame that animal. Do you know, on the coach I tried to wrench his head from his shoulders? I should have, too, had it not been such a strain to get at him. Honestly, I was quite disgusted with myself."

He shook his head, his eyes twinkling, "I cannot speak for Jarrod, of course, but I believe he longs for her. Right now he is quite busy with these plans, but I am confident that he will turn his full attention to her as soon as it is safe."

"I wish it will not be too late. She is sometimes mercurial and can be stubborn and proud. I worry about her."

It was more than he could stand. He took her into his arms and kissed her. "Who worries about you?" he asked.

She cocked her head and smiled with her whole face. "Perhaps I may allow it," she said, and pulled him back to her.

41

Maërlys stared at herself in the mirror above the vanity dresser. No matter which way she moved, no matter how the light fell, all she could see was the scar. She shook her hair to cover it but it blazed at her, even through that opaque curtain. She had hidden it from him during the journey, first with a veil, then on the boat, keeping her head turned, her hair over it, she was sure he hadn't seen it. He would never have approached her, else. What use could he have for her? Would he pity her and take her as his mistress? He had enough money to keep many mistresses, even a deformed one he felt sorry for and never visited. No. Never!

Only one reasonable path remained. She had heard them talking, and she knew Andre had escaped. She knew he must be back in England by now. She knew the name of the hotel.

She looked at the money on the vanity, the bills and coins she had filched from the kitchen housekeeping. She looked at the sealed letter, addressed to Emmeline Blanc. The children would be all right now. She listened. The house was still asleep and darkness enveloped the world.

Carefully she crept downstairs through the
silent house, out the back door, and into the stables.
No one was there. She saddled the gentle mare she
usually rode and was off. She would reach the post inn
long before she was missed, and would be in London
before anyone could stop her. They might look for her
at Emmeline Élégance, so she could not say goodbye
to Emmy. She would have her revenge. She hoped they
would not come to watch her hang.

They were sitting in the room under the stairs,
where their light could not be seen, when Jarrod
knocked softly. They said nothing, and after a slight
pause Jarrod put his head in.

"Now," he said, and they were instantly on the
alert. As Sarah reached for her sword, Henry put his
hand on her arm. She raised her eyebrows.

He looked into her eyes. "Who do I believe I'm
fooling?" he asked the air, removing his hand.

"Well, I should think," she muttered, drawing
the sword and following Jarrod from the room. Henry
admired the way her smallclothes fit her, particularly
in the rear.

They could hear the scratching as someone
worked on the lock at the back of the house, then the
door swung inward and a bulls-eye moved around the
room. They waited. The lantern found the boxes and
followed the outline of the four stacks.

"We'll come back to that when the house is secure," came a whisper. "Spread out and find them. There are only two. Cherille will be upstairs, but the darky may be anywhere."

Jarrod was relieved he'd sent Thompson away for the weekend. He was too old for such work. The three of them melted into the darkness as they counted the shapes of the opposition. One lingered near the boxes. Two went toward the kitchen, and a fourth headed up the stairs. Henry and Sarah followed the two, going around through the dining room. Jarrod went silently up the stairs toward his own room.

There was no one in the kitchen when Henry and Sarah got there. She put her hand on his arm, pointed toward the door which led to the servant quarters, then two fingers pointed to the doorway. Henry nodded and they took their positions on either side. They waited.

It was some time before they heard them, muttering in low tones as they returned. The door opened to the right as it was pushed, hiding Sarah behind it. She waited until the one in front came past. As he did, he turned to say something to his companion and saw Henry. He shouted a warning, and lunged. Sarah was on the move, but the man's attack on Henry spoiled her aim, and the dorge caught his shoulder. It drove him a few inches to his right, causing his blade to miss Henry, though it passed through his shirt.

Henry's luck with the dulodulo was better, as his opponent turned into the blow. It caught him on the point of his chin, not the point Henry had planned, but effective. The fellow's head jerked back and hit the door jamb, and he slid unconscious to the floor. By this time Sarah had abandoned the niceties and run her opponent through the breast. As he fell, his sword, caught in Henry's shirt, dropped from his hand and scratched Henry lightly on his left side.

"Is it bad?" Sarah asked.

"I'll do. We'd better move."

Jarrod had caught his opponent entering the master bedroom. The man had turned and engaged him, and they were fighting in the hall when Sarah's target shouted. The disturbance distracted the French agent for the moment Jarrod needed to pass his sword through him. As he fell, Jarrod turned and ran for the stairs. He arrived at the back door at the same time as Sarah, Henry moving slightly slower. The other man was gone. They dashed out into the yard and reached the gate in time to see the carriage turning the next corner.

"Do you know where he's going?" she asked.

"Probably. We'll need a cab." He turned and sprinted for the front of the house just as they heard the sound of a carriage moving on the square. He arrived as the cab pulled to a stop in the front of the house and a boy of about ten jumped out.

"Hold the cab," Jarrod shouted, and turned to the boy. "Who do you want?" he asked.

"Please sir, I 'ave a message for Lord Cherille."

Jarrod stared at him as Sarah came up behind. "Better give it to him, then," she said, pointing at the baron.

"'E don't look a lord to me," the boy said.

"Nevertheless," she said, "that's him and you're likely to lose a big tip while you're standing there."

The boy passed a note to Jarrod who unfolded it and scanned it under the stars. "From Nubbins. Been a signal."

He squinted at the paper, then at the boy, "Did you see the signal?"

The child nodded eagerly, "Bill told us to watch and not take our eyes off the window, and then the light come on, and the shade come up and down and up and down again. I run and told 'im and 'e sent me 'ere. What about this 'ere tip, eh?"

Jarrod thought for a moment, "Cabdriver, wait here. There's a gold guinea in it. Boy, come with me. Sarah, would you bring Henry inside and try to make him comfortable while I deal with this messenger? What's your name, boy?"

"Pardon."

"I said what's your name?"

"That is me name, Pardon. Pardon Jenkins."

Jarrod blinked, "All right. Come with me. Sarah, by the way, did you...?"

"One's sleeping," Sarah answered.

"Might be best to, ah, secure him," he said, glancing at the boy. Sarah's mouth twitched.

In the house, Jarrod scribbled a quick note, sealed it with the seal Sir Charles had given him, addressed it, and gave it to the boy. "Don't lose it," he said, fumbling in his pockets again. He took out a gold sovereign and handed it over. "Do you know this address?"

"Sorry, yer lordship, can't read. 'Cept numbers."

Jarrod read the address, and the boy nodded. "You must ring the bell and tell whoever answers that you're from Lord Cherille with a message for Sir Charles. Have you got that?"

"Yessir. Message for Sir Charles from Cherille. I mean Lord Cherille. Sorry."

"It's all right. Cherille will do. Give him that note."

Jarrod reached into his desk, pulled out a paper bill, and handed it to Pardon. The boy looked at it suspiciously.

"'Ere, what's 'is?"

"It's a five-pound note. It's for you."

"What am I to do wiv' it, eh?"

"Give it to your mother."

"'Aven't got one."

"Who have you got?"

"Got me sister, Betsy."

"Give it to her, then."

"Nobbut four. Likely she'll eat it."

Jarrod snatched the bill back, "Bring your sister Betsy around tomorrow, and we'll see what's to be done. If you want it."

"Awright, yer lordship. I'll be off then."

"Good lad, see you tomorrow. I hope," he added under his breath as the boy left.

Nubbins was waiting in front of the hotel when they reached The Ambassador. "Got it bottled up?" Jarrod asked.

"Yessir, your lordship. There's been three in since I sent the lad. First one was slippery, almost missed 'im. Second one came in like 'e 'ad a fire to put out. 'Ad a cab but it was gone before my man could catch it. Got a look at the driver though. Seen 'im before. Little Irish chap."

"Excellent, good work. Do you know for sure they both went to see this Facteau?"

"Oh, aye."

"What about the third?"

"Dunno what to make o' that, sir. I should explain this fellow was 'ere before, and my people saw 'im leave. Just as 'e were getting in 'is carriage, a woman runs up to 'im like she's gone to hit 'im or somethin'. Said she 'ad 'er 'and in 'er bag, fumblin' for summat and 'e kinda grabbed 'er, like, took the bag away and assisted 'er into the carriage. My man says it were more like he threw 'er in. When 'e comes back 'e's got 'er with 'im. Brings 'er inside, kinda holdin' 'er up, like maybe she were drunk."

"Young? Old?

"Very young, sir. Said she were an eyeful, never mind the scar."

Sarah leaned past Jarrod, "Scar? Where?"

"Right cheek, Miss. My man said it were noticeable but 'e wouldn't pass 'er up on account o' it. Funny, but the man 'ad one too. More like a powder burn, 'is were."

"The poor little fool. She must have followed me. Now they've got her." She drew her sword. Jarrod and Nubbins both held up their hands.

Nubbins beseeched her, "Please, Miss, put it away. I can't answer for it if we're seen waving weapons about in this 'otel full o' Frenchies. You know 'ow they are, foreigners, begging your pardon, Miss."

"Which room?" she demanded, but sheathed the sword.

"You know this woman?" Jarrod asked.

"So do you. It's Maërlys."

"But Maërlys doesn't have a scar."

"You know Maërlys, but you don't know the scar. Think. Have you seen her right cheek since...," she glanced at Nubbins and jerked her head toward the west.

"They injured her? They cut her? The devils." Suddenly his sword was out and Nubbins' hands were raised again.

"No, no, no, no, no, please sir, no. Please. In the room, possibly, but not 'ere. Please."

Jarrod turned to Henry, "Can you do this, old fellow?" Henry said nothing, just cocked his head to one side and gazed at Jarrod, smiling. "Then let us go. Nubbins, you wait here. Send Sir Charles and his men up as soon as they arrive. Sooner, if you can." Jarrod led the way, followed by Sarah and Henry.

It was nearly one in the morning, and the clerk did not even look over toward them. Whether he was asleep or not was unclear. A porter, snoring in the corner near the stairs, was more obvious. The three paid them no attention. When they reached the hall, Sarah put a hand onto Jarrod's shoulder, slowing him to a walk, then even slower.

"If they've got her, we're just putting ourselves in the same trap," she said.

"What do you suggest?"

"Trade for her."

His eyes went to the ceiling for a moment while he thought about it, then he nodded. "I'll go in and stall as long as I can. You will have to find a way to get us out."

"Will Sir Charles listen to us?"

Jarrod reached in his pocket and took out the seal, "Give him this if he balks. Now get out of sight."

He waited until they were gone, took the pistol from his pocket and reached for the door. It was unlocked. As he walked in, the three men in the room turned to face him. Maërlys was on the couch, across the room in front of him. She was bound and gagged, her hair disheveled, her clothes disarranged. He saw the scar on her cheek just as the man standing next to her cocked his pistol and pointed it at her head.

"Welcome, your lordship, welcome," he said. "Please place the pistol on the desk. And your sword with it, if you don't mind."

The man nearest Jarrod brushed past him, looked out at the hall and closed the door. Jarrod saw the powder burn on his cheek Nubbins had mentioned. As Jarrod followed the other man's instructions, laying his weapons on the desk, the scarred man turned to him.

"You come alone?" he asked. "Where is your friend, *le noir*?

"One of your men killed him," Jarrod answered.

"Then our visit was not a complete waste of time," the man with the powder burn said. "Now we will kill you and return for the goods."

"If I may make a suggestion," said the man holding the pistol, "we should wait until you have collected what you were sent for before we dispose of these people. There has been too much hurry and we have so far nothing to show."

The third man spoke, "You are right. Jules, bind this fellow and let him sit next to the dressmaker. Then you will go and see if what he says is the truth. When you have loaded the coach, as you should already have done, you will return and tell us. Then we will depart."

"And them? M. Facteau, they have caused us much trouble. They should be repaid for their efforts. This, this, *putain*," he pointed at Maërlys, "attacked me on the street with a knife. In the public street." His outrage was apparent, almost comical.

Facteau shrugged, "Did you not tell me her scar was your doing? She can no longer hope to be part of society, even on the lowest levels. No doubt she will become a whore, just as you say. Are you not avenged?"

"Bah. I wish to make her suffer. When I return, I will kill her slowly, and this one will watch." Having bound Jarrod's hands behind him, he pushed him onto the couch next to Maërlys. "Only then will I let him die."

"You will all do as I say," Facteau said. "I have had enough of wild actions and bungling. Go now, Jules, and secure the treasure. We will discuss the rest when you return."

42

"M. Facteau, you are a gentleman. Please remove the gag from this poor girl's mouth. It causes her much suffering."

Facteau glared at Jarrod, "What do I care? She has caused us enough suffering since we met her."

"Since you kidnapped her in Portsmouth?"

Facteau looked thoughtfully at the ceiling. "Not I," he said, "you are thinking of M. Caron. Tell me, is he dead?"

"Remove her gag and I'll tell you anything you like."

"You will answer for it that she will not scream?"

Jarrod looked over at Maërlys' tear-streaked face and raised a brow. She nodded. "There you are," he said.

Facteau looked at his companion. The man went over to Maërlys and removed her gag. Maërlys shook her head so that her hair fell once more over the scar on her cheek, then looked down.

"Thank you, Mr. Argent," Jarrod said. "It is Mr. Argent, is it not?"

Argent looked startled, "Have we met?"

"No, but I thought it would be you. Sadler spoke of you often. Poor fellow. Thought you his greatest friend, and all the while you sucked on him as if he were a pipe of good tobacco. Even with Caron's sword in his belly, he believed in Mother England and its good men and true. Men like Thomas Argent. Some of the things he said made me wonder, but it is all clear now."

"Sadler's a fool."

"Yes. But not a bad man. Not a traitor to his country."

"My country. Indeed. Easy for you, your lordship, to speak of your country. It is yours, isn't it. Lock, stock, and barrel as they say. You lords and peers, making the rest of us bow and scrape in the streets. Idiots like Lincoln, gaining their places through their family connections, grateful for the crumbs they get while the rest of us starve."

"It was my impression you have a good place at the War Office."

"Which I worked hard to obtain and which could be taken away without notice if some lordling wants it, qualified or not. If you knew the idiots I work with, men like Sadler—"

Facteau cut in, "Caron is dead, then?"

"Yes," Jarrod answered, "along with his coachman. We left them in the crypt to amuse the admiral."

The ghost of a smile played on Facteau's face, "I approve." Jarrod bobbed his head in a brief bow. "Who did it? Sadler? You?"

"As a matter of fact, it was a woman."

"The Malay. Of course. Constantly she appears when she is not wanted."

Jarrod bowed again, "Miss Dane is a remarkable woman."

Maërlys looked up and turned to Jarrod, "You shouldn't talk about her to them. They will hurt her."

"No, my dear, they will not hurt anyone in this country again, saving perhaps our poor selves. They will leave the country by tonight or they will face trial. I do not believe they would come off well at trial. Am I right, M. Facteau?"

"Quite right, your lordship. Fortunately, we will never know for sure about your English justice. Our escape is long arranged."

"They're going to kill us, aren't they?" Maërlys did not seem overly upset at the prospect.

"Possibly, my dear. Certainly, that fellow Andre seemed to have an attitude about us that did not bode well. But M. Facteau is a pragmatic man. He will recognize that our deaths will serve no purpose except to heat up the chase."

"The chase will be hot enough that another degree or so will make no difference," Argent said.

"*Au contraire, mon ami,*" Jarrod said. "I may be only a lowly baron, but I do have a seat in the House. And the English do not approve the murder of women, particularly gentlewomen like my lovely companion. She is no daughter of the street, whatever malicious slander your friend Andre throws at her. She is companion to her respectable cousin who owns a dress shop frequented by any number of fashionable women. They will see themselves in her, and their husbands will ask impertinent questions in the House, demanding justice for this poor woman, hounded to her grave by the Jacobins who drove her from her native soil. You yourself will go from a mere unhappy office-holder seduced by French gold to a peericide, if there is such a word, possibly the most famous English traitor since that American fellow, Arnold. He too had a friend named Andre, as I recall. A name known on both sides of the channel."

"Of course, you would prefer we leave you here to guide our pursuers," Argent snarled.

"Indeed I would, but, as M. Facteau will point out, we could offer no guidance of any kind as we have no idea of your plans. There are at least fifty ports I can think of, possibly a hundred, where passage to France could readily be arranged. It would be impossible to warn them all in anything short of a week, and the chase would have to be exceedingly frantic to allow for so much manpower. More likely, it would take a month. Unless, of course, the bodies of a murdered gentlewoman and a peer of the realm were left as, shall we say, spice to pique the appetites of your pursuers? At this stage, notoriety does not serve your purposes that I can see."

"Humph," responded Argent, as he and Facteau withdrew to the far side of the room and began to speak in low tones.

"It's my fault, isn't it?" Maërlys asked. "You came here to rescue me and now you'll die with me."

"I could wish nothing more, my darling," Jarrod responded.

"Please don't be nice to me," Maërlys said. "I've been a fool. I've made a mess of everything and you and Sarah have had to fix things for me time after time. If it were left to me alone, Reynard and Ambre would be in the hands of these fiends even now, perhaps dead. Oh, why would you be nice to me?" Tears flowed down her cheeks.

Jarrod shrugged, "Haven't any choice, my dear. I love you madly and wish to marry you. If we are to die, I could ask no greater favor than to be at your side when we pass into a better world. If we survive, my fondest wish is that you will marry me, and we will live happily ever after, as they say in the fairy books. Now, if you can manage it, I would like so much to see one of those brilliant smiles, such as I remember from Portsmouth, and which brighten my dreams each night."

"Oh, you are so kind," Maërlys sobbed. "I told Emmy. And Sarah. The kindest man I ever met. I don't see how you can even look at me, after what that man did to me, but it is just that you are so kind, and you make me cry, and, and...." She began to sob even harder, and her voice was lost in a sort of choking.

"Rest your head on my shoulder, my darling. I would pull you close to me but these fellows have made that impossible, for the moment, with their ropes. Do forgive me, won't you, and just lay your head where I can feel it. Ah, yes, that's my girl," he said, as she sank down next to him and laid her head on his breast.

They sat like that for what seemed a very long time. For Jarrod, it was barely a sweet moment and, regardless of the situation, he was pleased to feel her closeness, her head on his chest, her sobs slowly dying away as if she were going to sleep. This is the way I would spend my evenings, he thought, except for the ropes, of course.

He had been trying them for some time but had made little headway. Andre may be a vicious, dreadful man but he knew his knots. Jarrod watched as Facteau returned to his desk and began going through his papers, destroying some things, placing others into a case.

Argent glowered at Jarrod, which the baron took for a hopeful sign, but Facteau said nothing. Argent took a seat nearby and began to look to his weapons. He had two pistols and Jarrod watched him check his flints, then lay them aside on the table at his right hand. The chiming of the clock on the table near the inner door allowed Jarrod to track the time. He believed it must be almost four in the morning when there was a knock at the door.

Argent picked up one of the pistols. Facteau nodded, walked over to the door and opened it a crack. He appeared nonplussed for a moment, then looked down. The door was pushed open wider, and the boy, Pardon, came in, pushing past Facteau, heading directly for Jarrod.

"'Ere, yer lordship, this ain't no good." He held a coin in his hand. "I shoulda bit it when yer give it me, but I di'n't, so when I did, it near broke me tooth, like. Brass, it is, I fink."

As he said this, he was proceeding across the room toward Jarrod and Maërlys, on the couch. Behind Pardon, Facteau closed his mouth, which had opened in astonishment. Then he waved at Argent who turned, first toward the boy, then back to Maërlys, cocking the pistol. As he moved, Jarrod jumped off the couch. The pistol swung in his direction as Henry hit Facteau low from behind, and he fell backward. Sarah Dane, running past Facteau, leapt through the air, passing over Pardon's head. The child ducked and rolled toward the desk.

Argent, presented with too many targets, began to turn the pistol toward Sarah, but he was too late. Her fist, holding her dorge, caught him on the chin just as Jarrod barreled into his stomach. The pistol went off, the ball burying itself in the couch where Jarrod had been a moment before.

Facteau rose, stumbling slightly as Henry grabbed at his ankle. He stepped through the open door just as Sir Charles came in, pushing him back.

Behind Sir Charles were two other men who held Jules Andre between them. Another pair followed this trio, closed the door behind them and took up stations on either side of it.

Jarrod looked at Andre. His left eye was puffy, there was an ugly bruise on his throat, and a new mark striped his cheek, this one leaking a line of blood.

Sarah lay on the floor, reclining as if at ease, one elbow resting on the chest of the unconscious Argent. She winked at Jarrod.

"Glad you moved, your lordship," she said.

He smiled at her, "As am I, Miss Dane, as am I. Could someone help us with these ropes, do you think? Is that Henry, playing with Mr. Facteau? It's a mercy he's my friend and not my servant as he's always pretending. Have to fire him, then, always lying about while others do the work."

He winked back at Sarah, who smiled as she got up and went to untie Maërlys. Henry silently came over and did the same office for Jarrod. The two men holding Andre set him in a chair and one, producing a pair of manacles, set about arranging Facteau in another. The other went to where Argent lay, fastened his hands behind his back and left him. Jarrod picked up the extra pistol from the table, removed the cap, and replaced the pistol.

"Gentlemen, if you will secure that case of Mr. Facteau's, I believe you will find it contains many items of interest to the Foreign Office."

"So now it is Mister Facteau," hissed Facteau. "It was *monsieur* when you were in our hands."

"It is always well, I believe, to be polite to those who hold your life in their hands. But now, the hand is on the other foot, so to speak, and you may wish to remember the lesson." He turned to Sir Charles, "I believe Mr. Facteau had decided not to have us murdered after all, and would perhaps..." he frowned warningly at Facteau, "...be willing to so testify at his trial."

Sarah walked over to Facteau and gazed down at him. Her voice was cold, "He ordered the assault on my home. He ordered the death of myself and everyone else who lived there, including that lovely child on the couch, who never did him the slightest harm. If you wish to speak for him at his trial it is your right. I am quite ready to speak against him."

"Witch," hissed Facteau.

"Mr. Andre seems a little the worse for wear," Jarrod noted. "Did he resist?"

Again, it was Sarah who spoke, "I might have wished he had resisted a little more. I was fully prepared to wrest his head from his shoulders."

Henry said, "I have been trying to reason with her in this regard, but she seems to have taken against the gentleman."

Sarah's eyes glittered, "You did not see Maërlys, how he had tied her to trees and cut her face so she would not be too pretty for their beastly attentions. I would cheerfully eat his liver."

Jarrod walked over, stood next to Sarah and looked down at Andre, "I would be honored to prepare it for you and serve the wine." Andre refused to meet their eyes.

Sir Charles said, "We will go now. Jarrod, Mr. Andre spoke of a load of boxes of treasure, which he was on his way to transport when we accosted him. He says these boxes are at your house and would be of interest to the crown. I trust they will still be there when I call on you tomorrow morning?"

"Why not come on tonight, Sir Charles. There are also a pair of corpses and a prisoner you could assist me with, was you so inclined."

He turned to Maërlys, "Come with me, darling. I will see you in a comfortable bed tonight, then tomorrow we will go to your cousin and discuss terms for our marriage."

For the first time, Maërlys took an interest in what was going on around her. She stood and faced Jarrod, "Sir, you are very kind, and it may be that your kindness sometimes outruns your good sense. I trust you to understand that I would never hold you to any promise made under duress." She turned to Sarah, "May I stay with you tonight, Sarah, and tomorrow may we journey back to the High Weald so I can rejoin Ambre and Reynard?"

"Of course, my love, of course. It shall be as you say." She put her arm around the younger woman, and they started for the door.

Then Sarah stopped, and looked at Jarrod, "I swore an oath to myself, long ago, that no woman under my protection would ever be subject to any coercion, however well meant; that she would be free to make her own choices, with or without my approval. I will keep that oath, though it may sometimes seem to me to add to, rather than subtract from, the world's large store of unhappiness."

Jarrod bowed his head and she went on, "I have come to think more highly of you than I once did, not least because this man," she indicated Henry, "values you. I know he would not do so were you not of great worth. So you have my respect and I wish you well. I hope you may find a way to that which your heart truly desires. Call on me at any time."

She turned to Henry, "You know the direction of both my houses. Call on me soon. Please." Her smile held a trace of melancholy but two dimples made themselves known. Then she turned and walked out with Maërlys on her arm.

Jarrod looked around for Pardon, but the boy had vanished.

43

Dawn was breaking when the carriage containing Jarrod, Henry, Sir Charles, and one of his men arrived at the house in Berkeley Square. The coach was driven by another of Sir Charles' men. The other two had left with Andre, Facteau, and Thomas Argent. The prisoners would probably eventually reach prison and the gallows, but it was likely they would spend a long, unpleasant time in the sub-basement of the Foreign Office first.

Inside, Jarrod pointed out the two men on the kitchen floor and Sir Charles' men made short work of the living one, fitting him with manacles and stowing him in the carriage. Then they all turned their attention to the boxes.

"Let's have that one open," Sir Charles said, pointing to the top case on the second stack. The box was opened and examined. It contained bars of lead, as used in the manufacture of shot. A second case was opened, this time second in line on the third stack. It, too, contained lead. The bottom crate on the first stack, the top box on the fourth stack, each was opened in its turn. All contained lead.

Sir Charles frowned at Jarrod, "Are you making game of me, sir?"

"My dear Sir Charles, ask Henry. Henry, are these not the boxes you brought with you from High Weald?"

"Yes sir," Henry said.

"And are they not the same boxes you saw transferred from the boat to the house in High Weald?"

"Transferred at least half of them myself, sir."

"And in France? The same boxes?"

"Yes sir. Absolutely."

Sir Charles broke in, "Were the boxes opened in France?"

"Only the top one on the stack," replied Jarrod. "It contained gold and was used to repay the sailors who rescued us from France. Is that not correct, Henry?"

"Just so, sir."

Sir Charles continued, "Then someone has been defrauded, and it may be that you have prevented the fraud from being discovered. Do you suppose the French captain who brought the stuff from the West Indies stole it from the admiral before ever it reached France?"

Jarrod raised his eyebrows, "Very possible, sir, now you mention it. I do hesitate to trust a Frenchman, at least, without I know him well."

"Well, I suppose the admiral can make as much use of the corpses of two French spies as he could with this lot of lead. And at least it will not come back at us to hole our ships below the waterline, eh?"

"Just as you say, sir. Always a silver, or in this case, lead lining."

"Well, I'll have 'em send a wagon around for your corpses. Probably sometime in the afternoon. Dispose of these boxes of lead as you see fit. Perhaps you can realize something by selling 'em to a shot manufacturer. Then we'll return 'em to the French, eh?"

"An excellent idea, Sir Charles, excellent."

Sir Charles bustled off, leaving Henry and Jarrod to remove the corpse from the upstairs hall and lay it on the floor of the anteroom, next to the cases of lead. Henry frowned at the cases.

"What's to be done with 'em?"

"Ask me tomorrow, Henry. Now, I am for bed."

"The sun is up."

"So it may remain but, for a while, I will not join it. I—" He was interrupted by the ringing of the front door bell. "Damme."

"I'll see to it," Henry said.

"No. You see to that scratch on your belly. I will take care of the door."

"You are a baron," Henry said stiffly.

"And you're a damn nuisance, but I never hold it against you. I can answer a door. At least, I used to do, sometimes, when I wasn't a baron. Go to bed."

"And what of my curiosity?"

"T'will be the death of you, someday. P'raps of us both. Very well, answer the door and be damned."

He followed Henry as far as the front parlor, then collapsed in the desk chair to await developments. Henry returned in a moment with Pardon Jenkins, who had a small girl in tow.

Pardon doffed his cap. "We're 'ere, sir, just as you asked."

"At six in the morning?"

"Well, we di'n't wish to be lite, beggin' yer worship's pardon."

"No, of course not," Jarrod said. He turned his attention to the girl, "I am Lord Cherille. Are you Betsy?"

The girl nodded, wide-eyed. She had been staring around at the room. Suddenly, she seemed to gather herself.

"D'yer live 'ere?" she asked.

"Sometimes," he said. Do you like it?"

"Coo. I should say."

He turned back to Pardon, "What about you? Where do you live now?"

"Got us a plice at Missus Black's, we do. A corner, down a bisement. It's a little cold come winter, but I bin working for Bill a w'ile now and we might get somefing, like, come October."

"Have you ever thought of coming to the country?"

The little girl's eyes narrowed, "Wadda yer mean, country? W'at's that like, eh?" she said.

"'Ush," said her brother. "Naow. Ain't got no bidness ina country. Never bin."

"I will make you a proposition. I intend to return to my country house tomorrow. If you like, you may come with me and I will find work for you. Your sister can come too and may start school if she likes. You can go to school also, but I leave it to you. Either way, I promise you will be warm in the winter and have plenty to eat. If you do not like it, you may come back to London whenever you say, and I will give you five pounds, no ten, in gold, to do with as you like. Is that fair?"

The boy's eyes were now as narrow as those of his sister, "Whuffor, eh? You wouldn't be plannin' any bidness wiv me sister, would yer?"

This question nonplussed Jarrod for a moment and he looked helplessly at Henry, who was struggling to contain his laughter.

Finally, he said, "No. Of course not. I swear on a bible, or anything you like, that neither of you would ever be asked to do anything of which you did not approve."

Slowly, the boy nodded, "Well, 'at's all right, then."

"Excellent. You go see Bill and make sure all is right with him, and he pays you up to date. Then gather your things and be back here tomorrow morning. Will that do?"

"Right. And after we gets to the country we can come back 'ere if we don't like it?"

"I promise, and here's my hand on it."

The boy wiped his own on his shirt and shook, took his sister by the hand, and they left. She was still staring around at the appointments of the house as the door closed behind them.

Henry raised his eyebrows.

"She's only four," Jarrod said. "She may do very well."

"But the lad'll go crazy."

"We'll find him something. Perhaps he likes horses or other animals. He's still young. Have faith, Henry."

"How is your faith, sir?"

Jarrod's smile was rueful, "Failing, Henry, but we will see what can be done."

The trip to Cherille was uneventful, or would have been except for the children. They sat in the coach, and Pardon continuously asked questions of Jarrod. Betsy said almost nothing except "Coo," uttered at frequent intervals.

Changing horses at Reading and Newbury, Henry kept the coach moving as quickly as possible. Jarrod had initially suggested they take it in two days, to spare the children, but Henry had balked, "You'll see, best get it over," and Jarrod eventually admitted he was right. After supper at Newbury both children went to sleep, Pardon with his arm curled protectively around Betsy. Eventually, Jarrod nodded off himself.

When they arrived at Cherille the children were given over to the care of Marrin, who quickly called his wife, the housekeeper, into consultation. Since Christian's death, the staff had become a bit relaxed, as Marrin put it, and the two chief servants saw this as an opportunity to correct this incipient problem.

The next morning Jarrod had a brief conversation with Pardon, who readily admitted he was satisfied with his accommodations and agreed to accept guidance from Herbert and Patience Marrin. Betsy nodded enthusiastically but said little, other than a request to "see the 'orses."

"I'm sure that can be arranged," Jarrod said. "Henry and I have business elsewhere and must be away, but we will come back in a few days, or possibly a week. Then, if you are dissatisfied, we can discuss what situation you might prefer. Will that be all right?"

"Aye, yer lordship. I reckon we'll do. Might be they'll 'ave work for me by then."

"Indeed," Jarrod said, smiling at them both. He shook hands with Pardon and went in search of Henry.

"Ready for a visit to the High Weald?"

"Oh, Sarah, please, I simply cannot face him anymore. He is so handsome, and so kind to me, just looking at him makes me want to cry. I am afraid I will say something stupid and ruin both our lives forever."

"My love, if you feel so strongly about him, why not just marry him and be done? I believe he is a good man. Henry so assures me, and my confidence in Henry is, as you know, very high indeed."

"You do not intend to marry Henry."

"I do not intend to marry anyone, although I admit...that man...sometimes I think.... But no, I could never settle for any one love. But you are not like me; I know you enjoyed our time together, but you want something different. And I, well, I want you to have it."

Maërlys pulled back her hair to expose the scar on her cheek. "Look at this, Sarah. How could I marry a baron? How could I be his hostess at balls, knowing the ladies were whispering behind my back? We would finish as a laughing-stock. It would be the ruin of him, socially, politically, who knows? I do not wish to be the object of pity, his or anyone's, and to drag him down with me would be too humiliating. I would probably end in his mill-pond, my pockets full of rocks."

"Do you think it is pity that brings him here to see you? Simon advises me his carriage has been in the village and he will be here within the hour. I'm told there was an incredibly handsome man with dark skin on the box." She smiled, casting her eyes to the ceiling. "Will you not join me in happiness, kitten?"

"Do you think he comes to see me? He comes to see to those boxes you have in the cellar. By now, the ones in London will have been opened and he will have to take some action."

"Pooh. He is one of the richest peers in the land, and I have seen nothing to indicate he cares for money in the least. I make you a wager. If he does not refuse to take a penny for himself, then I will match every cent he takes and settle that amount on your Reynard. He cares only for you. I am sure of it."

She took both of Maërlys' hands in hers and looked into her eyes, "Come, my darling, will you not relent and consider his proposal? I am confident he intends to make you one, a proper marriage offer without any bonds or French agents to distract you."

Tears shone in Maërlys' eyes and she shook her head violently. "Please, Sarah, do not ask it of me. Do not leave me alone with him. I am so weak, I know I could not resist him, and it would be the end of everything. I must take the children back to London and we shall set up house with Emmy. It will be all right. You shall see. You have done so much for me; please do this last favor and I will always be your servant."

Sarah's face was grim, but she forced a smile, "I will not coerce you, my darling. Your life is your own, and so are your choices. When he is gone, we will make the arrangements and get you to London with your family as quickly as may be. It will be another month before we have to open the house for gambling but some of us may go with you to begin the process. You are to remember I am your friend always, and you know if there is ever anything you need, you must call on me. I will be very hurt if you do not, do you understand me?"

"Oh, yes, I promise," said the younger woman, throwing her arms around Sarah's neck.

44

Sarah came bustling into the parlor, where Jarrod and Henry sat at ease. They rose as she came in.

"Good day, your lordship, and welcome back to High Weald. It is good to meet you at last, with no menaces threatening us." She curtsied to each of them, making a point of doing her honors to Henry first. He glowered and she laughed.

"Sir, your friend rebukes me for not properly honoring a Peer of the Realm. I hope you do not take offence."

"No indeed, ma'am. By now you surely know that Henry is far prouder of my position than I could ever hope to be. It is all I can do to make him sit at table and not stand behind my chair. As if such a position would not make me too nervous to eat."

She laughed. "Well, we are glad to see you here so soon. We had not looked for you for at least another week."

"And yet no one seems at all surprised. Your man Simon opens the door as we draw up, the groom is standing by to care for the horses, we are led in here where hot tea awaits us on the sideboard. No one asks our names or our business. Anyone would think we were expected every moment."

She laughed and shrugged her shoulders, "You brush aside the wool we drag across your eyes. My business interests are, shall we say, far-flung, and it would be very silly of me not to know what goes on in my neighborhood. Your presence in the village was noted and preparations were duly made. I trust they will be to your liking."

"Indeed, I have no doubt of it. And may I know how our traveling companions fare, now that they are come safely to dry land in such a commodious house?"

"Though still abed, Mr. Sadler grows stronger by the day, under the watchful eye of Clara de Tiffauges. The children also are well, sir, and enjoying themselves immensely. They look forward eagerly to the sights and sounds of London town. Nor do I imagine for a moment that any of these are the voyagers to whom you refer." Her eyebrows came to a point above her eyes.

"I admit to a great curiosity regarding your fair companion, Maërlys de Brissy."

For the first time in his acquaintance with her, Jarrod found he had embarrassed Sarah Dane. Her complexion darkened, and for a moment she failed to meet his eyes. Then she gathered herself and once again gazed clearly at him.

"Despite my urging, Miss de Brissy has refused to meet with you alone, so I beg you will not ask it of us. She will join us for meals and other group activities, but asks that you importune her no further about personal matters. Do I make myself clear?"

Jarrod's face hardened and he struggled to compose himself. Finally, he said, between clenched teeth, "Quite clear, ma'am."

"Now I have made you angry. I promise it was never in my mind to do so. Please understand that, except in this one thing, the hospitality of my home is open to you in every sense. I have told you that I cannot be the instrument of coercion to anyone who seeks asylum with me, and must offer Miss de Brissy the same courtesy I would offer anyone. Indeed, I believe in my place, you, as a gentleman, would do the same."

Slowly, Jarrod's face relaxed and took on a rueful expression, "You are right to reprove me, ma'am. I bow to Miss de Brissy's wishes, and thank you for your hospitality. May I hope to return it, both at Cherille House in London and someday, at your leisure, at Cherille Hall in Wiltshire?"

Sarah smiled with pleasure and grinned at Henry, "Do you think we can persuade Mr. Winnow to allow you to fill your home with dark-skinned people? It will be your social ruin."

"Mr. Winnow will simply have to come to terms with it. I will be master in my own home." He looked at Henry and, in response to that gentleman's frown, added, "At least, most of the time."

Sarah laughed, "Excellent. Then let us go in to luncheon and afterward we will see what awaits us in the cellar. Will that be acceptable?"

"Lead the way. We are at your command, eh, Henry?"

The meal was a terrible trial for Jarrod. He was seated at some distance from Maërlys, and struggled to keep his eyes on anything else, but they would wander to her face. Worse, every time they did he found her eyes on him, although she would instantly look away. He felt his face burning all through the meal, toyed with the food on his plate, and was desperately relieved when the torment finally ended and Sarah led a large crowd downstairs to the cellar.

The two children, Reynard and Ambre, were also at luncheon, showing off the few English words they had acquired. Simon McInnis, Sarah's butler, bodyguard, and chief male support; Julia Harley, her secretary; and several others of the household joined the group in the cellar.

It was a large cellar, reached after passage through two false walls, and contained a great number of cases in addition to the ones of interest to Jarrod and Henry. Looking around, Jarrod noted an amazing supply of really excellent Cognac, and quite a few cases of the harder to acquire Armagnac. Looking back, he realized that Sarah Dane was watching him, smiling.

"Are you thirsty, my lord?"

"Not at the moment, but I will know where to come when I am," he smiled back.

"I am trusting you with this secret. I believe you understand the need for it, and will not betray us." She waved her hand to indicate the members of her household.

Jarrod bowed, "I am sensible of the honor, and swear in the name of my family to keep this and any other secrets you may require."

"Well spoken. Now, let us discuss these twenty-two cases. Henry and I did a quick audit when the contents of the boxes were transferred, but it might be as well to do a more complete one. Would you like to be present, or would Henry act as your representative?"

"Henry may speak for himself, but as for me, I leave any counting in the capable hands of yourself and your, ah, friends."

"What of your friend, Sir Charles? Need we be concerned about Government?"

Henry spoke up, "You would have been proud of his lordship, Miss Dane. Asked me questions like a lawyer. Always boxes this, boxes that, never a word about the contents, so I was never required to speak the slightest untruth. Sir Charles was a bit wild, had us open four boxes, or was it five? Lead in every one. Jarrod will sell them to a manufacturer of ammunition 'to recoup his losses,' as Sir Charles put it."

She looked at Jarrod, "Remember not to sell them all; one of them contains some of that Armagnac you have been admiring. A gift for you, as thanks."

Jarrod bowed again, "You are more than generous, ma'am. I thank you, and so, no doubt, does my butler. He is very fond of good brandy."

"Then, if we are to do the counting, how would you have us divide the, ah, spoils?" Sarah asked.

"Well," Jarrod replied, "here we are the representatives of two households. Would it suit you to divide the, ah, booty, evenly betwixt?"

Sarah glanced at Maërlys, and noted the look of triumph in her eyes. "Half to be distributed by me, and half by you, sir?" she asked.

"Oh, my half could be evenly divided into two parts, and I would leave their distribution to you. That would be half, or one quarter of the entire, to Henry, here, who, although the worthiest man in Christendom, to the best of my knowledge, has no fortune of his own."

Jarrod went on, "Everyone knows, I think, that I have quite enough money for any one man, so the remaining quarter should go to those who have protected it all this time. You will see it bestowed upon young Reynard and Ambre de Brissy, will you not? I am presuming that you will bestow some portion of your own share upon your friend, the lovely Maërlys de Brissy. If I presume too much, then I ask you to divide that quarter equally with the de Brissy family, to be administered by Maërlys."

This time, Sarah's glance showed her a Maërlys whose eyes were wide, her mouth opened in a soundless O. She watched as two hands rose to cover the mouth, and tears sprang into the eyes. Then Sarah curtsied to Jarrod.

"You are generous, sir. For my part, I believe the entirety of the remainder belongs to Maërlys, and although I am sure she will bestow some portion on poor Mr. Sadler, who has suffered so much, I am confident it will allow the de Brissys to live as they deserve, and not as they have been forced these last years."

Maërlys eyes were swinging wildly from Sarah to Jarrod, and back again. Her hands still covered her gasps, and her tears were flowing freely. Sarah smiled at her.

"So then," she said, "it will not be necessary for you to have even a farthing from me." She winked, Maërlys gasped again, her eyes rolled up, and she sank to the floor, or would have, had Jarrod not moved quickly and caught her.

Before he could stop himself, he kissed her lightly on the brow and murmured, "My darling, my love," in her unconscious ear. Simon and Julia moved to relieve him of a burden he unwillingly relinquished. He looked into Sarah's eyes and, before he managed to hide it, she found herself physically shocked by the pain she saw there. He looked at the floor, then watched as Maërlys was borne away, followed by her siblings.

When he looked at Sarah again, his feelings were masked, "You have told us that Mr. Sadler is improving slowly. May we be allowed to see him before we return? In fact, if you are agreeable, I believe Henry might like to stay for another day or two. If you can let me have a good saddle horse, a long jaunt across country would no doubt do me a world of good."

Sarah looked at Henry, who nodded. "Nothing could be easier, my lord," she said. "May all our blessings go with you. I will have it readied while Jenny here conducts you to Mr. Sadler's side."

Upstairs, they found Lincoln Sadler much improved from the near-corpse they had unloaded at Hastings less than a week earlier. He was closely, even possessively, attended by Clara de Tiffauges. Simon whispered to Jarrod that she was always by his side and would not allow anyone else to do anything for him. She bathed him twice a day, changing his dressings and lovingly seeing to his every need, no matter how squalid. They noticed that fresh flowers abounded and there was no smell of the sickroom, testament to Clara's constant attention.

"So, will you do, old fellow?" Jarrod asked.

"I believe I will, with help." Sadler smiled at Clara, who sat beside him, clutching his hand.

"How about the old trouble. Does it bother you to be here, in the Dane household?"

"I think," Sadler replied, smiling warmly at Clara again, "that is melting away. I have learned a great deal during our experience, and I thank you for allowing me to come. It is an educational thing, to go in search of something, and, finding it, realize it was not what you wanted at all. And lo, there is the real thing before your eyes. I know now what wonder is. I cannot thank you enough."

"You must get well rapidly and completely. Sir Charles apparently cannot manage without you and holds me responsible. I believe my family will lose one of its oldest friends should any more harm come to you."

"I believe the loss would be no more than I deserve," Sadler answered. "Had I not shared the secret of LeMay-sur-Èvre with my poor Clara, we would all have been much safer."

"I think not," Jarrod responded. "I think it was her possession of the secret that saved her life, and brought her back to you."

Sadler smiled at Clara a third time, and Jarrod felt his chest fill with a debilitating emptiness when he saw the love that was returned in the girl's eyes.

"I cannot imagine myself in better hands," Sadler replied. "Nor would I wish to be."

"I fear your parents will not find it much improvement."

"Then they can be damned," the young man answered, without rancor. "As I say, I have learned a great deal."

Jarrod laughed, though the sound was a bit hollow in his own ears. "Very well," he said. "Once you have got on your feet and finished all Sir Charles' papers for him, you will no doubt be exhausted. Come and stay a while in Wiltshire." He smiled sadly at Clara, who smiled back. "Bring a friend, if you like. It's pleasant country, we can shoot a little, and there may still be some very good brandy."

Standing next to the beautiful mare Sarah had provided for his return journey, Jarrod looked at Henry and took his hand, "Enjoy your stay, will you, and try not to insist on too many changes. Your friend will make a formidable enemy."

"She would that, but I know my place. You have been good to us, and I intend to stay by her as much as I can. However, I am not fool enough to think that she will take a saddle like this one." He patted the mare's neck.

"Well, I intend a quiet time of reflection at home, putting the estate's affairs in order. I would welcome your help any time but unless we are called to action, I hope you may find some little bit of peace, here."

"This business with the Leopard and the Chesapeake may cause a disturbance," Henry said.

"Yes, the damn fools. Napoleon is not enough of an enemy; they must enlist the Americans on his side. If that happens, they'll want us to go and use our contacts. I won't like it; it's mere stupidity. The Americans are our most natural allies. Damme, they're Englishmen after all."

He smiled, "See you've got me all wrought up. Well, it's good to feel something else, even if it's only the usual anger at military folly. You know my man of business, he'll see you right with that money. Or Nubbins will guide you, if you prefer. You'll find me in Wiltshire when you like. Take care old friend."

"You too," Henry said, watching him ride away. "You take care as well."

45

"Henry!" Sarah cried as he came into the room. "Where have you been?"

"Nubbins has been entertaining me. I thought you'd enjoy the rest." He went over to the fire and began to warm his hands. "Your obvious pleasure at my return proves I was correct."

She cocked her head to one side and showed him both dimples, "Are you implying that I was ever anything less than glad to see you?" She reached out and stroked his cheek, then withdrew her hand, "Goodness, you're cold."

"I fear London in December is no place for an 'umble native from Jamaica."

She shivered theatrically, "Nor a Malay either. I believe it takes five to eight years to grow accustomed to it. Come closer and I'll warm you up a bit."

He took her in his arms, kissed her thoroughly, drew back, looked into her eyes, and kissed her again. "Hmm," she said, "I believe we may make it through January, even February at this rate, forlorn displaced foreigners though we be."

He laughed, "I have hopes of lasting even longer and the best way I know is to deprive you of my presence from time to time. You'll never fully appreciate me, else."

"You'll not deprive me of your presence this evening, I hope, I hope," she said.

"No, nor tomorrow morning either, if you'll allow me, but then I believe I must go and see Lord Cherille. Christmas will be here before we are ready, and the last time I saw him I was positively fearful for his health."

She sobered, "Yes, you said. My friends tell me I am in the baron's debt. That man Facteau apparently tried to drag me down with him, using my name indiscriminately during his interrogation. Someone with connections stopped those insinuations from getting into court, sparing me from joining those evil men on the gallows. I know who that someone must be and owe him my life. It grieves me to hear of his despondency. Thin and morose were the words you used, I believe."

"At best. I fear he will waste away. As you know, I am completely enthralled with your lovely self. I have never met any woman I could love so completely, and I worship you as, I believe, any man in his right senses must, but I am fortunate. You are good enough to return at least a small part of this feeling, and tolerate my presence in your life—"

"Tolerate, is it? I'd like to see you get away. You may speak blithely of 'depriving me of your presence,' but I am not to be trifled with. Do it too often and you'll find yourself dragged back here, whether you

will or no. Bound hand and foot, if need be." She
caressed his cheek and ran her fingers into his hair,
her other hand placed possessively on his chest.

"Nonsense. I know how you feel about coercion."

"Coercion of women. Men are different animals."

He shook his head and smiled at her, "My dear, I
love you more than I can tell. If you refused me, as
Maërlys de Brissy has done the baron, I misdoubt I
would be the one wasting away for sheer misery. And
so I will go once more in hopes of offering him some
small cheer at this season. Speaking of the de Brissy,
how does she manage with her vast wealth? I've no
doubt she is the toast of London, beauty that she is."

"She is beautiful, indeed, although she does not
believe it. Instead of making a virtue of that scar,
which adds spice to what might otherwise be a
somewhat insipid, though lovely, countenance, she
decries it and blames it for her misery. I have begged
Julia, whose scar is much more evident, to speak
sense to her, but she finds every excuse she can to
make Julia's misfortune appear smaller and her own
larger. It is positively morbid."

"Cannot the money attract enough men to flatter
her out of this nonsense?"

"It is the most provoking paradox. The money
she keeps as a secret. She has hardly touched it,
except for small amounts to see to the education of the
children. I believe she feels herself unworthy of the
treasure, even though the scar she hates is proof that
she has paid for every *sou*. She has left it in my care,

so naturally it is Julia who manages it, a task she delights in. Making money grow is her talent and her joy, and I think Maërlys' fortune already exceeds its original value, despite the costs of the children."

"In the meanwhile, Maërlys continues to toil away in her cousin's shop, as if she were still dependent. I know she used a small portion of the money to eliminate Emmeline's financial worries, and I know her cousin urges her to consider living more elaborately, but she refuses and mopes, avoiding mirrors."

"What do you suppose is the source of this morbidity? Can it be cut out, as a surgeon might do?"

"I speculate upon it frequently. I am certain it has to do with this baron of yours, and I suspect were he still Jarrod Everly and not Lord Cherille, it might be possible to…, well, I don't know exactly, but I'm sure something could be done. I really believe it is the title which holds the key."

Henry frowned. "But they are related. We know that from the circumstance that Jarrod held the key to the de Brissy and Leissègues crypt. They must be some sort of cousins, distant as it might be. There could be no bar of rank where the same blood flows."

"Go ahead, if you like, and use logic on those who are in love. Well may it serve you. Tell me, since I am so rich, and you, until recently, were quite poor, would you have sought me so avidly had you not made your fortune in France?"

He smirked at her and winked. "Even more avidly, I make no doubt."

She laughed. "I know you better. You would never hunt for a treasure alone. Had this one not fallen into your hands, by accident as it were, you would still be begging from the mice at church."

"Maybe, but I would never let it keep me from pursuing the only woman I've ever met who carries a dorge."

"It is as I suspected. You are nothing but a slave to your dulodulo."

"And to you, my love, but never again to any man." He seized her and kissed her once more. They were both breathing heavily when the kiss broke.

"You must consider your friend and I will give thought to mine," Sarah gasped, "but for the moment I intend to forget them both and think only of you."

Henry said nothing but there was smoke in his eyes as he pulled her to him again.

Henry watched the groom taking his horse back to the stables as he pulled on the great bell rope. He was a bit surprised at how long it took the massive front door of Cherille Hall to swing open and was considering another pull when it finally did. The servant was not one he had seen before.

"Hello there," Henry smiled, "I don't believe we've met. I am Henry Winnow and would like to see the baron. Is he at home?"

"No, he ain't," responded the servant, starting to close the door. Henry put his hand on it, and it stopped, which disconcerted the servant a bit. He glowered at Henry.

"Perhaps you can tell me when he's expected," Henry said, no longer smiling.

"Dunno. Try around back," answered the man.

Nonplussed, Henry was considering a variety of responses when Herbert Marrin appeared behind the stranger, who turned to him, affronted.

"Dunno who he is sir. Somehow he's humbugged a groom into taking his horse, but now—"

"Pleased to see you, Mr. Winnow," said Marrin over the man's shoulder. "If you'll step this way I'll seat you in the parlor. His lordship is out riding at the moment but we will make you comfortable until he gets back."

"But sir, he's a—"

"If you wish to retain your place here, it would be best to return to the kitchen as quickly as possible. You may institute your inquiries there. At the moment you are blocking the entrance to the house, preventing his lordship's oldest and closest friend from entering."

"Oh, ah," the man said, obviously shaken. As he moved away he was heard to mutter, "No house I was ever in...."

Marrin gazed at Henry, concern in his eyes, but it was easy to see that Henry was trying to control his laughter. "Right this way, sir," he said, and saw Henry seated comfortably in the parlor. "By the way, if I may make so bold...?"

"Oh, for heaven's sake, Herbert," Henry said, "there's no one here but us. Unpack it for me."

The butler visibly relaxed. "Yes sir. His lordship only went out a little while ago and he is wont to ride for some time these days. Though it's not my place to say so, I think it helps him face the day."

"You're a good man, Herbert. He's lucky to have you keeping an eye out. How are those children he adopted?"

"Flourishing, sir, flourishing. The boy has turned into lord of the stables, when he's not following the gamekeeper. For a city lad, he's taken to the country like a duck in the rain. Slips away to the village if he's not watched, but so far has only gotten into three fights. At least, only three that we know of." He frowned, then brightened. "Acquitted himself well on each occasion, as far as could be determined."

"Ha," said Henry. "Pardon, indeed. And the little girl, Betsy?"

Marrin smiled, a thing Henry had never seen before. "Follows my wife everywhere, she does. Once she stopped saying coo to everything, she turned out to be quite bright. Might be a fine servant, someday, if she doesn't get snapped up above her station. Pretty little thing, though it's hard to be sure when they're so young."

He turned serious. "Would you like anything while you wait? A drink, some tea? Will you be staying? I believe we have your usual room ready but I'll make sure. And before I forget, Miss Susan Arville is also visiting. Shall I tell her you are here?"

"I would like a dish of tea, if you don't mind, and would be more than glad to see Miss Arville, if she can spare the time. In fact...," his eyes grew thoughtful.

"Very well, sir. I'll inform the lady of your presence. The tea will be ready shortly. If you like, I can send it with the man who answered the door." He raised one eyebrow.

Henry laughed, "No, thank you, Herbert. That poor fellow has enough to contend with, house full of, well, guests, and all. He'll need time to adjust."

It was only about five minutes before Susan came in. She was dressed in black. "Henry," she said, holding out both hands to him. "I'm so glad you've come."

"Oh? Is something amiss?" he asked, taking both hands in his own and bowing over them.

"It's just Jarrod; he seems so low and it's been months since that business was settled. Perhaps you can take him hunting or something."

"In December?"

"Well, you know what I mean. You're his friend. Can't you cheer him up?"

"Perhaps I should have made note of some witty sayings."

She frowned at him, "I should know better."

"I believe you do."

"Oh, very well, but something's got to be done. Wait till you see him. His clothes hardly fit him anymore."

"As bad as that? I'd hoped he might move on. Does he not tend the estate?"

"Of course he does. Have you ever known him to neglect work? It's just that he's so unhappy. It makes me want to swear at him."

"Have you tried it?"

She smiled at that, "Actually," she said, looking down, "I have."

"No effect?"

"Well, he did widen his eyes a bit, told me not to say such things, but then he just ambled off into his black stew."

"And the solution?"

"Well, of course you know he wants a wife."

Henry nodded, gazing at her. She stared back at him.

"Oh, no you don't," she said. "Honestly, you men are all the same."

"What do you mean by that?"

"He made the same suggestion himself, not long after the funeral. You never saw a man so relieved as when I turned him down."

"You turned him down? Why ever would you do that?"

"Make jokes if you like, but this is serious. I've never met this Maërlys de Brissy, but she must be a very special woman."

"Of course. That's it! You've never met her. Tell me, how concerned are you about Jarrod? What are the limits, exactly?"

She stared at him fiercely this time, "Well, the altar of course. I'm not the wife for him nor is he the man I need, though I love him dearly. I'd do anything for him that I would for a brother."

"Excellent. I've a sort of plan starting to form in my mind and we must discuss it. You see, I believe he is not alone in his misery. My friend Miss Dane advises me that Miss de Brissy is in similar straits. It is my belief that the difficulty lies in pride, but it is hard to know exactly where the edges of that pride may be found. So that it can be got 'round, if you follow me. We need a spy."

She was staring at him, her eyes wide, a frown beginning when the tea came in.

46

"Maërlys, it is simply too ridiculous, wasting your time here in the shop, when you know you've got money enough to set up your carriage, goodness, dozens of carriages, from what Miss Dane says."

"Sarah ought not to gossip so. And the children may need that money. Expatriates are ever so much more welcome in their adopted countries if they have money."

"My experience is that anyone is more welcome anywhere if they have money. Someday this Bonaparte will be history and they can return to France if they like. I'm not suggesting you throw it all away, merely that you make yourself more comfortable, rather than slaving away here making money for me. Miss Dane says—"

"If you say that one more time, Emmy, I swear to you, I will scream as loudly as I can. I love Sarah, as you well know, but—"

"And she loves you, and wants the best for you, as do I—"

"Well, if you want me to leave, you've only to say so—"

At this Emmeline put her arms around her cousin, "You know how much I love you, Maërlys. Your company makes the shop so much more than it could ever be without you. You know that, don't you? Please, say you do, I—"

The shop bell rang as a customer came in. It was Susan Arville, still dressed in black, who stood looking at the two women embracing for a moment, as they returned her stare. Finally, she ventured, "If I'm intruding, I can come back."

"Oh, no, no, no," Maërlys and Emmeline said in unison, then looked at each other.

Emmeline continued, "We beg your pardon. Just a momentary disagreement. In what way can we be of service?"

"You could begin by telling me how to end my disagreements with people in such an inviting way. I find we are usually mad at each other for ages. It's so unpleasant."

Maërlys and Emmeline both flushed. Emmy recovered first, "Well, we are cousins, and, being family, have not the luxury of being mad at each other for long. Besides, we do really love each other, and enjoy working together, but, sometimes, well, you know, we forget. But then it's all over, isn't it Maërlys? How may we assist you?"

Susan was staring around at the clothing on display, "I would like to buy some new things, and you do such beautiful work. I haven't been here in ever so long. I don't stay often in London."

"Will you need things right away?"

Susan smiled at her, "You are wondering about my mourning. My fiancé died six months ago and I have already been frowned at for clinging to my loss so long, but we were very attached. I had promised myself six months, and now must rejoin society, whether I wish it or no. I promise I will be very grateful for your help."

"I remember now. You are Miss Arville, are you not? I am sorry for your bereavement. I apologize for being so stupid, but it must be almost two years since we saw you. Please forgive me. Would you like to look around at some of our styles? We have a collection of French dolls you could examine."

Noticing that Maërlys had moved away, Susan followed Emmy to the counter. As Emmy reached under and began to bring up some of the fashion dolls, Susan leaned close and said in a low tone, "I was engaged to Lord Cherille." Emmeline's face went white, and the doll she was holding dropped to the floor.

She recovered herself before she recovered the doll, "Oh! I beg your pardon again. You startled me. You mean, six months...you must mean—"

"Christian Everly, yes. I am sorry I startled you. I was hoping to speak to you alone."

"To me? But...," she looked around for Maërlys, but the younger woman was not in sight.

"Yes, yes. I am told by mutual acquaintances that your cousin is not entirely happy. I know it is impertinent, especially from a stranger, but it may be of great importance to both of us. Is it true?"

Emmy considered the woman, thinking. Eventually, she nodded.

"I know the current Lord Cherille is also unhappy. May I speak to you about it?"

Emmy looked about her, then whispered, "Not here. May I come to you?"

"Please," Susan answered, and gave Emmeline a card. More loudly, she said, "Can you do that design in this fabric?" turning to a nearby rack.

"Of course, ma'am. It would be a pleasure," Emmy said. "Do you like this color? I believe this violet would bring out your eyes most delightfully. And the eyes of others, as well."

After that, it seemed to Maërlys that the new customer, this Susan Arville, was almost constantly in the shop. Hardly a day went by when she did not stop in and she often stayed for over an hour, sometimes even two. She was quite liberal in her choices of fabric and design and seemed happy to rely entirely on Emmy's discretion.

To be fair, she was relentlessly cheerful despite her mourning, and always pleasant. She never played the great lady or ordered them about, as some customers were liable to do. In fact, she was almost deferential, which puzzled Maërlys.

"It's the mourning," Emmy assured her. "She's just a little shy about coming out of it. I gather she was very fond of her fiancé and it feels like a betrayal, putting herself back on the market, if you will."

"Very well, but has she paid you anything on account? You've done an awful lot of work for her. You must have created eight dresses, all in different styles and colors, as yet unpaid for."

"As a matter of fact, Miss Suspicious, she has been quite generous. I believe she does not owe more than a third of the total at this moment, and I have not even begun her latest commission. As you know, that is more than we ever get out of some of our 'best' customers."

"True, but that is why you have to make the prices so high, to cover the defaults."

"If it keeps up, I shall have to give her the last two pieces *gratis* to avoid over-charging her. Honestly, Maërlys, you would not be so near about this were you not so unhappy."

"What makes you think I'm unhappy?"

"Just that you've been moping for the last four months, ever since you came back from France with the children. Honestly, if your face gets any longer, you could dust the floor with it."

"I'm just worried about the children."

"Nonsense. You're worried about that man, Lord Cherille."

"He means nothing to me!" snapped Maërlys.

"Then say his name to me in a normal tone of voice."

"Lord Cherille, Lord Cherille, Lord Cherille. There."

"You call that a normal tone of voice?"

"Oh, Emmy, what do you want from me?"

"It's not a lot to ask. Say 'Lord Cherille,' or better, 'Jarrod Everly,' in a normal tone of voice. As if you didn't care. Go on. Let me hear you."

"Please, Emmy, don't make fun of me."

"I am not making fun, Maërlys. I am in absolute earnest. I love you, and to see you unhappy eats at my heart. That man could have made you happy and why he does not is more than I can understand. I remember when he came about that execution and asked if you wished to see the death of that spy who gave you the scar. It was wise of you to say no, as it cannot be good for the spirit to watch the death of anyone, but he did it in case it would make you feel better. He honestly seemed to care about you and I'd take my oath he wanted to say more to you, but held himself in. And you were so cold to him, as if he didn't matter. Well, if that's so, if he doesn't matter, say it. Say his name. No one else is here. Say it."

Maërlys glared at her, then calmed herself. She pulled herself up straight and looked her cousin in the eyes, "Ja, Jar, Jarrod...," was all she could manage, then she was in tears, crouching at Emmy's feet, hugging herself and sobbing.

When Emmy knelt beside her, pulled her close, and hugged her, Maërlys laid her head on her breast. She looked at her cousin through her tears, "Oh,

Emmy, he was so kind to me. When I played the whore, he wouldn't let me; he treated me with respect and stopped, though it must have been painful for him. And always, he's been so kind. When I was, was, damaged, he offered to m-marry me. He offered again later. I think he feels pity for me because he is so kind. And, oh, I want him so much. I would be his mistress, if he wanted me, but I know he is too kind and good to use me that way. He already refused the chance."

"So why not just marry him?"

"Look at me. I am scarred; horrible, brutal men have stripped me and beaten my naked body; I shamed myself by trying to seduce him. If I were his lady, I would be hostess at his parties and the women would make fun of me, and refuse our invitations, and I would drag him down with me. I would ruin him. And all because he pities me. I could never marry him under duress, whether it is he or I who feels it."

"But how can you feel duress when you want him so much?"

"No, you are right. If he had not this pity, this feeling that he must save me, then I suppose.... But no, there is still his social position to consider. It can never be, Emmy, and I must accept it. I will try, but it may be some time yet before I can be cheerful. If you cannot bear it, just tell me, and I will go away until I am fit to be in company, however long it takes."

"No, my darling, you shall not leave me. We will face what must be faced together, and I will be by your side. I will see you through this miserable time, and stay with you until your brilliant smile shines upon us again." She smoothed the younger girl's hair, and kissed her.

And then, the other shoe fell.

47

"What do you mean, she's asked us to a ball?"

"Well, I think it's not a very large one, just a sort of party with some dancing. I think she wants to wear her new dresses, and perhaps have her friends welcome her out of mourning."

"But, Emmy, we're not her friends; we're dressmakers. People don't invite dressmakers to their balls; it's fantastic, bizarre."

"Well, I think she just likes us and wants us to be there. Perhaps she'll wear our dresses, and all the great ladies there will come to us and we'll become very rich. Well, I mean, I will. You already are. Rich, I mean."

"So, I have a great treasure which doesn't really belong to me and which I do not deserve. I am not in society and never will be. What would we do at this ball? Sit at table while the other people point us out? 'There are the dressmakers,' they'll say. 'Which one?' they'll ask. 'The disfigured one or the beautiful one?' It sounds too humiliating to be described."

"Certainly, when you put it so, it does sound humiliating. But suppose we went and sat quietly on the side during the dancing, admiring the dresses and enjoying the music. And when they go in to dinner, we can slip away to the kitchen and eat with the servants, then sneak out the back door. Oh, do come, Maërlys. We make these fine gowns and never see how they look in the dance. And we never get to wear them. We will have the loveliest dresses there, I promise you. They may look down their noses at dressmakers, but they will be jealous of our gowns. Please? Just once? For me?"

"It would certainly be just once, for we never have been asked before and will never be asked again. Indeed, it may be social suicide for Miss Arville. Just this once? Are you sure it would not be better for her if we do not go?"

"I love you like a sister, cousin, but you are beginning to tire me just a little. I ask you; does it make sense to deny ourselves a little pleasure in order to protect others who are perfectly capable of making up their own minds? People who can take care of themselves?"

"Very well, then, because it would be good for your business, but if it is horrible, you cannot say I failed to warn you."

"I will not say so, and I will allow you to say, 'I told you so,' to me every morning, every midday, and every evening for a month. Is that fair?"

Maërlys almost laughed, something she had not done since August. "I'll arrange for the glass slippers," she said.

"I see your friend, Miss Arville, has invited you to a ball. Will you go?"

Jarrod looked up from the note he was reading as Henry handed him the invitation. They were standing next to the hall table, which held a collection of such things.

"Susan? Let me see that." He took the invitation and scanned it. "It's tomorrow night. I'd hoped to be back in Wiltshire or at least well on the road. I've no intention of spending the end of the week in London."

"Seems a bit harsh. She was your brother's fiancée, was she not? Wore mourning for six months, though she was frowned upon for doing so. A frequent guest in your home. In fact she was there last time I visited, in December. Childhood friend, I believe?"

"Why don't you go in my place?"

"I believe that may be a bit above the odds. Possibly in a hundred or, perhaps, two hundred years."

"I suppose I must. Very well, but I'll not stay late."

"Duty to your hostess and a dance or two. No one can ask for more."

"I'll not dance."

"Must I go as your valet and put a pistol at your back? You must find some woman who is not dancing and do your duty. You are a peer of the realm. You have responsibilities to your country and your friends."

"Why do I put up with you?"

"Because I am right, as always."

"Being always right must get tiresome."

"True, but we all must do our duty in our own little way."

The ball was to be held on January twelfth, a Friday. In order to please her cousin, Maërlys had asked her friend, Sarah Dane, if they might borrow her carriage for the evening and Sarah had eagerly agreed. In fact, her eagerness had been surprising.

She had given Maërlys an arch look and asked, "A ball? Where?"

"I am not sure, somewhere in London, probably in Mayfair or Berkeley Square or somewhere like that. Emmy wants to go. I think it's silly, but I want it to be the best for her I can make it. She seems quite excited by it, for some reason."

"You are not?"

"It is unlikely to be anything but humiliating. However, we will do the best we can. Have you ever heard of dressmakers being invited to a ball?"

"Hmm. No, I cannot say that I have. They must think very highly of your cousin. And of you, as well." There was that strange look again.

In the event, Maërlys was surprised to realize that the house to which they were invited was not far from the house of Sarah Dane. Not in the same block, or even the same street, but around two corners, possibly directly behind.

Since they were unaccompanied by gentlemen, they decided that Emmy would act as chaperone to Maërlys, leading the way and making introductions as needed. Emmy had agreed to find them a quiet spot near the dancing where they could admire the dresses.

"Behind a curtain, if possible," Maërlys said.

As it happened, a curtain was not available, but there was an alcove with a window just off the dance floor, where two chairs sat alone.

"Perfect," was Maërlys' response to Emmy's look. They took their seats and turned. The band was warming up and a few couples had gathered on the floor to wait.

"Look," said Emmy, "there is Lady Montrose. She's wearing that piece we did two months ago. Oh, doesn't it look fine?"

Maërlys craned to see, "Oh. Yes, it does. But everything you do looks fine. These dresses of ours are exquisite and our hostess never looked so good. Speaking of that, what was that look that passed between you as we came in?"

"What look?"

"She absolutely winked at you; it was quite unnerving."

"She's probably nervous. Sometimes people get little twitches, when they're nervous."

"Hmm." Maërlys turned to the window, and when she turned back, there was a man standing there, a handsome man she had never seen before.

"I regret, *Mademoiselle*," he said, addressing Emmy, "that we have not been introduced. My name is Louvin, Charles Louvin. May I know your name?"

'Ah, Emmeline, Emmeline Blanc. I am pleased to meet you."

"The pleasure is entirely my own," replied Mr. Louvin. "Is it possible you would join me for the dance?"

"That's very kind of you, sir, but there is some mistake. We, I mean, I, am not a society person. You would be embarrassed."

"I would be embarrassed if such a beautiful lady refused my request for a dance. Have I offended you? If I have, I deserve the embarrassment and humbly beg your pardon."

"No, no, I am flattered, but I think you don't understand, I—"

He took her hand, "Then you must come and explain to me on the dance floor. I am perhaps a little stupid and it may take some time, but I promise to pay very close attention."

His smile was blinding and he was quite handsome. He pulled her to her feet and, short of actual rudeness, she was at a loss. He took her elbow and led her away. She glanced back at Maërlys, who shrugged. Then Emmy and the engaging Mr. Louvin vanished into the crowd on the dance floor.

Maërlys returned her attention to the lovely gowns whirling by, and cocked her ear to the music. Her eyes closed briefly, and when she opened them, there he was, looking as startled as she felt. His mouth opened, closed, opened again. He reached out his hand, withdrew it, reached it out again.

"Please, Miss de Brissy, will you dance with me?"

Maërlys glanced from side to side, but there was nowhere to look. There he was. He dropped to his knee next to her chair and looked directly into her eyes.

"Please?" he said again.

"I, I, I," she stammered but she could not make her legs work. He took her hand and stood up, pulling her with him. She stumbled on knees suddenly made of jelly. He caught her elbow and supported her.

"Come," he said, and they started across the floor. She felt as if she might collapse at any moment, as if she were held up entirely by his hand at her elbow.

Then they were on the floor, her right hand in his left, his right hand at her waist. She looked around and realized it was a waltz. She stumbled again, her left hand went to his shoulder, apparently of its own volition, the music began, and they were suddenly in flight.

Afterward, she was to wonder how he could move so cleanly through such a crowd, for a large number of people occupied the floor, without ever taking his eyes from hers. She was looking at him and he was so handsome and she wanted him so much, she could not think, she just let him take her, flying, flying.

She thought he would talk to her but he seemed as entranced as she, looking into her eyes, whirling, flying. She felt so light, she was sure if he let her go she would float up to the ceiling.

And then it was over. They touched down as lightly as possible, she never felt any jolt, everything as smooth as gliding on ice. He whirled her once more as the music died and his arms were around her and he held her close. Her head went to his shoulder and she was unable to raise it.

"Well?" he asked.

"Oh," she mumbled, "it was so beautiful. I wish it could go on forever."

"I wish that as well. The choice is yours."

"What do you mean?"

"Marry me, Maërlys. You must know I love you more than life. Please, my darling, let us not deprive ourselves any longer. Please. Marry me. I need you."

"But your social position. I am scarred."

"You mean scared. Face me and tell me you do not love me."

She looked up at him. "I, I...," she said.

"You cannot, can you?"

She found herself looking at his feet. "N-No," she stammered, "I cannot. But we could never have balls like this. No one would come to them."

"I may be only a baron, but I am very rich. Everyone will come to them."

"The women will laugh at me."

"Their husbands will not allow it, lest they ruin their chances of that occasional loan they might need."

"You are cynical, sir."

"But not about you. I love you so much, the sight of you takes my breath away. I did not expect you here. I have done as you asked and stayed away. I have tried and tried to drive your image from my dreams. Always before, I have accomplished everything I set my mind to, but this I could not do. I know now that I will never be able to do it. If you do not care for me, I must suffer it, but I cannot believe that you do not care. Tell me. Do you love me or do you not?"

She looked down, she looked all around, and finally, she looked back into his eyes. "I cannot deny it, your lordship, J-Jarrod. I do love you. I have loved you since first we met. We will do whatever you wish."

He pulled her close to him and kissed her. He was recalled to himself by a smattering of applause that turned quickly into a roar. He looked up to find Susan clapping, watching him and smiling, as the people around the floor looked at the two of them and applauded. Susan came forward and whispered to Maërlys. Emmeline was next to her, her eyes glistening with joy.

"May I announce the engagement?" Susan asked.

Maërlys looked at Jarrod and he smiled at her. She laid her head against his chest. "Yes," she murmured. "Oh, yes."

The End

Made in the USA
Middletown, DE
17 February 2022

61377850R00286